MEMORIES
ARE
MURDER

A Belle Palmer Mystery

by Lou Allin

RendezVous
Crime

Cover art: Chris Chuckry

LE CONSEIL DES ARTS | THE CANADA COUNCIL
DU CANADA | FOR THE ARTS
DEPUIS 1957 | SINCE 1957

We acknowledge the support of the Canada Council for the Arts
for our publishing program.

RendezVous Crime
An imprint of Napoleon & Company
Toronto, Ontario, Canada
www.napoleonandcompany.com

Printed in Canada

11 10 09 08 07 5 4 3 2 1

Library and Archives Canada Cataloguing in Publication

Allin, Lou, date-
            Memories are murder / Lou Allin.

(A Belle Palmer mystery)
ISBN 978-1-894917-33-9

            I. Title. II. Series: Allin, Lou, date- Belle Palmer mystery.
PS8551.L5564M44 2007   C813'.6   C2007-903842-5

To Jan, always answering the call

Acknowledgments

Thanks to all of you who have contributed to this last Belle Palmer adventure and those which came before. S.P. Hozy with an eagle eye for errors. Cousin Judy Ross, Sheila Ethier, and Dr. Evelyn Easton. The FEDS (Former English Department): soul sisters Nancy Jinot and Athena Christakos as well as Mary Ryan, new Queen of Speech. The hard-working library crew, Chris, Lucy, and Barbara. Vicky, who keeps the college working. My publisher and editor Sylvia McConnell, Godmother of the best mysteries in Canada. Dear Freya and Nikon, always looking for bears. The bush poodle, always looking for trouble. And the city of Sudbury and Cambrian College, who issued an invitation to join their community and gave me a home and a career along with unparalleled support. It's been a very fast thirty years.

PROLOGUE

The all-seeing lens of the sun was scorching and the blue sky so merciless that it made him dizzy. As he wiped sweat from his reddening brow, the warble of a swooping raven brought a smile to his face, and scarcely had he turned to follow the graceful wings than a stunning blow sent the world into such clarity that he gasped. There was no pain. Everything sped by like a silent film gone mad. A dizzying fall into the still mirror of the lake, the rush of the water meeting him like a merging twin. Bubbles blossomed from his mouth as he began to sink, his arms broken wings. The last thing he remembered was a tune from his youth. "I saw a man with his head bowed low./ His heart had no place to go./ I looked and I thought to myself with a sigh:/ There but for you..." As the words died in his mind, he blinked through the shadows to the light. And the raven flew on.

ONE

Over, under, under, under, over." Miriam MacDonald ran an inquiring finger down a newspaper page.

"Are you doing mental knitting or Sudoku?" asked Belle Palmer, as she entered the office and hung her navy trench coat in the closet after shaking off the moisture. Blessed rain— no need to shovel it.

A frizzy eyebrow rose, matching the Brillo-pad hair on her associate's greying head. Miriam engaged the wooden foot roller under her desk and gave a satisfied sigh as her baba's bunion legacy eased. "Remember those stats that called Sudbury the most dangerous place in Canada? How we live three years less than in cities like Vancouver where eighty is the norm? I'm clocking everyone in today's obits. So far we're only one down. Old Finns and Italians are tough birds."

"What was that marketing ploy you emailed the mayor during his last brainstorming drive to attract business? 'Move to Sudbury and get to heaven faster?'" Belle gave a quick genuflect, and they both laughed in the face of death.

As they settled in at their desks, Miriam's phone rang. She shoved aside a box of Timbits to pick it up, angling it between her ear and shoulder. "Palmer Realty. How may I help you?" A pause. "Yes, this is..."

Abruptly she stood, then braced herself against the desk, left hand on her ample chest as her cheeks went bone white. "In the hospital? How badly hurt? Don't tell me that Jack might…" Her rapid breathing punctuated the stuttered sentences.

Belle put down a pile of messages and came to her side. "Jack's injured? What happened?"

Miriam waved her off and listened, jotting notes on a pad, nodding and shaking her head. At last she hung up, by now only a slight hand tremor revealing her anxiety. Colour returned to her pleasant, round face, but a crease formed on her forehead, joined by another. Belle's elder by ten years, Miriam was like a no-nonsense sister who reminds you that your boyfriend eats with his mouth open even though he owns a BMW and has shares in Microsoft. "An accident in the shaft. He was pinned by machinery." Jack was a heavy-equipment operator at Kidd Creek Mines in Timmins, about two hundred kilometres north. The job was lucrative but dangerous. If not for helping to pay for their daughter Rosanne's teaching degree, he could have taken early retirement.

Belle put her hand to her mouth, had felt her heart dance in arrhythmia. "How serious is it?" Jack was a strong and vital man, nearer her age than Miriam's, quick with a joke and a bottle but quicker to help a friend. Thoughts of paralysis or brain damage trickled icicles down her spine.

"Just a fractured hip. He got off lucky. But he'll be out of commission for a few weeks once he leaves the hospital. *Tabernac."*

"That's a relief." In a nickel-mining community like Sudbury, Ontario, everyone knew someone who had been injured on the job, the fortunate ones with only a truncated thumb or aching back.

Spitting out more Frenglish curses, Miriam considered the in-box on her desk, the growing list of calls. Her small fist clenched in decision. "I have to go and help him, Belle. He doesn't have anyone else." As the penetrating grey eyes narrowed, quicksilver glittered in the iris. "He'd better not be collecting girlfriends, or the hospital will be his last home when I finish with him."

"I'll bet." Jack flirted with everything lacking an Adam's apple but meant no harm—Belle hoped. She still recalled an impulsive kiss aborted by a rifle shot.

Now that the crisis had eased, panic about the realities of Miriam's absence took over. Summer was nearly underway, the Victoria Day lilacs ushering in the blackflies along with her clients. Palmer Realty specialized in cottage properties, and no one wanted to buy a camp in the winter, which took up half of Northern Ontario's year. "What about a retirement home, where he can get meals and some attention short of actual nursing? Timmins is practically a ghost town. Health care is keeping the place afloat." At Miriam's shocked expression, she threw up her hands in surrender. "Sorry. Bad idea. He'd go bananas."

Miriam and Jack had been divorced for years but recently had been enjoying a renewed romance heated up by long distance. Nagging in the back of Belle's mind was the possibility that Miriam might move away to join him, an alarming prospect in a two-person business. Jack's connections might even land his ex-bookkeeper wife a job at Kidd Creek at top salary, not the "unshelled peanuts" Belle paid.

With the deliberation of a numbers person, Miriam riffled through an address book. Whereas Belle often jumped to hyperactive conclusions, nothing fazed Miriam. Her voice assumed a preternatural calm as the grindings of logic began moving her sharp cerebral cogs. "I wouldn't leave you stranded. You *know* that. I have a few people in mind."

"Jessie's still in Israel." Her venerable friend and the retired secretary of Uncle Harold, who had founded the business, spent many months a year teaching on a kibbutz. Figs and dates falling into her mouth, tropical plants and hot, dry sun.

While Miriam ummed and ahhed to herself, Belle concluded with a panicky shudder that running the office on her own was out of the question. An answering machine gave a fly-by-night impression, and she'd have to close when she took listings, held open houses, and did the myriad chores Miriam shuffled with the deftness of a keno dealer. The smallest realty office in a town with an historic boom-and-bust mentality, her business skated on the edge of the edge. A couple of bad months in prime time could ruin her, and the downhill side of her forties was no time to train for a new career. She'd rather wrestle bears than go back to teaching Grade Ten English.

Why was she sitting helplessly, waiting for rescue? Hadn't Canada's pioneer author Susanna Moodie advised souls lost in the wilderness to be "up and doing"? Belle grabbed the phone book to search for a temporary help pool. In a minute, she had located three agencies and started pounding numbers. Magna Personnel Resources had a listing no longer in service, Yours Temporarily had been hit with a bout of the flu and three unplanned pregnancies, and Bullworkers provided manual labour but nothing secretarial.

Hands on her hips, Miriam marched over with an annoyed look as Belle shrugged her shoulders. The older woman snapped the Yellow Pages shut. "Stop that. I told you I wouldn't leave you in the lurch. Those people aren't trained in real estate. Probably a bunch of yahoos. I'm sure I have just the person. Her number's busy, usually is, but I'll call you tonight. I know she's in town, because I saw her at Value Village last week."

Belle gave a sigh of relief. Value Village, too. Sounded like a sensible person. The used clothing store was no stranger to this loonie stretcher, who had grabbed a pair of Buffalo jeans for five dollars. Balancing optimism with fears, she nodded and tried to assume a grateful expression. Miriam was under serious pressure, and she deserved empathy and encouragement. In her youth, Belle had prized brilliance above all qualities in a friend, silver-tongued devils who cared nothing for feelings; now kindness was nudging into first place. "Jack will be okay. He's tough. And I don't want you taking the bus up Highway 144. Use the company car." She spread her hand in a magnanimous gesture. Miriam leased a pink Jetta, and with her book-cooking accounting skills, had also wrangled a tricky tax-deduction deal for Belle's Sienna van, complete with business logo, all-wheel-drive and automatic sliding doors.

Leaving at five, Belle climbed into the van and slid a Statler Brothers CD into the slot. Listening to "The Class of '57" always made her feel younger. She cast an eye at the mock Victorian home that housed the business on a shady cul-de-sac downtown. Massive cottonwoods were forming fluffy seed pods and mustering their leaves. Starting down the Kingsway, she ran into the only serious traffic in the Nickel Capital. Ninety thousand people lived in the core, though the City of Greater Sudbury served as healthcare and taxation centre, as well as shopping hub for another seventy-five thousand in outlying small towns.

As she took Falconbridge Road north, she passed through Garson, the bedroom community with the nursing home where her father lived. Tuesday, Tuesday, their lunch day, was coming up. She was getting used to his double language and often used it herself, either an ominous or comical sign.

Monitoring the landscape in this seasonal transition period, she blinked at the latest offering. At first a distant mist, the leaves were shy debutantes wearing spring-green dresses on the poplar and birch. The maple and oak foliage would be slower to unfurl but hung on stubbornly into the late fall. Approaching the airport, she gave a bemused glance at the venerable orange steam shovel that marked the entrance to a busy gravel pit. It was set up on crushed white stone and lit up at night like a proud icon of industry.

While operations had closed in Cobalt, Kirkland Lake and other more remote outposts, the gigantic Sudbury deposits, courtesy of a meteor two billion years ago, were revealing deep pockets. The lode of high-grade nickel, gold, silver and platinum ran thirty miles into the earth's core. The International Nickel Company (INCO) and little brother Falconbridge once had twenty thousand workers. Now the number had fallen below five thousand, but the tons of mined ore rose steadily thanks to modern machinery. Owned by Swiss and Brazilian consortiums, they were a combination powerhouse on the international scene, with the base metal at a twenty-year high.

Belle collected her mail at the kiosk and turned down Edgewater Road, passing Philosopher's Pond, a kettle lake left by glaciers, then reached the road to the former Blue Lake mine, now Nickel Rim South. Though the mine had closed in the Fifties, scientific advances were permitting deeper excavation. Nearly four hundred million dollars had been spent on the venture, including a massive complex rising from the crumbled foundations of the old site. But industry came with a price. The project was squeezing both people and wildlife. No longer could she ramble its wide, dozed roads to avoid bears and blackflies in the first weeks of summer. A massive parking lot had been backfilled onto a swamp, and above, a gleaming headframe bestrode the hill like a colossus, fed by an army of marching hydro lines.

As she drove along the ten-kilometre road skirting the western edge of Lake Wapiti, the rare conjoining of another meteor crater, she became aware of a shape behind her and tensed as a cheeky horn tooted. When she'd built years ago, only a dozen full-timers lived here. Now they numbered forty-five, buying cottage properties, tearing them down, and constructing monster houses even on toenail properties, windows a stone's throw from the road. She kept her speed at forty, fast enough for the blind turns and hills. Her rearview mirror framed a red Jeep Liberty. On they drove, the Jeep sniffing Belle's bumper. Though thoroughly annoyed, she searched her mind for a safe pull-off. Why enrage a neighbourhood jerk?

Time didn't permit her courtesy. On a wicked stretch over a high culvert with a creek tumbling freshets far below, the Jeep thundered past on the narrow, hard-surfaced road, its gravel and tar crumbling at the edges.

Belle read the license as the Jeep kicked up a load of dust: HOTTIE. Not likely a last name.

Another mile ahead, she saw the Jeep parked in a steep drive. She chuckled to imagine how that incline would strike fear under the demands of ice and snow. The house had changed hands three times in the last decade.

Finally, she pulled into her long driveway, passing her routed sign, "The Parliament of Owls", displaying the white, beaked Corny and brown, frowning Horny. Slamming the door, she could hear deep-chested barking, the world's cheapest burglar alarm. Freya, a senior German shepherd, bounded out, ran circles, and left for her ablutions. Ten hours was no problem for her elimination needs; she seemed to sleep the day away in yogic bliss.

Inside the two-and-a-half storey cedar house, Belle shook out chow, plus a spoon of fibre for the dog, refreshed the water bowl, and headed up to the master suite for a bath. Minutes later, towel-drying her short, red hair, now peppered with grey, she put on comfortable yoga pants and a T-shirt. The wood stove was on simmer, but it warmed the house like a bakery.

Dinner was a quick linguine puttanesca with black and green

olives, a fresh tomato, and tangy Sicilian olive oil, mounded with grated pecorino. Settled in the TV room in a pasha chair with massive ottoman, Belle tuned her television to her only satellite subscription channel, Turner Classic Movies.

Doris Day and Rock Hudson were starring in *Pillow Talk*. Remembering his death from HIV/AIDS, she watched the film with an ironic new subtext and an academy-award performance. So many of the screen's leading men had secret lives. Some, like Charles Laughton, arranged publicity marriages. Raymond Burr made massive donations to children's charities.

As the film ended, the gibbous moon began its silvery rise across the back of her yard. No word from Miriam. Should she succumb to nerves and call, or trust her cohort?

Half an hour later, she was immersed in the wilderness of Rocky Mountain National Park in Nevada Barr's *Hard Truth*. If she were to imagine herself an author, Barr, with her brilliant sense of place, would be her model. Then the phone rang.

"Still up? I knew you'd be fretting. Now you can relax, and I can leave to help Jack. Here's the answer to our problems." An old friend of Miriam's had agreed to sign on for three weeks or longer if necessary.

"And guess what? She'll do it for two-thirds of my salary. Am I a ruthless negotiator? Must have learned it from the master." Miriam knew that her boss loved spinning pennies into loonies and toonies like Rumpelstiltskin at his wooden wheel.

Despite the windfall, Belle had sudden reservations. She stubbed out her cigarette in the little catcher's mitt ashtray that remained from the old cottage. "Why so cheap? Does she know the real estate business?"

Miriam harrumphed in an affronted response. "Of course. A few years ago, she was a secretary at Crown Realty. We took computer courses together at Nickel City College."

Crown had gone belly up. Easy conclusions as to the woman's availability. Why wasn't she still working locally? "What about updating the website? We need to get those new listings fired up."

Miriam made a scoffing sound with her lips. "No worries. She's a master at Flash, she assured me."

Belle let a beat or two pass. "What's she been doing lately?"

"Just...got back in town from living down south in Milton. That's why she's happy to come on board. Yoyo has family here and needs breathing space to find a full-time permanent job again."

Belle finished the last dregs in the scotch glass. "I'm not sure I heard you right. Did you say Yoyo?"

"Short for Yolanda. Yoyo Hourtovenko. You'll love her. A laugh a minute."

"Lots of laughs? That hardly sounds like a—"

"Did I mention that she owns a German shepherd?"

Minutes later, turning out the light with a sigh of relief, Belle drifted into a baby-sweet sleep, prepared to adore Yoyo on sight.

TWO

The office was dark when Belle rolled into the yard. Yoyo was to arrive at seven thirty sharp, so this was not auspicious. With a grrr, she entered, nudged the coffee maker into action and sat down to polish ads for the weekend paper, normally Miriam's job. Barring the silly metaphor of her name, could Yoyo handle it? Not everyone could write good copy, fudge but not fabricate, plump but not lie, juggle the jargon. Doll house. Starter home. Retro kitchen. School nearby. Sharp minds knew what those innocent words really meant.

As the clock ticked past eight, Belle felt her pulse rising as steadily as a jet on takeoff. She'd give Miriam a call at Jack's tonight and tell her how unreliable her choice had proved. On to number two, a retired bookkeeper from H&R Block whom Miriam had also mentioned but who wanted full salary plus overtime.

Running her finger down her problem listings, Belle stopped at 1565 Edgewater Road, the Lavoie place. The unique log home had a high price and would appeal only to an appreciative and very wealthy buyer. Meanwhile, it would stand unoccupied, a dangerous status. If no dream offer appeared by fall, it might be an idea to have a firm like Tel-a-Fern keep an eye on the place, mow the lawn, rake leaves, make it look lived in until the snows rendered access impossible. Maybe next spring would bring them all better luck.

Then the phone rang. She cleared her throat and gave the usual cheerful answer, surprised at the voice. If she hadn't known Clifton Webb was dead, she'd have thought Mr. Belvedere had a twin. There was also eerie familiarity in the timbre and cadences, but different, as if an oboe had become a bassoon. "Sorry, but we don't handle rentals. Have you tried—"

"I know that, dear lady, but bear with me. Someone told me you deal in cottage properties." He explained that he had been seconded to the Ministry of Natural Resources on a contract to do elk research. "I've been bunking at a motel on Route 69 since March, but it isn't suitable. A real dive, with motorcycles night and day. Peace and quiet are important to me. If there's a lakeside property that hasn't sold for a while, perhaps the owners might appreciate a two-year lease. It could be a win-win situation for all of us."

His pregnant pause started one particular wheel turning in Belle's brain. 1565 Edgewater Road. Ivan was retired, and Maureen, a nurse, had joined Doctors Without Borders in Somalia. They wanted to return to their home but were afraid to leave it unattended for such a long period. Teary-eyed, they'd told her to sell. This might be the perfect compromise. She choked back thoughts of forfeiting a fat commission, but balanced that against losing jolly Maureen as a neighbour. Her New Year's Eve parties were legendary, especially her turkey on the barbecue.

"You *are* in luck. I have the ideal house, not far from mine. Can you meet me this afternoon?" That would give her time to call Maureen in Kismayu, where she was volunteering at a free clinic for women with fistulas. Giving birth at too early an age, they needed only a simple four-hundred-dollar operation to repair the ruptures. Cheap in the western world but beyond their means.

After she had given him directions and they had hung up, she realized that neither had introduced themselves. At her ineptness, Belle shook her head. Working alone had her rattled as a rainstick. Where was Yoyo? Grumbling, she sifted papers on Miriam's desk in quest of the name of that retired bookkeeper. With no success, she flipped the Rolodex and located Jack's name. Surely Miriam would be in Timmins by now.

Scarcely had she punched in five numbers, than at nine o'clock, the door banged open. In came a bottle blonde with cropped hair, pink-gelled in every direction, a walking strawberry shortcake with a dog leash draped around her neck. A few inches shy of Belle's five-four, she wore a silver mini-skirt with a wide chain-mail belt and a shimmery blue clinging top that lifted the veil over a bra that manufactured cleavage where no more was needed. A small mound of stomach riding high testified to...impending motherhood? At her side was a magnificent black-and-tan German shepherd with a Canadian flag bandana. Belle's mouth opened, but words wouldn't come.

After scanning the office, the woman stuck out a childlike hand, blazing with custom nail designs of cherub faces. "I'm Yoyo. You must be Belle. Meet Baron. Mimsy set everything up, right? This is a cute little place. Is that my desk over there?" She pointed to Belle's new fake-cherrywood workstation, a Christmas present to herself against her frugal conscience.

Only Jack was allowed to call his ex-wife Mimsy. Yoyo must be a very close friend. Belle tried to control her irritation. Yoyo might be the only solution to her personnel crisis. "You are a bit late." She glanced at the oversized watch on the woman's plump arm.

"Baron, down," Yoyo whispered, and the dog flattened with an oomph, massive head on paws, lively black brows darting. Laid-back must be his middle name. Yoyo tucked the leash into a capacious shoulder bag and met Belle's eyes with a wary challenge that didn't match her words. "Sorry, I—"

"Was there a problem?" Belle needed this woman, but she wasn't going to roll over and beg. A poor employee was worse than none.

Yoyo folded her arms, her back straight. "I said I was sorry. It won't happen again. And I did tell Mimsy that I'd *try* to get here at seven thirty, but that I needed to find Baron a sitter."

"A sitter?"

"My mom has an apartment in the Flour Mill. They don't allow dogs. I sneak Baron in and out by the back stairs. One bark could land us on the street."

Yoyo's situation sounded unstable, like trouble ahead. To compound the situation, at ten, Belle was due at a showing. "Yes, yes."

"Mom had to get some blood tests. So, is it okay if I—"

Belle rocked back in the chair. "You've already brought him to work. Why not let him stay? We have a kennel in the back room."

"For real?" Yoyo's blue-shadowed eyes widened, then chilled as she searched Belle's mouth for a smile that didn't arrive. "You're making fun of me. Forget it. I'm outta here." She turned on her sparkly spiked heels. Baron scrabbled up and followed suit. Belle hadn't even petted him, and he was a handsome beast. His nails were pristine, and his coat evidence of daily brushing.

"Wait—" Leaping for the door, Belle held up her hands. What was that saying about making lemonade? Why not let the woman show her stuff? A single day would tell. "We've had a bad start. Let's begin again. Miriam said you had realty experience." She waved the woman to a seat.

Yoyo sidled into Miriam's chair, crossed her shapely legs and pooched out her lower lip. "Ten years at Crown. Ninety per cent on the first two real estate courses. Best in my class. I'm gonna be a realtor, just as soon as I take the last course and pay my fee."

The easy ticket to wealth, a part-time job, many thought, but 24-7-365 was the reality. The assessment of several thousand dollars to join the hallowed ranks kept amateurs at bay. Belle nodded, blowing out a breath and leaning across Yoyo to punch on Miriam's computer. She coughed discreetly at a cloying perfume that smelled like cotton candy. "Then you know the ropes. I'll give you a brief tour and tell you what's on the schedule." She pointed to the coffee maker. "Still fairly fresh, comparatively speaking."

Grinning, Yoyo pulled a box of chocolate doughnuts from her purse. The dog drooled, and the phone trilled.

Later that afternoon, Belle drove down Edgewater Road and pulled into a large property bearing one of her business signs. At the entrance to the drive, Maureen had located a six-foot-high boulder, a "pearl", as rockwall builders termed the valuable commodities. She'd had a wrought-iron sign custom-made and drilled into the rock. "Pebble Beach," it read, casting artistic ivy shadows when the sun moved to the west. Inheriting the cottage property from her parents, then building a permanent home, Maureen had landscaped the place with a bevy of perennials, rock gardens and woven willow arbours with climbing gourds. A mass of parrot tulips raised expectations for the growing season. Daffodils were nodding in the sunnier areas. If this man...how maddening that they hadn't exchanged names...liked plants, he'd fall in love with the yard. Lilacs, white and mauve, were in glorious array, as were the pin cherry trees and a flowering crab. Their redolence filled the air, and each breeze off the water scattered papery petals onto the ground like wedding confetti.

The same balmy weather that coaxed that picture had also

brought a curtain of bugs. The bloody slaughter on her van's windshield was clear evidence. Belle retrieved a bottle of spray and a roll of paper towels to clear the massacre. Then she sat awkwardly in a slanted Muskoka chair on the covered porch, swatting now and then at a delta-winged fly that tried to burrow into her hair. Each winged destroyer had its signal features. And even the smallest, the no-see-ems, could creep through a large tent screen and leave exposed flesh burning like an iron had scorched it.

She heard the crunch of gravel. Into the driveway came a GMC 2500 Sierra 4x4. A tall man with ash blond hair got out. He wore sensible khaki work clothes and a red plaid light-wool shirt. She stood as he approached, noticing his trim Van Dyke beard. He polished his glasses with a white handkerchief, a nicety she hadn't seen in decades. Something in his cerulean-blue eyes summoned distant memories and left her speechless. Her mouth was opening, gaping, in fact.

"Ms Palmer, or am I presuming? Sorry, I didn't get your name. Things were happening rather fast, and I was excited about finding a house. I'm..." Then as he put on his glasses, he stopped, and the handkerchief fell to the ground like a forfeit in a medieval joust.

"Gary Myers." Her boyfriend from Scarborough Collegiate Institute in Toronto, or at least for the three months leading up to the senior semi-formal. At eighteen, he'd been much heavier, called Blubs by cruel peers, and yet his gifts had drawn her to his shining light. In the years since graduation, he'd been a cypher, a vanished man.

Gary had been the valedictorian with special medals in biology and zoology. More than that, he'd been a talented actor and a sparkling tenor. Goaded on by mutual friends, they'd started dating during *Brigadoon*, Gary as Tommy

Albright and Belle playing trumpet in the orchestra. How she'd gritted her teeth when he'd kissed the female lead, some blonde Swedish sophomore headed for Julliard. He also announced for the football games, sitting high in the box while Belle marched with the band.

And another oddity. Though they'd dated fourteen times, as tolled in her diary, he hadn't kissed her until date ten, when she'd summoned the annoyance and gumption to ask him. It had been a well-timed but perfunctory performance. She'd felt humiliated, despite the delightful experience of brushing his soft lips and smooth cheek. After that, he'd grasped the idea that a formal farewell was mandatory. How naïve had he been? Was it her fault? She brushed her teeth three times a day, swilled mouthwash, and had to fend off other comers with a handy knee.

He cleared his throat, offering his hand, strong and weathered. "Belle. It's been a long time. I've never believed in coincidences, but I've changed my mind."

The warm contact moved her, a deliciously uneasy feeling spreading from the pit of her stomach. "Despite the territory, the North can be a small place when it comes to people." She tried not to stare, but it was impossible. Whatever diet or metabolic reversal, he was now tall and lean. The clumsy black horn-rimmed glasses had vanished for trendy titanium models. He drew his fingers through a hank of silky hair, an endearing gesture she recalled with a pang. In high school, conversation had been difficult, fraught with teenage angst, double dates the salvation. Now perhaps they could communicate as adults. What kind of man had he become?

A smile grew on his face, coaxing familiar dimples. He cocked his head at her and firmed his lips as though trying to make a decision. "I do owe you an apology, long overdue. Things were...not as they seemed."

17

What did he mean? A hot flash moved from her neck to her forehead, and she feared that she looked like a cartoon. She stammered his last few words. He always had made her nervous, and the feeling had been mutual. She'd completely lost her appetite every time they'd sat together for a meal, had toyed with her food like an anorexic. He had lost the conversational flair he'd had with an audience. "Long overdue. You mean when we were, when we..."

Suddenly the curtain lifted. Hindsight had the clarity of a crystal blue morning at minus twenty-five Celsius, the birches eight miles across the lake as sharp as an Ansel Adams photograph. Belle nodded, then cleared her throat. "How long have you...I mean when did you..."

"Forever. Don't let anyone tell you differently. Cub scouts." He waved his hand. "Not that anything was happening at the time, but thinking back, I knew. Then there was Mr. Kluckhohn."

"Our Grade Seven geography teacher? Don't tell me he—"

"A sad old man, weeks from retirement. I told him I wasn't interested in his dirty pictures. Then I played the waiting game until university. It seemed safest, especially with HIV/AIDS on the horizon. I owe you one, Belle. It wasn't easy in the late Seventies. You helped me maintain a semblance of normalcy."

She took a deep breath, laughed in spite of herself. "Are you saying that I was your...what do you call it...beard?"

"Peer pressure is very powerful at that age. I couldn't take Richard Ralston to the grad dance, after all."

"The salutatorian? Whose father was an Anglican minister?" She took him up to the porch, digesting the information that was constructing a parallel universe.

They sat for over an hour, filling each other in on their careers. At long last, honesty and a mutual sense of humour made them fast friends. "So when a kid told me to kiss his ass,

I walked out of that school in Etobicoke before Christmas and came up here to take a job at my Uncle Harold's business," Belle said. "That was over twenty years ago. Since he died, I've been running it myself."

"Do you still play the trumpet?"

"Last time I tried to put on lipstick, and don't ask why, I couldn't find my upper lip. Anyway, I'm much too lazy to keep up my embouchure by practising." She wiggled the fingers on her right hand. "The muscle memory's still there. Guess I could play the fight song."

Together they sang, pumping their arms. "Fight on, SCI. Everybody's rooting for you. Crash right through that line..." Then they dissolved into laughter.

Gary had a doctorate in zoology from McGill and was a full professor at Brock University. Field work, not the classroom, kept him in love with the job. "Obviously, there aren't any elk down south. It's exciting that Nickel City College and Shield University have been involved in restoring the species to this area."

With a brief tour, looking out each window in approval across the eight-by-eight-mile lake, he agreed to take the house without persuasion at a thousand a month. "The Lavoies will be pleased," she said, explaining how to handle the utility bills. Sweet Maureen was cutting her in for ten per cent of the rent.

As Belle climbed into bed that night, she wondered if she'd done the right thing by asking Gary to dinner. Where was this new relationship going? Heady stuff, but would it only confuse them both?

THREE

Arriving the next evening for dinner, Gary presented her with a book. "I remembered you loved films. Didn't your dad take us to that screening room once? I wish my father had been a film booker," he said with a nuance of a smile on his expressive lips. A slight gap between his two front teeth had added a very human feature to the little idol she'd raised.

She looked at the cover, recognizing Buddy Rogers and Richard Arlen in a pensive but provocative pose in the 1927 *Wings*. According to the blurb, this "acclaimed history of homosexuals in film" documented over three hundred movies spanning eighty years. She leafed through it. "Wow. Edward Everett Horton as the poet-reporter in *The Front Page*. Bert Lahr as the cowardly lion? Are they serious? And all the way back to the silents, even before the Hays Office regulations. Incredible."

Freya showed much interest in the new arrival, and the feeling was mutual, as Gary scratched her ears. Somehow Belle wondered if he was measuring the dog's head for the boil pot, as he'd done before, assembling squirrel and raccoon skeletons in high school. They'd met as partners in biology, when they'd had to dissect a crawfish.

"Moose, deer and bear, sure, but I've never seen an elk," she said as they forked into one of her no-fail casseroles, made with lean ground beef, macaroni, tomato soup, red peppers and cheddar. Mâché salad with homemade blue cheese dressing rounded out the menu, along with blackberries topped with sweetened mascarpone.

Gary pointed out the window, where a party barge was making for home, chugging along with its pontoons parting the rising waves. Raindrops had begun splashing the panes. "Lake Wapiti, isn't it? 'Wapiti' is the native name for elk. Another coincidence." As he blotted his mouth with the linen serviette, he told her that the elk *(Cervus elaphus)* were native to Ontario, but extirpated by the late 1800s due to hunting and loss of habitat. The Thirties and Forties had seen efforts to restore them, but the unfounded theory that they were passing liver flukes to cattle had initiated a hunt that decimated the fragile herd.

"What do they eat? Do they compete with moose?" The extra glasses of the Sicilian nero red that was a bargain at ten dollars were winging her into a time warp with this ghost from her past. A generation had been born and raised to adulthood since last they'd met. If they'd had a child together... The spectre brought visions of prodigies, not that she'd been interested in motherhood. It would have been handy to have a teenager to shovel snow. She smiled to herself as he plunged on with his lecture. Her toes were tingling, or was it her imagination? She put down the glass and thought about coffee. Strong coffee.

"Not exactly. They're both grazers and browsers, but when the going gets tough in winter, moose head for dense coniferous stands and feed on balsam fir and eastern hemlock. Elk prefer cedar habitat along shorelines, pawing up buried grasses in early winter. A perfect compromise. Nature has a way of sorting things out, if we'd just let it."

Their own story in fewer than twenty-five words. "I've heard moose in mating season. Do elk sound similar?"

He arranged his lithe fingers, tossed his head back, and gave a fair imitation of a "bugle," which caused Freya to rise and come to his aid. Laughing, he ruffled her fur and accepted a kiss.

"Very different from the birch-bark-cone moose call." She poured the rest of the wine into his glass, sad to see it go, but glad that she wouldn't be running her mouth without inhibition. She was beginning to remember the feelings she had entertained for this man. Far more powerful than muscle memory. "What exactly is your project?"

"I'm based around the old Burwash area. Bump Lake. Sometimes I take the canoe into the more remote lakes. Cow/calf survival is my focus this time around." He had also published monographs on parasitology and foraging trajectories.

With cottages her speciality and over a thousand lakes in the region, Belle was familiar with every puddle and pond. Yet some areas were less habitable than others. "Burwash? Isn't that where a prison used to be? Or a correctional facility, whatever they're called?"

"So I hear. Nothing's left of the town. The jail's just a shell, not that I went near it."

"When did these elk arrive?"

"We did a pilot release here in 1998, and a few years later for a total of one hundred and seventy-two animals. A couple of hundred more in Bancroft, Lake of the Woods, and the Lake Huron North Shore. Moderate success, about four hundred and fifty in Ontario at last count. Ecotourism based on elk is a great possibility, too."

"Where do the animals come from?"

He drained his glass with an approving smile. "Elk Island National Park near Edmonton. They have a rigorous disease-management program, and their reproduction rate is solid."

Belle stifled a laugh. *The Sudbury Star* ran a story about those vaginal transmitters for pregnant cows. Ouch."

He tipped back in his chair with an embarrassed look. "They were supposed to help us track newborns, but the idea flopped. Small wonder."

Then he glanced at his watch with a sigh. A serious expression came over his face, and he smoothed his goatee. "Something else you should know. You'll meet Mutt later this week."

"Do you have a dog, too? No problem, as long as it doesn't dig in the gardens or scratch that pristine wood floor. Maybe we can hit the trails together. Freya can use the socializing."

"My..." He paused and gave her a wink. Laugh-lines around his eyes made him a man of self-confidence, far different from the serious boy with a secret. "...partner."

She should have known that he was no monk. Unlike her, he had a sex life. Being jealous of his soulmate seemed beyond silliness. "So he's coming up? Tell me more about Mutt. That can't be his real name."

"Malcolm Malloy. He's a murder-mystery author. Writes a series about Lucy Doyle, one of Canada's first female reporters. His books are set in Toronto in the Twenties."

"I'd love to read them, but I'm still focussed on the mutt part."

Gary laughed, deep and rich, with a spirit she'd never heard in the old days. "Mutt likes surprises. How about an open invitation for martinis? Bombay Sapphire suit you? Like them dirty? That's with a tablespoon of olive juice."

Would she have dreamed all those years ago that they'd be up in Sudbury having a conversation about elks and cocktails? It was comical. It was wonderful. With the final sigh she'd ever give about the colour of his eyes, Belle said, "Smashing."

Later that night, she pulled a worn, cracked-leather five-year diary from her bookcase. She'd kept one from the age of ten until she'd left university. A spyhole into the teenager she'd been. When was their first date? Once she'd memorized them like holy days. She leafed back through the middle entries for senior year, then stopped and smiled at the lurid lavender ink she'd chosen when she'd learned about Mary Astor's purple diary covering her affair with John Barrymore. March 6th. "HE ASKED ME OUT, SUGAR!" Then the writing got small and blurry. She grabbed her reading glasses: "In Eng, came up + bent down, saying, 'May I see you after class?' Then after, he said, 'I hope you're not busy Fri. Would you like to see a show?' WOULD I! I'd see a cremation with him. Doubling with Janet and John." Who were they? She couldn't remember their last names. And since when did she ever say "sugar"? She sounded like a deep-fried Southern...belle.

*   *   *

Later that week, she fielded a call at the office.

So far, Yoyo was working out well, except for her clothes and the occasional grammar error. She'd taken the coughing hint about the perfume, but Belle wondered how to broach the subject of those scooping necklines and clinging tops. Hot and humid summer weather would make the problem worse. Between the shrink-wrapped skirts and the décolletage lay mere inches. The spike heels beckoned and promised minimal flight. Nothing had changed since Betty Grable's pin-up poster to raise GI morale, among other things.

A hesitant male voice said, "My name is...Malcolm Malloy. I'm trying to reach Gary Myers. Your card was on the table, so I hoped that you might know where he is."

Belle shifted out of realtor mode as she introduced herself, wondering what this man might look like. How old was he? "Not since Monday, when I arranged for the house rental."

A worried sigh came over the line. "I just drove in from

Hamilton. Found the key under a rock by the door like he told me. A note on the fridge said he'd be back from field camp by ten."

"Did you try his cell phone?"

Malcolm, or rather Mutt, gave a snort. "He always forgets to top up. Don't know why he doesn't get a regular plan. Just cheap, I guess."

"Runs in my blood, too." A dose of Northern hospitality was in order. "I'm sure he's delayed. It *is* a couple of hours to Burwash. Cottage country traffic gets wicked on Fridays." She didn't mention that the infamous route was a killer highway with enough rock cuts to demolish two hockey teams per year. Her van sported a bumper sticker reading "Four-Lane 69". "You probably know that Gary and I were friends in high school."

"Oh, *that* Belle Palmer."

Suddenly she felt vulnerable. What had Gary said about her? Mocked their relationship? She remained silent, chewing her lip. Meeting Mutt now didn't seem like such a good idea.

"He said that you were the smartest girl in your class. Had him tongue-tied on every date." Mutt gave a hearty laugh. "You literally made him sweat."

She had waged quite a campaign. Staked out his house, followed him to the show, collected grade-school pictures from his collaborating friends. She even knew his locker combination and took an occasional peek. Now they'd call it stalking. Belle joined in the spirit, reading the unspoken undercurrent. "Guess I was a handful."

Yoyo returned from Muirhead's with a bag of stationery supplies and gave her a wave.

"I'm leaving early today to meet a client on the way home. How about taking a walk with me around four? I'll point out all the good trails. If Gary's back, all the better." As she told him where she lived, she had second thoughts. Gary was the nature lover. Perhaps Mutt didn't care for hiking.

Late that afternoon, Freya set up a roo-roo that heralded someone in the drive. A knock sounded at her door. When Belle opened it, elbowing the dog aside, she saw the vision of Laurence Olivier as Heathcliff, high brow, sculpted lips, flashing raven hair. His chinos and striped rugby shirt were neatly pressed, and his white sneakers immaculate. So "Mutt" was a joke, like a heavy person called Tiny.

"No car?"

"I just walked down. Got to stretch out after that drive."

"And Gary's not back?"

Shaking his head, he turned to stare at the glorious wraparound deck over the walkout basement, one side jutting forward in a tongue, two sets of stairs with platforms. "I like your Escher effect. What a view—180 degrees."

The lake was glassy, and they both swiped at their necks. "Wind's down. Bad news in early June." She explained that the freshly hatched blackfly swarm was too ravenous on the trails back of the house. "They were kissing me last week, but by now they've learned their survival lessons and are going for the jugular."

Belle flipped down the third row of seats to make room for Freya in the back of the van. Then they drove down Edgewater Road, headed north and pulled off on Station Road. In the bush were the remains of an abandoned mile of the old asphalt highway to Skead. It had served as an unofficial drag strip, with spray-painted starts and stops, but now the poplar and birch saplings encroached on the sides. "It's less dense here," she said. "We can hook onto a bush road and do a loop."

From her pocket, she pulled a bottle of industrial-strength bug dope. God only knew its long-range neurological effects, but nothing else worked. "This oily junk melts plastic. I hate it," she said.

"My parents have a cottage near Bracebridge, so I've been through the drill. It's a Canadian ritual. Don't leave home without it." He took a squirt, rubbed his hands together and patted his face as if applying aftershave.

"I'll take the risk for now," she said, tucking it away in her pocket.

On the scrubby trees that lined the road, miniature leaves were emerging. Mutt admired a bush with a delicate set of red seed keys dangling like a necklace.

"Swamp maple," Belle said. "One of five species in the area." She pointed out a birch conk, then a yellow shelf fungus. "Chicken of the woods. Supposed to be quite choice."

"Reminds me of shiitake. Have you ever tried it?"

"Some of my Italian friends comb the woods for mushrooms. Familiar though I am with many types, I don't have the nerve to risk a wrong choice." Sounded like much of her life.

Streaks of golden and green moss were making inroads on the old highway. They stopped to tune their ears to the location of a hairy woodpecker tapping for dinner. "So how long will you be here, Mutt?" she asked, feeling his odd name growing more familiar.

"The whole summer. I'm a writer, if Gary hasn't told you. Been having a bit of a block with the third book. It's common enough. A change of scene seemed perfect for a kick-start." With his clean-shaven baby face, he looked barely twenty, though she'd never ask. A gentle tracery around his hazel eyes bumped her estimate to thirty-plus. Gary wasn't a cradle robber, but she preferred companions her age. Who wanted a blank stare after mentioning a favourite musical group or pivotal historical event? Then again, with her classic film addiction, she should date octogenarians who remembered Joan Crawford as a jazz baby, not Baby Jane's sister.

Freya bounded ahead, flushing a grouse from the grassy

borders. The bird's nearby mate followed to the safety of a stunted oak. Scrabbling on the asphalt trimmed the dog's nails, a chore saved. Then they rounded a corner. "Watch the glass!" Mutt yelled.

Belle grabbed the dog's chain collar and steered her around a shattered windowpane. At the side of the road was a huge, fresh mound of construction material. Someone had been renovating and was too lazy and cheap to visit the town dump, even for a nominal fee. As Mutt watched, her keen eye tallied the totals. One truckload. Ripped up carpet, ten paint cans, guts of an old washing machine, scrap wood panelling, left-over pink fibreglass insulation floating on the breeze, and on top, a carton for a fifty-inch TV. For good measure, six bald tires lay in a ziggurat framed by an army of soft drink bottles. Green packing peanuts littered the landscape like toxic snow. The man who whispered "plastics" in Dustin Hoffman's ear in *The Graduate* was a seer. The world was drowning in its own garbage. An island miles long had formed in the ocean. "Damn. This has me seeing red. Why do people have to foul their own nest?" she asked, pounding her fist into her palm.

"It's disgusting, but what can you do about it? Check for tire treads?" He put his hands on his hips and bent over, Sherlock-style.

She waded into the field of scratchy blueberry bushes and leathery Labrador tea. "The smell's not bad. Let me peek into those nice black garbage bags."

He shuddered. "Be careful. There could be nails, or even needles."

"Medical waste? This isn't downtown Vancouver."

With delicate hands, she opened the bag and began sorting the trash, while Mutt watched her with a grimace on his face. At last she found a grocery store receipt from Garson. "A-ha.

Last week. That's why it's so fresh."

Mutt looked at the list. "Likes turkey, chocolate milk, Cheetos?"

Belle waved a debit card receipt. "Pure gold. I'm going to call this in to CrimeStoppers. Maybe they can trace the number."

As they headed for the van, she added, "This hasn't given you a very good impression. When the heat starts up in late June, the bugs will level off. Then I'll show both of you some great places." Mutt laughed as she dug a blackfly out of her ear, wiping the red smear on one sleeve.

"Down south we take visitors to restaurants, art museums, plays. I suspect here it's a favourite swamp."

"You got it, city boy. I have one for every occasion." She was beginning to like him. Her road needed its batteries recharged with new faces.

Near morning, Belle was dreaming of her last date with Gary. He had arrived in a white tux, wearing a carnation dyed to match her lace-and-satin Alice-blue dress with a strapless bodice and a hem just above the knees. An expert seamstress, her mother Terry had kept the extra cloth pressed in a drawer until the day she'd died. Gary presented the customary orchid corsage and pinned it to her with surprising dexterity, almost as if he had been practising. As he bent closer, she could smell the citrus of his 4711 aftershave. They walked down the stairs to his father's black Reliant, where another couple waited, laughing in the back seat. Then a phone rang. And rang. Why didn't someone answer their cell? She began to paw through the layers of sleep, remembering that even the car phone hadn't been common then. Sitting up in a fog, Belle craned her neck to peer at the green digital display. 4:35. She growled an answer into the receiver. A wrong number, or a crisis with her father?

"It's Mutt. I didn't know...who else to call. Gary's dead."

FOUR

Belle brushed the corners of her eyes, still groggy and barely coherent, preferring childhood memories to an ugly reality. "What are you talking about? An auto accident?"

His voice fell to a whisper, and she turned up the volume on the handset. "No. The OPP called here."

"I thought you said it wasn't an accident." The Ontario Provincial Police had jurisdiction over traffic outside of the Region of Greater Sudbury.

He cleared his throat, then resumed, strain apparent in the deliberate way he marshalled information. "It happened yesterday afternoon, probably about the same time we were talking. An air-ambulance helicopter was taking a kid to Toronto, flying over Bump Lake. Gary had an informal base camp there. A cooler. A little tent. Sleeping bag if he needed to stay over. They saw his canoe floating free and dropped for a closer look, then called it in. Thank God the boat was red, or it might have been hidden in the reeds. His...body wasn't far away. The OPP found his wallet and university information. It took a while to track down his chairman. He gave them the new number, and they called to see if anyone else was at the address."

These procedural details didn't interest her. "I'm not clear on what happened. His canoe was adrift in a quiet lake? How did he drown?"

A bitter bark of a laugh surprised her. "It's a cliché, isn't it?

Guy stands up in a boat to take a leak, overbalances, hits his head and farewell. Gary was a hell of a good swimmer, for all that mattered. We used to hit the pool at the gym every week. Olympic size. He could do laps until the place closed."

"Was he wearing a life jacket?" she asked, knowing the answer. Few canoeists bothered with the bulky creatures unless they were travelling in white water or with children.

"Are you kidding? He told me that Bump Lake's about as dangerous as a bathtub."

So fast in and out of her life after so many years of absence. Was there a message here? "Is there anything I can do? What arrangements do you have to make? Where is he, uh, the—" Somehow she couldn't imagine Gary as an *it*, a collection of periodic-table elements worth four dollars with inflation.

"I'm supposed to go in for the identification. The medical examiner, some doctor on rotation, will take a look at him. Then cremation, I guess. We never talked about our own plans, but for sure he hated funerals. Until the recent drug cocktails, nearly every month a friend of ours was dying of HIV/AIDS. I'll take the ashes to one of our favourite spots on Lake Ontario, or maybe the Botanical Park in Hamilton. He loved that place." At that, his voice broke, and she could hear quiet sobs.

"I'm so sorry about Gary. Keep me posted, Mutt." Not long ago, she had placed her mother's long-husbanded ashes around the rose bushes. It would be a banner year for blossoms.

Now wide awake, Belle left Freya sleeping on her sheepskin and went downstairs to boost the coffee maker, timed for 5:45. What was that old medieval verse from her lit survey? *"Timor mortis conturbat me"?* The fear of death confounds me. Gary's last breath had stopped long before Miriam's designated eighty years for a Canadian male. It was hardly fair, but she should be learning a lesson.

Taking her steaming mug to the living room, she sat in the blue velvet recliner and watched the apricot glimmers of dawn set fire to the leaden sky. A small compensation for rising early. To the northwest at the Wapiti Indian reserve, the same early flicker greeted her as it had done for years, neighbours yet strangers. Like Gary and her. Scarcely had their friendship ignited than it had guttered like a surfeited candle.

Dressing hastily in cream pants, loafers and a blue cotton sweater, she headed for the van. As she took off down the road, she saw a Prius in the Lavoie driveway. Mutt's? She hoped he was getting some well-deserved sleep, perhaps only out of exhaustion. The first two months' rent was paid. Would he be staying for the summer, or was that a grotesque idea?

At seven, she parked in the office lot and walked to the nearby Tim Hortons. She ordered a large coffee along with a ham-and-cheese scone, a filling bargain at less than two dollars. More customers swelled the lines, retirees prepared to nurse a cup for an hour, gossiping with chums, or working folk who blew by in minutes. "Help who's next?" one of the counter staff asked, an efficient question which put polite Canadians on their honour not to jump the queue.

"You're up early," said a voice in a grey coat. Bearing his own cup plus a virtuous bran muffin without butter, Steve Davis parked his six-six frame in the opposite seat. They'd met when he'd been a young cop moonlighting on security work for Uncle Harold. Now he was a senior detective. The long-abandoned blue uniform had done more for his smooth bronze complexion and jet-black hair, courtesy of an Ojibwa background with a dram of Scot added a century ago.

"Someone died unexpectedly. Guess I wanted to get to work and stop thinking about it." She explained the accident, wasting few words. Details were unknown at this point. She attempted a stoic shrug but felt her shoulders sag.

"Happens." He leaned back in his seat and fixed his dark pupils on her as one expressive eyebrow rose in a question. At his temples, grey was making inroads as fast as it was leavening her red hair. "An old boyfriend of yours, you say? Never heard you mention him."

Belle gave a wry laugh. As she shared the sorrow with her good friend, the irony of the little saga made grief secondary to reflection. "He wasn't one of my success stories. Now I understand why. All that time out of my life and thoughts, and then he reappeared as a reinvented person. But one that I liked much better." She explained her new perspective.

He spread his large hands, strong but gentle enough to cuddle his young daughter Heather, half-Italian and half-Cree, adopted a few years ago. "Hey, I'm with wise old Pierre. What any adult does with another in a bedroom isn't the state's concern. And as for the new marriage laws, who cares? Move on, world."

Belle stirred her coffee and finished the scone, the buttered fragments dry in her mouth. She wasn't solid enough this morning to ask him about Janet and their shaky marriage. Floundering on shoals on a monthly basis, it righted itself like an old galleon and sailed off. But a crease etched itself into his broad forehead. She met his eyes and let silence lead him.

"I might as well tell you. Now that Heather's nearly seven, Janet wants to adopt again to give her a sibling. We had some good luck with that agency in the Sault, so we'll see."

"How do you feel about that?" Safe enough question.

"Heather's been a miracle. Should we hope for two?" He sloughed off the concern with masculine brio. "The dynamics don't bother me. We might need a larger house, though. I'll let you know. Of course, I expect a discount."

Normally, the prospect of a sale cheered her, so she forced a smile at one corner of her mouth, wondering if he was joking about the commission. "Anything for the trade, Steve." Then, seeing that she still had a few minutes, she explained about Jack's accident. "You wouldn't believe my temporary secretary. Yoyo Hourtovenko. I'm not making up the name."

"Uh-hum." His strong jaw curved as he took a swig of coffee. "So Yoyo's out."

Belle digested the three words. Out. Was he confusing the situation with Gary's sexuality? "What do you mean?"

"I'm surprised you took her on. Or maybe not. Let me guess. Got her cheap, right?"

Belle spluttered, as too large a sip of coffee made her windpipe ache. "Well, I..." What was he implying?

"Yolanda was sent to the Vanier Pen in Milton for forging checks to feed her gambling addiction."

Belle stood up, knocking her paper cup and spilling a pool onto the table. She grabbed a serviette from the overstuffed chrome dispenser, pulling out a half-dozen to her embarrassment. "Gambling? You mean the slots? Sudbury Downs?" A sudden frisson of fear charged through her body, and her knees grew weak. Yesterday she'd given Yoyo the company chequebook and told her to pay the utility bills and the bi-yearly taxes. How could Miriam have done this to her, and what was the plan now?

"Slots, horses, blackjack, the lady's into everything."

She arrived at the office in marathon time, jayjogging across Paris Street. Yoyo's blue Ford Probe was in the lot, a rusty hole in one door, the trunk bearing wrinkles of an ancient accident and red cellophane mending the taillight. As Belle slammed through the door, Yoyo looked up from her computer. To Belle's horror, the outlines of a card game appeared on the screen. Gambling on the Internet? People lost their houses that way. For a moment she froze and rubbed her temple as Yoyo smiled and pushed forward a small plastic bag. On a boom box at her feet, a frantic song was playing.

"You're later than usual today. Isn't this humidity awful? I brought you some of my homemade dog bikkies. Baron's favourite." She opened the bag and proudly held up a brown heart-shaped cookie.

"We need to talk. What's on your screen? And what's that music?"

Yoyo turned it down to sotto voce and smacked a wad of gum. Spearmint tickled Belle's nose like a mocking retort. "Putamayo. Cape Verde songs. That's near Africa. They cheer me up. What groups do you—"

Belle waved her hand as if brushing a swarm of flies. "Never mind. I know all about your gambling habit. A friend of mine told..."

At that moment, into the office came a couple in their early fifties. Belle and Yoyo exchanged glances. "Are you open? We saw someone come in," the man said.

"Welcome." Belle ushered them to her side of the room and seated them in comfortable chairs, offering coffee. She leaned forward on her desk and gave a penetrating stare as Yoyo clicked off and began sorting mail.

Belle took the information from the Suvaks, who wanted to sell their Mallard's Landing house to move into a smaller place now that the last teenager had left for college. While they were filling out forms, she noticed Yoyo rise to greet a man dressed in an Armani suit and silk tie. With his brown hair slicked back New York-style, he seemed quite interested in her anatomy.

"I'll be with you momentarily," Belle called, acknowledging his presence with a wave.

"No problem, Ms Palmer." Yoyo grabbed a binder of listings.

"Follow me, sir. It's way more comfortable in the back."

The small office *was* getting crowded, but entertaining customers in the rear? Belle ground her molars as she jotted prospects for the Suvaks. When she finished and saw the couple out, she found Yoyo and her client sipping Perrier in the lounge, knee to knee on the couch. The binder was open to one of Belle's most problematical properties, the Adams horror. No road access. One had to park then climb up and over a rock outcrop the size of a whale.

The man rose and shook hands. "Yoyo told me about this fabulous camp on Digger Lake. I'm very interested. Can we go out this Friday, say around four?"

When he left, she followed Yoyo back to her desk. The woman was smiling like the Mona Lisa on Prozac. "That was good. How did you sell him on the camp?"

"The trout stream over the hill. He loves fishing. My granddad used to go to Digger all the time."

"This isn't a reprieve. We need to resume our talk. The subject is your gambling, common knowledge to everyone in town except for one." She stabbed at her chest with an index finger.

Yoyo's chin quivered. "I did my time. And I'm on medication. Compulsive gambling is a disease. You wouldn't fire someone with—"

Belle put up a hand in protest. "If the meds are working, what were those cards I saw?"

Yoyo hit a few keys. "Solitaire. Comes with Windows. Totally innocent." She put a hand on her belly, which reminded Belle of the elephant in the corner.

"And that's another problem. How...pregnant are you? Forgive my asking." Pregnant is pregnant. Why did she phrase it that way?

"Only five months. Long time to go." She blinked, and Belle

could swear that her soft, round eyes were filling. "Please, I need this job. My mother's—"

"Consider yourself on probation, and not because I'm soft. It would be too difficult to replace you for such a short period. And about that medication. Are you sure it's safe for—"

Yoyo nodded. "Not to worry. It's only St. John's Wort."

With Gary's death and this revelation about Yoyo, Belle had forgotten about reporting the Skead dumpsite. She dialled CrimeStoppers and to her consternation was routed to Toronto. How efficient was it to describe a bush road to someone four hundred kilometres away who would boomerang the information back to the Sudbury police? "Can you find out anything from the debit slip?" she asked.

"I only record the case, ma'am." The dispatcher also suggested that she take pictures of the site if possible.

Early the next morning, Belle finally reached Miriam at Jack's apartment. Apparently he was leaving the hospital tomorrow. "Cantankerous as ever. That's my boy. So how's Yoyo working out? A gem or what? Didn't I tell you—"

"About her gambling addiction?" Belle repeated what Steve had told her.

A worrisome silence made her squirm. Had she gone too far? Miriam's voice sounded hurt. "It must be a strain being as perfect as you are. Most of us make a mistake now and then. Like human beings, you see? She paid back every cent. Yoyo was one of those rare birds who actually made a profit."

"And you omitted the fact that she's pregnant."

Miriam cleared her throat. "Plenty of time before she's due. Have a heart for a fellow female. She's walked a tough road lately."

"What's tough about getting pregnant? I hear it only involves lying down."

"Miss Cynical, listen. A year ago, Yoyo fell in love with her social worker at Vanier, Tom Hourtovenko. When she got out, they married, moved into his apartment. Needless to say, the family resented her. Bunch of hoity-toities who show up at charity events but neglect their own backyard. Tom died in a multi-vehicle auto accident on Highway 400 last winter. Ice fog."

Belle lowered her voice. "That *is* bad." And to think that Yoyo never mentioned any of this. She had a new respect for the woman.

"It gets worse. He hadn't changed his will or insurance. Just careless. The family turned its back on her. She was left without a cent."

"What about the baby?"

"Yoyo is a proud girl. She never told them."

Belle nodded her head, a small door opening in her heart. "Sounds ruthless, all right. I don't blame her for writing them off."

"She is doing the job, isn't she? Results are what count."

"To be honest, she's got talent. I think she's unloaded the Adams camp."

Miriam gave a low whistle of admiration. "That *is* a miracle. I'm starting to worry that you'll replace me."

"No fear. Every other firm in town would give you a raise." She paused. "Something else has happened." She told Miriam about Gary.

"God, I saw the story in the *Timmins Daily Press*. Friend of mine's dad died the same way. Sometimes I'm glad we have to stoop to pee, even if we do hit our shoes." A silence fell. "Sorry. I'm not exactly commiserating. But you never mentioned him. And it's unlike you to carry a torch and not tell."

"The torch never caught fire. I got my wish. Went to the grad dance with the valedictorian, and I have the pictures to prove it."

"Really? Love to see them sometime."

As the CrimeStoppers agent suggested, she drove to Station Road and revisited the ugly place. While she snapped Polaroid shots of the soggy carpeting and panelling, her reoffended sensibilities gave her another idea for faster action. She headed down the road into Skead. At the turn of the century, it had been a lumbering town, thousands of tons of sawdust at the bottom of Kolari Bay still burbling at the site of the old sawmill. Now it was a peaceful enclave on the lake where a few hundred people lived in a permanent vacation half an hour from Sudbury.

Inside a clear plastic cover, she tacked three pictures to the wooden bulletin board the local seniors had constructed at the mailbox kiosk, then added a handprinted sign: *Know anyone renovating with this decor?* To be on the safe side, she gave only her cell phone number. Skead was a very small community, and word would travel fast. She had confidence that public sentiment was on her side. People would welcome the opportunity to police their streets for the greater good. Spotting a collection of business cards on the side, she added hers.

As noon approached, she was late for lunch with her father. After calling in the order, she decamped from the office and hurried over to Garson.

At the Big Nickel, a small restaurant that changed hands every other year, in competition with taverns and pizza delivery, their meals were ready. Her milk and a tuna sandwich on rye, his chopped chicken, mashies, peas and gravy. Cherry pie to follow. Since a near-fatal choking incident, he was on the gummer's special, but he never complained.

Balancing the clamshell boxes, she made her way up the wheelchair-accessible ramp of Rainbow Country, the two-storey building run by the Finnish community as a stopgap before finishing their Minnow Lake complex for the aging.

Shabby around the edges, but whistle-clean, it was cosier than the generic high rises that warehoused the elderly. She'd been lucky to whisk him back from Florida with minimal immigration problems, a bit of fact-fudging aside. At American nursing home prices, his mutual funds would have evaporated like the Jays' chances at a pennant, and the logistics of travelling across a continent to check on him made her shiver.

She picked up silverware and linens in the kitchen, then passed the nurses' station. Cherie was on guard, a curly blonde sparkplug who never missed flagging the slightest change in her charges. "George's skin is getting worse. Our doctor hasn't a clue. I know you took him to Vonnie, the skin specialist, only last month."

Belle paused, nuances of worry on her forehead. "He said it was bullous dermatitis. Nothing serious."

The nurse snorted in contempt. "Another kind of bull. That's Latin for blisters. A description, not a diagnosis."

"Ouch. Guess I shouldn't have taken Spanish." Belle nodded, appreciating the woman's sharp eye. "Even my father said the man was senile. Vonnie must be in his eighties."

"We need every specialist we have up here, but sometime I wonder." She turned as a frail man in a walker lurched by, his bum crack exposed by pants that hung on him like a scarecrow. "Here, Jim. Let me tuck you in, my man."

In the bright, private room with easy-care linoleum, Belle found her father in his gerry chair, the jailer designed to keep him from falling but also from walking, since he wouldn't cooperate with physio attempts. She doubted whether the trade-off was worth it, but he enjoyed his television, magazines and newspapers, and especially his food. Every meal her mother had placed before him had been the "best". He wore a clean blue sweatsuit and Labatt's slippers on his feet, an ironic touch.

He was a teetotalling Methodist, but Belle and her mother had made up for that with their mutual predilection for scotch straight up.

He brushed a shaky hand through his thick mane of white hair, cheeks pink with a fresh shave. Staff knew when the family would be visiting and made the extra effort. He tapped his watch as if to coax the hours to pass more quickly. *Jeopardy* and *Wheel of Fortune* defined his evenings. "Late. I thought you weren't coming."

She arranged the bib and food. "Neither rain nor snow nor sleet nor earthquakes nor tsunamis can stop me."

As he dug in with a will, she winced at the large black blisters branding his mottled hands. Suppressing an urge to roll up his pant leg to check further, she turned instead to her sandwich, making sure he stopped now and then to drink water.

When he had finished ten minutes later, she let him attack the pie, carefully mashed. "Remember Gary Myers?"

"Of course. Of course. One of those blond German lads you favoured. Were you trying to recruit your own Wehrmacht?"

She smiled at the quirkiness of his memory. Sometimes sharp, recalling Dunkirk with his Churchill imitation, dull some mornings when he forgot having breakfast and wanted another. Who had been her troopers? Wertman. Gall. Erhart. Stretching from Grade One to university. Was she a Teutonic magnet or vice versa? Then she explained what had happened.

"We never know when the grim reaper is going to come calling. Only the good die young, your sainted mother aside. Gary, now. I could see you wondered about that boy. Why he never came around again." He tapped his temple. "But parents know."

She cocked an eyebrow. "You never mentioned it."

"None of my business. My cousin Ab's daughter, Tracy the vet, she lives in Lethbridge with a female dentist." He waved his hand.

"Asked Ab about it. That's what he said. None of his beeswax."

Belle sat back in wonderment at a curiously twenty-first-century attitude for a man alive during the Twenties. "Tracy? I guess that wasn't a topic for discussion while I was growing up."

He gave a low whistle. "As a kid, you sure were confused about *The Children's Hour.* Your mother was at Massey Hall the night it showed at the screening, so you had to come." He had been a booker for Odeon Pictures in Toronto, and they'd seen four new releases every week together once she reached Grade One. "You cried because Shirley MacLaine was so sad."

The large clock on the wall was sending her a message. She turned with reluctance to a more alarming subject. "Cherie says your blisters are getting worse. Let's see." She rolled up his pants and nearly gasped in horror. Huge, watery black sacs covered his lower legs.

"They don't hurt. Not one bit."

"A saving grace." She tried not to shudder. Was he merely being brave, or was some more pernicious condition festering, like diabetes?

Making a note to tell the nurse to have the doctor check her father on the weekly visit, she left the nursing home. Something was very wrong here. For once she wished she lived down south with a lion's share of specialists...or in the States, with money up front and no waiting.

FIVE

It's all still a nightmare, but I can't wake up," Mutt said, sipping coffee on her deck. A slight breeze ruffled the needles on the huge fir that loomed twenty feet above the railings. The poplars and birch in the greenbelt to their right wore a bright cloak of new leaves, but he didn't seem to notice. His handsome face was battling the signs of stress. Circles had appeared under his dulled eyes, and his hand shook. "When I saw him on that table..."

She leaned forward. "I've never had to do that. Must be painful."

He shook his head, his dark curly hair close around his neck. "I write about this stuff. I tried to be objective, but it's different in real life. His face was untouched. Almost serene, pink from the sun. The illusion of warmth. I wanted to touch..." His voice broke off.

A minute passed. "What about his family?"

"I had to call his mother. She's in a retirement community near Hamburg. Even three Valium didn't do the job for me. Maybe I should have driven down, but I didn't trust myself on the highway."

Like her, Gary had been an only child. Belle tried to recall his parents, seen at a distance at concerts and plays. He'd never introduced her, a bad omen. His father had been a lithographer, his mother a housewife like most women in Scarborough of that era. Gary had inherited his father's blond hair and his mother's

43

chubbiness. "And his father?"

Mutt drained his cup. "Liver cancer. Didn't make it past fifty. Gary connected the condition with his work, all those toxic chemicals. Of course, they didn't know in those days."

"Did you get any more information from the OPP?"

"I took a taxi and picked up the truck at the impoundment lot." He gave a bitter laugh and drummed his fingers on the table. "An empty bottle of scotch on the seat."

"I don't believe it." This was turning into a B-movie.

"Cheap stuff, too. MacKay and Whyte. Gary wouldn't drink that on a bet. It was his only splurge. Glenlivet or nothing."

Belle winced at the trashing of her bargain brand. "Did he usually carry alcohol along when he was working?"

Mutt shrugged. "I wouldn't deny that if he stayed over in the tent, he might enjoy a few toddies around the campfire, but leaving an open bottle on the truck seat? No way."

"Reminds me of Tom Thomson." A friend of the Group of Seven, Canada's foremost pantheon of painters, he had drowned in Algonquin Park.

"A famous mystery," Mutt said. "There was a theory that he had been murdered by a local and that someone else lay in his grave. When a skull was unearthed, it showed signs of a bullet. Then the skull was identified as an aboriginal's. Some said the family had relocated Tom. No one knew where, or they weren't telling. I wrote a short story about it."

"I know it's tempting, but let's not get carried away." She imagined that with his crime writing, he juggled forensic possibilities on a regular basis.

Mutt stuck out his jaw, a faint stubble giving him the appearance of a high-priced model, probably through neglect, not affect. Belle preferred men clean-shaven. "The booze doesn't make sense."

She shifted to another subject. When her mother had died in Florida, Belle was fast on the scene with twenty garbage bags for her closets, burying her grief, as women often did, by turning to chores. By the following week, someone who needed them was wearing her mother's stylish clothes. Mutt would have his own sad duties arranging the evidence of a soul. "Are you going over to the Ministry to clean out his office?"

"This afternoon. He was only there a few months, but someone at Brock might be able to make sense of his elk research, if I can put it in order. Shame to throw it away...along with his life..."

He turned aside, and a hand brushed his eye. Then his broad shoulders straightened.

"Do you know much about zoology? And what about your own book? Don't you need the time for that?" Did it make sense for Mutt to get involved in the research? Maybe a mission would ease his pain.

"Minored in it. An odd combination, but it gave us a connection. And as for my book, let it go for the moment. Nothing's worse for an author than forcing a story." He paused and frowned at a fresh thought. "Gary was especially excited about something lately, something that bothered him. We talked on the phone nearly every night."

Belle shook her head, trying to remember what Gary had told her about his studies. Survival rates, was it? "A new disease? Or maybe someone poaching the herd?" Despite the ruinous penalties, which included heavy fines and confiscation of vehicles, the North was full of people who regarded the bush as a free supermarket.

Mutt walked to the edge of the deck, his velvety black hair stark against the pillowing cotton clouds in the distance. A raven warbled and swooped past. A marauding group of crows, smaller but dangerous, cawed shrilly from the tops of a high cedar, likely protecting their nests from the larger bird. "It was a white elk. A calf he found."

She blew out a breath. "Sounds rare. I wonder if it was an actual albino or just a hybrid. I've read about moose with pale fur. Did he tag it? Take pictures? He must have carried a camera."

"It was dead, that's all I know. He said he had to make a few calls. Get someone to look at it."

"So he was carrying the body around? My God." The idea made her shudder, which explained why she was no scientist.

"Not carrying it around." He looked at her with an amused turn to his lips, as if she lived on another planet. "He brought home specimens whenever possible. It wasn't gruesome to him."

"I guess not, and there's an ancient deer head in the woods that I am fond of. But surely no one would shoot a baby elk. There's no meat to speak of, and it makes a poor trophy." Then again, dogs and cattle and even people were shot every year by overeager hunters. Maybe it looked like a wolf to them.

"He didn't mention any wounds. Died from natural causes, I suppose. But he wanted it documented." He sat back down in the chair and crossed his legs, Noel Coward-style. North of Sudbury, it might have earned glances. But he was an author, and a theatrical side helped the mystique. More than that, he was adjusting to a savage loss, and he had trusted her with his heartache.

"How, uh, long were you and Gary together?" she asked. Perhaps she shouldn't have intruded, but once Mutt had left, how could she fill in the gaps?

"Seven years. Wasn't there an old film about that? Marilyn Monroe? Gary said you liked the classics."

The Seven Year Itch. What else about her had been dinner-table conversation?

He stretched out his left hand, where a simple gold band gleamed. "Gary was the sentimental one. He insisted on a ceremony. Gladioli in every colour of the rainbow, even cinnamon. Four of our friends in tuxes, including two women. A string quartet. Catering by Mildred Pierce. And down the aisle to Bach's 'Sheep May Safely Graze'. Kind of an inside joke. But it was quite the occasion. Even if my family didn't come. All of them were conveniently in Europe."

"It's a lovely song. Gary had a beautiful tenor voice, too." They were mourning two different people, a boy and a man. "How did you two meet?" she added, her prying on a forward roll. It seemed that he wanted to talk about their life.

"Over a bag of garbage, oddly enough. The annual initiative to clean up the hiking trails around the Niagara escarpment."

"Sometimes I think half the world's out to trash the planet, and the other half's cleaning up. It's a stasis."

Mutt cleared his throat and looked at his watch. Men's styles were getting larger every year, a metallic command centre. A present from Gary? "I'm due at ten with the truck at the Ministry to clear out his office. If you'd come with me, that would be great. I don't know my way around town."

An hour later, they turned off Route 69 into the Ministry of Natural Resources on McFarlane Lake Road. The complex lay in a low valley of emerging boreal forest punctuated by the occasional conifer. Mutt parked in the lot, and they headed to the main office.

A tall, older admin assistant looked up from her computer. A metal sign on the desk gave her name as Marj Brousseau. On the walls were advertisements for environmental initiatives, hunting and fishing regulations and topographic maps. Taking their names and shaking hands, she responded to their inquiry with a sad smile, as she removed her slim, wire-rimmed glasses and rubbed the bridge of her aquiline nose. Tumbling strawberry-blonde hair streaked with grey was gathered at the back of her neck by a colourful paisley scarf. "I didn't know Gary long, but he was a nice fellow. Serious about his job but with a good sense of humour. What a terrible accident."

Mutt swallowed, shuffled his feet as he looked at a poster of duck species. "We came to clean out his office, Ms Brousseau. If you can—"

"Of course. It's Marj. I'll call Dr. Rosaline Silliker. She's our supervisor." She punched in a few numbers.

Minutes later, a tall, dark chestnut brunette around forty with short, artistic curls entered the office, her arm extended from a tailored silk suit that brushed her mid-knee. Her legs were muscular without being overbearing, as if she worked out in Pilatian control of each group. "Thanks for coming so promptly at this sad time. We'll miss Gary. His research was critical to the survival of these local herds. He had such a commitment to bringing back the elk, both for tourism—"

"And hunting?" Belle added, one corner of her mouth rising. She'd visited the Ontario Fur Managers website last year in connection with a trapper in her woods. Despite the occasional garbage raid, she and her resident bears had crossed paths many times without incident. No question that encounters were on the rise since cancellation of the spring hunt, a hot button that pitted gun-toting Northerners against Torontonians who had nothing but the odd raccoon or skunk to bother them.

"Animals are a resource. We're here to keep them renewable. Farther north where jobs can be scarce, outfitters rely heavily on the traffic, and a few family lodges have suffered." Rosaline's tone was pleasant, but with a tinge of a bureaucratic lecture. The Ministry attracted criticism trying to please both sides, but Belle suspected that money was the bottom line.

Following her down a long corridor, they came to an office crowded with two battered oak desks, filing cabinets and floor-to-ceiling bookcases. One shelf held toothy skulls of small mammals, rabbit, porcupine, a weasel. A few jars of formaldehyde held mysterious objects, which Belle wasn't sure she wanted to examine. Mutt coughed as a musty smell tweaked their noses. At one desk, a young man of about twenty typed information into a computer spreadsheet. He wore jeans and a sweatshirt, the sleeves cut roughly to reveal an eagle tattoo on one arm. A mop of buttery hair, the kind that made mothers spit on their fingers and tamp cowlicks into respectability, gave him a pleasantly boyish look.

"Dave Watson," he mumbled, as they introduced themselves.

"Dave's a master's degree intern at Shield University. He can tell you what belonged to Gary." Rosaline looked around with a helpful smile. "Do you need a cart or dolly? How about some boxes?"

Dave seemed rather cool. Busy though he might have been, he didn't offer to shake hands and offered no commiseration about their friend. Shortly after, a handyman arrived with packing material and a flatbed wagon. Working slowly and carefully, Belle and Mutt emptied Gary's file cabinets. "What about the books?" Mutt asked.

Dave looked up and pointed out two shelves. A bibliophile, with her mother's Pauline Johnson's first editions of poetry as a prize, Belle watched Mutt touch them like old friends, the last remnant of a life that ended halfway to the finish line. *Ruminants of the Boreal Forest; Introduction to Zoology; North American Elk: Ecology and Management; Mosses, Lichens and Ferns of Ontario;* piles of *The Canadian Journal of Zoology* and *The Canadian Field Naturalist* as well as her own favourites, Peterson's *Animal Tracks* and Stokes' *Nature in Winter*.

In another cabinet Dave indicated, Mutt turned up several plastic baggies with dry brown shapes. He wrinkled his nose, but Belle had no reservations about examining them. Similar to moose droppings and virtually odourless, thanks to a meatless diet, these pellets someone would dissect in a more complete analysis.

On Gary's desk was a silver-framed picture, face down. Mutt turned it over to reveal himself in star quality from a Toronto studio. With a rising colour to his cheek, he tucked it under his arm. Then he asked, "Do you know what he was working on recently, Dave?"

"Naw. I've been out in the field the last two weeks." He didn't look up from his computer, presenting merely a hunched back. "Listen, if you can finish, I need some quiet in here."

Mutt and Belle exchanged eye rolls and gave the office another scan. Mutt opened a deep cabinet and found a few more files. Then he reached over his head onto a seemingly empty shelf, fumbling at first with a quizzical expression, then retrieving a strange object. "This is weird. Is it yours, Dave?"

Dave turned with a sigh and grunted. "Do I look like a garbageman?"

Mutt and Belle examined the old Pepsi can. The design didn't look recent, but neither did it appear vintage. The aluminum had begun to fade and corrode, more than sun damage. "I wonder why he kept this? Or maybe it belonged to someone else here years ago." Mutt spoke so loudly and pointedly that the man had to answer.

"I saw him with it. God knows why it interested him."

Mutt shrugged, and he fingered it gently so as not to cut himself. "Gary never did anything without a reason. Let's take it." To wrap the can safely, he found an empty plastic bag in a wastebasket.

As they were leaving, they saw Rosaline Silliker embrace a tall, balding man with a clerical collar. "I'll get an oil change for the car and come back at five, dear. You make the reservations at Verdicchio's." Sudbury's premier restaurant, a doctor at the table on the left and a lawyer on the right. A minister's and a middle-ground civil servant's salaries? Either they'd won the lottery, or there was money in the family.

"Finished already?" asked Rosaline, turning to Mutt and Belle. "Did you get everything? Is there any other way I can help?"

Mutt nodded thanks, but Belle could tell that his voice was breaking. He soldiered his way outside, hauling the cart, as she exchanged female glances with Rosaline.

"I couldn't help wondering why Dave was so unfriendly. Is he normally like that?"

Rosaline raised one professionally plucked eyebrow and folded her hands in front of her. Her nails were short and buffed. "Homophobic, I'm afraid. He was surly to Gary from the beginning."

Belle put her hands on her hips in a gesture of incredulity. "What? Such a young man? Hard to believe he'd be so judgmental."

"A very provincial attitude. He comes from way northwest of here, where they're not very...enlightened. Sioux Lookout's the nearest town. Maybe I was wrong, but I refused to buy into it by reassigning him to another office."

"Some people want to turn back the clock."

"You and I both remember how women had to fight for equality even in our lifetimes." Rosaline nodded. "Gary was a brick about it, though. Not a word of complaint. His approach must have worked, because things quieted down."

Belle managed to pass Rosaline and Marj business cards before she left the site. An hour later, back on Edgewater Road, as they unpacked, a large, hairy animal snuffled its way around the yard, pawing at a clump of sage in the herb garden. "Get out of here!" Mutt yelled. The beast bared its yellow teeth, one incisor chipped.

"It's Bill Strang's dog. Has he been bothering you? Sometimes he chases cars." She bent to scoop up a handful of gravel, a gesture any canine understood.

"Damn right," Mutt said, as the animal slunk off through the caragana hedge. "I spent an hour rebuilding what it dug up in the irises. And it left a pile smack in the driveway. I went next door to complain, but the guy's never home."

"Put the pile in *his* driveway. Saves time and effort to send a clear message. Everyone recognizes their dog's productions."

"God, you take no prisoners up north."

The remote road was "conflicted" about the subject of dogs. In the city, they were strongly regulated with registry and leash laws. Here, the new residents thought they had moved "to the country," negating any responsibilities. Dogs often ran free on the road, a danger to drivers and to themselves, not to mention walkers. Strang was a retired codger with few friends. His wife's death from congestive heart failure a year ago had made him even more reclusive.

"Or call the Animal Control. They'll check for a license and give him a warning by phone. Too bad you can't catch the dog and take him to the pound. That's my usual solution. But Buddy's too cagey."

"Buddy. Hah. Normally I'm not afraid of dogs, but that one is a monster."

That night while reading CNN online, Belle noticed a review of a new book that suggested Abraham Lincoln was gay. Apparently he had shared a bed with a storekeeper's son early in his career, a common occurrence on the frontier, but the boy's diary made startling suggestions. How had anyone ever found the diary or Abe's doggerel poem on same-sex marriage?

Upstairs in her waterbed, as the first loons of the year began duelling across the lake, Belle gulped a handful of vitamins, including calcium bombs, then tucked a cigarette into the jewelled Adolph Menjou holder her father had bought her at Universal Studies Park in Orlando. Before the TIA's rendered him unable to live on his own, they'd had some wonderful times in Florida. She made a mental note to call the nursing home for an update.

SIX

Belle toyed with a pencil, its point dull as chalk. Yoyo had broken the office sharpener that morning and was off to Staples. She wasn't that clumsy, just careless, wanting to do everything as fast as possible. As a multi-tracked Gemini and a minimalist, Belle understood the phenomenon.

"I knew you were concerned, so I read the files on your friend's drowning," Steve said, coming in the door and putting an attaché case on a table. "Detective Ramleau filled me in. Seems that the autopsy found alcohol in the stomach."

"That's not surprising. Mutt said that they found a bottle in his truck. But I didn't want to believe that he'd been drinking."

"Mutt. That's some name. Only ever heard of one. Shania Twain's husband."

"Mutt's a sweetheart. He's very...sensitive. But strong." She added what he'd said about the cheap brand.

"It wasn't as if he were boozing all day. Nothing in the bloodstream. The liquor was raw. Undigested." He leaned against the wall and sipped from an aluminum car mug.

Belle snapped her fingers. "So doesn't it rule out his being drunk?"

"Let's say he took a swig just before getting into the boat. Maybe he was coming down with a cold. As for the unusual brand, he could have bought it at some small outlet on 69 where there wasn't any choice."

"Any prints on the bottle?"

"Inconclusive."

"I hate it when they say that."

A glowering shadow came over Steve's face. "It's not all *CSI*, you know. Shows like that are perverting the legal system. Everyone wants DNA, hard evidence. Juries, like in the Robert Blake trial, aren't convicting without it, even though witnesses testified that he solicited the killing of his wife."

Tread lightly. Professional to his core and taciturn about his responsibilities, Steve usually dragged his feet on the details. So far he was being more than cooperative, perhaps because of her former relationship with Gary. "I see your point. Can you tell me more about the autopsy?"

"I'm only letting you in on this because it seems to be an accident, nothing more. No worries about compromising a case."

Steve opened the case and passed her a photocopied file with scarcely ten pieces of paper. Was this all there was to a life? She scanned the jargon. Major contusions to head. Occipital bone reveals compound fracture and haematoma measuring six centimetres by ten centimetres. Bruising on ribs. Haematology was normal in the blood profile assays. No toxicology concerns. Victim has no appendix. Additional examination unremarkable. Cause of death, drowning. Lungs full of water. Pond water, not tap water. Daphnia. Other organisms she couldn't pronounce.

Belle remembered when Gary's appendix had been taken out. He'd been in pain for days but insisted on finishing his midterm exams, collapsing as he turned in his math paper. In trying to preserve his valedictorian status, he'd been half an hour from a rupture.

Steve took back the report. "So it appears that he fell. It would have rendered him unconscious, or at best too confused to save himself."

Belle blew out a sigh. "Occipital?"

"Back of the head."

"But in that case, wouldn't he have been more likely to have come down in the boat?" With her fingers, she formed an area the size of the haematoma. A massive blow.

"Canoes are tippy. The fracture's consistent with hitting the gunwale more than the seat. You're letting your emotions carry you away...as usual."

Belle bristled and tried to stifle a frown. "Can you make a few more inquiries? Accidents often aren't what they seem in more ways than one. Think about that medical examiner in Toronto who misdiagnosed cause of death and sent parents and relatives to jail for killing children."

Twenty seconds passed before a wry smile came her way. "Ramleau's wife won a trip to Costa Rica, and they have to take it before July or lose the opportunity. Maybe I can muscle in and keep the case open. I wouldn't do this for anyone but you. And don't mention intuition, because your track record's wobbly."

Belle gripped his arm. "What a guy."

He opened a small notebook and took a pen from his jacket pocket. "Now tell me everything you know about Gary, his partner, and what the hell they were doing up here."

"For heaven's sake, take a chair."

"I'm used to writing standing up. Besides, my back is killing me. A whack of yard work on the weekend. I'm on my way to the chiropractor, as a matter of fact."

Belle made a commiserative face. Dear Steve.

After he left, she pondered the simple words in the report. *Unremarkable.* She knew what it meant, but the idea stung. Gary had been anything but unremarkable. Wasn't everyone's son or daughter? At least he'd known a committed relationship. When the role was called up yonder, she'd check in as a dog's best friend. Meanwhile, bills had to be paid. A lucrative apartment appraisal on Kingsmount was scheduled. Uncle Harold had been wise to suggest that she qualify for her appraiser's credentials. It kept the place solvent in lean times.

Fifteen minutes later, the door opened, and Belle blinked. The woman of sixty plus wore Capri pants, which exposed sinewy lower calves with a roadmap of varicose veins, a loose paisley top, and battered flip-flops. Her hair was a thin nest of home-permed curls, unnaturally black with silver roots, and she wore mirrored sunglasses like a wizened trooper. She gave the room the once-over and clumped to Belle's desk, tapping on it with a carved cedar cane. A cigarette dangled precariously from a cerise mouth sucked back into wrinkles. "You Belle? How ya doing? Yoyo around? I need a ride."

"She's...out for the moment. I don't think we've met." Belle fanned blue smoke from the air.

"Coco Caderette, her mother." Beery fumes surrounded her like a cloud of fermenting barley. She leaned forward for a handshake, her fingers thin and cold as turkey tendons and her nails chipped.

"I can't say when she'll be back. Half an hour's a guess." Belle couldn't help watching as an ash dribbled down the woman's blouse. "May I call you a taxi? I'd drive you, but I'm all alone here."

Coco guffawed, swiping at the blouse. "Oops, clumsy me. That reminds me of an old joke, honey. But shit, no. I can hitch down Notre Dame from here. Thumb, don't fail me now." Brandishing a digit gnarled with arthritis, as she turned, she noticed the picture of Freya on the wall, the noble sable head emerging from a greenery of ferns. "Gotcherself a nice shep. Female. I can tell by the nose. Very refined. *À bientôt.*" She lurched towards the door, leaving it open as she exited.

Belle blew a sigh of relief as she clicked the handle shut. No doubt there was quite a story in that family. Her own life was so uneventful, all the better for amassing funds on the march to retirement. Only lately had Gary's return wakened her from her doldrums. Then there was the dumping in the bush. Would anything come of her report to CrimeStoppers? Maybe she'd been a bit hasty in putting up those pictures. Steve would have slapped her wrist.

She picked up the phone to check on her father, but the line was busy. As Belle listened to the weather, Yoyo returned, grinning broadly. "That place is as dangerous as Costco. They had a special on Turtles. Have one. So yummy," she said, revealing a dozen luscious morsels.

Between nutty chocolate and caramel bites, Belle mentioned Coco.

"No sweat. I saw her get into a panel truck at the lights. Woman never needs a car. The North is so friendly."

"It's still not wise. Even though women of her age aren't usually abducted."

"Abducted? Maybe with a stun gun. Ma says she has a nose for people. Never wrong. Isn't she a character? I love her to pieces. She's my inspiration and the reason I'm not afraid to be a single parent." Using a compact, Yoyo applied a fresh coat to her glossy red mouth, pursing her lips and giving herself an air kiss. She wasn't using lipstick, but a kind of paint with a miniature brush.

Belle cleared her throat, speed-reading the sales slip and filing it. The candy must have been separate. Had Yoyo paid herself, or was shoplifting another habit?

Though Belle had enough discretion not to pursue whether Coco had ever been married or even supported by a man, Yoyo continued. "Old bastard took off thirty years ago. Mom had just lost her job as a cook at Burwash when they closed. Got another position at Pioneer Manor with the old folks. Damn, could she whip up meals. Vats of mashies. The bestest gravy. Homemade is nothing like that gluey, tasteless stuff that they—"

Yoyo's phone rang as Belle was about to tell her to get back to work instead of reminiscing about gravy. Suddenly she craved one of the hot beef, turkey or chicken sandwich rafts that floated the North through winters.

The rest of the afternoon was quiet. Picking up a strawberry sundae from the convenience store on her way home, Belle stopped at Rainbow Country to check on her father. He dove into the ice cream as if he'd been starving, even though she knew dinner had already been served. Afterwards, dreading the truth, she checked his legs. A jungle infection. The blisters were oozing and broken.

"Still doesn't hurt, though. They put bandages and cream on every day. The cowards look kind of scared. Am I contagious? Is it beri-beri? Remember Edwina Booth from *Trader Horn?* When they shot that film in Africa, she caught malaria and nearly—"

She took away the empty plastic container and spoon, her temples pounding. Belle hated making scenes, but enough was enough. "We're going to find out. I promise."

Down the hall she walked, choosing her words carefully. Passively accepting her father's medical treatment had led to this crisis, but the staff wasn't to blame. "Ann," she said to the nurse at the desk. "My father needs to get another opinion. I think he should be in the hospital. Do you agree?"

"Cherie and I were going to suggest that," Ann said with a relieved sigh as she picked up the phone. "I'm glad you're insisting. The way the system works, the family has to make some healthcare decisions. Frankly, I don't have much confidence in our Dr. Davison. If he had a decent practice, he wouldn't have to pad his payroll with nursing home visits. Makes you think."

Back in his room, Belle put an arm around her father's thinning shoulder, once so muscular. She owed him the same care he'd given her, even if he had pinned her to a diaper once. Recalling how at only five she could twist him around her finger to take her for milkshakes made her glad her mother had tempered the spoiling with an occasional wooden spoon to her bum. "You're getting a ride to the hospital. Someone will take a look at you. Let's hope they have better credentials than Vonnie and Davison."

"Will I get any food there? When will I come home?"

And Rainbow Country was home. "I'm not sick. I'm just old," he'd grumbled when he'd arrived, an accurate assessment.

Still worried about the delay in her father's treatment, Belle stopped at Mutt's. The soft, warm June evening had brought him to a lounge on the covered porch, where he was sifting through a pile of papers. Gary's massive pickup sat in the driveway. As she got out, he hoisted a beer. "One for you? Light okay?"

"Perfect."

When he returned, she let a cool trickle run down her throat. Today had actually passed twenty-five Celsius. Who needed to live in the banana belt? "How's everything going?" she asked, forced to lean backward in the angled chair until her neck muscles hurt.

"I'm just getting started. It's weird, though. Gary always typed up his field notes within a few days. There's nothing from the last two weeks. It's as if he stopped working." He shrugged. "Of course, I have his little pocket notebooks. He left a pile here on the desk. From the dates, it looks like the most recent one might be missing. His writing is terrible, though. Could be I have the dates wrong."

"I didn't see any small notebooks at the office when we picked up the supplies."

"Maybe he had it in the canoe, and it's at the bottom of the lake." Mutt sounded discouraged.

She told him about the autopsy. "The details are pretty spare, but they're always upsetting." She recalled reading her mother's death certificate. Everyone died from heart failure. The cause made the difference. A massive infection after chemo had triggered Terry Palmer's final collapse.

"So I heard. Detective Ramleau again. Cold bastard. I didn't care for his line of questioning." He gave a disgusted look. "The jerk asked me about any insurance or wills."

The thought hadn't even occurred to her. Belle swallowed another few ounces and gave what she hoped was a contemptuous laugh. "That's absurd. Are you saying that they're investigating you?" Maybe she shouldn't have pushed Steve to keep the file open.

"The old *qui bono* has them back on the case. Gary left everything to me. Double indemnity on insurance from the university."

"But everyone needs a will. And accidents happen. Surely they can't be—"

"He told me about it when we first got serious—$200,000 on the policy. Then of course our house in St. Catharines. A friend's occupying it while we...I'm away. My name's on the deed, though I didn't contribute much. Gary insisted on making us equal partners. Everyone thinks writers are all rich, but I'm just getting started with a small press."

"So that's all, then?" She tried to minimize the totals, but the remains of the day would be considerable. Down south, especially in the Golden Horseshoe, house prices had gone to the moon. Half a million dollars bought an ordinary bungalow.

"He'd invested quite well. Mutual funds. All that stuff's at home, though. I don't know anything about the exact figures. Frankly, I never paid attention."

Belle nodded. "Stocks fell into the toilet after 9/11, but values are soaring now." Mutt waved aside the financial complexities. Was he that naïve? Still, not everyone cared for money as much as she did.

"So how bad was the interview?"

He seemed charged with anger and humiliation as he recalled being taken to a windowless cupboard of a room at Police Headquarters at Tom Davies Square, running long fingers through his thick hair, a pulse pounding in his temple. "I can't believe they grilled me on where I'd been that day. And listen to my crime jargon. It might be funny if it weren't so personal."

"Routine." Belle thought about the logistics of the trip north and spread her hands. "But you were driving 69 all the way, right?" Had he stopped off at Bump Lake? She felt guilty for her suspicions.

"I had no idea about how to get to where he was working. Why would I have cared until now? But the police say the road goes by the Burwash turn, and how can I prove I didn't know?"

"I see. The point is that you could have reached him without much difficulty...if the time frame was right." She noticed four hummingbirds duelling at the feeder. They were aggressive little creatures, territorial and war-like. Mutt must have filled it. That a murderer could mix hummingbird nectar seemed like a grotesque joke. "They sound like they're bluffing."

"It was beyond belief. They asked me some very intimate questions about our relationship. Whether anyone else was involved. Who was living in our house. A Cecilian nun from Zaire who's taking courses in microbiology at Brock. Even the HIV/AIDS question lifted its ugly head."

"How awful. Why is that relevant?" Trying not to be obvious, she scrutinized Mutt. With the modern drug cocktails, no one resembled the archetypal skeletal victim any more, but another crease had etched his forehead.

He squared his broad shoulders. "You can bet they wouldn't have handled it this way in T.O. Bunch of rednecks." He saw her grimace. "Sorry. I don't mean you or any of the others I've met up here. Ramleau made my blood boil."

"He's off the case soon." She told him what Steve had said.

"And this guy Steve's a friend of yours? That's a break."

Too many ideas were arriving without notice. Belle didn't know how to interpret that comment. Did he expect special treatment? She finished the bottle of beer, touched the cool glass to her cheek. Were the police right? Did Mutt have the opportunity?

Belle pointed at a road map he had spread out. "Show me where he was working. I know a bit about the region from my real estate travels."

Mutt indicated Bump Lake, several miles west of the former Burwash facility grid, deep in a swampy area with a maze of dirt roads and old logging trails tapering into savage, uncharted wilderness. "Here's where they found his canoe floating loose and his...body. His truck was parked a mile back at the turnaround."

"So he must have portaged." No wonder Gary had become so fit. Muscling even a light canoe was a task she couldn't handle alone for more than a few hundred feet.

Suddenly he gave his head a pound with the butt of his hand. "Damn. I forgot about the canoe. Gary joked that it was his woman, sleek and fast. It's a Prospector Chestnut."

Belle knew that brand well. Old Town had been making them since 1910. "I have a Grumman. No mystique, but it

62

can take a collision with a jagged rock. Anyway, we can use the truck and pick it up." She paused. "Unless the police have it." If it had been left in the open when the death had been thought accidental, how likely would it be that fingerprints or other forensic evidence like blood would remain? She kept quiet.

"Those Keystone Kops again. But then I guess you don't get much crime up here, not like down south."

"We kill people with roads. Sudbury has two of the worst twenty in Ontario."

He looked at his watch with sudden embarrassment. "Sorry, but I'm expecting a call. I've been in contact with a few of his fellow professors at Brock. They're excited about getting the notes and promised to answer any questions. If I can get this project tidied up, then at least I..." He looked out over the lake, where a merganser skidded across the glassy surface, its mate probably in the shoreline rocks and weeds guarding their nest. "Remember that baby elk? I dreamed about it last night. We should start there."

The inadvertent "we" had made her a partner. She noticed a pile of periodicals on the table. One anomaly caught her eye. *The Environmental Pollution Journal.* It seemed well-thumbed and had strips of paper marking pages. "Pollution? I thought he was a zoologist."

"Scientific disciplines often overlap. One time he did a study about metal levels in fecal pellets of moose. Around the ore smelters in Sudbury, I think."

Once Sudbury's core had been a wasteland the size of New York City, timber gone, vegetation scoured from roasting beds at the turn of the century and acid rain to finish the job. Soil had run from its hills, leaving black rock. Then in the Eighties, a government-industry-civilian re-greening initiative had brought rye grass and small pines back, leading to a United

Nations reclamation award at the Earth Summit in Brazil.

"So question one, where is the baby?" Suddenly she had an eerie thought. Zoologists were quirky enough to keep carcasses in the freezer. Maureen had a power-chugging monster in the basement. "You didn't look downstairs—"

He tapped her hand. "My first thought. It's empty and unplugged. But I got a clue from a zoologist at Shield University. He said that Nickel City College has a dissecting room in their new tech complex. Paul Straten's the contact name. Apparently he's one of Ontario's top elk researchers."

"I gather you haven't reached him yet."

Mutt folded the map carefully. "We're still playing phone tag."

That night Belle ate a frozen pizza for a change. With a whole-wheat crust, low-fat mozzarella, and topped with spinach, it sounded better than it tasted. A call to Rainbow revealed that her father indeed had been ferried to the St. Joseph Health Centre Emergency Room. Ann suggested that Belle call to check his progress before driving in.

"He's being seen by the doctor now," the nurse said when Belle finally got through. "We're full-up, but we're going to keep him overnight, even if it's on a gurney. Best thing is to call back in the morning."

"Can you get him a sandwich?"

The woman laughed. "He's already had three. Plus coffee, a doughnut and snacks from someone in the waiting room. He's not allergic to peanuts, is he?"

SEVEN

Preoccupied by her father, Belle hadn't slept well and was out of the starting blocks at five with no more than coffee and juice. As dawn broke, she was passing the airport, watching the plume of the Superstack in the distance, the world's largest free-standing chimney, which supposedly scrubbed the air ninety-five per cent clean of sulphur dioxides.

Slowing down after the Falconbridge Road railroad overpass, before she turned right into Tim's for another java, she glanced at the large billboard warning about "The Silent Killer" and urging people with gas installations to install carbon-monoxide alarms. Hers was in the TV room. Recently when the window had been open and the van had been running outside, the unit had started beeping like gangbusters. Most houses had smoke alarms, but how many older homes added this precaution?

At the hospital at seven a.m., she talked to the heavy-set nurse in the Emergency Room, bleary-eyed after a long shift and blowing her nose. Belle stepped back from the germfest. "Yes, he was seen by Dr. Cowl, a very sharp resident. Spotted it right off. Pemphigoid, an auto-immune disease of the elderly."

Not mere blisters, then. Belle put her hand on her chest, felt her heart play timpani. Her blood sugar needed a top-up. "Can they help him?" When she got to the office, she'd check the Internet for treatment options.

The nurse smiled in reassurance. "Not to worry. A regimen

of steroids, Prednisone probably, will clear him up fast. He's a sweetie. Talked on and on about how he'd seen every film ever made."

Belle laughed. In nearly fifty years of working, so he had. "Then he'll be going right back to the home?" Routines were so important to him.

"High doses of Prednisone can cause anxiety and other disorienting symptoms, especially in seniors. They'll keep him here to assess his initial reactions for at least a week. And now I'm sorry, but I—"

"Thanks for your patience." Belle looked around at the many cubicles separated by white curtains. "May I see him?"

"They took him out half an hour ago for some blood work. I'll tell him you came by."

At the office, Belle noticed by the trademark shepherd snore that Baron was making himself comfortable in the back room. He was quiet and well-behaved, despite his manly assets. Was Yoyo hoping to breed him? That was easier for the owner of a male. One-stop shopping, and a share of the pups. Still, he had a few conformation flaws.

Yoyo had settled in. The hustling temp had not only helped unload the Adams place, but like a veteran in the trenches, she had cold-called forty people that week, a chore Belle likened to successive root canals, and lined up four eager to sell. Her outfits had toned down. Today featured a tasteful linen dress (high hemline and Lucite platform heels aside), and she'd nearly memorized the stylebook Belle had loaned her.

"I was still having the worst time with this 'me' or 'I' stuff with prepositions, until I figured out that if it sounded wrong, it was right," she said with a comical smile. "Between you and me. Duh."

Belle laughed until her stomach hurt. "And vice versa. Now why didn't I think of that?"

Yoyo applied herself religiously to the keyboard, tapping up a symphony that rivalled Miriam's in speed. When she finished, she reached over her shoulder to rip off another "Word a Day" page from her calendar. "Fossil," she read, pausing with some surprise. "Hey, do you know that word can refer to a living person? Weird."

"Not really," said Belle.

Around ten, Mutt called, his voice more perturbed than worried. "There's been a break-in here." He gave some details, but with a client coming in the door, Belle didn't have time for the whole story.

"I'll stop by on my way home. Meanwhile, call the police and the insurance company. I think Maureen uses Royal on Paris Street." As the go-between profiting from the rent, she felt a responsibility to expedite the matter. Not that she was totally surprised, because occasionally a tiny crime wave hit the road, usually teenaged snowmobilers breaking into camps just to raise hell, or in summer, the disappearance of prime movers like boat motors, shotguns, and small electronics. One real danger was vandalism. Maureen had some lovely antiques and very expensive small-paned windows for a country look. As for Mutt, she didn't imagine he had brought much in the car, except for clothes, books, a computer and a printer.

Late that afternoon, Belle was at his door. "Knock, Knock," she said, as he put down a journal and got out of a recliner.

The beamed, open-concept great room had a kitchen and dining area at one end, the massive fieldstone fireplace from the original cottage reaching two stories at the other. Building a house around a chimney had been a tour-de-force, but Maureen had installed an insert for safety. Nothing seemed out of place at first glance. Maureen's father's handmade snowshoes were crossed on the wall, along with two rusty leghold traps purely for decoration. The large wine cooler in the corner was burbling as if it stood at the bottom of the ocean. "Are the other rooms okay? When do you think it happened?"

"Hold on. I'll explain." He sighed. "I went into town last night to see a film at that Silver City. Didn't get back until midnight. To be frank, I just unlocked the door, went upstairs, had a brandy, and got in bed. Slept in. I didn't notice the broken window until this morning."

The house had an open, wraparound porch, which made for easy access for intruders. Belle walked over to examine the pane he'd blocked with a piece of cardboard and duct tape. "You can get a glazier out for that. Bestway Glass on Notre Dame is good. But was anything taken?"

"I didn't pay much attention to what was in the house. Obviously, the big television's still here, that old stereo. My laptop was in the car. Gary's camera is gone, along with his new laptop."

She blew out a breath. "Those are typical targets. The Hock Shop will be the first call for the police."

"One other funny thing." He paused, scratching his head for answers. "Seems like the den was their real focus. They opened a portable file cabinet of Gary's. Rooted around in his papers. Do you think that they were after cash? Looking for a safe?"

"What else? Anyone can tell that there's money in this house. It's no fish shack." She'd never forgotten her one and only burglary, when she'd rented an apartment. A gold coin worth five hundred dollars U.S., a birthday present from her mother, was in her underwear drawer, the first place any respectable robber checked. Lucky for claims, the empty case was left behind. "I'll ask Maureen about valuable property, and we'll check off the items. Have the police come out?"

He shrugged and batted at one shoulder of a blue cashmere

pullover, where a mosquito had landed, sneaking in with Belle. "An hour ago. They told me that unless they get a tip, these kinds of robberies are hard to solve. If it's a ring of juvenile delinquents, sometimes they get lucky if the kids brag at school."

"Not likely. Kids don't roam in gangs here, hauling skateboards or doing wheelies on their bikes. That's typical of suburban areas with malls."

"Now I see why you have a dog for a burglar alarm. Maybe I can rent the one next door." He cocked his thumb towards the adjoining property, then had a second thought. "Say, you don't think that guy would—"

Belle shook her head. "Bill Strang's a loner, but he has a healthy respect for the law. Used to be a security guard at Memorial Hospital."

Mutt's mouth gave a suspicious twitch as he flipped back his hair from his eyes. "Then he'd be wise to the ways of break-ins, wouldn't he?"

"Let's be logical. For nuisance purposes, he would have trashed the place, not just mucked around in the den."

Mutt folded his arms and leaned back on the sofa. "Guess so. I'm used to city life, with five locks on each door."

"Anything new on Gary's research? How are the missing camera and laptop going to affect your work?"

"I checked his files before the theft. Everything was backed up on disks, and they were upstairs. The Nikon had nothing saved in the memory when I first looked at it. But the good news is that I'm meeting with Paul Straten at the college tomorrow morning. Do you want to see that white elk baby? Gary took it in a week ago."

"So it wasn't lost after all. Oh, my God. What kind of shape is it in?" Her stomach had been rumbling for its dinner infusion.

Now, any appetite was flying off as quickly as the shrieking seagull that flashed by the shoreline in search of a minnow.

Mutt chuckled, his eyes crinkling like foil at the edges. "Frozen. Eleven tomorrow at the college good for you?"

As she was leaving, she noticed a stunning framed etching on the wall. "Irish elk," the brass caption at the bottom read. "Was this Gary's?"

Mutt swallowed and looked out the window. "I gave it to him. Took a trip to Dublin last year. I found the engraving in a shop. Circa 1810."

"Beautiful creature. Extinct?"

"Went out of production eleven thousand years ago. Gary said they weren't elk, but giant deer. Seven feet at the shoulder and twelve-foot antlers, according to fossil reconstructions."

"I wonder why their antlers got so big."

Mutt laughed from the belly. A sound of resilience. "Sex, of course. True then, true now. Females chose to mate with the best displays, and finally their necks couldn't sustain the weight, or the horns got entangled in trees and killed them."

Belle rubbed her neck. "Fashion's a killer, starting with hooker heels."

She was unable to reach Maureen at the main number for the clinic in Kismayu that night but left a message on the answering machine telling her about the break-in. The house was safely occupied, and that's what counted.

*   *   *

The next day, finishing some paperwork, she left the office at ten thirty, passing the latest mall expansion revitalizing the city. After over a decade, the higher unemployment rate was dropping toward the national number. Chapters, Staples,

Costco, and up the hill, the gigantic Home Depot and the Sears HomeStore. Joining them were more American chain restaurants: Kelsey's, Montana Bar and Grillhouse. She preferred lunching with the rain-snow-or-hail sausage vendor set up at Canadian Tire. The complimentary sauerkraut was a meal in itself.

Turning onto Barrydowne, she passed LaSalle Blvd., then made a right into the Nickel City College complex. For decades, it had offered practical training in business, health and social sciences, and technology. Passing a few pay lots and the ever-growing Special Needs Centre, with its metal sculptures of clients in wheelchairs, she parked at a string of meters, moved to one showing half an hour, and dropped in a loonie, calculating to the minute.

At the foyer doors, she saw students puffing happily in front of the No Smoking sign. Her nostrils flared at an herbal mix, and one eyebrow rose as she got a wink from a young man dressed in black semi-Goth apparel. A music student? Still, a bit early for the wacky tobaccy, as her older neighbours Ed and Hélène called it. Inside the main lobby, she met Mutt, sipping a coffee and offering one to her. Behind him, up the stairs to a mezzanine, a long line waited. "This place has more wings than an octopus has tentacles," he said. "I've been roaming around. Found the coffee right away, though. Regular okay?"

She'd ignore the sugar to spare his feelings. "Perfect. Lead on, Macmutt." She bent back the plastic tab for a slug as they began walking down the hall. A few girls in short shorts had admiring glances for Gary's partner. She preferred that word to lover, consort, even husband or wife. A clean, Western-movie sound, someone you could count on. Like Randolph Scott. Then she remembered a *Vanity Fair* article that had run a picture of Hollywood's two most virile men setting up house together in the Forties. Thirty years later, a maître de had claimed that Cary Grant and Scott had met for supper in a famous restaurant and had sat together in a darkened banquette, holding hands like an old married couple.

"Belle, are you coming?" Mutt looked back in amusement over his shoulder.

She hadn't been in the building for over ten years, when she'd last taught a realty class, and the latest addition led off to NORCAT, the Northern Centre of Advanced Technology, with glassed bridges to the Trades area. Mutt directed her left to another set of endless corridors, past the Native Friendship Centre and an art area with paintings. A depiction of granite shores in the style of Bruno Cavallo attracted her. Rocks were this town's middle name, including a sportswear store and even the college's new student centre, On the Rocks. The bare-bones honesty of the Cambrian shield made the farmlands of the South seem sleepy and unchallenging.

"E-dome this way," a sign read as Mutt pointed to the next turn. "Paul's meeting us there. This place is state-of-the-art. All sorts of high-tech electronics for long-distance education, too."

"U of T never looked like this," Belle admitted. The post-modern techno effect was far from the halls of ivy and its hundred and fifty years of traditional lecture rooms.

The E-dome was a huge circular room with tiers of desks and accommodations for projectors and audio-visual presentations. Automated screens and a theatrical lighting system hung from the ceiling. The unpainted cement floor facilitated machine movement and portable seating but seemed cold and unwelcoming to Belle. What would it be like at minus thirty-five outside? With all that glass, the heating bills must almost bankrupt the college. Two men were talking, one a technician, who was making notes on a clipboard.

Joining them, Paul Straten reminded her of Gary sans beard, fit and at home in the field. Short and muscular like Mutt, he wore chinos, a denim shirt and hiking boots. His chocolate-brown eyes sparkled as he shook hands, and Mutt made the introductions.

"I'm so sorry about what happened to Gary. I liked the man, and I looked forward to working with him."

Mutt blinked and nodded while Belle stared out the window, to where a huge teepee had been erected on the student green. This was a Sioux concept, not Ojibwa, a tribe which made birch shelters over branch structures. More romantic, though.

Paul cleared his throat. "Anyway, I've got our little friend all ready. Just out of the freezer."

They followed him down another hall, around a corner past plaque-dedicated electrical and instrumentation labs, then through a door to a lower level. There he took a key from a ring and unlocked the door of a large room with stainless steel cabinets on one wall. One end led to a loading dock area with roll-down doors. Mechanical hoists moved overhead from one oversized table to another. This was no ordinary autopsy room. Fans shifted the cool air, spreading a slight smell of antiseptic. Belle shivered, although she knew no human bodies rested in the drawers. This queasiness didn't run in the family. Her father's first job at fifteen had been attendant at the Toronto Morgue.

On a steel table with drip grooves lay a draped form no larger than a dog. Paul pulled back the sheet. Nearly all legs, the animal was pure white, with a large cut up the middle. Belle found herself transfixed. Paul directed their attention to the eyelid, pinned back in a bizarre effect which made her cringe. The eyeball was pink. "A true albino. Don't see many of these in any species. They usually die long before puberty."

"Why is that?" Belle asked, softening toward the small form, scarcely weaned from mother's milk to taste briefly of spring's soft grass. One snowy March, she'd found signs of moose birth on her snowshoe trails, a welter of clotted blood and tissue with tiny calf hooves following the cow's, rushed into a cold, cruel and shrinking habitat.

"Easier for predators to spot. Wolves. Coyotes. Hunters. And genetically they're prone to disease or burdened with a weak immune system. Parasites are also a problem."

As a dog owner aware of the usual suspects banished with an expensive monthly pill, Belle asked, "What kind of parasites? I know ticks have become more prevalent with our warmer summers."

He gave a light laugh. "Where do you want to start? Wild ruminants are subject to helminths, which are worms, protozoa, arthropods such as flies, and also ticks and mites. Farmers dread the crossover diseases like brucellosis because they're afraid their herds will be infected."

Silence filled the room for a moment, almost like a church. "What were the results of the autopsy, or whatever you call it?" Mutt asked quietly.

"It wasn't shot or injured. That was obvious on first examination. Heart and lungs, all the organs looked in good shape. No evident defects. It is underweight for its apparent age, according to our standard figures." He traced along the rib cage much as a vet would check a dog or cat. "So much guesswork, with many factors. Perhaps something happened to the mother."

Belle asked, "I don't know what I was expecting. Is there nothing definitive?"

"Don't give up yet. This gets top priority. Tissue samples have gone off to Waterloo, where they have a comprehensive lab. We don't handle complex toxicology here. My program is aimed at Sustainable Outdoor Resource Management. The students get hired by the MNR or work as guides."

Touching the shoulder of the small beast, thinking of how Gary must have felt at the sad discovery, Belle asked, "When do you expect the results?"

"Not for several weeks. It's no rush job like a murder investigation." He pulled a small notebook from his pocket. "I have your number, Mutt. I'll give you a call."

Belle passed him a card. "Here's mine if you can't reach him." Maybe Paul had a family and was in the market for a house.

"Poor little creature," she said, as they left the college. "Alive enough to have strength to die."

Mutt stopped in his tracks and looked at her. "Great line. May I steal it for my next book?"

"It's already stolen. Thomas Hardy." She didn't mention that it came from "Neutral Tones," a poignant poem about two lovers standing near a pond in bleak midwinter, realizing that their relationship was over. The *sine qua non* of pathetic fallacies. She thought of it especially in bleak December, where the quicksilver sun fell below the barren hills at scarcely four o'clock.

As they parted at the entrance, Mutt turned to her. "Paul's given me some hope. I'm going to start transcribing the earlier field notebooks. Maybe they'll contain a clue to what Gary was working on those last days. It's really odd that nothing turned up at his office. He was never late with deadlines."

"Could be the elk autopsy report was holding him up." She watched a muscle work in his jaw and added, "Is there any other way I can help?"

He gave a sigh. "I can handle the data. I'm just not familiar with the landscape where he was working. And I think I need to be."

Belle brightened, searching for a way to make a contribution. "I have plenty of topographic maps."

"There was a roll of them in a fishing-rod case in the truck. The Bump Lake one was on top, marked up at first glance. But if I have any questions, I'll bring them over." He gave a grim laugh. "Meanwhile, if you don't see me, I'll be under arrest."

*   *   *

A few hours later, Belle's cell phone rang as she headed home down Radar Road. Driving and talking was not her habit. The act reduced reflex times, and she needed all she had. Pulling in to the North Star Confectionery, she answered.

"You the one who put up those pictures?"

Someone had taken the bait about the dumpsite. An informer or the felon himself? Despite the warm breeze sending lilac perfume her way from a neighbouring yard, she felt a sinister chill as her pulse quickened. "Yes. Do you have any information?"

"For a price."

Forget Good Samaritans. Show me the money. "What about service to your community? Do you like looking at garbage in your own backyard?"

"Hell, being a nice guy don't pay the rent." A rude bray hit her ear. She wouldn't be surprised if he were blowing snot over the speaker. She could nearly smell him. The Great Unwashed. "I got no time for this shit. Meet me at the airport in thirty minutes. First luggage carousel. Got sixty bucks?"

She nearly laughed. A couple of cases of beer. Information came cheap. The rendezvous sounded safe enough. A woman rushing into a meeting with an unknown man in a dark alley was third-rate mystery material.

Shoving in a Diamond Rio tape, she geared up for the meeting by singing along. "Gonna get a doooooooooog." Soon she was parked at the meters in front of the airport, spotting a clunky old beater chugging down the road. She slipped into the new, improved terminal. The waiting room was between arrivals, empty except for a nun in full white regalia reading *The Life of Pi* and sipping a soft drink. She looked up at Belle and beamed, receiving a thumbs up.

Dressed in baggy workpants and a ripped leather jacket, a young man slouched in and motioned with his head. Towering over her, an asset wasted on such a slob, he held out his hand, the shovel-nosed fingers yellow with nicotine. His face was ferret-sharp, and she could smell stale sweat. "Seventy-five." He looked around as a beer-bellied officer with a grey crew cut finished a coffee in his stroll and headed for the washroom. "Hurry up. Security's gonna think this is a drug deal going down."

"It's sixty." She waved the high-tech metallic bills with the aging queen's portrait, retooled for perhaps the final time. "The name first."

He glanced around, greasy threads of dirty blond hair tickling his eyes, the sclera yellowed and unhealthy. His breath made her think twice about continuing to smoke even five cigarettes a day. "Remember, you never heard this from nobody. Joey Bartko's your man. Lives on Pine Street in Skead." Then, snatching his prey and walking quickly outside, he was gone like a bouncing thief in the night, muffler sparking under the car, one window skinned with plastic. Belle breathed a sigh of relief and went to the ladies' to wash her hands. She felt dirty just thinking about him.

At home shortly after, she called the CrimeStoppers' toll-free line again and gave the new information, citing the case number they'd assigned. "We couldn't do anything with the debit card slip. Only the last numbers are recorded for security reasons. Now that we have a name, we're in business. Sometimes there's a reward for information when stolen property is recovered," said the clerk, a woman with a hoarse voice who kept clearing her throat. "Sorry. Another smog alert."

"Rewards don't concern me. This idiot needs to be stopped before the bush turns into one giant landfill." She paused, biting her lip. "This is all anonymous, right?"

"Certainly. That's part of our mandate. The police will visit the scene then go to his home tomorrow. We have your pictures of the trash site. That carpet is distinctive, and if he has a JVC television to match the box, all the better."

"What's the fine for dumping?" Life in prison, as far as she was concerned.

"For household waste, up to five thousand. Jail time for a second offence."

As a soft rain pattered on her roof and a rising wind from the north tinkled the wind chimes outside her patio door, Belle fell asleep quickly, the t's and i's dotted for the polluter. If only coordinating Gary's research were so easy. Mutt was working overtime. She didn't envy him his task of tying up loose ends, but Paul Straten's information had provided a few threads. Like Mutt, she dreamed of the white elk calf. Was there room at Rainbow Bridge for wild souls?

EIGHT

With the blackflies and mosquitoes in temporary abeyance after a helpful rain, Belle grabbed the window of opportunity to take Freya on a short walk to Freedom Hill. The bear bell attached to the dog's collar jingled a warning to any foraging bruin. For extra security, she sang "O, Canada", "God Save the Queen" and "The Maple Leaf Forever", chuckling at how young Morag in *The Diviners* imagined words in the last song to be not "dauntless hero" but "donkless".

Along the way, the groundcover arbutus had bloomed, and she picked a delicate white flower to savour its spicy smell. The rose-twisted-stalk was emerging, and a shy nodding trillium could be seen in a shady nook under a massive yellow birch sprouted during the French Revolution. Goldthread, one of the first to emerge, blanketed the cool green moss. Each plant was answering summer's call in preordained progression. Spring in the North was a blink of the eye, a flick of the calendar page. Not quite the cruellest month, but snowmobiles roamed the lake as late as April, and the giant ice cube six-feet-thick that was the lake left a chill and kept temperatures two weeks behind those in town. Patches of snow nestled in the darkest woods, shielded from the sun by hills, rocks or trees. Yet the tide was gathering in the backcountry. The brook was heavy with freshets as the dog paused to drink. Letting the peace of the forest envelop her, Belle heard the mournful cry of the dove, usually a city phenomenon but moving closer as civilization stretched its tentacles. A familiar drumming, slow, then picking up speed like the stuttery start of a lawnmower, reminded her that grouse were seeking mates.

At the summit, she re-erected her inukshuk on the top of a rocky chimney shape and looked over low hills punctuated with distant hydro lines marching across miles of wilderness. Gary could have walked these trails with her, learned about her secret places and natural altars and cathedrals. They had taken different paths to appreciating the bounties of nature but had arrived together. She'd taught herself more in the two decades up here than she'd ever learned in school. A passion for understanding the natural world grew with each discovery. She stooped to pop a teaberry into her mouth for a burst of flavour. Overwintered, they were tangy and tart, a memory of a gum long discontinued.

Freya sniffed a small taupe bundle on the peaty path. "Leave it," Belle said sternly and found a stick to flip the stiff, blunt-nosed carcass of a shrew into the brush. Rodents carried parasites, an expensive proposition at the vet's.

When Belle emerged onto the pavement from the sheltering willow bushes that camouflaged the entrance to her trail, she met Ed DesRosiers on his quad, his dog Rusty ambling alongside. Ed was pulling a small trailer, probably headed for the amazing disappearing hill, a tall esker, to fetch free sand and gravel. Quads she hated with a passion, but she knew his joint problems didn't allow him to roam the bush with her any more. His cane was once again strapped to the bike. "I thought your hip was better after that operation."

He grimaced. "Now it's my knee. Doc says I gotta lose forty big ones." In sweatpants and a light Sudbury Wolves jacket, Ed wore his poundage like a sack of rice, favouring suspenders over a useless belt.

"I haven't seen you guys in weeks. How was your cruise?"

"I gained ten pounds. Hélène lost five. 'Course, while she was doing this spinning stuff, I was lifting weights at the buffet table." He shrugged good-naturedly and patted his belly.

Rusty splayed upside down in the submissive posture until Freya finished her requisite nosing. Belle gave the chocolate-red mutt's groin a gentle rub. "So what have you been up to?" Ed asked. "See any grouse in there? I was meaning to get a few birds for the wife."

She filled Ed in on Gary's drowning. No need to add the details about Mutt and his quest until they knew something substantive, nor to churn the gossip mills with their ancient dating history. She'd been embarrassed enough with Steve's and Miriam's reactions.

Ed pulled a battered stogie out of his pocket and gave it a pondering chew. He knew better than to light it, even if his wife wasn't in sight. "Sorry to hear that. Down around old Burwash, you say?" He scratched his grizzled chin. No shave yet today on the jolly round face. Retirement had its perks, even if he continued his plumbing profession on an ad hoc basis for friends. "Cousin of mine shot himself by accident down there must be about...the year our first grandson Todd was born. '88. Mike got to boozing around the campfire and tripped over a root or something. Left five kids. Damn shame."

She smeared a blackfly on the back of her ear, turning up a crust of blood. Insects were the true rulers of the world, if only in numbers and resilience. "Tough break for everyone."

"It wasn't pretty. I was with the search team." He squinted as the sun came out from behind a silver streak of clouds. "Funny thing, though. Never knew him to have more than a beer or two. Didn't drink hard liquor either, but there was a bottle in his tent."

She checked her watch. Getting late. "One other thing. I

don't know if you've heard through the grapevine that the Lavoies' house was broken into. Double-check your alarm system when Rusty's not on guard."

He gave a pound to the quad. "Man, what is this road coming to? Myron Zippel opened up the camp and found his ice auger gone from the boathouse. Four hundred bucks. Someone had a party in the living room and left a pile on the carpet."

"A pile? Oh, I get you." Belle winced. Steve had told her about that atavistic side of vandalism. The ultimate humiliation from cave dwellers to dot.commers.

"When does he think it happened?" Zippel wintered in Florida, like many local snowbirds.

"Maybe a week ago. 'Cause he was out here on Victoria Day, and all was A-OK."

So the robbery might not have been an isolated incident. Belle had a mental picture of the property. "His place is hidden from traffic by those thick cedars. Easy pickings by car or boat." At the beginning of Edgewater Road was a Neighbourhood Watch sign with its alert eye. On six miles of winding hills with acres carved out of the bush, the warning was a token gesture.

At the office, Yoyo was working on the week's ads, her tongue cleaving her blossom mouth in a pose of deep thought. Belle gave her a wave and went to her desk, dialling up a client with an open house. "Drop of vanilla on the oven racks. Then set it at three hundred degrees for an hour. Gives a homey touch. I'll be there tomorrow at one. And it's a good idea to take the Dobermans out with you."

Yoyo, who wore a demure cardigan over her cherry-red vinyl bustier, came over with the copy for the weekend newspaper. "How's this? And I updated the website, put up pictures of all the new listings." Her voice sounded odd, as if she were working her tongue around something or unable to open her jaw.

"What have you got in your mouth?" To her credit, Yoyo wasn't a gum chewer.

"Tooth-whitening strips. Another five minutes for the uppers. Then I get to have a reward. One of these cinnamon pinwheels my neighbour brought from a boulangerie in Sturgeon Falls. Help yourself."

Belle nibbled the rich pastry, full of brown sugar and spice. Then she turned to the text. "Perfect. I think you've got it, my fair lady. Nice job with the pictures."

"Noooo problem. Comes with the territory." Yoyo basked for a moment, then inspected her nails. "Ummm, there is..."

Wiping a fleck of pastry from her mouth, Belle asked, "What is it?"

"I need to leave at three today."

Belle tossed down her pen with a sigh. She'd been buttered up but good. "What for? Things are heating up. We've had people in every afternoon this week."

"My mom has a...bail hearing. Got into a little fracas at the National last night. Didn't like no...I mean anyone calling Elvis a fat pig. Her bedroom's decorated with those velvet pictures, and she even bought a cool rug of the King off a guy who had a display on the street corner."

Coco was her daughter's cross to bear and probably vice versa. Flipping her daybook, Belle said, "You're very lucky. I'm clear. But never again. Someone else will have to rescue your mother."

Yoyo headed for the back room and returned with the dog on leash, a plastic bag in the other hand. "I'm taking Baron for a whiz."

Mutt called that night as Belle was drying off from a kiwi bubble bath that soothed the knots in her neck caused by opening the latest property tax bill. Hers had gone up nearly eighteen per cent for no water, no sewer, no sidewalks and no streetlights. Just a view, frozen five months of the year. "Want to go down to Bump Lake? The police said they left the canoe on shore. Belonged to the Ministry for all they knew. Could be it's gone already."

She flopped into the waterbed. "I agree. What a shame to lose it. Count me in."

"Are you busy on Saturday?"

"Morning's open, then a quick listing on Richard Lake. That's on the way back from Burwash, so it would be convenient. Are you an early riser?"

"When I'm writing, I sometimes start at dawn. It's great to watch the sun come up here on the lake."

"How's the research?"

"I need to go back to the Ministry for another look around his office in case something turned up about those last two weeks. Hope I don't run into that Dave guy. I wouldn't put it past him to sabotage Gary's work, now that I think of it."

Belle blew out a breath. "That would be dirty. Too bad Gary had to put up with him." And how much more harassment through the decades? Only recently had gays been included in the Charter of Rights.

That night Belle awoke at three o'clock, as Freya began a roo-roo. She walked out onto her tiny papal-blessing balcony and peeked around the corner at the deck below. The moon was full and bright, illuminating the empty lot. A hunched black figure was pounding the garbage can by the door, with moves rarely seen outside of the WWF ring. She yelled and banged the railing. "Get out, bear! Go away!" Freya's howls added to the chorus. The animal bumped its rump down the stairs and disappeared into the McNairs' yard next door. She feared telling Jeannie about the visit, even though the family wasn't out for the summer yet. The retired principal wouldn't even walk the road, much less dare the bush. Bears were creatures of habit, too, returning again and again when rewarded by a bacon wrapping or yogurt container. Despite the inconvenience, she would now lug everything up to the locked box by the road. It had a metal top and was fastened with chains to a pair of four-by-fours driven into the ground.

The next morning, she shook her head at the fang and claw marks in the plastic receptacle. The weight of the animal had popped off the top and scattered coffee grounds, eggshells and corn husks on the deck. After she cleaned up, she drove down to Mutt's with Freya, and they left in Gary's truck at seven. For maximum storage, the back seat had been replaced by a level platform covered with a blue tarp. Mutt had added cushy towels for a pasha effect, leaving the dog in comfort.

They pulled into Connie's on the Kingsway for a truck-stop breakfast. Three eggs in each selection, stacks of dollar pancakes, bacon, sausage and home fries. Connie's would never offer Egg Beaters, but at least the brown toast added one healthy touch. As she filled up on breakfast, Belle wished she had worn comfortable sweatpants instead of jeans. "I should have had a bagel."

"Gary had a tough time keeping his weight down, he told me. One diet after another when he was in university. Once he got into the field, things got easier. Apples and jerky were his favourite lunch. Of course, I didn't know him then. It's hard to imagine."

She'd hardly recognized him herself. "I have some old school pictures, if you'd like to see them." They'd been in a shrine on her desk through school, but she'd put them away when she'd graduated. Not thrown them away. Perhaps she had kept them all these years for just such a karmic moment.

Mutt took one hand off the wheel to rub his jaw. On his lips was a bittersweet smile. "Good thing someone was his curator. He told me he didn't want anything around to remind him of the porker he used to be."

Belle closed her eyes for a moment and saw the dust of freckles on Gary's nose. The deep tan of the man would have covered them. And always the striped shirt, whether at twelve or seventeen. His mother's idea to achieve a thinning effect? Hair carefully combed and parted on the right. A shy smile, but never hard to coax. "He was boyish, cherubic. Not that heavy." Some of her favourite silver-screen actors were on the portly side. Laughton, Ustinov and Greenstreet.

"His voice changed, too, he said. He used to be quite a tenor."

"I can help you there. I have a bootleg tape of our high school's production of *Brigadoon*. Would you like to hear him?"

"You're amazing. You kept it all these years?"

She cleared her throat as a Greyhound bus with a Vancouver sign roared by. "It hasn't been that long."

His eyes darted her way, as if aware of twitting an older woman. "There's a tape deck at the house. I'd like to...hear him again." He turned to her as he slowed for a red light. "Do you think that's morbid?"

She pondered her answer. Technology was changing the world of grief. Videotapes were common. It wasn't as if he was watching it every night. "Not at all. I'd like to hear it, too."

As he switched to Paris Street with its monster potholes, Belle felt the truck rock, its heavy suspension demanding a price. "The City of Crater Sudbury. You can't imagine this in winter."

Mutt adjusted his legs in the wheel well. Wearing cargo pants and a jersey mariner's top, he had chosen a light musk aftershave. "Down south is no picnic. Toronto gets a foot of snow, and they're paralyzed until the mayor calls in the army."

At the Four Corners, they took Route 69 South, after gassing up at Canadian Tire. Mutt tucked the store's bonus money in a compartment overhead. "Gotta keep it sorted like Gary did. Nickel bills at the bottom, five-dollar ones at the top." Soon they were at the bypass, then passing the Tourist Board Welcoming Centre and the last motel. At the long hill overlooking Rock Lake, the treacherous nature of the only artery to Toronto flexed its muscles, with an occasional centre passing lane, invitation to a head-on for impatient motorists. Sharp rock cuts and the occasional swamp punctuated the forests of fir and spruce. The azure sky was broken by lazy cumulus clouds, a painter's dream. Except for transports, most of the traffic was headed to camps on one of two hundred lakes, or along the Wanapitae or French Rivers.

The area had a colourful history as a connecting point for the Voyageurs. In 1613, Seigneur Champlain had taken the traditional canoe route to Georgian Bay and Superior by coming down the Ottawa River to Lake Nipissing, then being paddled down the French itself, losing his astrolabe navigation system in the process, uncovered in a farmer's field in 1867. After that, except for sending its lumber to Chicago to rebuild after the Great Fire of 1870, it had slept until the railroad came through in 1883. Sudbury might have become one of many temporary construction towns had a workman's pick not revealed the nickel payload. Capitalists had struck quickly, buying rights for a dollar an acre, and within three years, blasting had begun at the Copper Cliff mine. Life was rugged, and so was the lifestyle for the six thousand citizens. "The people of Sudbury are, one might say, as rough as their surroundings" was a contemporary commentary from the outside world.

As the road widened for a passing lane, Mutt pulled to the right to let a speeding van streak by. People got frustrated waiting their turn at death's roulette wheel. Not a kilometre later, the pair laughed and traded satisfied smiles as they saw the van pulled over by an OPP cruiser.

At last they turned west past open hay fields and a golf course, snow-covered half the year, but a tourist draw for cottagers. One distant hill had been used for military training manoeuvres and bore a large set of bullseye targets. They drove in several miles to Burwash before parking at a turnaround overlooking the remains of the old town grid.

"Years ago, I came here to dig up perennials. Even asparagus. It's a hardy plant," said Belle. "Maybe we can get enough for a meal." They parked and wandered along a street to nowhere. Many of the houses had been post-and-beam construction, without foundations, so their traces had vanished, except for the oddment of broken glass or demolition debris. Gardens and flowerbeds were long overtaken by wild raspberry canes and stubborn weeds like goatsbeard.

In a sunny, sandy area, with the shoulder-high dried plumes of last year's crop to guide her, Belle located a dozen luscious shoots and plucked them. Mutt seemed amazed as he placed his hands on his hips. "You forage, too? What other talents do you have?"

"I'm developing them even as we speak," she said, flattered into a rare blush. They returned to the truck and wrapped the vegetables in paper towels for protection.

Mutt opened up a bag of sweet-sour jerky and offered her some. "So where to now?" he asked.

"Let's check that topo to locate Bump Lake. A number of dirt roads branch out from here, and we don't want to scratch this pretty truck," she said, patting the dash.

He reached behind the seat for a fishing rod case. "Kept his maps rolled in here nice and tight," Mutt said. "Here's the one we need right on top. Seems to have been tracing water routes from Bump. See his pencil marks?"

"Is that usual for elk research, or just a way to reach the interior?"

"Both, I suspect." Mutt nodded as he scanned the paper. "Game trails often follow the water. Animals know what spots dry up and which ones keep flowing."

Belle watched the compass attached to the dash and made some educated guesses about directions. "Take that track to the right. It's the best used. We'll drive as far as we can go."

After another half-mile on a rutted road that would have challenged her van's undercarriage, they dead-ended in a field of daisies and hawkweed. Belle shielded her eyes as she studied the trees on the border. "Uh-oh. Hold on a minute."

"What are you looking for?" Mutt asked as Freya nosed a clump of vetch, and a grasshopper jumped into the air. The dog's teeth snapped, and she swallowed in satisfaction.

"A tag or blaze to show the portage." She pointed to the left. "Good thing it's not fall. Red and yellow are hard to spot when the leaves turn. Blue is best."

A red plastic "flag" circling a sturdy sapling brought them to a well-trampled trail. Belle looked at the topo. "Shouldn't be that far."

Twenty minutes on, the leaf-mould path wound a serpentine way past early mushrooms like velvet shanks sprouting near a dead oak. The Ojibwa had feasted on them, along with the choice meadow and horse mushrooms and the occasional monster bolete. Finally they reached the edge of weedy Bump Lake, a perfect spot for browsing moose or elk. The sun warmed them, and a pleasant breeze wicked sweat from their faces. Insects were asserting their dominion on the water, striders on the surface and clouds of gnats massing above. A purple glow of pickerelweed bloomed a few feet out, surrounded by white and yellow water lilies. Mutt pointed to a school of minnows, a clear sign to Belle that the acid rain that had decimated lakes nearer to town had not reached this far. Some had been "buffered" back to a normal, life-sustaining PH balance. Birds were the best judge. The eerie ululation of a loon broke the absolute quietness, and from the other end of the crystal waters came a sensual reply in kind.

"Mating season," Belle said. "They have a different set of calls for this time of year. Yodelling and laughter. At night or before a storm, ha-oo-ooo."

Mutt breathed deeply, his eyes crinkling in delight. "I heard them last night. Going to bed and waking to that sound instead of sirens is a privilege. Northerners are lucky."

If Gary's last heartbeat had stilled in a place as beautiful as this, it was a fitting background. Far better than ticking life away on a hard hospital mattress, wired to a collection of whispering machines. She dreaded such an end for her father. But he was on the mend, now, wasn't he? She needed to visit the hospital.

They spotted the canoe overturned under a silver birch near the water's silty edge. Belle admired the sleek lines of the red Kevlar canoe, a perfect blend of art and utility. She lifted one end. Not too heavy. Still, returning was going to be rough. Portaging was not her favourite activity, especially in bug season. And she'd forgotten to bring the bug dope.

Mutt rubbed his hands together in preparation. "Fifty-eight pounds, Gary said. A cinch."

The blast of a gun in the woods to the left made them duck on instinct. Freya's ears flattened. She hated the sound and, though scouted by a neighbourhood cop when a pup, would have washed out of any Canine Unit.

NINE

Mutt pulled Belle to the ground with him, one arm over her shoulder. In turn, she reached for the dog's collar. "Down, girl." Together they huddled, faces pressed to the fresh grass. When another report sounded, she tried to home in on the direction. Sounded more like a shotgun than a rifle. It wasn't hunting season, but that mattered little out here. In nearby St. Charles, forty-eight hunters had been arrested and over one hundred and fifty charges laid. Then again, someone might be after partridge or rabbits.

"Stop shoooooooooooting!" she screamed, and Mutt joined her with a baritone haloo. After a long silence, they struggled tentatively to their knees, their heads craning around and their hands up.

"What the hell?" yelled a voice from a thicket seventy-five feet to their right. Then the pesky alders rippled alive like an optical illusion, and Belle nearly squeaked in alarm. Head to toe, the man looked like a walking leaf pile, or perhaps the Creature from the Black Lagoon, only his eyes alive in the matching balaclava. She'd seen the gear in an outfitter's catalogue. He carried a shotgun safely broken over one arm. From the other hand dangled the iridescent plumage of a partridge. A jolly springer spaniel trotted at his side in perfect heel. Pulling off the headgear, he appeared to be in his sixties. He gave them a serious stare as he assessed their pants and shirts, variations of green and brown. "Sorry for the scare. You folks ought to wear red or something. Coulda gotten plugged."

Mutt spoke up. "What about you, then?"

The man shuffled his shoulders as he stuck the partridge, purple feet first, into a canvas game sack slung over his shoulder, its head lolling out, tongue poking through its beak. "I'm the hunter, aren't I? It's my job to disguise myself. I've got a blind back there, and the birdies come to me. So what are you all doing here, anyways? It's not hiking territory."

As her nose worked, Freya narrowed her eyes in a primitive gesture. In one quick move, she nipped the head off the grouse and began munching. Belle grabbed her collar, but the dog had already swallowed her snack whole. "I'm really sorry. She's a sucker for grouse."

The hunter grinned. "Saves me the trouble. Does she skin, too?"

Still mortified at her dog's bad manners, Belle made the introductions, then said, "We came to collect that canoe over there."

He closed the sack with a wink to Freya, then extended a horny, weathered hand. "Patch Wells. Sorry if I sounded unsociable. Don't get many visitors."

"Especially not if you shoot at them." Belle let a smile soften the warning.

He toed the ground with one boot. "You say you're after the canoe? Nobody showed, I was gonna make off with it myself. Nice boat."

"Yes, but it belonged to the man who drowned here. He was our...friend." Mutt said, his eyes searching into the distance.

Patch nodded sombrely, waved his cap at a mosquito. His balding head ringed with curly steel hair afforded no protection. A black eye protector gave him the appearance of a pirate.

"Myers, eh? Coulda knocked me over when I heard about it where I gas up the quad. Had many a chat with Gary when I fished Bump Lake. Shared a mess of perch one time. Only fellow other than me I ever saw eat the little buggers. Tasty if you don't mind the bones."

Belle had seen no vehicle in the area. The quad explained that. "Do you live around here?" she asked, bending down to pet the spaniel's silky fur.

He pointed with a truncated thumb, likely another hazard of bush life. A belt-knife rode on his hip. "Little Josie and me got a cabin back in the woods apiece. Just a shack. It's Crown land, but I don't even lease it or nothing. Nobody bothers me, except for in October when moose season opens. Have to watch my tail then."

Belle cocked her head. It wasn't wilderness she would have chosen, unless she wanted to raise blackflies. "What brought you here in the first place?" Perhaps he'd grown up on the few hardscrabble farms in the area by Highway 69.

He smiled, exposing one jagged tooth and a couple of gaps. "Saw old Burwash on the way in? I was a correctional officer there, guard they used to call it. Place closed down in '74, not a dry eye among the staff, though I expect the cons looked forward to incarceration in a more civilized location, especially in bug season. No jackrabbit parole here. Drive 'em nuts in an hour, and they'd come crawling back." He told them that Burwash had been constructed in 1914 on over 35,000 acres and expanded at the end of World War Two. It housed up to 670 criminals sentenced to two years less a day. The town, self-contained with churches, stores and schools, was built for the prison's employees. With 150 families, it had a great spirit of camaraderie.

She wondered how he survived out here year-round. Wood heat, of course. No utility bills. Canada pension, the Old Age four-hundred-dollar freebie, and perhaps the extra supplement of meat and fish provided for a simple but fulfilling life. "I like solitude, but this is too lonely for me."

"I get along. Whittle up pretties to pass the time. Sell them on consignment at the Science North shop." He took one from his pocket. "Happen you might admire one. Keep 'er. I got lots."

"Thanks." Belle considered the delicate willow instrument. Tourists were suckers for homemade items like blueberry jam, polished rocks and maple syrup. As she blew a shrill note, Mutt covered his ears. "Loud," she said with a grin. "A great way to warn off bears."

"Pea's the secret."

"Pardon?" She and Mutt spoke at once.

"Dried pea inside." He put a finger to his large, fleshy lips, his flinty eyes crackling with mischief. "Can't tell how it got in that little place. Might want to patent the idea some day." His eyes wandered to a couple of pop cans and an empty chip bag in a fire ring of rocks. "Damn kids picnicking at the lake now that school's out. Not sure if picnic's the right word for what they're up to." He bent down and collected the litter, stuffing it into his sack with the grouse.

Mutt looked around for a moment in slight confusion, as if he had forgotten something. "Was there a tent here, maybe a sleeping bag?"

Patch cleared his throat. "The tent blew down a few days ago, and some animal got into the sleeping bag. I have them both back at the camp. A bit of stitching and washing, and they'll be good as new. If you can wait about ten minutes, I'll—"

"You might as well get some use out of them." Mutt locked eyes with Belle and gave a nod toward the canoe. "Nice to meet you, Patch. Guess we'd better get going. It looks like a long haul."

They walked over to the canoe and stooped in preparation

to lift. Patch followed and put a hammy hand on Belle's shoulder. "Hey, now, pretty lady. That's a man's work."

She bristled but calculated the shoulder pain ahead. Five years ago, she would have declined. Now, discretion was the better part of bursitis. "A hand would be great. Thanks, Patch."

After the men hoisted the canoe into the truck bed, Belle rounded up yellow polypropylene rope to secure the boat against wind gusts and damage from movement. Patch waved goodbye as he gave a whistle to his dog.

"That old geezer would have grabbed the canoe if we hadn't arrived," Belle said.

"He's welcome to the other gear, especially if it's in as bad a shape as he says. He did make the offer to return it."

"Which he knew you'd refuse after that convenient story. Pretty crafty."

Driving back to Sudbury, still out of range of radio stations, Belle settled into the comforts of the large truck, especially the seats. Sweet lumbar supports and three-way adjustments. She wouldn't be happy gassing up, though. With the recent price hikes, a brown hundred-dollar bill would bring little change.

Mutt fumbled through Gary's CD selection, frowning. "We never did agree on music. Copland is as modern as I want to get, and don't get me started on jazz." He slipped *Appalachian Spring* into the groove.

"Jazz seems to be an acquired taste, like pickled eggplant. I like the classics, but the odd guitarist like Jeff Beck makes a break for me." Belle went on for some minutes telling him about Yoyo's Putamayo recordings. He made a good listener, the secret of making and keeping friends, from Dale Carnegie to Dr. Phil. Then she realized that she'd never bothered to ask about his writing. With the emphasis on Gary's research, she'd quite forgotten that she was talking to an author.

"Tell me about your books. How did you happen on Lucy Doyle? Was she a real person?"

His smile showed that, like all writers, he was flattered by the questions. "Absolutely. She started with fetch-and-carry jobs at the old *Toronto Telegram* in 1890-something. I came across her in a History of Canadian Journalism course."

"A woman working at a newspaper when Victoria was still queen. I like Lucy already."

"She became a reporter later on, also a drama and music critic, a gossip columnist and editor of the women's page."

"Quite a resumé. What happened to her?"

"It wasn't the path to riches. In her seventies, she was allowed to live free in a little cabin in a local artist's colony, the Guild Inn. She was still doing research for her books. Never published, though."

"My mother told me about the Guild Inn. Rosa and Spencer Clark collected statuary for their mansion from some wonderful buildings under the wrecking ball." Belle nodded at the trip down Memory Lane. "I grew up in Scarborough. We used to drive through that spot of parkland on Lake Ontario. It ran as a hotel for awhile."

"It's demolished now. And that statuary's all that's left of parts of old Toronto."

Mutt waited for the thirty minutes it took her to list the Richard Lake cedar Panabode with double garage. Roll the dice, and let's try $399,000. Later he dropped her off at home with a complimentary copy of his first book, *Murder in Corktown*. Born and raised in Toronto before it had boomed into Metro, her father might remember that historic area near Parliament and Queen.

Belle made a sandwich and considered her next step. She hated driving back into town, but she needed to check on the old man. Mutt had waited long enough for her. She hadn't wanted to ask for more indulgence.

After settling Freya into her overstuffed chair, with a sigh she got into the van and headed back. Half a mile later, the red Jeep Liberty came chasing her tail. Not again. She flicked her right blinker and slowed, pulling to the side with a slow seethe and a selection of Miriam's Frenglish curses, ending with *sacrifice*. The brake pedal seemed a bit soft. Wasn't a tune-up scheduled next week? The Jeep flashed past, up a hill, and around a corner as if on fire. If anyone had been coming, a head-on would have sent everyone to an orthopaedic surgeon, if one could be found. Sometimes only an accident taught the right lesson. Too bad the innocent victim paid the same deadly price.

At the gravel pit, she bumped over a trackless former rail crossing, now part of the TransCanada Trail. Packed with rough slag and smelly creosote, it attracted quadders and snowmobilers, not more fastidious hikers. Then she headed down the long hill that bottomed out passing Philosopher's Pond, a small-trout paradise. Preoccupied by the idiot who had passed her, she forgot to ease up on the gas. Suddenly she found herself stomping on the brake with no effect. Sweat glazed her brow, and her heart trip-hammered while she watched trees fly by in a green blur. Where in hell was the emergency brake? As she fumbled with the controls, the vehicle teetered and charged up the steep hill like a bee-stung bull. With her luck, either the courier man or a delivery of propane would be her next and last vision. But the woodland spirits smiled, and the van slowed as gravity asserted its domain.

Ever so gently, she tickled the gas enough to reach the crest by the mailbox pavilion. "Pretend you have no brakes, because that's the case," she told herself. Easy. Easy. She sidled off in the deeper gravel and slowed to a stop, her leg shaking from the adrenaline rush. Safesafesafe. Belle pounded the dash in relief. If she'd been anywhere else, she'd have been a statistic. Life was a crapshoot, and this time she'd rolled sevens. Blowing out a breath, she grabbed her cell phone, then rummaged in her wallet for her CAA card. But Saturday? Bad time for mechanical problems. Still, she was alive, and the van was in one piece with only brush scratches.

Riding into town an hour later in the cab of the tow truck, she told the driver what had happened. "Just gave out on you? Like stepping on a ripe plum? Only 20,000 klicks on the van? Brakes should be okay. Sounds like a busted line. Run any rough roads?"

"Every other day." She cursed her own luck and wondered if she had damaged the vehicle on one of her excursions up humped cottage lanes. She had the van dropped off at Robinson Automotive on LaSalle and asked for a ride to Enterprise, where she rented a van. If hers wasn't ready by Monday, she would need a large vehicle to ferry clients. One of the curbside car lots had boasted a yellow Humvee. That would give Palmer Realty a distinct image, but at two miles per litre?

Her father had been moved to Laurentian Hospital, the new megacentre eclipsing the older hospitals. Belle parked in a far-flung lot, wondering how heart and stroke patients fared walking uphill to the main entrance. Perhaps many never made it. Outside in a rudimentary plastic shelter, two women dangling portable IV's puffed up a storm. Some vegetarians felt that Sudburians' shorter life spans were due to the habits of fat, retired miners who loved their tobacco and beer. Perhaps the diversifying economy and the new fitness boom would turn the tide. Even Miriam had bought a treadmill. Belle preferred the bush, but in the long winters, often darkness or a week's worth of minus thirty-five degree temperatures made exercise difficult, if not impossible for all but the extremists who thought frostbite was a badge of honour.

At the Tim's in the foyer, she purchased two coffees, milk and sugar for him, and a soft jelly doughnut. She found him in a double room on the third floor, the other bed occupied by a man with a bandaged head.

Her father was napping, but she could see an improvement in his blisters. The dressings were off, and the purplish-black was fading as new tissue took over. "Wakee wakee," she whispered and touched his arm, remembering those biceps big as a grapefruit.

His cornflower blues snapped open, and he grinned, fewer teeth every year, a side effect of nursing homes, where brushing was low on the list of priorities. Then again, on a bad day, she wouldn't put it past him to bite a rough hand. "Terry, is that you? When's dinner?"

Had the Prednisone disoriented him, or had he had another TIA? "It's Belle. Your blisters, remember? We finally got you a diagnosis and the right medication. You'll be fine. Palmers are tough. Remember those Crusades." Trekking from Scotland to Jerusalem and back bearing green fronds must have taken years.

"Oh, Belle, stupid, stupid of me. Told you that damn skin doctor was senile, didn't I?" With his voice strengthening, he blinked and rubbed at a crust in his eye. "But the food is terrible, terrible. Cold tea. Cold toast. Cold everything. Cornflakes. I hate cornflakes. Your mother never had a box of cereal in the house, except for oatmeal, and that doesn't count."

"One strategy to get people out as fast as possible. But look at what I've brought." Weight was not a problem for him. He'd dropped from two hundred to a healthier one-eighty since leaving Florida. The occasional sweet treat wasn't forbidden.

"Thank God. But only one?" he asked with a pout. She helped him manage the coffee and fed him small pieces of doughnut, wiping the jelly that dribbled down his chin. He was wearing a set of white whiskers. No time for amenities when nurses were being laid off. Hospitals expected the family to pull its weight. As for family, she was it. If he wasn't out soon, she'd bring his electric shaver. Dignity was second only to comfort for the elderly.

Mentioning the near-accident might agitate him. "Soon you'll be back at Rainbow watching Alex Trebek, one of Sudbury's finest citizens."

"Oprah, too." He gave a cough, and she backed up on instinct. A frightening survey had showed that one out of three patients developed complications just from being in the hospital. Infections, even broken hips.

Meanwhile, his roommate was watching a game show on a mini-television hanging from a metal structure. "Say, do you want a TV? I didn't think about that."

"How much does it cost?" He narrowed his eyes, coughed again and was handed a tissue. She hadn't snatched her frugality from the sky.

"Never mind that. You're a rich man. We're riding a bull market, and the loonie is headed for the bald eagle. I'll see to it. What about that cough, though?"

He waved his hand in dismissal. "It's nothing. Bad air in here. Why don't they open the windows?"

"Be glad you're in the only air-conditioned hospital."

"I miss your mother's cigarettes. Harold's, too." Her uncle had reached eighty on three packs of unfiltered Camels a day.

On the way to the elevator, she saw a familiar figure. Dressed in a cashmere skirt and cowled sweater, Rosaline Silliker was exchanging air-kisses with a lady in a faux python-skin jacket. "Darling. You're looking wonderful. How's your father?" the snake woman asked.

Rosaline gave a brave smile and arranged a shoulder bag. "Same as his father, I'm afraid. Congenital heart disease. Now a little stroke. They're making him comfortable. He's pain-free and cognizant. That's something."

Belle felt a certain kinship with the woman and wondered if once again it wasn't a case of withholding expensive procedures from the elderly. To paraphrase a neighbour, "We have the technology. We just can't afford it."

After arranging for a mini-television at a maxi-cost, she saw a *Sudbury Star* on a table in a waiting room, folded it, and left the hospital. When she remembered about germs, she dropped it onto a bench for the smoking brigade.

Monday morning after breakfast, she headed down the road. The rental, a bare bones basic Pontiac Montana, was a pale imitation of the sophisticated Sienna. And it rattled. No sign of Miss Liberty, the red Jeep in a hurry. A good omen for a good day. As soon as business hours opened, she called Robinson Automotive. The owner answered. "Saw your note on the windshield. That tow guy was right. It was the brake lines."

"Did you say *lines,* as in plural?" That sounded like serious damage. Was it that last accordion trail by Lake Penage?

"Both of them cut neatly in the same spot."

Her stomach lurched. "Cut? Are you sure?"

"One hundred per cent. This isn't a case of kids fooling around. I'd say somebody doesn't like you big time. Better report it to the police. Can you keep the van in a safe place? Next time it could be worse."

Told that the vehicle would be ready by five, Belle hung up. "Safe" was a problem. For once she wished she had splurged and built a garage, despite the extra property-tax bite. As for the suspect, she gave a bitter laugh, knowing she was *non grata* to one *persona*. Joey Bartko. No matter how she rationalized that she was unhurt and that the repair cost was minimal, it had been focussed, deliberate, and in a legal definition, attempted murder. Somehow he'd found out, perhaps seen her at the bulletin board or heard the buzz in the village of Skead. What had she unleashed when she'd played environmental cop? Would he be satisfied or ratchet up the agenda? Even were the charges proved, with the long delays in the court system, he might not go to trial for months, and certainly, he'd be out on bail. She needed advice, and only one big brother came to mind. She balanced peace of mind on one hand with a humiliating lecture on the other. The scale tipped toward security. She wasn't a family of one.

When she got to the office, Yoyo was standing by the front steps. At her feet were the shattered plastic remains of the Palmer Realty sign. She turned to Belle with a shrug. "Guess the bolts gave out. Lucky no one was underneath."

"I should have replaced it long ago. It's over fifty years old. I'll call Ernie's Signs to get someone to haul the mess away. This is not going to be cheap." She bent to examine the corpse. The bolts were rusty, but had they been given a head start?

On a lunch break, she walked over to Tom Davies Square to the Police Department on the hunch that Steve might be in. As he rose in rank, he said that he spent more time typing reports than he did collecting criminals. She gave her name to the sleek brunette receptionist in the modern lobby, a world away from the typical jowlly sergeant high up on a pedestal platform in Thirties films. With shiny floors and glassed walls, it looked like a five-star hotel. Where did they hide the ne'er-do-wells?

As a vase of mauve and burgundy carnations sent spicy fragrances into the air, the woman punched buttons on the phone. "A Belle Palmer here to see you, Detective." Listening to his reply, she delivered a world-class smile. "He'll be right out."

Steve appeared from a corridor to lead her back to his office. Nothing like the rabbit hole he'd once inhabited, a basement burrow crowned with asbestos-covered heating pipes. He popped a small bag into a sleek new bullet-shaped coffee maker. "A single cup at a time, but it's great stuff. Jamaican Blue Mountain. Keeps me from drinking too much or inhaling sludge, too. One for you?"

"I'm on overload already, thanks." She took a seat in a familiar battered and duct-taped leather armchair that looked like it had seen duty during Mackenzie King's tenure. "Couldn't part with the old beater, eh?" she said, gyrating around a loose spring as he doctored his coffee.

"It has my bum memorized."

"That *is* important."

His office was crowded with organized mayhem. Graduated piles, file cabinets open and ready, bulletin boards of Canada's Most Wanted, and post-it notes on every available surface. The usual pizza box was in the overflowing wastebasket. On the wall were pictures of Heather, "graduating" from kindergarten, racing down a soccer field at Lily Creek, braids flying, and grinning from a roller coaster ride at Canada's Wonderland. None of Janet. Understandable but sad. Was that what marriage was all about?

Steve took a sip of coffee, placed the mug on a copy of *Blue Line* magazine, and said, "If you're here about Gary, sorry to report that we've pretty much closed the book. It's true that Ramleau liked the boyfr—"

Seeing her eyes sharpen, he added, "I mean partner, but the time frame was too close."

"I heard that the questioning was offensive." Belle drummed her fingers on the chair arm. "And how ridiculous.

Mutt loved him. Seven years is a long time to be together."

He shrugged. "Take it from an old pro. Passions can run high in any relationship. I've had a few murderous thoughts about Janet, and she'd say the same."

"Oh, come on. Divorce is easy enough. No-fault." Suddenly she felt presumptuous, pontificating on the subject, not to mention teasing the raw wound that was his union. Then again, she couldn't recall any wedding she'd attended where the couple hadn't split. All those toasters and blenders jousting in the marital settlement. Twenty thousand dollars would have fared better in mutual funds instead of bankrolling a wedding album headed for a landfill.

"You know that spouses are always the first suspects."

"And the leading cause of death for pregnant women is murder." Belle leaned forward. "But the time frame cleared him?"

He opened a file folder, leafed through a few photocopies, and tapped a pencil at one entry. "June 5th. Malloy used his Visa in St. Catharines at eleven that morning gassing up. Got cash at the TD bank next. Nice camera shots. He's one handsome boy. The Medivac helicopter that saw Gary's body called in the report at two o'clock. Given the time to navigate around Toronto at high noon, up the 400, onto 69, and then over to Burwash, walk to the lake, kill Gary, then get to Sudbury and out to your road at...when did he call you?"

"Kill Gary." Frank enough, since Steve's job demanded cool objectivity and time-slicing syntax. Friend to friend, bluntness was laced with tact as thin as the two per cent milk he'd added to his coffee. At least he wasn't always talking about "perps". Taking off her glasses, she massaged the bridge of her nose. "Points North was on the radio. Just after four."

"There you are, then. Couldn't do it unless you were flying. And cottage traffic is thick in the summer. Wasn't that a Friday, too?" He spread his hands in a *fait-non-accompli* gesture.

Belle nodded, glad that Mutt would get no further aggravation. "Case closed, then. Thank God. An accident was bad enough. I came to see you about something else, Steve. My van was sabotaged yesterday."

"Broken windshield? Flat tire? Vandalism always rises when school's out. Sorry about your new baby, though." He'd taken her to a special roast and lunch at the Apollo when she'd signed the papers.

She took a deep breath and told him about the severed brake lines. "I'm sure this all started when I called in a report to CrimeStoppers about someone who left garbage in the bush, and I don't mean a cigarette butt." Describing the mess, she paused, afraid to proceed. Steve was furious when she put herself in danger. But he had to know how she'd found a name. "Then someone gave me a tip."

"Really." A muscle in his cheek twitched as he stared at her, and his voice was flat. "That restores my faith in humanity."

She dealt out the details, reddening at the humiliation of sneaking around passing out twenties, playing private eye at the airport. "It made me so mad. How would you like it if someone trashed your backyard? That's the way I feel about the bush. I walk those roads during bug season, and now I never want to go there again. You know the municipal government. No one's going to clean it up. And those tires are good for a hundred years."

"So you put up a notice that said, 'Come get me, sucker'."

"But I only gave my cell—"

Steve raised his large hand in an "enough" gesture. "We have to talk this out before it escalates. Listen up. The fact that he came to your place raises big red flags. Think anyone might have seen him?"

Her neighbours, the McNairs, had opened their cottage that week and stayed for several days. Now that the leaves were out in the brushy area between their properties, her parking area was half-shielded. A greenbelt formed the eastern side. But people drove by all the time, and they loved keeping an eye out for activity. A leaning tree cut. A new vehicle. Roof repair. But what if he had come at night? "I'll make a few calls. What about dusting the van for prints?"

He shook his head. "Finding forensic evidence would be a joke, given that a hoard of mechanics worked on your van. We're in luck if he has a record or, better yet, is on probation. Then I can yank his strings."

She sat back, feeling like she'd had that cup of coffee after all, its rich aroma turning to acid in her churning stomach. An adult's version of the principal's office. Steve was riding to her rescue yet another time. The big brother she'd never had. "Thanks. I owe you...as usual." She felt like buying him a decent watch to replace his plastic Timex Sport, but wouldn't Janet love that?

The phone began ringing, and she rose to leave out of courtesy. He clapped her on the shoulder, giving it a squeeze that warmed her heart. "Just for now, even though it's inconvenient, leave your van with the DesRosiers and lock your doors. If Joey's behind this, he might be tempted to make a return visit."

"Should I keep my shotgun handy?" she said with a half-smile on her face, knowing that he suspected that it was unregistered. Belle found the cash-cow gun laws hard to swallow, even outside of Alberta.

Shortly after five, Belle exchanged vehicles, then drove home and left her van at the DesRosiers' for safekeeping. After dinner, she dialled the neighbours who lived farther down the road and might have passed her yard. Some were at their camps, some in town. No one had seen anything. A widow who didn't like staying at the lake unless her family was there, Jeannie McNair spent only a few summer weeks at the lovely home next door. When she heard about Belle's van, she tsked and said, "I was out working in the garden all afternoon. Rodney and I left after dinner and took the garbage with us. Those bears get into everything. Did you see the mess at Toivola's?"

"There have been a few robberies, too. Missing anything, as far as you know?"

"We just opened up and got the water running again. The girls have too many dance activities to come out. Thank God they're not into boys yet." She paused as if in thought. "Rodney's been looking for his chainsaw to cut a dead branch by the playhouse. Can't find it anywhere. Of course, I told him he may have loaned it to someone last year and forgotten."

Belle hung up, digesting the latest news. Prowling for property and cutting brake lines were two different animals. Still, she began sweating despite the chill in the room. Was a cruel June frost just around the corner?

TEN

Belle had spent the evening devouring Mutt's book. Her family had lived in Toronto since her grandfather had come from the Bowmanville area to set up a greenhouse on Runnymede Road in Lucy's days. She pictured the massive, buttressed churches still anchoring the downtown, St. James and Trinity. The St. Lawrence Market. Allan Gardens. Union Station. The dowager hotels like the Royal York and its counterpart, the King Edward. The majestic Romanesque red stone structures of Queen's Park. Historic villages like Rosedale and the Annex, layered over time. And finally, the brick, Gothic-style apartment still standing at Wellesley and Church where her parents had conceived her, the floors so uneven from settling that a marble could roll down the hall. So many landmarks had vanished since Lucy had seen the last milk-wagon horses clump down the streets. Belle smiled at the mention of Gish's *Orphans of the Storm*, a silent classic Lucy had seen with her detective "beau" Wilfred Pearson at the ornate Uptown, one of Toronto's since vanished regal theatres.

Over coffee at six, having left the last pages until morning, she finally said farewell to plucky Lucy. Mutt had played fair with the reader and spun a tidy puzzle. She should have guessed that the friendly neighbour had connections with the rum-runners. Why not stop by on her way to work to tell him how much she had enjoyed it? After breakfast, she went outside and stared, trying to understand what was wrong with the picture. She slapped her head. No van.

Hoisting her attaché case, she walked up the long drive and turned right as a mini-schoolbus chugged by. With a cool north wind forestalling the usual cloud of bugs, she inspected the ditches for the latest plant arrivals. The bracken was unfolding its tiny green fists alongside the leafy nautilus of the fiddlehead ferns.

Half a mile later, she arrived at the DesRosiers'. Last night, when she'd told them about the damage, Hélène had urged her to stay over, but she treasured her independence. More precautions made sense. Little help the clumsy shotgun was, wrapped in a garbage bag in the basement rafters. Willie Mann, a snowbird neighbour, had hinted that he had a .22 Saturday Night Special for dispatching skunks and coons. Should she borrow it until this mess was settled?

At the kitchen window, Hélène waved her in, but Belle shook her head and pointed to her watch. Coming outside with a plate, her friend handed Belle a bran muffin, steaming in the cool air. "Were you okay last night? I'm worried about you, not your van."

Belle suspected that the muffin was made with Sugar Twin and slathered with Becel, but she took a large bite, wiping the yellow product from her chin. Another triumph for Hélène, though Ed needed the diet, not his wife, slim in her purple velour robe. Savouring the plump raisins, Belle mmmm'd approval. "I was fine. Not a sound out of anyone, even my resident bear."

"We're used to that. Human beasts worry me more." Hélène's pleasant face amid greying curls reflected concern. "Why not stay here for awhile? Freya's welcome, and the guest bedroom is yours. Remember our gin rummy games?" She gave

Belle a quick hug, passing a scent of lilac talcum.

"This is very temporary. Steve's working on it. I expect to hear from him any minute." Not true. Steve had a job to do, and putting out her fires shouldn't be a priority. The DesRosiers were guardian angels, but their guest bed left a spine begging for chiropractic adjustment. She'd probably gain ten pounds from the meals as well.

"Did you get your garden in yet?" Near the small oak tree decorated with juice-bottle bird feeders, Hélène pointed to her neat vegetable and herb patch, finely tilled and planted with stakes bearing seed packages. "Last night it was only three degrees. Too close for comfort. I had a couple of old sheets ready."

"I was frosted twice last June. This weekend, maybe." Too many diversions. If she didn't get underway now, forget all those luscious zucchinis, beans and tomatoes. She felt like the laziest girl in town next to her neighbours, but retirement afforded far more than forty extra hours a week, what with the travelling time.

Accepting a refill for her car mug, Belle drove off. A few minutes later, she pulled into Mutt's yard. He said he rose early to write, leaving the afternoon free for plotting. Where did he get his ideas? She couldn't imagine sponging up life's experiences. Eventually, he had to fabricate something. Perhaps that was the genius of a successful writer, weaving facts with fiction. Yet even this little road had a plethora of characters in search of an author. Two convicted child molesters, one for each sex, a suicide, a husband returning like Ulysses after thirty years, one motorcycle death, suspected incest, countless cases of adultery. And that was only the public total.

From the passenger seat, she picked up the trade paperback with a cover picture of Edwardian row houses, admiring the studio photo on the back, the confident pose, the casual tailored clothes. Mutt must fend off advances from both sexes and anyone in between. The dedication read, "To Gary. It's about time." Brief and heartfelt. What an irony, considering that it had run out for him so soon.

With no boathouse, the red canoe was overturned down on the beach, paddles on top. Since Mutt was staying for awhile, it might be fun to take a run down the lake, visit Flowergull Island, Bear Inlet, check the progress of the blueberries on the sunny banks of the shore. A picnic could be arranged, and her 1.2 horsepower motor would save their sweat. Then, out of a corner of her eye, she spied movement in the burning bush bed, one of Maureen's hard-won prizes, zone five, closer to Barrie. Dirt was flying in all directions. She hustled down a wood-chip path and caught Buddy in the act. "Hey, you! Go bury your bones next door!" she yelled.

She waited until he had skulked back to Strang's property and made a mental note to give old Bill a call. Mutt was too polite to lay down the law. Stepping onto the covered porch, she peered in through the handsome blue door, its top half-stained glass. Only darkness. Maureen had no bell, so she knocked loudly. No answer, even when she repeated the gesture. Puzzled, she checked around the side of the house, where the car and truck were parked. Was he in the shower? How embarrassing if she let herself in and he strolled out in a towel...or less. Had he gone on a walk on the paths across the road? She noticed two wine bottles in the recycling box. Getting into the sauce to lubricate the wounds of such a devastating loss, or merely making up for a restless night? Looking in impatience at her watch, her foot tapping, she considered the choices. Should she come back after work, or leave the book? The skies were massing with overstuffed clouds edged with silver, a predictor of thunderboomers. The porch might get wet. Too intrusive to open a friend's door and slip it in? Time was ticking by.

She tried the door and found it unlocked. Mutt was adopting country ways, but in view of the break-in, a bad idea. As she entered and shut it behind her, the air seemed heavy and burdensome. She took a few tentative steps. An invisible hand clutched at her chest, and her eyes began to sting. Though the air was clear of smoke, she surveyed the fireplace. Swept clean. What was the heating system? Belle shook her head to clear her memory, recalling that Maureen also had a propane furnace. In the confusion of sorting information, feeling her knees weaken, suddenly she knew something was terribly wrong. Propane was essentially odourless, so producers added a disgusting smell for safety. She detected nothing but thought of that Falconbridge Road billboard with the cartoon character. Carbon monoxide fumes. The Silent Killer. She prayed that he wasn't inside, but the odds weren't favourable. "Mutt! Mutt!" she screamed at the top of her lungs as her hands grabbed the back of a kitchen chair for support. All was ominous silence. Fear charged down her spine like an electric rod, and she knew that if she didn't get out now, she'd drop where she stood.

She wheeled for the porch, leaving the door open and taking great gulps of air, bending over, arms braced on her knees. Her temples pounded as she forced herself to think, shoving the instinct to panic to a remote corner of her brain. Don't waste time calling an ambulance. By the time it arrived, Mutt would be dead, if he was still inside. She had to get him out. Yet it was suicidal to charge up the stairs to the master bedroom, only to asphyxiate herself. She'd take it in logical steps. Open the windows. Flip on the overhead Casablanca fans. Come back out. Breathe. Return. Open the back door and more windows. Turn the furnace off at the control by the fridge. She knew the layout by heart, had seen the blueprints and remembered each stage as the classic log home had been an entertaining creation on the road.

Breathing through a wet towel might allow her to reach the upper floor, she thought as she came out the third time. She couldn't hold her breath all that way, much less haul back a body. A body. A shiver prickled her neck. Had he already joined Gary?

Windows open, a dishtowel soaked at the sink, Belle had completed her work downstairs. Already the air seemed lighter, a cool north wind blowing through the cross-ventilated windows, their chintz curtains pulled aside. She tied the wet towel around her mouth and nose like a bandit. Then she charged up the stairs, bruising her leg as she slipped on the slick, varnished wood. The thick banister was a solid round of pine, impossible to grasp. Reaching the landing, she raised the window, pressed her nose to the screen and gulped in fresh air. After re-situating her mask, she turned. Six more stairs, two at a time. To the left was the master suite, complete with jacuzzi. Her eyes wild with terror, she rushed in.

Like Henry Wallis's Chatterton on the daybed, alabaster skin shining, Mutt lay on his back, one arm draped over the side of the king-sized memory-foam mattress. Soft beige flannel sheets and a patchwork quilt covered him from the waist down. With a fierce cry, she flung open the windows and switched on the overhead fan. Had she been wrong not to call the ambulance, or was it already too late?

She tossed back the covers and reached forward, shaking him, momentarily heartened at the warmth of his shoulder. Instead of the red she'd expected, his impassive face was oatmeal pale, and he didn't respond. If alcohol had compounded the poisoning, he might never come around. She had to move him, and fast. What did he weigh? One fifty? He was only a few inches taller than she but muscular in his navy silk boxer shorts, his well-defined chest smooth as a girl's, the vaunted six-pack testimony of workouts. A lion's head tattoo fit perfectly on his right pectoral, where perhaps a lover would admire it. The air was no longer pressing on her chest, so she moved quickly and with less panic. Tightening her towel again, she went to the large bathroom for a glass of water, returning to splash it onto his face, fashioning Byronic curls in his dark hair. No way could she haul a dead weight out of the room, down the stairs, and outside. Maybe she should have canvassed the nearby houses until she found someone home. Tears of doubt stung her eyes. Finally, she got a moan in response, then a cough.

"Wake up, Mutt. There's a gas leak." He was alive, but with every passing minute, chances for permanent damage increased.

"Wha?" His head lolled on the pillow, chiselled jaw slack, drool ribboning from his open mouth.

She pulled his arm and felt a slight resistance, a good sign. "Get up, or I'll have to drag you down the stairs."

Suddenly he lurched over the side of the bed and vomited into a pair of sheepskin slippers. She held his shoulders to keep his windpipe free. Then he was on his knees, and she was urging him out of the room. When he fainted on the stairs, she blocked his fall and eased his awkward weight down to the living room, wincing with each bump. Like most women contemplating the ravages of age, never had she imagined gravity as her best friend.

The air was finally safe. She sensed the difference and breathed deeply, forcing every molecule of oxygen to recharge her blood. Twenty-five more feet to the kitchen. With her knees trembling like Olive Oyl's, sweat poured down her face and trickled along her back. Thankful for the polished oak floors that Maureen kept slick as a bowling alley, she yanked

Mutt by his shoulders the last yards to the porch, bumped him over the threshold, and placed his head on a throw pillow from a wicker settee. Her lungs were wheezing with exertion. Each muscle flamed with lactic acid, and her lumbar region gave a warning twinge. Her head felt balloonish, detached from her body, and a troubling nausea roamed her stomach. A reaction to the gas or trauma? Every minute counted now. The temperature had risen a few degrees, but unclothed, he was in serious danger of hypothermia. Having saved him once, was she placing him in more danger?

The brisk wind swirled dead leaves around the yard in mini-tornados as a car sped by on the road, leaving a cloud of dust. She ran back for an afghan from the sofa, then for insurance, grabbed a heavy canvas coat from a Victorian hall tree and covered him. Still, the porch floorboards were cold. She rolled him onto a dog blanket snatched from the van and placed him in the recovery position.

Choking back a sob, she hunted for the cell phone in her console. A chemical taste coated the back of her mouth, and her nostrils were scorched with acid. For a moment she thought she was seeing double then realized that her glasses had fogged with sweat. Shoving them back onto her head, she squinted as she dialled 911. Driving Mutt to the hospital, even if she could get him into her vehicle, wasn't going to revive him any faster. In her frantic state, she'd probably land them both in a watery ditch on the swamp flats.

"A man on Edgewater Road has propane gas poisoning. Or carbon monoxide, whatever. The address is 1565."

There was a pause. "Which Edgewater Road do you mean?"

Belle rapped her temple. As a realtor, she should have remembered another Edgewater Road near Long Lake.

"Sorry. Up the west side of Lake Wapiti."

"Is he conscious?"

"He came to for a moment. Now he's totally out. Breathing but not responding."

The female voice was deliberate and calming, part of the job. "Keep him warm. Stay on the line." She put Belle on hold for thirty seconds, an eternity. "A unit's just leaving Radar Road after a false alarm. Arrival should be in twenty minutes. Have you turned off all the appliances? An electrical spark could be dangerous. And I hope no one's smoking."

Shivering from fear more than cold as she hung up, Belle gathered herself around Mutt to share her warmth and form an unusual Pietà. She held his hand, compact and artistic, monitoring his stuttering pulse. His face was too relaxed, flat-featured. Gentle slaps or shakes failed to bring him around. She lifted one flaccid lid and saw his eye rolled back like the baby elk's. "Help is coming, Mutt. But please talk to me. What about Lucy? Will she marry that policeman, or is she just pumping him for information?" Crazy ideas like driving a mile down to the Proctors, where she knew asthmatic Joyce kept bottled oxygen, crossed her feverish mind.

For some reason, singing seemed like a good idea, and she began a soft version of "I Dreamed I Dwelt in Marble Halls". When the thought of a mausoleum rose, she switched to "The Minstrel Boy" then to "The Wearing of the Green", some of her mother's Bing Crosby favourites. With his Irish background, Mutt might be familiar with the melodies. It was common knowledge that coma patients responded to touches and sound.

On the lake, a cigarette boat surged by, leaving a wake of rolling waves pounding the pebble beach. Lakefront was so picturesque. Everyone wanted to live there but usually couldn't imagine the pitiless nature of high water, especially when roused by wind. She realized that her mind was rambling again.

Soon the welcome siren of the ambulance punctuated the air, rising and falling with the undulating hills and curves. The vehicle slowed, turned into the yard and backed up toward the porch. A wiry young man with a pencil-thin moustache and a short blonde woman, both in trim navy uniforms, hustled out and rolled a gurney out of the rear.

"Thank God," Belle called, then eased away and hovered at the perimeter, watching every move as an omen.

The young man readied the stretcher, and the woman peered into Mutt's eyes with a penlight, next listening to his heart and firming her mouth at the results. What did that mean? Could he have damaged his cardiac system? In quick, efficient motions, an oxygen mask was affixed. Only then did Belle notice the bluish tinge of his skin. "His face is so...I mean I thought that—"

"Cyanosis. That cherry-red reaction is very rare." She listened to his heart again. "Have the defibrillator at the ready, Jim."

Trying to tune out the scolding chitter of an affronted squirrel in the cedars, Belle stood by, hugging herself. In the distance, thunder rolled, and a fat raindrop splashed onto her face. "Will he be all right? I mean will he have any serious damage? I don't know anything about gas poisoning."

The woman touched her arm, sending comfort with warm brown eyes. "It's roulette with these cases. Pray, if it's your habit. Good thoughts always help."

With Mutt blanketed in the ambulance, the paramedic jotted particulars on a form, then said with a polite frown, "Sorry to ask, but is there any reason to think that this was a suicide attempt, ma'am?"

"Usually people use cars or ovens, don't they?" Belle folded her arms in a defensive posture, not sure whether to be insulted for Mutt or confused. "It was an accident with the furnace. A leak or something." But knowing how regular Maureen was about maintenance, that made little sense. And despite his devastating loss, the idea that Mutt would or even could fool with a furnace to turn a house into a gas chamber was ludicrous. Why hadn't the alarm worked?

"Best get someone out here right away to fix it, then. You don't want a fire on top of this."

Belle felt a flash of heat across her brow, despite the cold, wet morning. A fire? She'd only turned off the main switch. What now? Follow Mutt to the hospital? Not without calling Campeau Heating. He couldn't return to the house until repairs were made. A crash of lightning brought a deluge of rain as she ran for the porch. And on top of a headache that was turning her brain into a clothes dryer filled with running shoes, she had a client due in twenty minutes. Quickly she dialled the office and told Yoyo to apologize and ask the woman to wait. Since she had an extra key for the house, she went to the basement to hit the main furnace breaker then locked the doors behind her.

In the habit of summer storms, the rain had stopped as quickly as it had started, leaving a smear of blackflies on the windshield. Halfway to town, Belle remembered that she had left the windows open. Changing lanes with this distracting thought, she was nearly creamed by a tandem of pulpwood.

Her arrival at the office after twenty-five minutes of low-level flying found Yoyo doing her nails, pots of primer and polish laid out with orange sticks and files, a major production. To Belle, nails were a tool, not an adornment that ate up time and broke when opening a jug of washer fluid at minus thirty. Living in the north, she'd abandoned fashion and beauty for clean and warm and had no idea where her iron lived. She hung up her trench coat and got a coffee. Maddened with worry about Mutt, she felt like talking. Yoyo didn't need a long-winded history about her relationship with Gary, but she could provide some commiseration about today's disaster. Came with the job, as Miriam knew.

"That appointment rescheduled for tomorrow anyway, so no sweat," Yoyo said, peering at her. "You don't look so hot, pardon me for saying. Time of the month?"

"I wish."

Hearing the scenario, Yoyo put her hand to her mouth, then realized it was fresh with paint and began waving it dry. Her round, bottle-green eyes saucered, the light brown tapered brows shaped like tiny rice-paddy hats. "My cousin went on a winter camping trip near Elliot Lake. Ran a propane stove in the tent and never woke up. Left three kids under ten. His widow should have sued the ass off the manufacturer. Sure would in the States. Canadians hate to rock the boat."

Biting off a patriotic retort because she half-agreed, Belle recalled canoe trips where she had cooked inside a tent amid torrents of rain. "I hope my friend'll be okay."

"Sure he will, honey. Big strong men always are." She flexed a mock muscle.

Yes and no, Belle thought. Once her father had been a powerhouse who used to carry his daughter on his shoulders. Age asserted its dominion, even though it beat the alternative. She dialled Campeau with a pitiful helpless-woman tale and received a solemn promise to meet her later at the house.

Around noon, they ordered pizza, agreeing to share a medium shrimp scampi. Seafood was brain food, high-fat mozzarella aside. Yoyo washed down a bevy of vitamins with her large chocolate milk. "Folic acid," she said, holding up a pill bottle. "Can you believe that it cuts the risk of Down Syndrome by eighty per cent? This little one's getting kid-glove care." On her desk was a copy of *What to Expect When You're Expecting*.

As they munched, Yoyo presented the monthly figures, looking good for a change with the freshening summer sales. Interest rates were low, and diversification of the local economy had fuelled a demand for housing. Belle had finally paid back the temporary loan she'd taken from herself to rebuild the dock, a dubious business practice. "So compared to last year, you're up a couple thousand this month. Do I get a raise?"

Replying with the same bland non-committal expression she gave Miriam at that nagging question, Belle turned to the wall calendar. How well she knew the long lean months of fall and winter, feeling like a stunted northern red squirrel husbanding nuts. With her luck lately, she'd forget where she left them. She watched Yoyo re-file the material, a slight pout on her heart-shaped face. "How's your mom doing?" How rude that she hadn't asked, as if no one else had problems.

Yoyo tapped her sharp nails on the desk in the rhythm of a snare drum. "She paid her fine with bingo winnings, the rascal. Runs in the family, I guess. But given her health, this won't go on much longer."

At the coffee maker, Belle stopped in mid-pour. "Is she ill?" With that wicked cane, the woman had looked capable of fending off a rutting moose.

"Naw. It's immaculate degeneration. Those dark glasses. She's losing her vision."

"Imm..." Belle gave a small gasp, blinking aside the annoying floaters that had begun to plague her, a sign of aging, the cocky young optometrist had said. Helen Keller aside, blindness seemed the cruellest fate. "I've heard of that. There's no treatment?"

Yoyo's padded shoulders sagged. Today she wore an imitation blue leather skirt and top, silver epaulets and a zipper up the front of the jacket, at the crest of the décolletage instead of an inch below. Perhaps impending motherhood was turning her from coquette to Madonna. "They have a treatment for the wet kind. That's hers. But Ontario is one of the few provinces that won't pay the shot. Too expensive or something. How much is your eyesight worth?"

"Cheap bastards." Belle had seen American ads trolling in major newspapers. Focussing on MRIs, virtual colonoscopies, and other scans that often took months to schedule, they encouraged wealthier Canadians to jump the queue.

When Belle called later that afternoon, the nurse at Emerg related only that Mutt was being seen. Given her appointment with the furnace technician, visiting him was out of the question. Belle hustled home at four, meeting the Campeau cube truck at the mailboxes and letting it play stalking horse for outgoing traffic. Maybe Miss Liberty was heading this way. She gave an evil chuckle. Jeep vs. truck today at the demo derby. Place your bets.

The truck slowed, as if to double-check the address on the green metal sign, then pulled in. She introduced herself to Colin, according to his name tag, who carried a heavy toolbox as he eyeballed the house with approval. "I see all the windows are open. Smart move. I don't want to walk into no Texas-style gas chamber. Good reason never to smoke on the job." His grey eyes crinkled at his joke.

"How often does this happen?" Of the three central heating systems, propane seemed cleaner than oil and certainly less expensive than electricity.

The grizzled man rolled a toothpick around his mouth with machine-tooled precision. "Over three hundred people a year die in the U.S. and Canada from carbon monoxide poisoning. Boats are a real killer."

"Boats?"

As a guttural roar assaulted their eardrums, they turned toward the lake, where a jet-ski was doing doughnuts as mindlessly as a ladybug in a lampshade. Colin added, "Cabin cruisers. Gets a bit chilly on August nights, and on goes the furnace. Faulty ventilation's a killer. No regulations up here."

After Colin had gone inside, she roamed the gardens that had won Maureen first prize in the Skead Horticultural Tour. The rose beds were producing shoots, and by the house a delicate clematis had begun its shy drift up the lattice. The tulip and daffodil bulbs had peaked and should be deadheaded.

As she sat on the porch wondering what to do next, Belle pulled out the cell phone and called Emerg again. This time she was told that Malcolm was still in critical condition and had been moved to Laurentian Hospital. Hadn't he regained consciousness? A pause. "I'm sorry. That's all I can tell you. Are you a relative?"

"No, I—" Then they were disconnected. She heard a croak and looked up to see Raven, the Trickster in Ojibwa mythology, hang-gliding the thermals and playing with a fellow bird. Normally she enjoyed the antics of the bird that amused itself, but all she could think of was Mutt. This sounded bad. She should call someone, but whom?

Twenty minutes later, Colin came out and walked to the side of the house, where ten-foot grey-green junipers, mugho pines and climbing roses lay in dense beds. He hunted one way, then another, tipped back his faded cap and scratched his head. "Where's the damn exhaust? Plants are so thick, I can't see a thing."

Belle laughed. "I think it's behind the lattice. The owner wants an authentic log-cabin look."

They inspected a squared box set out from the wall and floored with gravel. Inside were the clothes dryer vent and another polystyrene pipe. Colin unscrewed the lattice panel, brushing aside dead leaves from the Virginia creeper. Though the pipe angled downward, it seemed blocked. As his fingers probed, material sifted to the ground. Shaking his head, he rooted manfully with a straightened coat hanger and began clearing the pipe.

Curious, she joined him, wrinkling her brow. "Yuck. What *is* that stuff, and more to the point, how did it get there?"

He held small shards of what looked like cotton, paper, leaves and pink fibre insulation. "Mouse nest. Little buggers half-wrecked my RV once. Transferred the insulation to the kitchen drawers for their litter. They can find the smallest hole." Then, with a grunt of disgust, he flung the material into the forsythia bushes.

"I have a propane furnace too. Maybe I should check it." She shivered to think how easily a tiny creature could imperil lives.

"You're okay as long as you're using it regular. The mouse takes the hint. How about this place? Folks been on vacation?"

"The family left over a month ago. Someone else moved in, but it's been very warm until last night. If it got below twenty, the furnace probably came on."

He cleaned his hands with a towelette from his toolbox. "It's unusual, but if Mickey, or rather Minnie, was a six-pack short of a two-four, there'd be time enough to build a nest."

"So is the house safe now?" When Mutt was released from hospital, and surely he would be, he had to go somewhere. How long did it take to recover from gas poisoning? Should she ask him to stay with her?

Colin opened a pack of gum and offered her a chew, but she shook her head. "I'll clamp on a grid to prevent this from happening again. Then you're off to the races."

She had a final thought. "What about the propane alarm?"

He shrugged. "Dead batteries. I replaced them."

As he prepared to leave later, Belle gave him a cheque for a hundred and fifty dollars. "Got any more of that mesh?" She'd fix her own vent.

With a wink, he clipped off a square for her and saluted. Belle stood in the driveway. No time now to drive back to town to the hospital, especially when Mutt might still be unconscious. But his family should be told. Sadly, he'd never mentioned them, except to say that they'd refused to come to his wedding. Where did they live? Hadn't he said that they had a cottage in Muskoka? Blowing out a breath, she checked her watch. Six. Freya would be waiting. At the very least, she should give the house a quick search for an address book.

First she closed the windows, then went to the den, where on a large walnut table, he had set up a spiffy green iMac and a printer. A couple of DVDs read *Wellesley Street Whistler*, dated early in the year. Over on a roll-top desk were a few small field notebooks of Gary's as well as a yellow pad with what she imagined were Mutt's observations about the research. Determined to think positively, she gathered them up. On returning to consciousness, he might appreciate having them. Where would he keep his contact numbers? In his computer? She tried to boot up, but it was password-protected. Luckily, the desk drawer held an old address book with Gary's idiosyncratic angular writing. Her name wasn't in there, but why would it have been? In the M's, she found a Megs Malloy in Hamilton.

Belle didn't relish giving bad news, so she took a deep breath before picking up the phone and dialling the number. Time for a working person to be making dinner. A thin, nasal voice answered.

"I'm calling about Mu…Malcolm Malloy."

"I'm his sister. What's this about?"

Belle told the story briefly, without sugarcoating the prognosis. "That's all I know. Hospitals won't release anything specific except to immediate family, and then usually only in person. I didn't have a number for his parents."

"I can tell them, if that's your worry."

"When he…comes to, he could use some support. After all, he just lost his partner."

"I guess that's the acceptable term, but it sounds like a cowboy movie. Anyway, Mother and Father haven't spoken to him in years."

"Maybe it's time to mend fences. He could die." She felt like pushing the limits but was painfully aware that she might be scripting a prophecy.

Megs sighed, then seemed to be thinking, muttering to herself. "Dad's been diagnosed with late-stage prostate cancer. He doesn't have much longer. I guess I should come up. It's a hell of a drive, though. A cowpath from Barrie, I hear."

Belle's opinion of Megs was growing frosty as the dilemma unfolded. Someone needed to be at Mutt's side. The woman could stay at Maureen's now that the furnace was fixed. "Not quite. They've four-laned fifty more kilometres. Should be finished about 2025." To simplify matters, Belle gave directions to the business, where she could provide a map and a key to the house. Did Mutt's sister look like he did? She certainly didn't have the same warm personality. What kind of a name was Megs? It reminded her of a rabbit. Yoyo, Coco and Mutt. Was she writing the screenplay to a Little Rascals comedy? She turned for the door and realized that she was ravenous. Time to go home and fatten up Porky.

ELEVEN

The next morning, Belle sat at her desk sneezing as dust motes roiled in the strong sun coming through the window. "How about some dusting, Yoyo? I gave you a Swiffer set."

"Sorry, out of sight, you know. I've never been house-proud. Mom handles that." Yoyo went to the cabinet, slipped on a fresh cloth, adjusted the wand with elaborate gestures and made a show of covering every surface, humming Faith Hill's "This Kiss". Belle shared her opinion of the joys of cleaning. They both should own naked little non-shedding Chinese cresteds.

The clock ticked past two. Megs was overdue, but traffic might have delayed her on such a long trip. On a sheet of foolscap, Belle began drawing a simple map to the lake. She had mixed feelings about meeting the woman.

On a break, Yoyo slurped a yogurt drink and flapped a tabloid. "Unreal. Do you know a woman had cosmetic surgery to resemble a cat? And even worse, a guy wanted to look like a snake. So he shaved his head, got scale tattoos, and had his tongue cut in—"

"Enough already. *The Island of Dr. Moreau* come to life."

"Right, I heard about those islands where the rich and famous go for secret operations."

Then the door opened, and in came a woman in her mid-thirties, her eyebrows arched like Gothic windows, giving her a perpetually surprised look. Her upper and lower lips appeared to belong to two different people. "I'm Megs Malloy," she began, planting herself in front of Yoyo's desk as she scanned the area. "I thought this was a business. What do you sell here, anyway?" Her snarky voice implied that they were running a Ponzi scheme or rerouting Nigerian spam.

Clearing her throat from across the room, Belle drew herself up, still six inches from the woman's height, always an unpleasant sensation. Her eyes flashed to the patent-leather stiletto boots. How did she drive in them? "Belle Palmer. As I told you, this is a realty company. We specialize in cottage properties."

"Then where's your sign? My father always said that a business without a sign is a sign of no business."

Belle and Yoyo exchanged glances. "It, uh, blew down in a storm. It's taking awhile to replace. Custom work." And about two thousand dollars. Ouch.

Against her will, Belle stuck out her hand, finding herself enveloping a two-day-old mackerel. Retrieving it, she wiped off the moisture on her back, then pasted on a smile.

Megs frowned at her surroundings and gave an obvious shiver. She wore a purple linen tunic over pink tights and a long-sleeved turtleneck. Her unnatural ash-blonde hair hung in layers, kissing her shoulders, a casual look running to the triple digits. A monogrammed suede bag rode her shoulder like a bandolier. With a pointed motion, she checked her watch, a slender diamond model that flashed "old money" in Belle's eyes. "That traffic was outrageous. People up here drive like bloody maniacs. I've got to settle somewhere and put my feet up. A nap. Then a meal. What decent restaurants are nearby the house?"

Belle smiled at the naïveté. "You'll have to pick something up en route. Going down the Kingsway, you can find Greek, Chinese and the usual chains. There's also a small supermarket in Garson a few miles later with an LCBO next door."

Megs gave a cursory glance to the map Belle provided, then pulled out a pearl compact and scowled at herself in the mirror. "Can I use your little girls' room?"

Belle pointed toward the back. "You may."

As the woman left, Belle and Yoyo issued a dual groan. "As you can gather, that's Mutt's sister."

"Shut *up!*" Yoyo's voice rose in pitch, and she made a scoffing gesture with her hand. "How did she get Michael Jackson's nose? And did you see that forehead? Botox city. Some people don't know when to stop."

Belle straightened, wondering if she had heard correctly. "Did you tell me to shut up? What the—"

Yoyo gave a merry laugh, covering her mouth to contain herself. "Not that. It means, like, are you serious?"

Belle returned to her desk, feeling a few bones squeak. She knew why she was comfortable with Miriam; they had the same set of references. "Some of us...older folk might get the wrong idea."

"Hey, even Julie Andrews says it in *The Princess Diaries.*"

"A good reason to watch *I Was a Male War Bride* instead."

Yoyo attacked her keyboard with a passion. "Oh, you and your old movies. My mom told me about those black and white ones. Boring."

Hair moussed into respectability and fresh fuchsia lipstick applied with a trowel, Megs returned. "I'm out of here. I have your home number from last night. If anything's irregular, I'll call."

This isn't the Harbour Castle Hilton, Belle thought, and I'm no concierge, lady. She said, "You might want to visit the hospital now. It's forty-five minutes to the lake."

"He's still in a coma, isn't he? Or do I need an update?"

Belle replied, "Last I heard. That was this morning."

Megs closed her purse with the snap of a mousetrap. "I'm much too tired. Tomorrow is another day."

"But you never know. Maybe by tonight he'll–"

"Listen here." Megs put one hand on her snake hips and with the other stabbed her finger like a striking cobra. "Before I got into local politics as a councillor, I was married to an ER doctor. The usual treatment is to put the subject into a hyperbaric chamber to clean the gasses from his blood...if you country folk have one here in the back of beyond. As for a coma, the brain often needs a rest after a trauma. Perfectly natural."

Not perfectly natural to be so nonchalant, Belle thought, as she clenched a fist on her lap. And what kind of a person thought of a patient as "subject"? It reminded her of the terminology used in Nazi death-camp experiments.

As Megs headed for the door with an impatient stride, Belle added, "The Lavoies have a lovely house. You'll be quite comfortable. But they're on a septic system, not a sewer. Don't flush any paper and especially not tampons."

The stricken look on Meg's face was worth the ugly scene that had preceded it. "Then what do..."

"You'll figure it out."

Finishing at five thirty, Belle braved rush-hour traffic down Paris Street en route to Laurentian Hospital. If Megs wasn't going to check on Mutt, she would, and see her father at the same time.

George Palmer looked flushed but happy. Despite his earlier complaints, he'd polished every compartment on his dinner tray. Once he knew what to expect, he adapted. "I'm going home in a few days," he said. "Skin's nearly all better."

She inspected his arms and hands. Not perfect, but the blisters were drying up and heading for recovery. Why did it take a crisis like this, at the prohibitive costs of a hospital stay, to diagnose an obvious condition? She felt like filing a malpractice suit against Dr. Vonnie.

Knowing how he relished a good story, she told him about Mutt and the accident.

"Are you rounding up the usual suspects?" His eyes twinkled, and he rubbed his gnarled hands together. From a past rich with silver-screen whodunits, he liked to dramatize events.

"No, this really was an accident. I saw the mouse nest myself."

He gave a small cough. "Your old beau and now this man in the same week? Sounds like a bit of a coinkydink. Edna Mae Oliver would know where to poke her long nose." *The Penguin Pool Murders* was one of his favourites. He identified with crotchety James Gleason.

She gave him a kiss and made a lunch date for Tuesday at Rainbow Country. In Mutt's room on the next floor, a wren of a dark-skinned nurse was changing his IVs. Belle tiptoed in, the smell of a recent Lysol application strong in her nostrils. Yet in the corner, an olive from someone's tray had rolled to a stop. "Is he...conscious?"

The woman cocked her lustrous black head as she affixed the lines, tapping them for air bubbles until she was satisfied, then making a note on his chart. "He's come up another level. His blood work is good. I thought I heard him mumbling earlier. That's a good sign. Somebody called Ben. A friend or relative?"

"I don't know. We just met recently." She looked at his athletic form, covered by sheets, now weak and vulnerable. Someone, perhaps a female aide admiring his beauty, had given him a recent shave and applied a soothing balm from the bottle on the bed table. Outside, she could hear cheers from a kayak race on Lake Ramsey. "Is this the first time you've seen carbon monoxide poisoning?"

The woman nodded, checking a round watch pinned to her

uniform. "But I read about a tragic case in the States a few years back. A whole family. The father told their GP that the ancient furnace was faulty, but he said they had the flu and sent them home. Next morning they were dead, all five of them."

How lucky Mutt had been, Belle thought. She drew closer and laid a hand on his shoulder, careful not to brush the tubes. "You're close, Mutt. Keep trying. Swim back to us." And who is Ben, she wondered, brushing a tear from her cheek and taking a tissue from the dispenser. An old flame? A pet? Megs might know. No doubt they'd meet again, despite her best efforts.

Aneetha, according to her name tag, ran a gentle comb through Mutt's clean hair and gave a girlish sigh. Belle saw no ring on her hand. "I shouldn't say this, but he is a gorgeous man, isn't he? I'll keep a special eye on him for you."

On the way home, Belle let the speeding Francophones pass her in droves on Radar Road as they headed for Valley East and Hanmer, fertile plains of potato fields, berry farms, and newer subdivisions. Her father would soon be going home, so to speak. He hadn't complained that she didn't sit with him for hours on end. Work he understood. Only at seventy had he reluctantly retired, and a year later, the company had begged him to return. As for Mutt, his condition sounded guardedly optimistic. On the darker side, Megs would be descending soon enough.

Before turning onto the Airport Road, she noticed overflowing boxes of petunias lining the driveway to Freskiw's Greenhouse. She pulled in past the tree and shrub selection, went inside, declined the hanging baskets for twenty-five dollars a pop, and filled a cart with six-packs of ready-to-go vegetables. June 12, now or never.

At seven, she opened her front door. As she stood on the deck while the dog streaked out, Belle noticed something strange about her garden. It was prepared in rows as neat as a packet of pins. Minutes later, she hit her answering machine. A message from Hélène: "Got Dad a tiller for his quad for an early Father's Day, and he had to try it out. He's done every garden this end of the road."

Her friends had come through again. Stressed from the long day, Belle felt no compelling urge to cook. She popped a beer as she opened a friendly blue box. Kraft Dinner, comfort food, with a side of sliced low-fat Spam sprinkled with sugar and fried to a crisp. Typical camping fare. She compensated for the cholesterol bomb by adding a salad of avocados and the delightful mesclun mix which reminded her of the days when only iceberg bowling balls rolled down the alley to Sudbury.

The heaping plate was ferried to the video room to watch *Walk on the Wild Side*. In 1962, MGM had been uncommonly gutsy to present the doughty Babs Stanwyck in an implicitly gay role as the madam of a brothel and the lover of lithe Capucine. A stalwart man had to appear to "save" Capucine, but in noir fashion, the exotic French starlet's character died in an accidental shooting. Later Capucine said that she might have been interested in the queen of the screen, but that Stanwyck had been otherwise engaged. How tragic that as a victim of depression, the stunning Capucine had committed suicide at fifty-seven by leaping from a tall building in Paris.

In bed that night, Belle noticed Gary's pocket notebooks, which she'd taken for Mutt and left on the dresser. Curious to see if she could make sense of his jottings, she began reading them in order, cross-referencing them with Mutt's observations. How meticulous Gary had been in documenting habitat, time and place, temperatures and weather. But where was the one with the dates from his final week? Had he gone camping somewhere, perhaps at nearby Killarney, the jewel of Ontario's parks, with its blue lakes and white quartzite mountains? The last time they'd talked, just before his death, Gary hadn't mentioned taking time off. Somehow she felt an intimate contact with him in these letters from the grave. Feeling nostalgic, she hauled out her senior yearbook to find his one message to her.

In the centre of the right-hand cover page, the place of honour, she read his parting words like visiting Sybil in her cave: "It's been an interesting relationship. But we've had support from dozens of genuinely concerned and benevolent sources—so how can we lose? The psychological ramifications are truly magnificent; quite a study. May the Higher Being bless you." The message, contrasted with all the usual puerile good wishes and in-jokes of other friends, had confused her eighteen-year-old brain. Higher Being? She'd never met the word "ramification", and what about that show-off semi-colon? Considering that she hadn't heard from him after their prom date, the "so how can we lose?" now struck her as a bit cruel, and the condescension was galling, despite the hint that he knew about her network of information from his so-called friends.

As Freya snored on her sheepskin, Belle sat back in the waterbed and did a slow burn, as much at herself as at him. Had she had no pride? What an embarrassment she'd been, sneaking around on his street in the dark, digging grass from his lawn to plant in her mother's rose garden, preserving that dried carnation. She filled the shot glass with scotch and sipped slowly. How much had he known or suspected? All her friends had been sworn to secrecy, but that meant nothing. A similar obsession today could lead to a restraining order. Instead, he'd been faithful to his temporary role.

A gale rushed through the bedroom. She closed the patio doors and cranked the window to an inch. Then shivering, she hauled out the down duvet from the closet to buttress the patchwork quilt she used June to August. Northerners never knew when the weather had a custard pie up its sleeve.

*   *   *

The next morning, every inch covered with clothing, even her socks pulled over her pant cuffs, and her hands sticky with dope, Belle donned her bug hat and began to plant the garden. The heavy white cowl flowed onto her shoulders and had the murky face screen of a nuclear clean-up crew.

Freya kept shaking her head until Belle took pity on the crusts tipping her velvet ears. "That's enough punishment, girl," she said and took the dog to the basement patio doors, shutting her inside.

Sweating in her Canadian burqa, she sat on the edge of the thirty-foot-square wooden crib, site of the old cottage, sorting herb pots of summer savory, thyme and basil when she heard an odd scuffle behind her. Something sniffed at the back of her neck. On instinct she froze. A wangy smell twitched her nose, then came a gentle butt. No question as to what had come calling. It wasn't Bigfoot.

TWELVE

Should she leap up and yell? This bear-aversion technique worked well at a hundred feet. Playing dead was a tactic for grizzlies. Like an automatic camera shooting five times each second, Belle stared at the lake, the dock, her rockwall, pictured herself sprinting to the boulders then forced into the water, still icy enough to kill. Bears were exceptionally fast, and not only did running excite the prey drive, but they were excellent swimmers with more padding.

The moment drew into eternity. Then as she felt consciousness slipping away, Freya began a frantic bark. Dog noses were 500,000 times as sensitive as a human's, the olfactory part of the brain a sizable lump. She'd smelled the beast through the open windows, and her claws scrabbled on the sliding glass doors. There was a huffing sound and a series of retreating thumps and scritches on the patio stones. Barely breathing, daring to turn at last, Belle watched her furry boyfriend disappear up the driveway and across the road, galumphing in a fluid and graceful manner like Jackie Gleason dancing his bulk in a slapstick routine.

Her lungs were threatening to break through her chest, and sweat stung her eyes and pooled under her arms. Hyperventilating, she flung off the hood and flopped down heavily on the grass, lowering her head between her knees. It had considered her and found her wanting, a choosy beast.

When her pulse dropped to one hundred, a dyspeptic chug

sounded, and a ramshackle truck bounced down the driveway. Cyril from Ray's Firewood had a delivery of ten cords of maple. He gave her a wave, then positioned the truck carefully so that when he lifted the box, it wouldn't hit the overhead wires. A squeal from the hydraulics, and out thundered the wood chunks. "No short cuts, I promise. Want me to pile it, too, madame, or do you need the exercise?" he asked, making a mock bow.

Curly-headed Cyril was a Francophone in his late fifties. Laid off when Canadian Pacific shut down their Capreol engine shop, he'd been too old to retrain and instead made a living at one of Canada's oldest professions, hewer of wood. She never begrudged him the forty bucks for the piling. He was a demon with his hook, and her back would thank her.

Belle felt heat flush her face, still winding down from her tryst. One leg was shaking, and she batted at it to behave. Sweat still trickled from her temples despite the cool breeze. When she tried to reply, her voice stuck in her throat. "Sure. I...have to go to town now, but I'll give you the cash. Ten per cent government discount, right?"

Cyril cocked his head at her, his grey work clothes pressed with sharp creases and a bandana tied around his neck, revealing a patch of chest hair. "Feeling all right? Look like you had a scare."

"You could call it that." She described her close encounter.

"*Moi*, I've had plenty meetings when I go pick the blueberries." He made himself a few thousand selling Sudbury's bounty to middlemen who sent the baskets south. "And a friend of mine years ago, Eino Kallimaki, he got eaten by a bear."

Belle willed her confidence to return to normal. "Come on. A bite maybe, but not eaten." Bear attacks were rare, but sensational. A female jogger in Quebec had been killed a few years before by a mother protecting her cub. Two boys in a tent, their clothes stinking of fish, had died in Algonquin Park.

He gave a Gallic shrug, lit up a cigarette and offered her one, which she declined. "Went checking his trapline down in the old Burwash area. Some thirty years ago. Never should have been off on his own. Losing it upstairs. He had angina, too, so we were thinking maybe the heart gave out. Could be the bear didn't actually kill him but just cleaned up later. They like that dead stuff, *charogne.*" He waved his hand in frustration. "The English, she's—"

"Carrion," said Belle. If she didn't get over this, the bush was closed to her. How many times did such a close encounter happen in one lifetime? Burwash, too. Hadn't someone else mentioned an accident down there?

While he set to work, singing a tuneless song in time with each thwack of the hook, she looked at the sky and remembered her own chores. An hour later, the vegetables stood in promising rows. With luck, a gentle rain would start the germination process. No time now to set up sprinklers. Showering off and dressing in a crisp beige pantsuit, she left for town.

En route, she saw Strang's rusty Mazda truck in the yard and pulled in. He was splitting birch by his woodshed, Buddy dozing in the sun on an old tarp. Strang's small but choice property, bought by his father in the post-war period before the road had even arrived, had an ancient clapboard cottage, sleep camp for kids, and an old-fashioned wooden swing set. Giving it an eyeful, she figured that the lot itself might bring eighty thousand. The buildings would be razed. "Progress," and she was part of the process.

"Bill, I need to talk to you about Buddy."

Setting down his maul, he spit out a long chew of tobacco in expert fashion, clearing the chopping block. "That guy next door complained, eh? Shouldn't have shut the door on him, but I'd had a few. Truth is, Buddy chewed his rope again. I need to get him a chain."

Belle blinked at his response. Normally on a wave-only acquaintance, he was friendlier than she'd expected. Like the rest of the neighbours, she'd gone to his wife's funeral and made a donation to the Heart and Stroke Foundation. "I have a light metal chain that might serve. My boathouse is open. It's hanging on the wall by the life jackets. Maureen will kill me if anything happens to her garden."

He nodded. "'Preciate it. He's not a bad dog, just following his nose. Half-Lab."

"I don't know if you've heard about what happened...to the men next door." She gave a brief précis of the two incidents.

"Saw the story about the one that drownded. But the other guy, too? Tuesday, you say?" He rubbed his chin, a heavy growth of whiskers discoloured like old ivory. His nose resembled a poorly peeled potato. "Jeez, that was the night I ate something gave me wicked cramps. Caught a bass off the dock and didn't gut it fast enough. Got to going at both ends."

This was more information than she needed. Swallowing, she glanced at his leaning outhouse, facing Maureen's property. Class Five septic system. With a raspy scream, a red-tailed hawk swivelled on the drafts, eyes tuned to the possibility of a rodent dinner.

Bill wiggled a finger in his capacious, hairy ear, then wiped it on his overalls. "Back and forth all bloody night. Might as well have brought a pillow. That's how I seen the car pull in."

Was it Mutt coming back from the show? "A Prius?"

"That silly, half-electric golf cart? Watch him try to start her at minus thirty-five. Naw. It was a nice white Buick. Showed up under the full moon. Thought it was odd. Parked at the end of the drive. Maybe got lost and went down to get directions, but at two in the morning?" He gave her a crooked smile, his top plate missing-in-action. "I was sick as a poisoned pup. Wasn't thinking straight. No way in hell I could see the license or who was driving. But I love those Buicks, and I know that shape like the sweet curves of my late wife."

Belle drove off more intrigued than before. The idea that someone had been visiting Mutt seemed unlikely. Had he met someone in town? But why the furtive behaviour of the driver? Meanwhile Gary's research was in limbo. At the first stoplight in Garson, she had a sudden idea. What about going to the Ministry herself? That Silliker woman had been helpful.

Back home by late afternoon, she sat at the dining room table and sorted the mail. With the sun returning, a double rainbow had formed across the lake, putting the pot of gold at the airport. Then her phone rang.

"What kind of a zoo is this? I took out some trash and saw a wild beast cross the road. A black monster. You never mentioned bears," Megs said, her voice tremulous. "Do you shoot them or call Animal Control?"

Belle laughed, remembering the Ministry's huge wheeled cage parked at the turnaround last June. They'd nabbed their boy in a few hours, lured by hunks of smelly meat, and packed him off to points north. "If one broke into a camp, maybe. Maureen has a locking garbage box, but you're better off keeping smelly stuff in the freezer until trash pickup on Tuesday."

"How primitive." The shrill voice rose like a V-2 rocket. "I don't feel safe. Coming up was a big mistake. Maybe I'll leave in the morning."

My mistake, too. Belle looked at her watch. Freya was scrutinizing her empty food bowl, a crease of annoyance on her brow. No way in hell was she asking this harpy to stay with her, but she was interested in what Megs knew about Gary's past, sordid though it might sound through her filter. "Stop worrying. No one on this road has ever been killed or even injured by a bear. And Mutt will be glad to see you. Family is important."

When Megs whined about forgetting to pick up groceries, Belle took pity on her. "Plenty for two here. Why not drop by for dinner around seven?"

Megs agreed with surprising haste. Hanging up, Belle slipped in a CD of Mary Martin in *Hello, Dolly*, advising Walter Matthau that "On cold winter nights, you can cuddle up to your cash register. It's a little lumpy, but it rings." That line had made her smile at sixteen. Romance had never been on her to-do list, despite a few Gary look-alikes at the U of T, a stuffy physicist with a yappy Jack Russell and an angst-ridden psychologist, who'd said she reminded him of his dead sister. Giving all to her career, she retained independence but missed the partnership that bonded the DesRosiers, and Mutt and Gary.

Meanwhile, she did a frantic tally of her cupboards and freezer. Rainbow trout marinated in light soy, ginger root and garlic for the BBQ. A rice pilaf. The asparagus from Burwash. All in half an hour, vacuuming the high-traffic paths included and running a towel around the dusty living room. Now for some calming music to sooth the savage breast or beast. Sprightly composers like Delius and Delibes.

*   *   *

A mauve Infiniti rolled silently into the lot as Belle peered out the TV room window at 6:59. Megs arrived at the door soon after bearing a bottle with a VQA label. "Call me patriotic. I drink nothing but Ontario wine. This one has a rating off the charts," she said, sweeping in dressed in slender designer jeans and a chartreuse silk shirt. When Freya trotted around the corner of the hall, she shrank back. "Aren't these dogs banned?"

Belle nudged her pal aside, giving a hand signal to cease and desist. "You're talking about pit bulls. A well-bred shepherd is a pussycat. Bad dogs have bad owners."

They walked past the compact kitchen, where Belle gave the bottle a second look. A cabernet/merlot reserve. Thirty-five dollars, if she remembered the bin correctly. Megs turned to the stove, touching the grey handle of a pot, picking it up and peering underneath. "Martha Stewart? I love her cookware. Did you get this up here?"

"Half price. When she was in jail, Sears panicked and discounted everything."

"They're a bit small, but you're not cooking for a family." The woman craned her neck toward the living room, perhaps expecting a tour of a home in the hinterlands.

Choosing to accept the comment as an observation, not a judgment, Belle noticed the mass of welts on the woman's face. "Need something for those bites?" she asked.

Megs paddled her thin fingers over the angry skin. "I was outside only for a few minutes. Allergies. The Benedryls I took should kick in any minute. At least the medicine cabinet was stocked."

Belle left her for a moment and returned with a white tube. "Try this. It stings a bit but eases the itching."

Megs began dotting herself with the ammonia-based product, wincing as she proceeded.

"We'll be eating on the deck. It's practically bug-free right now thanks to those natural-born killers." She pointed at a helpful squadron of dragonflies as they exited the patio doors, helicoptering around like delicate bats. A square wooden table on rollers had been set with placemats, her Santa Fe-style dishes and flatware, and centred with a miniature vase of lilies of the valley, their aroma sweet as Dior perfume.

She went back in to pour the wine, tasting a sip and getting a shock. For the first time, she found an Ontario wine acceptable. Blackberry and pear overtones. Now she'd have to bring out her prized Amarone, should a second bottle be required. She arranged a ceramic platter of smoked oysters, a slice of brie, and buttery crackers full of trans-fats.

Returning, Belle clinked Megs' glass as they sat. "To Mutt's recovery."

Megs nodded in approval as she scanned the lake, her lips smacking at the wine. "This view *is* lovely. One compensation for living outside civilization. Those tiers with crushed stone and shrubs are attractive. How do you get a gardener to come all the way out here?"

"The same way I get the maid and butler." Belle forced a smile. "Think what it would cost in Toronto. And you can't even swim in Lake Ontario. They close the beaches every second day."

Megs' mouth screwed into a semi-colon. "Sometimes you can nearly walk on it, though. That's why the hydrofoil to Rochester went belly-up."

A dry sense of humour. Maybe the woman wasn't a total loss. "Soooooooo," Belle opened with as casual a pose as she could manage, "I knew Gary from high school, but we...lost touch. How did he meet your brother?"

After nibbling an oyster, Megs finished the glass, picked up the bottle, and poured another. Belle winced at the rapid consumption.

Megs tried to crease her brow in thought, but the injections fought the effort, leaving it smooth. "Let's see. It was about eight years ago. Mutt was engaged to a gorgeous debutante. Related to the Eaton family. He'd been at Upper Canada

College. She went to Havergal. Had her coming-out party after graduation."

Break-the-bank tuition. And debutante "coming out" of what? Belle's eyebrows rose at the mention of the family behind Canada's fabled flagship department store. "Really? What happened?"

"The wedding was all planned for after Mutt got his MA. St. George's Country Club in Etobicoke. Lovely historic place. Honeymoon on Nevis. Then a house in Rosedale. So generous of Brittany's parents." She gave Belle a knowing nod. "Mutt could have written full-time. None of those humiliating sessional jobs at Mohawk teaching Bonehead Grammar to future veterinary technicians."

A death sentence in itself. Belle took a cracker and a slice of the creamy cheese. "Then he backed out? Must have taken quite a lot of nerve."

"I wish he'd known his own mind from the first." Megs shook her head. "It was embarrassing. Then Father cut him off without a dime."

Belle felt her pulse accelerate as fast as a mallard taking off at the crunch of a fox on the shoreline. "That seems extreme."

"You know the older generation. But even I was confused. Brittany Crawford was so beautiful. And very sweet, too. I did charity work with her, finding homes for abandoned Yorkies. What was he thinking? He didn't even give it a try."

Belle lifted an eyebrow. "I call him brave. Even today, there are social pressures to conform to the so-called normal family unit. At least he didn't marry her, have a few kids, and then bail out. And his relationship with Gary was stable. Seven years, wasn't it?"

Megs gulped the last from her glass. "Do you think he and Gary were a poster couple? They had some battles royale."

"Gary? I can't believe it." But the boy of eighteen was not the man in his late forties.

"Listen, far be it from me to talk against my brother, but he's always spent everything he made. *Carpe* whatever. Made Visa rich. Dad bailed him out now and then. But Gary was quite thrifty, cheap even. They were always arguing."

Belle thought of their dates. A movie, a hamburger. Her father's complimentary passes to theatres. She'd been so enamoured that a simple picnic in his company would have been as good as a steak dinner at Barberian's.

"Lord, what a day. Those bites have stopped tormenting me. I think I'm finally relaxing." Megs drained the bottle, pointedly waiting for the last drips and sucking them like mother's milk. Her hand was none too steady, and the roadmap of veins in her eyes glowed pink. "Thirsty girl. I'm going to need a refill."

"Me, too." Belle got up with reluctance and brought back the Amarone, a hefty 14.5%. They both ducked from reflex when a giant yellow plane roared overhead, heading north across the lake.

"What in Christ's name is that?" Megs cried.

"Ministry plane. It picks up water here and takes it to a forest fire."

"Don't tell me I have to worry about an evacuation, too?"

"The airport nearby is command central. That plane could be heading for somewhere a hundred miles away."

Megs took a deep draft of wine, without savouring the rich aroma or commenting on the full body of leathers, tannins and plum the label promised. "Where was I? Oh, yes, their arguments. You don't have to look at dear Malcolm twice to see that he's film-star material. He did some modelling during university. *Toronto Life* magazine. And you know that territory."

Where was this heading? "Are you talking about affairs?"

Megs waggled her finger, flashing a band of emeralds. "You've seen him. What do you think? Men followed him like the pole star." A light burp escaped her lips, and she patted herself on the chest like a naughty baby.

"He was mumbling something in his sleep. It sounded like Ben. Any friend or relation?" Belle asked.

"Certainly not family. But friends? You might say we ran in different circles," she said with a haughty turn of her head.

The last bite of salad went down with a bitter taste unrelated to the arugula. Megs finished everything on her plate and mentioned that she hoped the trout wasn't fish-farmed. "All sorts of worms and parasites." Then she gave a pointed sniff, rubbed her nose and asked for a Q-tip.

Belle used them to clean the water-filter containers. "In the bathroom cabinet. Lower right." Megs tottered off for a few minutes on a mysterious mission.

After dinner, during which Megs slurred her words and laughed at everything, even comments about the weather, they moved inside to escape the night chill. With her bare feet on the blue leather couch, Megs drank a coffee with Courvoisier and had fallen asleep when Belle returned from the bathroom. An icy cloth got the woman up and into her Infiniti, Belle bracing the storkish body with one arm. Megs slumped in the seat, lipstick smeared on her mango mouth, while Belle rummaged through her purse and found the keys, starting the motor with a delicious purr. What were we driving here, half a bungalow? Leather seats, probably heated. Directional program. Like the cockpit of the Challenger in wood grain.

At Maureen's, her back screaming, Belle deposited the woman onto the couch, tossing a blanket over her, placing her keys and purse in plain sight. What kind of shape would Megs be in tomorrow to see her brother, she wondered? The last half-mile of the walk home, the air hit her like a tonic. At least the star show was worth the trip. Without the bowl of city lights, Ursa Major flexed his claws toward Lynx, while Ursa Minor watched from above, learning lessons from mother. Lynx and bear she understood, but what about Drago lurking between? There were no dragons any more, except in human form.

So Megs recalled no Ben, hardly surprising given the family estrangement. Once at home and in bed, Belle picked up the notebooks, some water-spotted pages, a tiny fly wing, hazards of the field, trying to decipher the scientific jargon, the abbreviations perhaps only Gary understood. Water PH numbers done on site. That she understood. Acid and alkaline. Something about diatoms and daphnia. Far from the city and never in the destructive plumes, the water should be healthy. Colour was no indicator, though. Lakes clear and blue as sapphires had a high acid content.

With a gulp, she came to the day that he had found the dead baby elk, the first albino he had seen. "No sign of the parents in the herd I observed near Pine Mountain. No obvious damage on the body. Slightly underweight. Dead less than a day," he had written. Sad, but exciting. Question marks appeared, and a word was repeated, but the ink was blurred. She squinted, cleaned her reading glasses. Test? What was the word? Bent? No, benthic. Then benthos. There it was again. She saw that Mutt had jotted it on his yellow lined pad, along with a "Min? Go back?" This made her sit up and reach for a drink. Had he been able to return to the Ministry as he'd intended? Most important, when he came to, would he recall the thrusts of his analysis?

Nearly eleven, an hour past her bedtime. But she couldn't resist the puzzle. Freya rolled her head up and gave her a sharp look as Belle levered herself out of the waterbed. Downstairs in the computer room, she searched her Oxford dictionary but couldn't find either "benthos" or "benthic". Scanning past Benedictine, Bengal and Bennett Buggy, a car pulled by horses, named after the Depression-era Prime Minister, she stopped and gave herself a neural rap "upside the head". Though at first, it might have been a logical assumption, "Ben" was not a person. As she thought about booting up and accessing Google, vampiric winds were shaking the ancient lines that linked Alexander Graham Bell to Bill Gates, slower than molasses in January, as her mother used to say. She'd use the high-speed access at the office.

As Belle turned in, she shivered and got up to close her window. Temperatures had dropped to less than five degrees as a sudden Arctic blast from the northwest rushed across the lake like a killer tornado. Too late now to cover her plants.

THIRTEEN

The unseasonably cold weather had merged with the warming lake to brew up a pea-soup fog the next morning. Belle could barely see twenty feet as she inched along Edgewater Road, braking for the occasional stupefied grouse freezing at her approach, then making a roadrunner dash. No letup until Radar Road, she knew from experience. Planes were grounded, the radio said. Then she switched it off to concentrate on driving, appreciating the fog lamps' eerie glow. As she rounded the corner at a stretch bordering a swamp, she slowed and blinked to appreciate the rare moment.

Standing beside a cedar log was a majestic blue heron, cloaked like an exiled king to a romantic eye, but in all practicality, merely seeking a frog. Solitary diners often guarding their territory, they became more social in heronries during egg-laying time, when they built their massive twig nests on dead spars. Though the majority of young herons failed to reach their first birthday, survivors were often good for over twenty years. Perhaps this one had lived in the area longer than she had. She recalled lines from Charles Sangster's ponderous "The St. Lawrence and the Saguenay". "All night the Fisher spears his finny prey;/ The piney flambeaux reddening the deep...Like grotesque banditti they boldly sweep/ Upon the startled prey, and stab them while they sleep." As if reading her intrusive thoughts, the heron ruffled his feathers and lifted off into the haze on purple wings, wispy streamers in his wake. Only then did she notice that behind a flattened stand of scrub willow, a vehicle lay wheels-up in the shallow water twenty feet from the road.

Abruptly, she pulled over and punched on her flashers. The last thing she needed was a collision. Should she use her cell phone to summon help or wade in like a maritime Samaritan? Seconds counted. Plunging into the shallow, stinking muck, she winced at soaking her sneakers, pushing aside the burred grasses which tugged at her pants like tiny goblins. Small hillocks provided purchase for marsh marigolds, their cheerful yellow-globe spring announcements long gone. The icy water crept to mid-thigh. A splash made her yelp before she saw the dark olive box of an alarmed turtle scrabbling over a log. Small comfort that Ontario had only one poisonous snake, the Massasauga rattler, a diminutive creature located farther south. Her shoes sucked mud with each step. For purchase, she grabbed at a sturdy clump of reeds, cutting her hand. Sedges have edges. Closing in, she recognized the red Jeep. Miss Liberty, an accident whose number had been called at road bingo. Would the door open, or had the crash bent the frame? For an irrational and guilty moment, Belle wondered if wishful thinking had become reality.

Visibility was poor, but the Maglite in her van would have confused the issue with its reflections. Belle glanced up. Amid dull patches of fog, the insistent sun was clawing itself a window. In the front seat, a young girl about her size hung upside down, still in harness, long honey hair trailing in the water, her pale, expressionless face inches from drowning. An eerie glow came from the dashboard, green footlights to a drama. Wrenching open the door on the fifth pull, Belle tugged on the belts, trying to find the clasp. The device refused to release its burden.

Damn it. Why mmmmmeeeee? Her teeth chattering like

the taps of a three-toed woodpecker, she slogged back to the van and seized a Swiss army knife from the glove compartment. Back at the Jeep, standing on ice-block legs, she braced the girl with one arm and sliced with the other. As the body came free, Belle supported her against the side of the vehicle. In this awkward embrace, she felt the beating of another heart. The cold water shocked the girl back to consciousness, her sparkly-shadowed eyelids fluttering as she kicked out in confusion. "Huh? Where am I? I'm friggin' freezing!"

"No place you want to stay. Let's go to my van." Belle helped her to the road, marching together like Napoleon's defeated army, crushing the fragile pink, hexagonal flowers of the bog laurel, and eased her into the rear cargo area, covering her with the handy dog blanket.

She could hear small whimpers as she called 911, and her heart raced. The girl might have suffered internal injuries. Pulling her from the swamp had been a calculated risk the same as rescuing someone from a burning car. If she had vertebral problems, would Belle face a lawsuit? So much for the Golden Rule.

Before launching into a lecture about driving habits, she'd better check for injuries, ask a few definitive questions. Belle moved into the back of the van beside the girl, trying to ignore the organic goop that coated the carpeting. She tried to wiggle her toes, but the effort was painful. Flicking on the overhead light, she looked at the girl, now strangely silent. "What's your name? How do you feel?"

"ZZ Bryant." Pulling the blanket closer as she shivered, she brushed back her sodden shoulder-length hair. She wore a skin-tight, V-necked cashmere sweater and hip-hugging jeans that began four inches below the waist, leaving a swath of fishbelly-white skin. One ear sprouted five rings, the other a pearl stud. A tattoo of a black rose circled her belly button and matched the dark lipstick. Clunky purple Doc Martens loaded with swamp muck were on her feet. Then she rotated one arm with a wince. "I'm okay. But Mom will kill me for flipping her Jeep. I'll be grounded until graduation next June. Maybe even longer. And I was getting a trip to Europe." She sniffed and rubbed her pug nose on her sleeve. Mascara dribbled down her high cheekbones.

Only seventeen? And Belle Palmer collected another eccentric name. "How is that spelled? Zee Zee? Like Zsa Zsa? Are you partly Hungarian?"

"Just the two letters. My mom wanted me to have a cool name." Her bee-stung lips reminded Belle of Clara Bow, the silent era's Angelina Jolie. Collagen treatments already? The Yellow Pages were stuffed with cosmetic surgeons at a time when people were waiting two years for a new hip or knee.

Grateful that the conversation seemed to reveal no ill effects, Belle narrowed her eyes and introduced herself, feeling that she represented the sane neighbours. "Listen, ZZ. I've seen you on the road, and you drive like a total idiot. Frankly, I don't care what you do to yourself, but I don't want to meet you head-on or get forced down an embankment. In a strange way, especially since you're not hurt, I hope this accident is a wake-up call for you."

ZZ's lower lip quivered. As an affectation, it was effective as hell. Adding that shy dimple made her a drop-dead-cute manipulator. But she reminded Belle of Miriam's spoiled mini-poodle with a handmade four-season wardrobe.

"It wasn't my fault. I swerved to miss a fox. I'm always late for something. We live so far from town." She shrugged and gave a sigh. "Guess I have a heavy foot. I got a ticket last week. Paid for it the same day so that Mom wouldn't find out."

On a roll, Belle leaned forward and tapped her knee. "This

might be the time to fess up, clean the slate. Your mother will be so glad you're unhurt that she'll forgive you. And by the way, Jeeps are known for their instability on curves."

ZZ managed a smile and looked at her reflection in the window, frowning as she ran a hand through her dishevelled hair. "Some of those ETs are cute guys. Did you get my purse?"

Not long after, the ambulance made yet another turn down the road. ZZ was headed to the Emerg for a thorough examination. She had answered the paramedic's questions, and there were no signs of injury other than the sore shoulder from the belts. Belle marked the spot in her mind. A bad banking angle had caused her to swerve into a snowbank here last winter during an ice storm. Still, ZZ had probably been doing over eighty kilometres per hour. She gave Miss Liberty's sorry vehicle a salute. *Ave atque vale.* Future home: Rock City Wrecking.

Freya was sleeping on the hall rug when Belle returned and woke up with a snort. "Fast day or what?" Belle said. Stripping off her smelly clothes and runners, she took them to the laundry and put them on "soak", with a dab of bleach. Then she went upstairs for a shower, a fresh outfit, and a bandage for her hand, which was stinging from the sharp sedge.

An hour later, when she arrived at the office, Yoyo looked up with a devilish expression. "That Steve Davis was here. Wants you to call him back. Where you been hiding that man? He's a hunk. Reminds me of an old boyfriend who joined the Mounties. Six-foot-two, eyes of blue. Too bad he got his old girlfriend pregnant with triplets. Better her than me, though."

Belle sorted her mail, a frown tickling her brow. Like Miriam, this woman knew which buttons to push. Another side effect of having no mystique. "Really, Yoyo. He's married." Not happily, she neglected to add, fearing further speculative comments.

Diamond chips seemed to glitter in Yoyo's smile. "Big feet, too. And you know what they say about a man with big feet."

A trap was being set, but crabby about the day so far, Belle was not in a teasing mode. Jokers had to run their course. If they sensed a weak spot, they plunged in the skewer and twisted it. "I give up."

A roar of laughter erupted as Yoyo slapped the desk. "Big shoes!"

Then she stood and stretched, her small belly shielded in a tasteful dirndl skirt with a peasant blouse. Flats, too. Belle glanced at the calendar, nervous about Miriam's delayed return. What if Yoyo was farther along than she'd stated? At this stage, pregnant women loved inviting people to feel the baby move, but Yoyo issued no invitation, perhaps sensing her employer's disinterest. Women took their cues from their mothers, and Terry Palmer had never cooed at babies. Now if Yoyo had been a German shepherd...

"Ooo, my aching back. And I have to pee every fifteen minutes. Don't ever get pregnant." She went to the coffee machine, hoisted Belle's cup, got a nod, and made one for each of them.

"It's nearly too late for that, but I promise not even to get married, not that there's any connection these free-wheeling days," answered Belle.

"You're missing out, sweetie. When you find the right guy, it's the greatest job on the planet."

Where had she heard that before? That annoying television advertisement, as if good male parenting could be legislated. Their merriment over for the moment, Belle reached Steve on his cell. He was starting off for Algonquin Bay to pick up a suspect in a recent confectionery robbery. "No worries on Joey Bartko. He has bigger problems than trash dumping, and he's skipped. There's a warrant out for him for passing bad cheques in every bar in town and failure to appear. He did some time a few years ago for running a meth lab in the bush, so this second offence will put him on ice. His mother in Skead swears he hasn't been around, but it's just a matter of time before we track down his last living cousin or no-account trailer-trash friend."

"Thanks for the update, but I'm not sure I feel that safe. I mean he's still on the loose, after all." Didn't Steve get the point? Or was it that he'd never been physically afraid in his life?

"Then move into town. You said it's getting too crowded out there anyway. Might as well have the conveniences of civilization." His voice was speeding up, as if he had other business on his plate.

"I appreciate your help. Give Heather a hug. Maybe you can bring her out for a swim in July when the lake warms up." She pulled back from the disturbing drift of the conversation like the retreating horns of a slug. Steve's lecture was on the mild side, but she didn't feel like defending her lifestyle on a weekly basis. He'd relax only when she moved next door. Wouldn't Janet have a cow...or an elk?

That night after grabbing a hot beef sandwich platter at Rudy's on LaSalle, Belle turned into her drive later than usual. Darkness had pooled in the corners of the yard. Hélène had come down to feed and water Freya at six. On 105.3, the only station she could pick up in the last few miles, the radio was blaring Anne Murray's "Snowbird" in a Canadian top hundred contest. "Spread your tiny wings," she bellowed as she exited the van with a pirouette. Then her voice trailed to a whisper as she froze halfway to the deck. Was that a vehicle parked under a spreading maple or an optical illusion? The matte battleship grey sky bore no moon, and an eerie absence of wind gave the landscape a shadowless, two-dimensional effect. Her gaze swept the property as the hairs on her neck rose, and cerebral neurons left her legs waiting for directions. No weapon, no backup. A perfect time to regret that she hadn't enrolled in tai chi. Like a trapped animal, she calculated the logistics. Too far back to the van. No man's land.

She dropped the attaché case and rushed for the stairs. Once the door opened, her guard dog would come to the rescue. The slavering jaws of a ninety-pound shepherd, grey-muzzled or not, were quick persuaders. "Freya!" she screamed. But as she gained the deck and barking started, a rough hand reached out and grabbed her ankle. She fell, twisting in an iron grip, her shins bruised and lacerated.

"Not so fast. You and me got business, babe. Or maybe you should butt out of mine." Smoke dribbled from his pinched nostrils.

One billion, give or take a million, synapses in her brain pointed to one man. "Bartko."

"Joey to my friends. But you're not on my Valentine's list. Nosey bitch. What's the skin off your nose if I dump some shit in the fucking bush? That's what it's for, stupid." He coughed up a loogie and discharged it onto the deck.

"Let's talk about what you did to my van." Speaking loudly, she heartened at Freya's maddened barking, aware that the dog heard their conversation and knew from the tones that it wasn't friendly.

"Prove it. You got dick-all on me. Accidents happen."

Backlit by a peach-melba glow lighting the western sky, Joey was a paunchy forty. He wore a Harley Davidson T-shirt that bulged over a studded leather belt, baggy jeans slit at the knee, and unlaced work boots. His thin, dirt-brown hair was either slicked back with gel or needed a Comet dip. He was a polluter, a cheque kiter and a drug dealer. Careers close enough to assault and even rape. What was in store for her? Her frantic eyes glanced at the unlocked door. She needed only to distract him long enough to open it and unleash the canine tornado.

As a broken-toothed grin spread over his face like a disease, he squeezed her arm. Belle winced but didn't beg. Tomorrow there would be a bruise. What about a tomorrow, period? Junk psychology told her to keep talking. "You got me good on the van. That was smart. You must know cars."

He snickered and flicked his cigarette, which spiralled off the deck onto the gravel, then pulled her close, grinding his hips against hers. A stale male-musk smell came wafting along, as if he bathed once a week at gunpoint and changed his clothes when they shredded off. "Damn right. I've beat the system all my life. And don't bother telling the cops about this friendly visit. Even if they do find me, which they won't, I got a hundred gold-plated alibis for tonight."

Freya was aiming for a world record of consecutive yelps and growls, jumping and scratching at the door. Joey pressed his temple. "That goddamn dog is giving me a headache. Needs a good lesson with a two-by-four."

The crunch of tires, and a bicycle wheeled down the drive, startling him into relaxing his grip. "Hey, what the..."

Belle charged the door, pushing it open and falling into the hall. "Get him, girl!"

Joey was standing tall when Freya lunged at him, massive paws against his chest, her snarling face spitting drool. "Yaaaaa!" he yelled as he flailed wildly and tumbled down the stairs, hitting his head with a sound like a ripe melon on a concrete post base at the bottom. His features tightened, then relaxed as his breath subsided. Out cold, and a face only a weasel mother could love.

Belle gave Freya the signal to sit and wait. Her ruff raised in prehistoric wolf mode, the old dog narrowed her eyes at the body as if she'd like a taste. Belle stroked her head. "Easy, sweetie. You'd have to get your stomach pumped."

A shiny mountain bike pulled up and ZZ got off, bearing a huge bouquet like an Olympic torch. "Guess I should have called. Dad told me it was too late to come, but you didn't answer the phone all evening. I was going to leave these by the door. Hope I didn't barge in on anything."

"Barge away."

Then ZZ looked down. "Eeuw. What's the matter with him? I hope he's not your boyfriend."

Belle came down the stairs and patted her on the back. "Consider your debt paid in full. This guy's been bothering me ever since I reported him for dumping in the bush."

"Good for you. Some pigs left a bunch of clothes by the mailboxes last year. Me and my bro cleaned it up." Dressed in a leather vest over a T-shirt that read "Will Work for Shoes" and pyjama-style shorts, ZZ put her hands on her hips and twisted her head to better investigate Joey. "What are you going to do with him? He looks stupid but dangerous. Does he belong to a motorcycle gang?"

No telling how long Joey would be in slumberland. Minutes perhaps, then what? "He's not organized enough for that. I'm going to the boathouse for some rope. Tell the dog to 'get' him if he wakes up."

"No problem. I'm a black belt in karate. When you're short like I am, it helps. And I love dogs. Here, girl." ZZ knelt and cuddled Freya's head, scratching her ears to deliver pure bliss.

Puffing from haste, Belle returned with a large coil of polypropylene rope and tied Joey as uncomfortably as possible. Then she speed-dialled Steve at home. His wife Janet answered.

"It's Belle. I need to speak with Steve. Police business."

A telling moment of icy silence. Belle looked at the receiver, wondering if they'd been cut off. Then Janet's childlike voice assumed a studied innocence with a heaping tablespoon of umbrage. "I'll just bet. He has an office and regular hours. Why do you insist on—"

"I'll apologize to *him,* if you don't mind."

"Hon-bun, it's that *woman,*" Janet called over the noise of a television and Heather's musical laughter in the background. The receiver landed on a hard surface with a decisive crack, but the connection wasn't broken. Anyone would think they were having an affair. Janet probably did. Belle doubted that he reported their occasional lunch dates, since he always paid in cash.

She explained about Joey's visit, squirming at first but proud at the results.

"You what? I don't believe it." She imagined him passing a hand through his thick hair, thunderclouds gathering on his broad brow. Silver patches at his temples were spreading, thanks in part to her.

"Take it easy. I've already heard lecture 322. All I was trying to do was clean up the bush. How did I know I was going to unearth a psychopath? And you told me he was gone from the area."

"That's not what I said, and you know it. Ten points for not turning him into meatloaf with your twelve-gauge."

"I hate to ask, but can you handle this yourself? You've been checking his records and know the situation." She felt like patting herself on the back for her citizen's arrest.

"You're lucky I finished dinner. What a pot roast!" His dramatic tones conveyed the idea that someone was listening. Steve took guff from no one but his wife, and that he did for Heather. "I'll clear it at headquarters, get another officer to assist, and be there in an hour. You said he's tied up? Nice and tight?"

"Granny knots by the pound. And I have a star witness to the assault." She shot a glance at ZZ, laughing as she tossed stones for Freya. The dog always suckered visitors into doing her will.

Flipping on the deck and yard lights after disconnecting, Belle went inside to make cocoa, a teen choice, and set the bouquet in water in a crystal vase. Huge red roses with ferns and babies' breath, they must have cost.

"I think he's coming to," ZZ said later, dipping into the Peek Freans as they sipped from warm mugs on the deck stairs. Rolling over, Joey shook his head like a wet dog and began exercising his lowlife vocabulary, spitting at them just out of range.

"I'm sure you've heard worse, but it's so ordinary," Belle said. "Shakespeare made swearing a fine art. Away, you cut-purse rascal. You mouldy rogue. You filthy bung." She shook her fist at Joey, who scowled and squinted at a foreign language.

Laughing in a musical cadenza, ZZ launched her long hair over her shoulders like a cape. "That's way better than *Julius Caesar*. It sucks big time. We had to memorize fifty lines. 'Friends, Romans, Countrymen. Lend me your ears'? Give me a break."

Her perspective was refreshing for Belle, but she supposed it might pall when Brad Pitt or Paris Hilton entered the discussion. She sipped the chocolate, made from melted semi-sweet blocks.

"Is he, like, going to jail? Cool."

"He'll be, like, cooling for a long time."

Grunting like a warthog, Joey twisted himself into a sitting position. "I got friends," he said.

"In high places, no doubt. Gets his ideas from country music." Belle tapped ZZ's arm. "We'll add uttering threats to the report."

An hour later, true to his word, Steve arrived in the passenger seat of a squad car, a beacon light in the coal-black night. He and Officer Kelly Size, a short-haired blonde woman in her thirties, gave Joey the once-over. Kelly stifled laughter despite her no-nonsense attitude.

"Don't expect bail, Joey. That warrant shows that you'll run," Steve said. "And as for two-years-less-a-day, you're into the big time now. Got any buddies at Millhaven?"

Joey gave a theatrical moan. "I need to go to the hospital. Think I got a concussion. The bitch nailed me with a shovel."

Steve craned his head around as he winked at Belle. "What shovel? You must be hallucinating. Sampling too many of your own wares?"

Kelly knelt to inspect the maze of knots, tipping back her cap. "We need to cut this mess, or we'll be here all night." Steve wore civvies, and her belt was shy of cutlery.

Belle reached onto the top of a beam underneath the deck where she kept hand tools for the garden and pulled out a paring knife. Kelly cut the Gordian knot, then with an efficiency of purpose, slipped Joey into a set of plastic cuffs and leaned him against the stairs for a body search, turning up a tiny .25 calibre in an ankle holster.

"A gun, too? Very bad idea," Steve said. "I suppose it's registered? In Texas?"

After Joey was safely in the back seat of the cruiser, Steve took them inside for a preliminary statement. "You spell it how?" he asked, scratching his head.

After the cruiser left and ZZ promised to return some weekend to teach her a few defence moves, Belle was finally alone, trying to wind down. At least Bartko was in custody. Turner Classics was showing *Rebel Without a Cause*, starring James Dean and Sal Mineo, two young men whose sexuality burned like comets. Nubile Natalie Wood aside, a superfluous character, director Nicholas Ray had made subtle use of the chemistry between the men. On that fatal night, as if studying his future, Sal as Plato looked with puppy eyes at Jim Stark, played by Dean. Their careers had guttered quickly, an early death by Porsche for Jimmy and a fast knife in an underground parking lot for Sal.

Then the phone rang. "It's...Mutt. Sorry to call so...late, but—"

FOURTEEN

Belle let out a war whoop that echoed through the house. Freya picked up on the mood and joined the pack howl, her silken head thrown back in abandon. Apparently Mutt had awakened late that afternoon. Cognitive and physical tests had kept him busy, along with eating everything in sight. Two young nurses had even fetched submarine sandwiches.

"What have you got there, a bunch of wolves?" His voice was slow and deliberate, but stronger than she'd imagined.

Belle laughed. "Freya, that's enough. And you're fine now?" she asked, hoping that a positive question would win a positive answer.

A few seconds passed before he answered, hardly the eager conversationalist she recalled. "Those hyper...whazzit chamber sessions did a number on my claustrophobia. When I came to, I thought I was in a horror movie buried six feet under. Screamed like a girl. They had to give me a shot of Valium before I calmed down. Then I conked out for awhile."

Briefly, she told him about the furnace. "But it's all fixed. Safety measures in place."

"That is weird. Sure, I've seen the occasional mouse under the bird feeders, but I never gave it a thought. You didn't put any poison around, did you? A couple of cats—"

"Never. A poisoner is the lowest life form." The notebooks sat in a pile on the table. Would Mutt be offended to learn that she'd been rummaging through the desk, if only to get a contact number for his sister? "When I looked for the address book, I saw Gary's notebooks and planned to bring them to you at the hospital. You circled a couple of terms and made notes. 'Benthic'. When the nurse said you mentioned a Ben, at first I thought—"

She heard a long and frustrated groan. "God, that seems so long ago. It's like my mind has been journeying from one end of the galaxy to the other."

Belle chuckled at the Mutt she remembered. "You sound sharp enough."

"In the present, sure, but I don't remember much from the last couple of weeks. The doctors say that it's going to take awhile for my memory to return. Isn't that great news for a novelist?"

Her heart plunged at the thought. In a series, continuity was everything. Would Lucy Doyle become a footnote in Canadian crime writing? "You just woke up. Don't rush it. Take life a day at a time." Now she was doling out canned advice like a pop psychologist.

"I wanted to pull his research together, but honestly, don't ask me to add four and four. Maybe you can make sense of the notebooks. As for my novel, I'll never make the October deadline if this keeps up, and my publisher will have a fit. It's like juggling six tennis balls." His voice trailed off.

The conversation was growing grim. She needed to ask him about that white Buick, but if he couldn't remember that night at all, it might depress him further. Then she remembered Megs. "Has your sister been by?"

"An hour ago. She managed to offend everyone within a hundred yards, especially the doctors. But I owe you for getting in touch with her. She told me about your dinner, too."

"Hey, you don't get to pick your family. And she did come

to see you." Not to mention telling me intimate details about your life. Had he and Gary really gotten into physical fights? "I hope you still intend to stay for awhile. Do you need a lift back to the house?"

"Those were my original plans, and this development has cinched it. Maybe lying on the dock catching a few rays will help. As for the ride, Megs is coming tomorrow morning. Double-decker broomstick." He gave a half-hearted laugh, then started to cough. Had his breathing been affected, too?

He gave a long sigh. She could feel the weariness. "Listen, Mutt. You'd better rest—"

"Dad's in tough shape. I need to go to Hamilton as soon as I get back on my feet. He's not such a bad guy. Maybe this will give him second thoughts. Megs said that Mom's coming around, too."

After hanging up, Belle bit her lip. With Mutt *hors de combat*, any progress with that elk research was up to her, no matter her limitations. The Internet had been too generous about "benthic", giving her ten thousand hits and hundreds of pdf pages. Maybe she could nail two chores at the Ministry by checking to see if more of Gary's material had turned up.

The next day at Canadian Tire on Barrydowne, where seasons alternated between garden tractors or snowblowers lined up at the door, folks were muscling out boxed air conditioners. Belle picked up more water filters. She should start drinking only bottled, but it was so expensive, as were decent reverse osmosis systems. Her line emerged a hundred feet out into the lake, where the water was deep and cool, and sat on a tripod to keep it from sucking muddy sediment. Even so, creatures unseen to the human eye might lurk in the warming water.

At the Ministry, the same pleasant older woman greeted her at the reception desk. "Hello, again. Is that handsome Mr.

Malloy with you?" She peered past Belle, searching with some disappointment, and why not? He was a treat for the eyes, no matter your preference.

"No, he's—"

"He came back to check the office again. Friday last, I'm sure. My, didn't he get into a row with Dave. And then..." A crease appeared between Marj's calf-brown eyes, and she clucked in disapproval.

Belle took a moment to digest that news. So Mutt had forgotten that he'd been to the Ministry. Had he found anything of value? If so, where was it? "We're still trying to track down missing parts of Gary's research," she said.

Marj teased a tendril of hair out of her face, a faint aroma of vanilla in the air. "I shouldn't tell you this, but Dave's gone," she said with an effort to keep her voice low as a trim man in his thirties dressed in a khaki uniform with Ministry patches came down the hall.

"Jeff, did you get one of my cookies?" She reached onto a shelf and passed him the plate.

Jeff slipped a few into his pocket. "Another bad day for Bullwinkle. Blood and gore all over Route 144 near Cartier. No human fatalities. Used to be that the soup kitchens could take the meat. Now it'll be wasted. Go figure."

"Possible lawsuits, I guess. Times aren't as simple now," Marj observed.

Belle accepted a cookie as well. Oatmeal and chocolate chip. "So Dave's gone? Did he finish his project?" she asked between bites.

Marj put a finger to her full cranberry-red lips and ushered Belle down the hall to the office, bare from wall to wall. "Turns out Dave wasn't doing very well at the university. One day last week he didn't turn up. Seems like he left town. Took our new Nikon D100 with him, along with a seven thousand dollar long-distance lens. Rosaline was beside herself."

"Quite a haul. I can well understand why she was upset." If any records remained in files or as copies, enlisting Marj's aid would be critical. Belle flashed a pleading smile. Time to tweak the maternal instincts, or something hotter. "I'm here alone because Mutt's had an accident."

Marj gave a small gasp, but Belle held up a reassuring hand. "He's going to be fine. I'm taking over for now. Obviously everything's gone from the office, but I'm sure you have a finger on the pulse of this place. My office assistant knows more about my business than I do." Did she really say that? Shameless flattery.

The woman's eyes crinkled, and she smiled, so Belle added, "Is there anything else you can tell me about Gary's routines? Something that doesn't make sense?"

Steepling her slender fingers in thought, Marj gave her memory a scan. Her lips pursed at a sudden thought. With military swiftness, she unclipped a PDA from her belt and plugged in a few numbers, nodding to herself. "There *is* the water." As Belle pricked up her ears, she explained that Gary had sent test tubes to their lab on a regular basis, never missing a week.

"That surprises me. He was a zoologist. Why this great interest in water?" She was absorbing information like a three-year-old at a Baby Einstein unit.

Marj chuckled and patted her arm. "All life is about habitat. Food, water, shelter and predators. We're all dependent on our environment. That's why our work here is so important, dear. Do you watch David Suzuki's show?"

"Wish I could, but I have only one channel. As for habitat..." Belle wondered at the "dear." Good thing Marj was older. When a younger person called her that, she'd get in line for a room at

Rainbow Country. She tapped her temple in a "duh" gesture and grinned. "Right. As a realtor I should understand — location, location, location."

"We'll see what we can find. I have a few ideas. Follow me." Back at her desk, Marj consulted a sheaf of papers in a tiered tray and looked up with a puzzled expression. She disappeared around a corner and came back minutes later with a shrug. "How odd. There's no record of the results of his last tests the Friday before his accident, and I checked the duplicates. I wonder what could have happened to them."

Belle folded her arms. "Sabotage from Dave, maybe. With his dislike of Gary—"

"Dislike? My goodness, I'm sure *I* never mentioned... Did Rosaline—"

Down the hall came the sleek, teal-suited form of the director, Rosaline Silliker. Her low, white slingbacks were stylish yet comfortable. Belle wouldn't have minded adding an inch or two to her own frame, but the need to tramp cottage properties put strict conditions on footwear. "Did I hear my name? Speak of the devil and all that." She regarded Belle with a broad smile and shook hands. Her buffed nails were short and practical. Perhaps she still did field work.

"Ms Palmer, was it? You left one of your cards."

Belle looked from one woman to the other, sensing that she might be making a pest of herself. This development was interesting, and she wanted to follow it up. "Sorry to bother you kind people again." She repeated her intentions about the project.

The phone rang. Rosaline gave Marj a boss's eyebrow and checked her slim gold watch, making Belle feel distinctly in the way. "We're expecting a delegation from Michigan today. All about new strategies for those tent caterpillar invasions that don't respect borders."

"Unleash the government flies." Marj's eyes assumed a pixie look as she picked up the receiver.

Rosaline gave a gentle laugh at Belle's confused face. "One of our jokes. Nature sends those flies to attack the egg cases of the caterpillars, but everyone gives us credit."

Belle said, "Even my neighbours believe that urban legend." Friendly flies, some called them. Or lazy flies, fat and easy to swot. They left their little poop markers wherever they landed and had her roaming with a bottle of spray cleaner and a disgusted snarl.

"Come to my office, where we'll be more comfortable. I might be able to send some business your way, too. I was going to call you."

Perking up, Belle followed her like a puppy scenting bacon on the fry. Some people thought her pushy, passing all those cards around, curbside-car-dealer style. It was merely good business. She griped about buying nickel-and-dime ads while Cynthia Cryderman, the largest realtor in town, with a pink limo, hair to match and an advertising budget to rival Molson's, drummed her phone number into local brains with an annoying but effective radio ad.

"Water? Sorry there's no coffee. I'm trying to cut back. High blood pressure and heart problems run in my family. And a little elegance helps the illusion." From a tray with a white cloth, she picked up a delicate goblet and filled it at a large cooler.

The Ministry wasn't air-conditioned, and Belle had started to sweat. A cold drink would be welcome. She accepted a glass and drank deeply, tinging a nail on the thin crystal. She decided not to mention seeing Rosaline at the hospital. It seemed intrusive. "Guess I should start buying bottled water. I've been spoiled by living on Wapiti and taking the lake for granted. But the population explosion on my road, complete with dogs, fertilizers, questionable septic systems, has to have an impact."

Rosaline turned her patrician head, her long brown hair shiny in a complex but perfect chignon. "Word to the wise. Don't tell anyone where you heard this, but statistics are coming to light on nickel content in our water, too. I recommend Crystal Springs. Costs a bit more, but *vive la différence.*" She kissed her slender fingers as a ruby ring instead of the conventional wedding band cast a stained-glass sparkle on the white wall. Weren't rubies bad luck for marriages? Probably a medieval superstition.

Belle drained her glass with appreciation. "It does seem clean and sharp. Now I sound like a wine connoisseur."

"Makes President's Choice taste like Cleveland's tap water, and I should know. I spent a week there one night at a conference."

Belle laughed at the rare, laid-back humour of a government official. Rosaline's office was the same size as Gary's, but its picture window overlooked a pleasant meadow with maples, oaks, and birches in full-leaf. At picnic tables and park benches, workers chatted on their breaks. A stunted northern red squirrel leaped from one tree to another, chased by a giant black relative. She blinked in surprise and pointed. "I've noticed that eastern grey squirrels have started moving into town. Not in the bush so far, though. In comparison with ours, they look like King Kong."

The director pointed to a wall map of climate zones. "Global warming's no fiction. Our scientists have recorded many plants and animals moving slowly northward." She reached for a specimen box containing an insect that resembled a walking stick. "Look at this creature."

"I've seen those in my bay."

"It's a brown waterscorpion. Normally only found down south. Its beak can puncture your skin. As for plants, sumac grows here in micro-environments. Hop hornbeam, too."

"There's a small hornbeam stand on one of my paths. The bark reminds me of shaggy hickory."

"Very secluded, right? Probably a few degrees warmer all year round. If it goes on, maybe we'll see those comical American magpies. My husband and I visit Taos, New Mexico, where his parents live. Missionaries. What a life. God bless them." She motioned Belle to a comfortable blue suede armchair. Her own executive model was ergonomically designed in black leather. Crossing her shapely legs with a silken schuss, Rosaline sat back and smiled, plucking Belle's card from a bulletin board and tapping it on the desk. "Here's the good news. My mother is looking for a condo. Waterfront view would be ideal. Price is no object." She gave a theatrical grin. "And I'm not just 'talking through my hat', an expression of hers."

Belle's heart thumped as she leaned forward, hearing the sounds of a teller riffling a wad of crisp hundred-dollar bills. "Thanks for thinking of me, Ms Silliker."

"Please call me Roz," she invited with a classic toss of her head.

The polish and quick wit reminded Belle of Roz Russell. "The timing is perfect. There's a fabulous new project in the south end on Paris Street overlooking Lake Ramsey. Maki Cove Condominiums. Extremely exclusive. Top-of-the-line fittings. Private health club. Prices range from...$280,000 to over $400,000." She stopped for a quick assessment of body language. Nothing changed about Rosaline's pose or expression. This was going to be one whopping commish, if it went through. When Miriam came back, they'd wing off to the Bahamas in December. Make that Aruba. She hadn't enjoyed rijstaffel since leaving Toronto.

Rosaline clasped her hands together, at one knuckle a

touch of knobby osteoarthritis Belle hadn't noticed before. Perhaps an old injury. "It sounds ideal. Mom spends the winter playing golf in Boca anyway. Wants to walk out the door at the first flake of snow and return at ice-out with no worries. I live on Indian Road on Lake Nepawhin, so we'd be quite close."

Belle was one breath short of singing the "Hallelujah Chorus", but she made an effort to remain cool and professional. Dream deals often melted like May snow. "I have brochures at the office. Shall I pop everything into the mail?"

Rosaline agreed, and they both stood. Behind her were framed diplomas from the University of Calgary and a Ph.D from McGill. To rise to senior management in her early forties meant that the scientist was made of stern stuff. Her maiden name had been Gable. Belle thought of the true king.

"Sorry not to be of more help about the research. Gary's office is pretty much cleaned out with...Dave gone. Thank God for that. I didn't accept this position to lecture sanctimonious bigots about civil rights." With her hands on her hips and her brows flashing fire, she had the demeanour of a gunfighter.

Belle banished the scene with a throat-clearing. "There is one thing. Marj mentioned that some water sample results never made it back from the lab."

Rosaline sighed and shook her head. A silver streak ran through her hair on one side, a striking effect. "Half the staff takes water samples on a regular basis. Especially with our sad history of acid lakes, it's like a religion. Mix-ups can happen. Poor labelling, wrong dates. Breakage, spillage. Or perhaps he was concentrating on another part of the project."

"Marj said he never failed. Every Friday." Another word popped into her mind. With all their gabbing, she had forgotten that mission. "Benthic. I keep finding that word in

Gary's notes. My dictionary is no help, and the Internet is overkill. What does it mean?"

Rosaline pointed to a tiny stuffed greyish-brown owl with no ear tufts. "As you can guess from my magpie comment, ornithology was my focus. *Migratory Flight Patterns of the Northern Pygmy-Owl in the Rockies*. Of course, Wilf over there died of natural causes. Let's see, though." Turning like a captain at a console, she ran her finger along a set of reference books, plucked one, and returned to her desk to put on a pair of half-moon reading glasses. As she searched, her almond-shaped, butterscotch eyes scanned like a machine. "It's been a long time, and I hated organic chemistry or hydrology, wherever we studied that stuff. I'll try to translate. The benthos refers to the bottom-feeding organisms in an ocean, estuary, or lake that provide food for fish." She leafed through a few more pages. "Hmm. Hold on. Then there's benthic flux, which is defined as the rate that fluid, chemicals, particles or energy flows through a surface. And—"

Belle held up a hand. "I surrender! Not only did I fail physics, I cheated on a biology exam. Science was not my cup of tea. But you've pointed me in the right direction."

"Many women feel that way, unfortunately. I've always felt that a female hand could direct the discipline in a more custodial and less damaging direction. I often speak at high schools during Career Week to encourage more young girls to join our ranks." Rosaline closed the book and replaced it. "Come back and talk to our zoologist in a few weeks if any other questions come up. Right now she's up in Red Lake on a marten habitat project."

"You've been very patient. We hope to send this to Brock." She didn't want to drone on about Mutt's accident and his problematical prognosis. Why would Rosaline care? She'd met him only once. As for the white elk, she could talk to the zoologist once she learned the test results.

Dropping by the Land Registry Office to search the suspicious title of a camp on Onaping Lake, Belle grabbed a quick and early lunch at Black Cat Too, the bookstore cum coffeehouse on Durham Street. Their chili was hot and spicy, the way she liked it. Blotting her mouth after finishing and heading for the door, she saw Steve at a rack with *Photo Life*. He'd gotten into digital photography since Heather's arrival and appreciated the store's large selection of magazines. Under his arm, he carried a periodical about scrapbooking. Janet's latest hobby? It certainly didn't appeal to Belle, and maybe that was the point. No one would inherit her memories.

"Free time? What has law enforcement come to?" she said with a grin.

"We are allowed lunch...every other day. By the way, Joey's getting arraigned at ten tomorrow morning," he said. "No more of Mom's perogies for him. Grilled cheese and wieners instead for lunch and dinner."

"Thanks for coming out yourself that night," she said. "I owe you."

He put down the magazines and folded his arms in a squared stance like a high school vice-principal, the designated disciplinarian. His liquid black eyes drilled into her, and one thick eyebrow rose on auto-pilot. "You got yourself into trouble, and by a lucky coincidence, back out. It's not going to happen again. Promise me that you'll mind your own business, personal and professional."

Gently she punched his arm. "Don't I always? And I'm a one-woman-plus operation, remember, so I have to be—"

"Speaking of the plus, how's Yolanda working out? Or is she gone already?"

"Far from it. She has a great future. Lots of initiative and plenty of...nerve." She thought of the dreaded cold calls, a realtor's *bête noire*. Yoyo seemed to greet them with the challenge of a lynx on the hunt.

He nodded slowly, barely suppressing an ironic smile. "A perfect personality for a criminal."

At the office, she breezed in at last, making a note to send that Maki Cove condo info to Rosaline. She had neglected to get a home address. Would the name be in the directory? Reaching for the white pages, she stopped short as she saw Yoyo with her head buried in her arms on the desk. Muffled sobs shook her shoulders.

FIFTEEN

Bad news about Coco? Belle went over and placed a tentative hand on her back, realizing that Yoyo had a small frame, despite her mammary assets. The simple, embroidered flax peasant top over slacks added an innocent Old World vulnerability. "What's wrong? Not the baby, I hope."

Yoyo's head pulled back, and the tendons in her neck stretched. Her deep-shadowed eyes squeezed in a paroxysm of pain. Despite her make-up, her face was pale as chalk. "Jesus, Mary and Joseph on a snowmobile. These cramps started last night after dinner. I hardly got any sleep at all. Now my head's pounding like a jackhammer. I *never* get headaches."

Belle heard sirens go off. "Cramps? Have you had any bleeding?" Sounded like an engraved invitation to a miscarriage. But what about the headache? Stress from the pain?

Yoyo balled up her child-sized fists and pounded the desk, overturning a paper clip holder. Then as a spasm passed, she exhaled in relief, her breath ruffling her wispy bangs. "Nothing. That's why I'm not that worried. Could you get me a couple of those painkillers from the bathroom cabinet, the ones with codeine?"

Wanting to help, her stomach tensing at the obvious suffering, Belle knew medication might confuse the issue. She folded her arms. "Forget it. You need to get to the hospital. Don't take chances with two lives at stake." Something else

175

occurred to her. "How about your appendix?"

"It's out. Do I have to show you the scar?" In her frustration, Yoyo's voice assumed the cross mantle of agony.

Belle narrowed her eyes and gave the woman one last assessment. Half of Canada was clogging up Emerg with ingrown toenails and harmless sniffles, and this woman wanted to play Brunhilda. "Why not call your gynaecologist?"

"I just moved back. You know the system. The earliest appointment was next month." Yoyo stood with difficulty, balancing against the desk, her brow etched with agony. The bulge below her waist, barely the size of Miriam's belly pack, remained unobtrusive, except for Belle's imagination.

Was Yoyo lying about her due date? Perhaps she'd miscalculated. At five-foot-two and a hundred-ten pounds, Terry Palmer had said that she never looked pregnant. In her eighth month, the doors of the Queen Street trolley had closed over her ocelot coat as she was exiting, pinning her in their grip. George had run alongside the car yelling and waving in panic until it had stopped. Prairie-born, Terry had been tough as a gopher.

"I'm getting worried. Are you sure about this?" Belle asked.

"Just give me my jacket. Then take me home where I can lie down. I'll get the car later, or take the bus tomorrow morning." She pulled a tissue and wiped a sheen of sweat off her face. No eye shadow today, nor foundation. Only a trace of a pale cinnamon lipstick. Probably too sick to care.

Belle checked her watch. "Well, if you're—"

"Nothing's scheduled for you this afternoon. I'm sure I'll be fine once this passes." She clenched her jaw in silence, pride warring against practicality. "All the correspondence and ads are done. Not one possessive error. You'll see."

"Of course I will. But promise me that you'll go *tout de suite* to the hospital if this gets any worse. Your mother's home, isn't she?" She realized that she'd grown strangely fond of the unconventional young woman and her pal, Baron.

After putting a "Back in twenty minutes" sign on the door and saying a prayer for once that no business would arrive, Belle helped Yoyo down the steps to the parking lot. "Want to lie down in the back? I keep the third seat folded under for Freya, and there's a soft pad." Thank God she'd given the carpet a thorough treatment with the shop vac after ZZ's swamp incident.

Waving off the suggestion, Yoyo climbed into the other captain's chair, and fastened the belts with pained sighs. Belle headed for the Flour Mill, an old section of town abutting hills of black rock. Full of cheap tenements and blocky houses four-square to the north winds, it was Sudbury's low-rent district, near the Goodwill and across from secondhand furniture and clothing stores.

They passed six cement grain silos nearly ninety feet high. Erected in 1910 along with a long-gone brick mill and commercially abandoned for half a century, they had been hastily refurbished with planters of petunias and a brass plaque paying tribute to Francophones who'd settled in the area. Now the stucco was crumbling again. Getting more exact directions, Belle turned down Queen Street and passed a small historical museum. "Take another right," Yoyo said.

Along the narrow street, a hoard of children played tennis-ball hockey, dragging aside goalie nets to let the van pass. Another PD day for teachers? They approached an apartment building, perhaps an original rooming house for bachelor miners. "Stop here."

Vinyl siding had replaced the clapboard, but a rusty stain dripped from the leaking eaves.

"I can read your mind, Belle," Yoyo wheezed as she stopped for breath, her face red with exertion. "It's broken. Surprise, surprise."

Broken like the hopes and dreams of those who took refuge here, a way station between poverty and life's next stage, down or up. Belle felt ashamed to witness the woman's home, especially with no advance warning, but what did that say about her?

Heat was building like a sauna the higher they climbed. Finally they emerged into a dingy hall with only a stuttering twenty-watt bulb dangling like a moribund tarantula from the flaky ceiling. The shabby linoleum and crack-patched walls were clean, but nothing could erase the toil of a century, nor the whiff of urine. Odours of fried cabbage and sausage from frugal tenants battled microwaved pizza in the stuffy air. Yoyo fumbled for her key, and they entered 4C.

Roo-rooing, Baron shoved his muzzle between his mistress's legs in typical shepherd style, his tail swishing against a standing fan that Belle rescued from a crash. "Quiet, baby. You know the rules." Bending over awkwardly, Yoyo buried her face in his thick ruff.

Then Coco emerged from a small galley kitchen, an apron over her faded print dress and a wooden spoon in her hand. "Home early? I baked a spice cake, and I'm making macaroni salad, your fav—" As Yoyo collapsed onto the couch, her mother came to her side, kneeling stiffly. "What's wrong? Tell Mom."

Belle said, "Stomach cramps. Pretty bad. I wanted to take her to the hospital, but she re—"

"Damn it, girl. Why didn't you wake me this morning?" The women exchanged a few words Belle couldn't decipher. Then Coco's wizened hand smoothed her daughter's hair. "She'll be okay, and junior, too. Didn't I have six children, all born at home? Acted as midwife for Olga one January when we were snowbound. Do you remember that, sweetie? You were a big help, even at five."

Belle took in a long breath, savouring the luscious aromas

of cinnamon and nutmeg. If anything, they ate well here. "You mean she's not—"

The woman folded her arms across her bony chest. A small silver cross hung around her fissured neck. The grey hair was curly, but thin at the crown, exposing a pink scalp. "I bet it's something she ate. Chinese takeout last night. Had a coupon. I'm allergic to seafood, so she took the shrimp while I had the kung-po—"

"Stop!" Covering her mouth, Yoyo charged from the couch as if possessed and headed through the kitchen. A door closed, and they could hear retching, then the flush of a toilet and the rush of water in the sink. Baron followed his mistress, whining softly.

Coco settled into the couch, folding her hands like a mother superior. Hot air swirled around the room courtesy of floor and window fans. A pigeon landed on the windowsill, and she tossed a pillow at it. "Scram. In France, they eat the likes of you. I'm already dreaming up recipes."

Belle gave a light laugh. "Don't tell the Minister of Health. It might replace tuna fish as a menu suggestion from the government."

Coco got up to check on her daughter. Reluctant to leave until she was sure Yoyo was recovering, Belle gave a cursory glance at the apartment. Barely five hundred square feet. A worn couch in a nubbly Danish Fifties' pattern, along with companion loveseat. Chrome dining table and two chairs. A pile of magazines on the coffee table, *People* along with a few tabloids, but a copy of *Feed Me, I'm Yours* lay open. On the wall, a winter scene with a frozen brook romanticized the savage weather of the North. A Coke bottle on a side table held six daffodils. Scavenged from some innocent and befuddled gardener? Aluminum-painted radiators delivered steam heat, a nice touch if you could imagine the gurgling as babbles of a serenity pool. She did the math. Sixteen units, four per floor, probably with a custodian in the basement, where sunlight never shone. The owner would have bought it for a song and done minimal maintenance. To be fair, often low rents brought a failure to pay, long legal hassles with evictions, and once the riffraff disappeared, costly damages like holes in the walls and ripped-up plumbing nudged the bottom line. It touched her heart that pressed calico curtains framed windows cleaner than hers, and the place was dusted and vacuumed to perfection, not one shepherd hair on the threadbare beige carpet.

Coco returned with a smile the size of the Alberta oil fields. "Am I right, or am I right? She's asking for some soup already."

Belle saw the cuckoo clock on the wall pushing her margin into the red as lost opportunities passed. "Guess I'd better go. Tomorrow's Friday. Nothing's on. Tell her to take a long weekend if she needs it."

Coco touched Belle's arm. Inside the house, she wore no dark glasses, and her eyes were flaxflower blue, much like George Palmer's, a colour that implied an honesty, real or imagined. It was hard to believe the woman was the barfly that Yoyo had portrayed. But with failing vision, her world would shrink. "You're a good boss. Had one like you when I worked at Burwash."

Belle turned in the doorway. "So Yoyo said. Weren't you a cook?"

"And do I got the recipes. Oughta write a book. Hey, there's an idea. I could make a mint." She brandished the wooden spoon in concert, cackling like a jolly witch. "Shepherd's Pie. Lasagna. Beef stew."

"Rough country down there. How did you stand it?"

Coco's eyes assumed a dreamy look, one crinkle in each corner for every decade. From next door through the paper-thin wall, a screaming baby took wing, but the old woman didn't seem to hear. In tenements, deafness was a blessing. "Had me a sweet little house. One and only time. Good place for kids, living in the bush with our own school. Keeps them out of trouble with drugs and what-all. I raised the whole bunch there, Yoyo coming along twenty years after the first. Damn husband of mine never did hold down a job, then went off to Yellowknife with a waitress and never sent me a nickel. That garden was my prize. Asparagus patch with stalks thick as your thumb. Takes years to get 'em going, but how I do love it. Costs the moon at the grocery, though. I haven't ate it for so long."

Who would have thought prison life so bucolic? "A job like that must have had some drawbacks. What about the inmates?"

"Hell, those boys weren't no trouble." She gave a scoffing gesture, but then her face grew dark with a troubling memory, and her pace slowed. "It was—"

"Mom, I could use some tea before I try the soup," Yoyo called as the bathroom door opened.

Belle took the cue and hustled herself out and down the hall. How did Coco run Baron up and down several times a day, or did Yoyo come by on her lunch hour? As Dietrich said, "You can lie about your age, but you can't beat a good flight of stairs." She arrived in the foyer, wondering if she should report the landlord to the authorities. Then again, he might tear it down and sell out to a fast-food franchise. Affordable housing was hard enough to find for the working poor.

The rest of the overcast afternoon was quiet. Belle thought about the close call with Yoyo and resolved to give Miriam a shout to see when she might be expected back. On the way home, she stopped at Mutt's, noticing with a sinking feeling that the Infiniti still sat in the drive. Windows were open on the sultry night, and Jann Arden was singing "Ode to a Friend". She knocked at the door, and Mutt waved at her from the sofa. Craning her head as she entered, she spread her hands in a question, her lips forming his sister's name. "Winding down in the jacuzzi," he said. "Coffee coolers are in the fridge. Megs hit Starbucks for Costa Rican. Pour yourself a cup."

Belle again admired the pink-oak designer kitchen with Italian-tiled counters, a double-doored brushed-aluminum fridge and matching Jenn-Air stove. Her own two voltage-guzzling appliances came from the original cottage. Pouring a frosty glass and hitting the ice cube dispenser with childish glee, she took a refreshing gulp, returned to the living room and sank into a distressed leather chair. Overhead, the fans hummed in rhythm.

Mutt put down a book and leaned forward to take her hands between his. A few pounds lighter, an Omar Sharif hint of shadow under his eyes, he'd also lost some conditioning lying in bed for those days. "It's great to see you. How can I thank you for saving my life?"

"I rented you the house. Comes with the territory. Did I leave many bruises bumping you down the stairs?"

"By the time I was out of the coma, they were hardly noticeable."

"You're reading. Is your memory coming back?" If cognitive abilities were sharpening, it boded well.

"It's Gary's. He took a book to bed each night, one of his habits." He showed her the cover. Konrad Lorenz's *King Solomon's Ring*. "The ways animals communicate has me laughing. Good medicine."

"I've read it. That's why I'm glad Freya can't talk." She and Gary had shared many common interests.

"One odd thing." He picked up a newspaper clipping from the lamp table. "I found this folded inside the book. What do you make of it?"

Belle read the *Sudbury Star* headline from a month ago: "Markis Reserve mortality rates 30% higher than rest of province." If any group was dying off faster than Sudburians, it was First Nations people, with growing epidemics of diabetes, substance abuse and suicide. What tragic gifts the whites had brought with their so-called civilization. In this latest incident, two boys returning from a canoe trip had developed a mysterious rash and bumps on their legs and arms as well as breathing problems and dizziness. They denied sniffing solvents such as gas or glue, an ongoing problem in more remote Northern communities. The issue of contaminated water had been suggested. A government report from over ten years before had shown serious water problems on hundreds of reserves, a national disgrace. But Markis had tested its drinking water and found it safe.

Mutt asked, "Why did he keep this? Is this reserve near where he was working?"

Belle searched her geographical memory. The region had many reserves, one on the north shore of Wapiti, another bordering on Lake Nipissing. On a general scale, Markis was located to the southwest, and its eastern edge abutted the southernmost portion of meandering Long Lake, a duplication of Edgewater Road with its collection of old cottages and new brick monster homes. "Let's check his topos to get oriented."

He got up a bit stiffly in his black silk pyjamas and matching robe, and they went to the den. "Here's the Burwash map we used for Bump Lake," she said, then shook her head as her fingers traced locations. "We need something farther west. He probably portaged into other lakes or went down the rivers in his habitat research. Then again, maybe we're way off base. He could have saved the clipping for someone else. Does he have friends who work with native people?"

Mutt's lips formed a tight line, and he turned away. Then he cleared his throat. Had she struck a nerve? Was this the jealousy Megs had implied? "For a short time, he lived with an older man, a professor of sociology at Brock. An expert in native diversity issues. Max Leaver. Even after we began our relationship, they still had coffee together once in a while and sparred over politics. Max is a bit right wing, which has to be an anomaly for a gay man, like those Log Cabin Republicans in the States."

"So you could ask him? Or—" She wanted to pursue the matter but worried about the intrusion.

"I'll give him a call. Out of courtesy, I tried to contact him when Gary...died, but got his machine. It's a bit awkward."

"Maybe the article has no bearing on his research." She still wasn't clear on that benthos phenomenon. Mutt was recovering but a long way from total function. To press this too much wouldn't be good for his self-esteem.

He levelled his hazel eyes at her. "Gary never did anything without a reason. He was the perfect scientist."

Belle saw the copy of his novel that she'd returned that terrible morning. "I loved your book, especially the silent films you mentioned. Got the next two at Chapters." In truth she'd picked them up half-price at Bay Used Books. "Which is your favourite?"

Mutt smiled shyly. "That's like asking a parent which child is the golden one. But I like to think I'm getting better, so I'd say the latest. It'll be out in the fall."

"Great. You met the deadline?"

He shook his head with a brave smile. "We're always about eighteen months ahead of time. My deadline is for next year's book, and I'm stuck in the middle."

She stood to go, sorry that she had mentioned his work and the ongoing problems. "I can get that topo for the area west of Burwash. Maybe we'll notice something significant."

"I promised his chairman at Brock that I'd have a package to send on by the end of the summer. They can sort it out." From upstairs they heard footfalls. Belle hastily twiddled her fingers at Mutt and slipped out the door.

When she got home, she went downstairs to replace her water filters. No water bills arrived, but she had to maintain a pump and a heated water line, continuously threatened by hydro outages in sub-zero weather. She turned off the valve and unscrewed the clear blue plastic tubes, taking them to the sink. Out of each came a white cartridge to collect debris and sediments. As she held a container to the light, small creatures swam like brine shrimp. Belle flushed the residue down the drain, stifling the urge to retch. What bottled water had Rosaline recommended? Crystal...Springs? Those monster bottles would be the best buy. Still, she'd have to purchase a water cooler, too.

Miriam was next on the list. If Yoyo was going to be off for more than a few days, or in the case that something dire happened with her pregnancy, she'd better check for back-up. She dialled Jack's number, but a strange male voice answered. "Uh, a friend of Jack's came in with a float plane, and Mimsy and him hitched a ride over to Lake Abitibi for some fishing at the guy's camp. They'll be back next Sunday."

Fishing. One step beyond rehabilitation. It sounded like a vacation. Belle gave the table a light pound as she rang off. But should she really blame Miriam? When they'd talked only a week ago, Yoyo had been holding down the fort like a legionnaire at Fort Zinderneuf. A bush trip sounded like good medicine for the pair. They'd camped all over Northern Ontario during the first years of their marriage, before their daughter Rosanne had come along. Belle would keep her fingers crossed about Yoyo. At least Jack sounded like he'd soon be on his own again. Then an alarming thought struck her critical brain. Maybe they were getting back together for good, and she would soon lose her cohort. The idea made her stomach turn cartwheels.

SIXTEEN

At the office the next morning, having been delayed by a multi-car accident with ambulances and tow trucks converging from all directions, Belle was surprised to see Yoyo under a full head of steam. Her colour was healthy, and she marshalled her body like a midget staff sergeant, bustling around with lemon furniture spray, loading the coffee machine. A gleaming smile lit up her face, and it wasn't just the whitening strips. Perhaps the glow of pregnancy wasn't a myth after all.

"Back to normal?" Belle asked, shaking her golf umbrella onto the commercial carpet. A soft, warm rain had been falling since dawn, ideal weather for germinating the seeds in her garden. With recent events, she hadn't even checked for telltale green sprigs.

"Mom was right about those damn shrimp, the old doll. Good thing I didn't panic. Our neighbour with a bleeding ulcer had to wait eight hours at the Emerg." She handed Belle a list. "Four more prospects. We might move that water-access camp on Trout Lake. Ryan is willing to drop another two thousand, and a buyer called last week asking about a place in that range."

"Good work." She checked her docket. Two free hours. Joey would be arraigned this morning, a sight she wanted to witness for atavistic satisfaction. Watching him led off in leg irons or the plastic equivalent would give her a boost. Then she'd get Ed and his ancient truck and clean the site so that she felt like walking there again. "Back in a few hours. I'm going to the courthouse. Call the cell if anything urgent comes up." Suspecting strict protocol, she'd set it to vibrate.

Ten minutes later, heading down Cedar Street, she parked the van far down the block in a free spot. A short hike brought her to the halls of the old provincial courthouse. Near the wet and drooping Canadian flag, a granite obelisk stood proudly in commemoration of those fallen in the two world wars. Hosts of red geraniums and perky zinnias had been planted to celebrate summer's all-too-brief tenure. Asking a security guard, she was told that arraignments and bail hearings took place in Courtroom One, along the hall to the left.

She seated herself in the back row, surprised to see almost a hundred people. Cases of all pedigrees appeared on the docket, from spousal assault to armed robbery to the rare murder. Sudbury had had only two so far that year, including a man left dead on frozen Lake Ramsey, par for Canada's 3.8 per hundred thousand. Recently the long-awaited ban on pit bulls was creating a monster caseload of defiant owners turned in by fearful neighbours. Wives and mothers sat, wads of tissues to eyes. Surly teenagers skipping school had come to support their buddies, lounging long legs in the benches, their ball caps backwards, never wondering why the sun got in their eyes. Seeing the bailiff pass, she asked about Joey's hearing. He consulted a clipboard. "Bartko? Alphabetical order. Your lucky day, miss."

To pass the time, she opened Mutt's second book, anticipating a treat. In *Death in Bluffers Park,* Lucy was involved in a hot chase after liquor smugglers, boating their booty across Lake Ontario to lawless Buffalo. Though rife with its own blue laws, Canada had never signed on nationally to Prohibition, allowing cities to vote wet or dry. Rough-and-ready Sudbury's preference had been a foregone conclusion. She smiled to read about Lucy watching *The Gold Rush*. Charlie Chaplin devouring his boots with a knife and fork was a comedic milestone. She made a promise to herself to read her father a few passages about his old stomping grounds.

The courtroom was stifling, with only ceiling fans urging the heavy, humid air. Some muttering and movement at the front attracted her attention, and when Joey scuffled in wearing an orange jumpsuit with SPD on the back, she whispered an inner "yessss." The days of wine and roses, or beer and chips, were over for this character.

"All rise." The courtroom came to its feet as the black-robed judge entered, a woman with sleek, razor-cut reddish blonde hair, a trace of grey at the temples and a simple black pearl on each ear. Judge Betty Dean, a no-nonsense lady similar to Miriam in age and deportment, rapped her gavel smartly and brooked no interruptions, dispatching Joey's case with a flare of her sharp nostrils and a staccato delivery. The docket was so heavy that he would be getting free rent for the next nine months. Bail was denied because of his high risk, not to mention the breach of probation.

Sneering at the decision, Joey had a few choice but cautiously mumbled words for the judge, tossing back his greasy hair as he stuck out his stubbled jaw. Two young men in caps, jeans and T-shirts gave Joey a "right-on" fist salute. Down came the gavel like a judgement of God. "That'll do, Mr. Bartko, unless you want to be held in contempt. And that includes your ignorant friends. This is a court of law, not a tavern." His lawyer, a fresh-faced woman from Legal Aid, her hair gelled in a flyaway fashion and wearing a ruffled blouse and a short skirt that displayed matchstick legs, whispered in his ear. Suddenly, all heads turned at a wail.

"Don't take my boy. He's all I got. I put up my house for

security like last time," called a care-worn, wrinkled woman in the front row who spoke hesitantly with a thick accent. Getting up slowly to thump her walker toward the bench, she was nearly as wide as she was tall, a fireplug in a nondescript brown raincoat. She reminded Belle of Maria Ouspenskaya in countless films where a salt-of-the-earth Slavic woman was needed. Her steel-grey hair was covered by a bright red babushka. Orthopaedic shoes and heavy lisle stockings were on her feet. With a firm nod to the bailiff, Judge Dean sent the woman back to her seat, where she buried her face in her hands and keened in grief, comforted by a woman with Heidi-style white braids who patted her bowed back.

Joey stood in cuffs, watching his mother with a concerned crease on his brow. Moving his manacled hands to his face, he brushed a tear from his eye. Then his gaze went to the back of the courtroom, fixed on Belle, and hardened into an ugly and feral expression. His friends caught the change and turned like a hyena pack to look at her. Lowering her head, she slipped out of the courtroom, feeling exposed and endangered. This had been a very bad idea. Joey had bragged that he had friends. What might they do for him?

When she got to the office, she noticed Paul Straten's card still on her bulletin board. She'd nearly forgotten about that baby elk. Had he received the autopsy report? Would anything conclusive appear, or would the death be unexplained? Mutt would be interested in any developments. Her call was routed to the departmental secretary at Nickel City College. "He left last week for Toronto with connections to Moscow and Siberia, where he'll be working on a grizzly bear project in the Kamchatka Peninsula for the summer."

"Darn. I should have called earlier." Belle bit her lip, then explained her connection with Paul and the visit to the college. "Did he get any test results?"

"Pardon me." The woman spoke to someone else, muffling the phone. "Sorry, a student came in with a late paper. You were asking about the elk, that poor little baby?"

A surge of hope fluttered in Belle's ribcage. "Yes. Did he mention it?"

"He was gone when the fax came in. But he told me to call a...let's see...Mutt Malloy." She tittered at the name. "I tried, but no one answered. You'd think everyone would have an answering machine. Where is that consarned report? And the print was so small. Do they think we're all thirty? I'll need my..." She grumbled to herself amid sounds of drawers opening and closing and riffling of paper. "Here it is. The tissue samples showed signs of arsenic poisoning."

Belle sat up, posture at full alert, pencil poised on a pad, its point now history. Who would poison an elk? Farmers were no fans of the ungulates when they wandered into their fields around Massey to munch produce, but they were more likely to shoot first and ask for a trail permit later. Even so, Burwash and points west were thick bush, not succulent hay or alfalfa fields. "Arsenic? But how..." Her voice trailed off.

"It does sound strange. I'm afraid I don't know the first thing about those animals. I got transferred from the English department when it was eliminated in a cost-cutting..."

As she rambled on, Belle heard less and less. Here was a development worth pursuing. "Maybe I can contact Professor Straten and ask him a few questions about these results. Does he have a cell phone number? Satellite access?" From tundra to tundra.

"Dear me, no. He's in a very remote location. I shouldn't think he'd be in touch for weeks. They go in by helicopter and live in tents."

Belle left her number and sat back in her chair, testing the possibilities. Could the animal have encountered poison bait for wolves or coyotes? Hunted to near extinction, wolves were only now making a comeback. She remembered the lustrous silver pelt on the pine-log wall of an exclusive lodge catering to rich American hunters. On a snowmobile jaunt, she'd wandered in, and the owner had been polite enough to make her a coffee. Later that winter, she'd been privileged to witness the haunting sight of six beasts loping across the ice at dawn. The pelts belonged in action, form and function, not decorating a wall like a lifeless memory.

Then the phone rang. Mutt said, "Sorry for the short notice and for calling you at work, but would you like to see a play at the Theatre Centre? My treat. Megs is going bonkers in the bush. It's the least I can do, seeing that she did come up here."

Watching the two of them interact might be even better drama. "What's playing?" A quick glance at her cotton blazer and slacks made her glad she'd left the jeans at home.

"Ibsen's *An Enemy of the People*. Megs was surprised at the choice. She thought the locals went for nothing but fluff."

A theatre history minor in university, Belle would have preferred *Hedda Gabler* or *A Doll's House*, all of which she'd seen at Stratford. Ibsen was a century ahead of his time in his attitude toward women. How he burrowed inside the skin of frustrated Hedda or revealed the bold yet feminine spirit of Nora was a tribute to advanced sensibilities. But *An Enemy of the People*? She couldn't recall the storyline. Sounded very political. Ibsen never scrupled about pointing fingers where scrutiny belonged.

"Starts at seven thirty. We're eating at Respect is Burning. Got to love the name. You're welcome to join us."

"Better not. It's going to be a squeeze. Meet you in the foyer? Oh, and I have some unusual news about the baby elk. It..." A couple came though the door. From his tailored suit to her stylish dress, they were cash on the hoof. Belle wouldn't recognize Donna Karan if she fell over her, but it was a good guess. Yoyo greeted them with a dazzling smile and a handshake, nodding at Belle. "Clients. Catch you later, Mutt."

Her business concluded a short while later, a quick call to Hélène got Freya an invitation from the DesRosiers, her number-one babysitters. A tasty porketta was on the menu. Belle would have to do something special in return.

With a spare hour, she drove to the Ontario Map Company, located in an unprepossessing bungalow at 463 Clinton Street. She always bought her topos for canoe trips there. Passing through the peeling white picket fence, she entered the house as a bell jingled. The narrow front room was dedicated to maps of all sorts with the emphasis on hunting or fishing.

On a giant squared grid of Ontario, the clerk helped her locate the area west of Burwash then searched the corresponding drawer. The Copper Cliff number she pulled had INCO's headquarter town at the upper right corner, but proceeded southwest all the way to the Markis Indian Reserve and the Penage Lake system. In between were numerous uninhabited lakes as well as the Burnt River. Did that explain why Gary had kept the clipping? She had no doubt that as a field scientist immune to weather and terrain, he'd canoed and portaged his way into the deep bush in pursuit of his beloved elk, but the reserve was rather far from Bump Lake. Water samples. Now arsenic. Was there a connection? Perhaps she could make time to see that zoologist Rosaline had suggested.

At six thirty, she ate downtown at a sushi restaurant. This time she tried the surf clam and left with her taste buds winging from the pickled ginger and stinging from the wasabi mustard, a perfect combination.

Centrally located on Shaughnessy Street across from Tom Davies Square, with its modern metal human sculptures, the

Sudbury Theatre Centre was a magnet for the city's intelligentsia and social climbers. She couldn't imagine live theatre ninety years ago in a rough-at-the-edges mining town, yet drama had been an entertainment mainstay before films and television. The Chautauqua circuit had visited Sudbury on a regular basis. Oscar Wilde might have received the same rave welcome that Leadville gave him on his American tour, tossing back rye whiskey cup for cup with the boys and holding impromptu court deep in the mine as they christened the new shaft, the Oscar.

As she entered the front doors, Mutt waved the tickets at her, spruce in his light charcoal suit with a red striped tie. In a backless black dress that exposed her bony skeleton, his sister was inspecting artwork on the lobby walls, many by Ivan Wheale, a local painter who specialized in the rocky shorelines of Georgian Bay. "Hello, Belle," she said, joining them. "This optimistic brother of mine promised me some culture. I think half my brain cells have withered since I've been up here."

Gritting her teeth, Belle said in a hushed voice, "Don't start a stampede, but we even have latte now."

Megs tweaked a corner of her narrow, fire-engine-red mouth. "Starbucks, probably, but they don't carry Kopi Luwak from Indonesia. I treat myself once a week. Raven's Brew has everything."

"Never heard of Kopi..." Suspecting that she was setting herself up, Belle didn't attempt the rest of the name.

Mutt gave an indulgent sigh, as if accompanying a rude child. "Gary told me about the process. This is hard to believe, but the palm civet eats the reddest berries, then they pass through its digestive system, with only the soft outer shell dissolving."

"Oh my G—" Belle put a hand over her mouth as the sushi repeated. Should have stuck with the California roll.

Megs smirked, clearly enjoying a moment of triumph as they moved from the lobby. "The fermentation process adds a fabulous caramel flavour."

On this Friday evening, they settled into their seats amid a full house. The lights dimmed. Belle leaned into the plush seat and was transported to nineteenth century rural Norway. The plot is carried by Dr. Stockmann, who discovers that the runoff from a tanning mill upstream is polluting the local health spa. Yet instead of applauding his life-saving research, the local businessmen and mayor pressure him to cover it up. Corporate malfeasance over public conscience. Nothing had changed from *The Jungle* to *Fast Food Nation* to *Sicko*.

As the act proceeded, Mutt, sitting in the middle, spread his arms along the backs of their chairs, ever so lightly touching her shoulder. The slight pressure and the citrus scent of his aftershave took her back to her first date with Gary, though Old Spice was *de rigueur* in those simple days. They had ridden the subway and trolley to a Fellini movie at the Runnymede. No one she knew then had owned a car, except for a few toughs who took auto shop instead of French and could fix junkers. When another boy slipped his arm around his girlfriend, Gary no doubt felt prodded to follow suit. She swallowed a lump in her throat, thinking about how he'd forced himself to act against his nature. It had been stifling in the old theatre, his hand lightly sweaty against her bare upper arm. Mutt's gesture was a matter of posture, ingenuous and innocent, and it sent a message that he felt familiar with her. Given the option, you didn't touch someone you didn't like.

At intermission, Belle read the liner notes, chuckling to herself. In a letter, Ibsen had written "the minority is always right. Naturally I am not thinking of that minority of stagnationists who are left behind by the great middle party which with us is called Liberal; but I mean that minority which leads the van, and pushes on to points which the majority has not yet reached. I mean: that man is right who has allied himself most closely with the future." How many politicians were so brave, especially when safeguarding the environment hit the corporate wallet? Even the dinner table wasn't safe. Spinach, carrots and tomatoes had been indicted, and now seafood would be off the menu in a few decades. Could even the Green Party save them?

She pointed out the letter to Mutt, who had brought glasses of red wine from the bar, and he nodded. "Gary liked Ibsen. Told me he played a few roles in university theatre."

"He was a good actor. In more ways than one."

A sheen filmed Mutt's eyes as he responded with a bittersweet memory. "His favourite role was Osvald in *Ghosts*. He drew parallels between the themes of venereal disease and the current HIV/AIDS situation. 'Mother—give me the sun', that killer line. Blind, doomed and begging for release. It brought down the house."

Over at the bar, Megs, décolletage edging ever south, had corralled a balding man in a casual tuxedo, his comb-over a *trompe l'oeil*. By rough count, she was on her third glass of wine, and she tossed her tiny head back to laugh like a rooster exposing its neck on the block. Mutt's face had a "what-can-you-do?" expression. Had he bailed his sister out of many uncomfortable situations or watched from the sidelines? Belle wondered why these siblings were so different. As an only child, she had no yardstick.

Megs had disappeared when the chime to return came, though they waited until the last minute. Perhaps she had gone off to play doctor. No doubt she considered the acting third rate and planned to make a few acid remarks. Just as well she was "missing in action". Belle turned to Mutt. "Does she pull this often?"

He finished his plastic cup of wine and put it in the trash. "Even as a teenager, she was a man-eater. Disastrous marriages. An alcoholic lawyer and an accountant who did jail time. Maybe one of your tough northern guys will give her a run for her money."

When the curtain fell at last, Belle wasn't surprised to see that Mutt had nodded off, his head against her shoulder. So soon out of the hospital, he shouldn't have overstretched his resources. "Wake up, sleepyhead."

"Huh!" He came to with a snort, rubbing his bleary eyes. "Sorry about that. I guess even one glass of wine was too much. Always was a cheap date."

They filed out and headed for the parking lot. Belle was still pondering the timeless theme. If Ibsen were alive today, he'd be leading the charge toward universal acceptance of the Kyoto Agreement. Where were the visionaries when you needed them? Drones and managers. It was depressing.

Mutt reached the car and spread his hands, looking around the parking lot with a frown. "Where is she?"

An ebony Jag XKE pulled up, and Megs leaned out the passenger window as if she were in a French film, batting her thickly-mascaraed eyes, a cigarillo dangling in her hand. She flipped it onto the pavement, then tossed Mutt her car keys. "Don't wait up. Colin, I mean Dr. Marsh, is going to show me his house on Lake Ramsey. It's a Frank Lloyd Wright design." Before they could respond, the sleek vehicle merged into traffic like a cheetah parting a herd of wildebeest.

Mutt stood with his mouth half open. Clearly this crossed the line, even for him.

"I'll give you a ride home," Belle said, concealing her disgust. Didn't the woman realize that her brother was in no shape to drive?

As they forged down the Kingsway and exchanged the garish lights of town for the soothing darkness, an inverted bowl of ink with twinkling stars, she told him about the arsenic. "Did Gary ever mention elk getting poisoned by bait intended for other animals?"

They made the turn past the airport and climbed the hill. Overhead, a small prop plane swooped over, a bird with Christmas lights on its wings.

"Whoa. That's off the wall. Are you sure they got all the figures right?"

"How could they make a mistake? Arsenic's either there, or it's not. And these labs are independent. No axes to grind."

Mutt asked her to turn up the heater. After the ordeal, his metabolism was still on the slow side. "I think I remember from chemistry class that arsenic can occur naturally. Once it was used for cosmetics, even for health reasons. 'Eating arsenic', they called it. Small doses."

Belle eased off on the gas as they plunged down a hill. "You have quite a background. I guess that's a writer's territory."

"Got that tidbit from a mouldy old paperback, *The Shocking History of Drugs*. Plagues, poisons, things like that always fascinated me as a kid. Pretty morbid, eh?"

"As long as you weren't pulling wings off flies, I wouldn't have been worried." Putting herself in a parental role reminded her that fifteen-plus years separated them. In a strictly technical sense, she could have been his mother. She shook off the thought as she saw him lean back in his seat and relax.

"It's so dark out here. Don't you love it?"

As they turned onto Edgewater Road, piercing yellow eyes in the bush gleamed in Belle's headlights. An owl peered from the branches of a large poplar. Such a privilege to see one of these nocturnal creatures whose call was "Who Cooks for

You?" Thinking about birds, she recalled Rosaline Silliker's thesis, which triggered another thread. "You mentioned an idea about Dave sabotaging Gary's research. I'm starting to believe that." She filled him in on her visit to the Ministry, the missing water tests, and Dave's disappearance.

Mutt turned his head to her, his voice gaining confidence as his thoughts sped up. "Little fragments are coming back. I went to the Ministry, and...I think I got into an argument with him. The guy has a bad attitude about gays. I came close to shoving him up against a wall when he mouthed off about Gary. But the office was the same as we left it. The secretary was busy with someone else, so I missed her input. You might be right. He had access to Gary's work. Now he's gone under a rock somewhere."

Belle narrowed her eyes as she scanned the road. Oddly enough, darkness was the safest time, animals aside. "Could it be connected with the robbery? Someone did take the laptop and camera. Remember the interest in the files."

Mutt looked confused. "Not the guy next door, then? He was my choice."

"After I talked to Bill, I scratched him off our list." Belle tended to put dog lovers on the side of the angels, but she'd been wrong before. Something returned to her memory. She told him about that large white Buick.

Mutt gave a deep sigh. "That night's still one long wormhole between dimensions. All I remember is going to bed, then someone pulling on me. I woke up in the hospital with a royal headache."

"The car was there too long to be merely turning around. And not at three in the morning. Bill was too sick to notice much more. But in the dark, anything could have been possible."

"I don't know anyone with a white Buick. Can't say Gary

didn't. What are you thinking?"

Belle's chest tightened as a possibility emerged. "Maybe what happened to the furnace was no accident, my friend."

"The furnace? Why in the—"

At the sight of oncoming lights over a hill, Belle pulled to the side, wary enough to avoid the soft ditch but brushing a few willows. "Let's start with the break-in. Why would an ordinary thief concentrate on the study? Their chainsaw and generator were untouched, in an unlocked shed. There's two thousand dollars alone. And the last notebook missing? To give us just enough information not to get suspicious. If they'd all been gone, we would have seen a definite plot."

"You're way ahead of me, but the lack of sense makes sense, if you can follow that logic."

"You mean illogic." The van eased into the yard, and she reached into the back for the rolled tube. "Today I bought the topo for the territory west of Burwash. Are you up to a decaf?"

"I'm still pretty dry. A soft drink for me."

Belle made herself a coffee while Mutt took off his suitcoat, loosening his collar. "God, I hate ties. What a stupid idea."

"You ought to try pantyhose and spiked heels."

"That's what a friend of mine says." His grin made her laugh. Clearly he was close to normal again.

Shortly after, walking into the study, they placed their drinks on the desk. Belle looked at the cola, something emerging from the corners of her mind. "Remember the old Pepsi can we found? Sure was strange that he kept that." It reminded her of her mania as a teenager. She'd probably have put Gary's pencil stubs in her museum.

Mutt sipped from his drink, his Adam's apple working. "Must still be in the truck."

Given the keys, Belle turned on the yard lights and hit the

remote. In the extended cab, where the seats had been removed for more storage, she saw the plastic bag with the fragile can pushed to the side and picked it up carefully. A very odd souvenir. More to the point, what could have caused the aluminum to corrode?

Together they sat on an overstuffed chintz sofa in front of the fireplace, where Mutt had cobbled together a quick pine blaze. The night was cool. Staring into the leaping flames was a pastime as old as the first men with sticks and a rock.

She pulled over a floor lamp and turned it up to bright. "Spread out the topos on the coffee table and match them up. See if we can imagine where he went from Bump Lake."

Cracker Lake, Merit, Dooble, Brodill, Big Paddy, Paddy, deeper into the wilds as her finger moved west towards White Oak Lake. No roads, not even water-access black dots for camps. Occasional swamps were indicated by bushy symbols. Low elevations, the highest only a thousand feet. Perfect bug territory. Winding watercourses, Bevin Creek leading to Bevin Lake. This was barely charted wilderness, impossible to travel on foot, and hardly less ugly by canoe. No wonder Burwash had no escapees. The prison set one guard at each end of the nearby railroad tracks and one at the road to Route 69. West was the one impassable direction. What had Gary found?

Mutt put a finger on the legend. "I see what you mean. It's a nightmare, except by water. How often do they update these maps? This one's 1993—quite some time ago."

"From what the woman at the map company said, they don't bother unless the area's getting urbanized, like around Tilton Lake. It used to be summer cottages. Now people commute from there."

Mutt followed her tracks with heavy eyelids. She watched his profile as the resinous kindling sputtered behind the screen, a bank of quarry tiles protecting the shiny oak planking. "If we accept the idea of sabotage on Dave's part, could it have been just for spite, a random choice? Or did the dead elk mean something more to Gary?"

"The arsenic is proof that he was right to keep the body." A reactive smile died on Mutt's face. The corners of the room etched with shadows, they sat in a warm halo of light. "Do you want to take this all the way? As a mystery writer, I can see incarnations of evil everywhere. Go back to the beginning. Suppose his death was no accident."

"That was my first thought." Belle sat back into the pillows with electrical charges rising from her spine. "The booze never made sense. A set-up. Are we saying someone hit him?"

"The blow came from behind, remember? It was possible that he fell and hit his head, but I'm saying he would have landed in the canoe. So let's imagine he was struck on land and then taken out onto the lake."

"In the middle of nowhere? Who would he meet? Did they get into an argument, or was the whole thing planned? I can't see him inviting Dave into his boat." Belle stretched out her sock feet and enjoyed the warmth of the blaze. "Nobody's at Bump Lake except for the occasional teenager and sportsmen like that Patch guy. What's the connection? It's possible that Dave would have known his plans, though. I wonder where he was when Gary died."

Belle's gaze went to the mantel, where a handsome bronze urn sat. "Is that..."

"Came yesterday from the Cooperative Funeral Home. I was supposed to collect it, but they were helpful enough to send it out by courier when they heard about my accident." He stood and walked over to lift the container gently. "A few pounds. Dust thou art and dust returneth—"

"Don't forget the important part: 'Was not spoken of the

soul'." The fragile carapace around a person was as insignificant as the urn itself. Useful for its tenure but a temporary home for a spirit.

Mutt held the urn in his arms like a baby, but at last he replaced it and went over to the double tape deck. "I've played this over and over. His voice had deepened, but I recognized it. Like knowing him as a boy. I made a copy, so I can give yours back."

Belle swallowed a lump in her throat. "Play it for me. I haven't heard it since university. God knows why I kept it." But she knew.

He started the tape, and she was whisked back almost thirty years. First "Once in the Highlands", then "There But for You Go I." At "It's Almost Like Being in Love", she had to turn away. Almost. What does anyone know of love at seventeen? A trick of hormones aimed at procreation ASAP. Yet for the innocent she had been, a tear sneaked from her eye. "In thy valley, there'll be love." The final words faded back into the distance of time, where they belonged. Shangri-la was a place of dreams, no longer of this earth.

She could tell from Mutt's posture that he was close to exhaustion. The song ended, and he turned off the player. "Whatever fine points a serious investigator could have brought to bear on the forensics at the scene, everything's long gone now," she said.

One small ember of hope lingered in his voice. "Court TV is one of my favourite shows. Cold cases are often broken by someone snitching or a paper trail."

"And we're unlikely to find either, now or in 2025." Belle looked out the window. A lone houseboat lit by a lantern *Huckleberry Finn* style, putted down lake like a sedate dowager, except for the boom box sending "Love Me Tender" echoing across the still water. Ed and Hélène on a moonlight cruise. "The logical course is to ask Dave a few questions, but I don't even know his last name. Maybe Marj—"

"If the Ministry can't find him, how can you?" Mutt stifled a yawn. "Guess I should—"

"Sorry for rambling on. You need your rest. Anyway, we still have our mysterious Pepsi can. I'll show it to a friend of mine in chemistry at the university. What have we got to lose? And when Paul Straten gets back, we can follow up on the elk poisoning. That zoologist might be back, too."

"I wish I could do something." Double vertical lines creased above the bridge of Mutt's nose. "Bloody Words starts Thursday. I'll be gone for three days."

She nearly laughed out loud, despite the late hour and her growing sleepiness. Belle hadn't been up this long since the last election. "Bloody Words? What's that?"

"Canada's biggest mystery conference. Authors, fans, publishers, agents, the whole shebang. I reserved at my usual B&B on Jarvis months ago. And I can take time to see my father. He's doing better. This might be a breakthrough for us."

Belle touched his hand. Why was she tempted to make contact with him? She wasn't the touchy-feely type. "Are you strong enough? Is Megs taking you?"

"With her," she nearly added in high hopes.

He gave a tired laugh.

"The plane is fine. I'd bow out if I could, but I'm committed to speaking on a historical panel as well as the usual signings and manning a booth for the Crime Writers of Canada. Besides, that kind of activity energizes me, takes me outside myself."

"Tell you what. I want to read about Lucy's next adventure. You write, I'll investigate. Deal?"

When Belle returned home, Freya had long since been delivered by the DesRosiers, but she was unusually restless, rooing at the least noise, a plane, a passing vehicle, even a barking fox on night patrol in search of rabbit pie. Belle went into the computer room to check her answering machine. Two hang-ups, not that irregular, given the cold-calling machines that struck at six and disconnected after a few rings. She could still see Bartko's ugly, threatening face on her deck and in the courtroom. Better start locking her doors like Steve had suggested. With her luck, she'd probably lose her key, have to get a ladder to reach the roof, then leap the yawning abyss to her bedroom balcony.

After a quick shower, she rolled into the undulating waterbed, sailing on her favourite ocean liner to dreamland. Despite the hour and her long prayers including the quick and the dead back to age five, sleep avoided her like a terrified groom. Her grandfather had been obsessive-compulsive, by modern diagnosis, and she carried the genes, by now reduced harmlessly to closing a book on a "lucky" page that didn't have sevens or add up to thirteen. She was running through a scenario of being snowbound in a cosy cabin, heating beans on the wood stove, finally nodding off when the phone rang. Sitting up with a start, she grabbed the portable model on her night table. "Hello?" Seconds passed. "Hello?" She heard only the sound of heavy breathing, the absence of speech that struck a primal terror.

SEVENTEEN

"owardly bastard," she said, punching off the set with a vengeance. Then she flicked on the lights, put on her slippers, and stomped to the utility room in the basement. which contained the washer, dryer, small freezer, water heater, furnace and a host of handy cabinets plundered from the old cottage. Standing on a footstool, she stretched into the rafters for a black plastic bag with Uncle Harold's old twelve-gauge. She broke the gun and peered into the chambers. Empty, good citizen. Where were those shells? Ed had given her two last New Year's, when he'd fired his shotgun over the lake after she played "Auld Lang Syne" on her trumpet.

Upstairs in the china cabinet, she reached into the Toby jug of Merlin, who guarded her mother's seven Royal Doulton ladies, white elephants passed on to an unappreciative daughter. Her fingers found two cartridges. No one would find her defenceless again. She shook her fist Scarlett-style and went back upstairs to lock her doors for a change. Surely Joey's pals would tire of the harassment.

The next morning, Belle called a former client at Shield University, Athena Christakos. The sweet Greek lady with the best baklava in town taught basic chemistry to freshmen and was always perking by six.

"Sounds like you need a metallurgist more than a chemist," she said. "I'll be at the office all day until vacation starts next week. Drop it off here any time. If I'm not around, the secretary will take it." She paused and tried to muffle the phone, but Belle could still hear "Mira, leave your brother alone. If he doesn't want his yoghurt, that will be his problem when he's a bent old man at sixty."

With no access to a ski bag, minutes later Belle tucked the shotgun into the dog blanket in the van and left the yard. When she got to the office, Yoyo was arriving, a subdued Baron with his ears askew by her side. "Damn low air in a tire again. Happens all the time. Mom says I aim at every pothole in town."

"My road is a minefield, too. I even bought an air compressor. Try getting new valves installed."

Baron headed for the back room with a decidedly stiff gait. Tuned to canine conformation, Belle noticed it and frowned. "What's the matter with your boy? Did he hurt his leg?"

"Baron, come here. Show Belle your owee." The dog returned, lay down, and rolled over at Yoyo's hand signals. Belle gave her credit for taking time to train the large animal. His pink belly streaked with cream hairs led the eye to a decided absence of the masculine companions. Yoyo considered him with a mournful expression. "I finally did the deed. Petville Animal Hospital had a subsidized rate for the first five people to apply. But his poor empty purse. How tragic."

Never having had a male dog, Belle was unfamiliar with the finer points of the neutering process. "I don't understand. Was there some option?"

"Not unless I'd acted sooner. He is a very, very big boy. People turned their heads, especially in hot weather when his ballies dropped to stay cool." She wobbled her lip with a sigh. "They say it'll shrink."

An hour later, Belle took off for a walk over to Cedar Street then to Elgin to drop off ads at *Northern Life*. This seedy part of town included cheque-cashing outlets, a few scabrous bars, and alongside the railroad that bisected town in the least attractive spot, the huge new Farmer's Market, a glory of glass and metal designed as a year-round venue for the produce vendors that operated in tents during summer. Unfortunately, the higher rents were proving too rich for slim pockets, and many stalls were empty. She stopped at a Mexican food booth with a pleasant Chicano grandmother and picked up a double order of tamales.

The rich aroma of the spicy tomato/pork/corn roll-up was tantalizing her salivary glands when she saw a familiar figure emerge from a pawnshop and head toward her. The fugitive Dave? So he had stayed around town after all. After his theft at the Ministry, how paranoid would he be at her approach? Then again, how could he know that she'd heard about his crime?

"Dave! Over here!" she yelled, waving one arm, the other cuddling the package like a warm puppy.

He stopped and gave her a furtive stare. "I need to talk to you," she called, as a massive freight train with four locomotives blew its whistle and charged past, sending up clouds of dust and leaving the air perfumed with diesel fumes. Belle rubbed at her eyes, blinking.

When she looked up, she saw him on the run, heading down Elgin and turning sharply into an alley. She considered the delicious package. Swearing, she placed it on the doorstep of an abandoned shoe shop, probably some homeless person's sleeping spot. Running at top speed, dodging a few drifters lounging with paper bags outside May's Tavern, she reached the alley, then paused. At the end was an eight-foot chain-link fence and an overflowing dumpster. A street person rummaged through a discarded pizza box.

"Did you see a guy run past here?" She placed her hands on her knees and sucked back air.

The grizzled face had a crooked smile, several teeth missing, the rest rusty pegs. "Yeah, he went over like a pole vaulter. Got into that red truck. Want a boost?" In the distance, a Dodge Ram burned rubber and roared off. Running certainly indicated guilt. But as a thief, saboteur, or even a murderer?

"Thanks for your help." Belle passed him a toonie.

Returning to the doorway, she was dismayed to find her tamales gone. Some soul had good taste.

At four she drove down Paris, taking Ramsey Lake Road past Laurentian Hospital. Farther along, she turned into the Shield University complex, home to five thousand students and site of the province's new Medical School. At last the doctor-poor North could train its own. But would they stay?

Winding her way around campus, Belle parked at a meter near the Science Building. Stopping to admire the view of Lake Ramsey with its jewelled islands and monster houses, she saw a dragon boat team paddling in rhythm on the glassy surface.

On the first floor, in a cluttered office resembling a landfill, she found Athena, marking lab reports. How she found time to raise three children under twelve amazed Belle. Never one to fuss about clothes, she wore a grey jumper over a pair of tights and Birkenstock clogs. She looked up and stood to give Belle a hug. "The kids have grown six inches since I last saw you." On the wall were several photos of a birthday party.

Belle admired the sweet, candid shots. Like their beautiful mother, the children were modelling material, lucent light-olive skin from their Italian father, dark hair and laughing brown eyes with lustrous lashes. Examples of their crayon work were pinned on the bulletin boards.

"So let's see this legendary can," Athena said, holding out her hand. With the other, she brushed back a strand of streaked brown hair that had escaped from a leather ponytail clip.

Belle pulled it from the paper bag, holding it like the Holy Grail. "Careful, it's very eroded. Sharp pieces could cut you."

Athena paused, fingers pulled back. "Should we be concerned about fingerprints?"

"Too late now, but I don't think that's where the mystery lies. Even filled with cement, it would make a poor murder weapon."

With the delicacy of a scientist, Athena turned the can to catch the light from the floor-to-ceiling window. "Aluminum is a very sturdy metal. Doesn't rust like iron or steel. Out in the open, it can last for decades. Something's been at this."

"Been at?" Belle took a seat on a secretarial stool in front of a computer, rolling back and forth. "Not an animal—"

"No, something quite corrosive." Athena traced the faded metal, lacy in spots, with a feathered touch. "Clearly this has been in contact with an acid substance. Where was it found?"

Belle spread her hands. "That's the mystery. A friend of mine was working down in Burwash and points west. I can't guarantee that's where he found it, but it's an educated guess. And he kept it. That's the strange part."

"You have me intrigued. What did he say? Why is it so important to you?" Her pleasant manner showed concern, not annoyance.

With little time of her own, Athena penetrated to the core of the matter, a rare combination of empathy and logic. Belle decided to tell her about Gary and Mutt. One more therapist couldn't hurt.

"An old boyfriend of yours? I'm at a loss for words." She put a hand on her chest.

"I've taken enough wisecracks from everyone I've told. You wouldn't have recognized me at eighteen."

Carrying a report, a student appeared in the doorway, then pulled back, mumbling an apology. Belle felt guilty about taking up the woman's time. Imagine if someone barged into *her* office during peak hours. "Anyway, can you get me any more information on what caused the corrosion?"

Athena pointed out the door and across the hall where a sign on an office read, "Rick Cooper, Metallurgy". "Our man's usually here in the afternoons. One glance and he'll have an answer."

Fifteen minutes later, approaching her office, Belle saw a squat figure emerge, come down the steps with a walker and get into a waiting Neon, which chugged off. Was that Joey's mother or a local baba? Down the street was the Ukrainian Seniors Home, and the mobile ladies did regular walkabouts.

"Did a Mrs. Bartko stop by? I thought I recognized her," she asked Yoyo as she poured herself a cup of coffee. Ever since Megs had mentioned that specialty brew, she hadn't taken quite the usual pleasure in her daily cups. Missing Miriam more and more, she had started using her cohort's "Are We Having Fun Yet?" mug.

"Sure did, and I don't mind telling you that my grandma's Ukrainian comes in handy. *Vitayu.* Hello. *Dyakuyu.* Thank you. Chalk another one up for yours truly." Yoyo raised her arms in a double victory sign.

"So I guess she's selling her house. If Joey's going away for a long time, she'd be better off in a small apartment. And she probably wants the cash for a lawyer." Belle gave her credit for pride instead of a pump on the public purse. "But it's hard to believe that she chose this company after my problems with Joey."

Yoyo shrugged. "I don't think she made the connection. She asked for someone called Harold Palmer. He sold her the place decades ago."

Belle nodded as she pointed to a picture of a moustached, white-haired man with a fifty-pound muskie. "That's my uncle." Miss you, Pal Hal.

"My feet are killing me. It's this extra weight. I bet I've

gained fifteen pounds. That's about on course with Mom. You could hardly tell." Yoyo put Miriam's foot roller into action, savouring the sensation. "I told Mrs. B. that you'd want to give her place a once-over before settling on the asking price. She's not going to get a fortune over there on a side street, even with the recent renos she mentioned." Homes in the million-dollar range had been erected on MacClennan Drive along the hill overlooking the sheltered bay.

Belle grunted at the thought of those renos and their leftovers dumped in the bush. "Right, but you never want to own the most expensive house on the block."

Yoyo chortled. "What were you doing at the courthouse, by the way? Even the idea brings up bad memories and makes me nervous."

Belle squirmed in her chair, then explained her connection with Joey. "Can you can see why I want to keep a low profile?"

"Wow. Sounds like a dangerous man. Why not tell her to find another realtor?"

Belle listened to the siren call of the cash register and gave a dismissive gesture. "He's in jail, so he's not going to bother me. Why would I want to lose the commission? Not on your life." She neglected to mention the unsavoury friends. If she didn't think about them, maybe they would go away.

"What about *your* life? Even an idiot like that has connections, probably as nuts as he is. And he operated a meth lab? Sheesh." Yoyo aimed her finger like a pistol, cocked and dropped the thumb, and blew on the tip of the "gun".

"Don't worry about me. I have some..." Her words were drowned out by the roar of a motorcycle pushing decibels just shy of a jackhammer.

"What did you say?"

"I HAVE SOME PROTECTION IN THE VAN." The

211

noise outside dropped to zero halfway through her answer. With no clients around, she put her feet up on the desk, flicked a dog hair from the stretch jeans and unbuttoned her blazer.

Steve came around the corner from the bathroom, his voice a growl that would have done a cougar proud. "Did I hear 'protection' and 'in the van' in the same sentence? You better be talking about birth control."

EIGHTEEN

Belle tossed Yoyo an evil look and dropped her feet to the floor. "Why didn't you tell me Steve was here?"

"'Cause I know your priorities. Money first." Sticking out her tongue in a mischievous gesture, she rose, placing a hand on her back with an "oooo" in a classic pregnant pose. "No rest for the wicked. Gotta hit the bank for some deposits. Later, guys."

As the door closed, Steve arced a paper towel into the wastebasket and folded his arms. Round one was about to begin. She heard the gong. "What *do* you have in the van, or maybe I don't want to know. Tell me it's a hockey stick."

No time for charades. He was furious. Belle mumbled a few words, and he exploded, pacing back and forth like a caged man. "Are you crazy? It gets stolen, and then where would you be? Arming a nervous young punk to hold up a convenience store?"

"Okay, it's just..." When she started spinning her wheels, Belle knew she was in trouble. Why didn't she shut up until this blew over? She bit her lip and considered the ceiling. Was that a water spot or a ladybug?

"It's *just* about showing up at that hearing. Detective Burns told me he saw you scuttling out with Joey's buddies watching your stupid back."

"All right! It was a mistake. A stupid one. I'm stupid. Now I'm keeping a low profile." She didn't take issue with the scuttling, but it made her feel like a trilobite.

He gave the desk a pound that rattled her teeth, then added a glare that could scorch paint. "You couldn't do that if you changed into a garter snake. And as for the shotgun, it better be back in your rafters by supper, or I'll come get it myself."

"You wouldn't dare." Her heart beat a conga rhythm. Maybe he was right, but paternalism went only so far before her independence was compromised.

"The fine for an unlicensed firearm is two thousand dollars, and jail time in some cases. To use your own yardstick, take that to the bank."

Two thousand from the last commission. Already earmarked for the new sign. "I never said it was un—"

Then the door slammed, and she was alone. Except for Baron, snoring in the back room. Belle went to his side and stroked the soft fur, wiping unbidden moisture from her eye. She knew Steve's anger would flare out like a Canada Day sparkler, but this would take time. She didn't envy him, Janet on one side and her on the other. Scylla and Charybdis. Was she the whirlpool or the nymph?

Shaking herself back to action, Belle saw the Maki Cove literature, which she'd neglected to send to Rosaline. She put it into a large mailing envelope and searched the white pages. No Silliker. Unlisted? Or perhaps her husband preferred to get his calls at work or by cell. Addressing it to the Ministry offices by default, Belle added a note about arranging a tour for the mother. Then she wrote a postscript: *You might be interested to know that Dave Watson is still around. I saw him from a distance downtown.* Perhaps the police could do something with that information. With her luck, it would tailspin into another crisis like the one with Joey.

The next day, Belle met Athena for coffee. They were enjoying the doughnut of the month, a chocolate caramel variety. "All the fat in muffins, might as well enjoy one of these babies," Athena said, patting her stomach. "It's hard to get back into shape the older you get. When I think of the soccer I used to play..."

Belle accepted the bag with the can. "What did Rick say?"

"Lakes close to town that suffered in the acid-rain years had tons of cans like these, especially near the tailings ponds."

Belle searched her memory, recalling the geography on the new topo. "You mean like around Kelly Lake Road near Copper Cliff? My friend wasn't within seventy-five miles of there." Then she recalled that one of his studies had involved nickel content in fecal pellets of moose browsing near the core area. That might have been a few years ago. She couldn't recall the publishing date of the monograph. Ancient history? Yet he'd only been in the ministry office this summer. Had he found the can years ago on one of his trips and brought it with him? With the reason for the corrosion so obvious, why keep the object at all?

"Rick had another suggestion. What about an old mine back in the bush?"

Of course, Gary would be concerned about habitat if he'd found something dangerous, something toxic. Belle started making connections. The elk. Now the can. High acid content? "I'll check the topo, but offhand, I don't remember seeing any of those little crossed pick and axes used as a mine symbol. What about the arsenic idea?"

Athena beamed like a June sun on a sandy beach. "My own tests on a folded crease show arsenic residue."

Belle scratched her ear. She'd loathed every science course she'd been compelled to take. "Is arsenic a by-product of nickel smelting?"

Athena hmmed to herself. This wasn't her area of expertise. "From what I can recall from my distant studies, it's more a factor in gold mining."

"But INCO processes all kinds of trace metals. Platinum. Palladium."

"True. You need another opinion." She gave Belle the name of a mining and geology professor at Nickel City College.

On the way home later, Belle fell into a trance along Radar Road, hardly aware of making the turn up the airport hill until a gravel-hauler pulled out of the pit and forced her to brake. She'd promised Mutt that she'd make inquiries, but she could have used a second pair of legs. The elk, the missing water samples, now the can. Had they overlooked any other clue in Gary's last few weeks? He'd been such a solitary man, but that was what he'd loved about the job.

Approaching Mutt's, she saw him in the yard, filling the washer fluid reservoir in the Prius. He wore a crisp blue turtleneck over wheat jeans and slip-on hikers. Belle wondered about his future love life. Would he look actively for a partner or let life transport him where it would?

"Need a ride to the airport?" she asked, getting out of the van.

"Naw. Short-term parking's fine with me. Easier when I get back instead of taking a taxi."

She hadn't seen the Infiniti in the drive. "Megs?"

He grinned. "Seems she went to Vegas with her new boyfriend, Colin. He's a plastic surgeon."

"Kismet or what? I see discounts in her future." What would the woman try next?

"She seems pretty stuck on the guy. First time I've seen her this serious in a long time. But as for more surgery, she was told last time that her nose might collapse. Has to keep clearing it with Q-tips."

Belle gave an inward shudder as that memory clicked home. Then she told him what she had learned from Athena.

A shadow crossed his face. "Mining, eh? Gary and I took a trip to Yukon once to hike the Nahanni and heard some horror stories about contamination left behind at abandoned mines. By-products like arsenic and cyanide."

"I'm asking a specialist. When you get back, I'll have more information."

He nodded. "That Max Leaver I mentioned? He hadn't heard from Gary in years. Can't see why he'd lie at this point. He was quite upset."

Belle put a hand on Mutt's shoulder. "Take good care of yourself."

He took her hand, kissed it and made a mock bow. "Your wish is my command. And since I'll be in Toronto, can I bring you back anything?"

"Certainly no Kopi Luwak coffee. How about picking up a great bottle of wine at their big Vintages store by the waterfront? I'll go as high as...fifty dollars." Had she really said that? What were her feelings toward this man? Elementary psychology would probably say that she had transferred her affections from Gary to him, revisiting the mentality of her hot-blooded teenage years. Did he see her as ridiculous, or was he enjoying their friendship? As she watched him drive off with a wave, she was sorry she wasn't going along. She was beginning to feel like a schoolgirl, shoving work aside to play when they could have put their heads together about Gary's project. Would she ever know the truth?

The next day Belle had showings at the far reaches of town, from Chelmsford to Onaping all the way down to Lively. This was the best week yet for the business, a rising curve that usually peaked in mid-July. She was contemplating giving Yoyo a raise, a generous part of her mind duelling with the usual pesky scruples about finance. The woman would probably be gone in a few weeks. Why not toss a few more dollars her way? Belle thought of Coco's macular degeneration.

When she came in to drop off a load of paperwork just before five, she passed a crowd on its way out of the office, a happy sight. Yoyo was copying information from a couple from Windsor who had taken teaching jobs at Nickel City College. A wave of recent baby boomer retirements had thinned the ranks. Belle sat them down, glancing at the coffee machine. Nearly empty. "I used to be a teacher," she said to break the ice. "What are your subjects?"

Judy Johnson said, "I'm in math. Ted is in psychology."

Good choices, she thought. One was cut and dried, or so she imagined. And, unlike English, no one ever said that they hated psychology. That would be disliking yourself.

After she'd shown them pictures and data about two choice properties on Atlee Street, a stone's throw from the college, she pencilled in a visit on Monday. As they left, she turned to Yoyo, who was cracking open a container of chocolate milk. "Busy, I take it?"

"It was a mob scene. People coming and going. Half an hour ago, there must have been a dozen at once. Mrs. Bartko came in again. Says her neighbour is going to give the outside a coat of paint this weekend. She didn't look so good, poor lady. Very short of breath. An aunt of mine—"

Why did women love to gab about health concerns? You got old, you got sick, you died. Why dwell on it? Belle checked her watch and made a Papal blessing. "Ten to five. I declare a holiday. Go forth and multiply."

"One will be totally enough." Yoyo broke into a wave of laughter. "You're getting soft, boss. On the other hand, you know I'll take some of this home." She fluttered a pile of papers on the desk.

Belle yawned. "I didn't get my portion of coffee today with all those showings. Want the last of the pot?"

"No way. I've been having some reflux lately. Had to lay off. Another perk—get it?—of approaching motherhood." Yoyo pressed her breastbone and gave a tiny burp. "'Scuse me."

Belle smiled. Yoyo was fun to have around, but a little went a long way. She appreciated Miriam's steady, no-nonsense approach to the job. Pouring herself the black dregs, swirling it to cool, she gulped it down too fast, nearly burning her mouth. Usually Yoyo made great coffee, but this must have been sitting for hours. It was faintly bitter, too, like espresso. She finished it as her lazy lot, then sat down and gave her agenda a quick scan.

Yoyo returned from the bathroom, where she'd scoured the coffee pot. Walking over to Belle's desk, she tapped her plaid watch. "One minute after five. Got your pound of flesh after all. So you'll lock up?"

"Nope, all through." Closing her daybook, Belle stood abruptly, then reached out a hand toward the desk as the room tilted like the Whirlygig at Sunnyside Amusement Park.

"You okay?" Yoyo asked, grabbing her arm. "Was your leg asleep or something? I love that phrase. Sounds like it has a mind of its own."

Shaking her head, Belle sat back down. "Just a bit...dizzy. Happens sometimes when I stand up too suddenly, or I've been travelling at a high speed and stop to get out of the van." She had always moved fast, a dervish valuing velocity over perfection. Was this a warning? When had her last check-up been?

Yoyo regarded her with an analytical eye. "How old are you, anyway, if I might ask?"

Mind reader? Belle flushed slightly. Not that she cared, but every woman had a kernel of vanity, especially when confronted by a younger specimen. "Somewhere between forty-five and death," she replied, paraphrasing a line from *Auntie Mame*.

Yoyo's brow wrinkled, and she raised a grim, warning finger. "Aha. Sounds like high blood pressure. My mom had spells like that, but she's on metoprosomething now. Has the readings of a two-year-old. Don't be stubborn about needing medication. That's called denial."

"It wasn't a 'spell'. You sound like I'm in my dotage. And besides, hypertension doesn't run in my family until seventy-five." She blinked a few times, then spread her hands. "I'm fine now. Really. A splash of cold water will wake me up. And Yoyo..." The other woman set her expression to neutral, as if not knowing what to expect. "Thanks for your concern. I mean it."

A few minutes later, still wet around the ears, Belle got into the van, and driving with extra prudence, pulled into the street and headed for the Kingsway. Yoyo was a decent sort, old indiscretions aside. With this latest rush of business, why not toss a few hundred dollars her way? Profit-sharing was a motivator, even for the short term. And it was possible that she might need her services again. Losing Miriam to Jack was unthinkable, but it could happen. Romance did that to people. Just because Belle had chosen a career over a relationship didn't mean everyone did.

Traffic was exceptionally heavy, and she stuck to the right lane, despite the curbside potholes that gave ball-joint manufacturers and alignment shops happy faces. The dizziness was gone, but she still felt lightheaded. What had she had for lunch? A couple of cheese-and-cracker snacks from Mike's Mart. And the cherry fritter, Tim's biggest doughnut, had probably sent her blood readings into toxic overload.

At least the weekend was here, and she'd be able to broil a steak, relax on the deck, soak up a few rays. Not too many, with her reddish hair and fair complexion, like her father. She blew out a disgusted breath. Everything was bad for you lately. She watched traffic wing off like colourful bats into consecutive fast-food caves, Harvey's, Wendy's, McDonald's, the local Deluxe Hamburgers that had its hardcore fans and sold luscious gravy to go with fries and a chicken sandwich cut on-site from the bone. Somehow the thoughts made her nauseous, a rare condition. Too much stomach acid from the coffee? What a person got away with at twenty, she paid for down the road. Then as Belle reminded herself to merge left at Falconbridge Road, a dangerous construction bottleneck, she nearly sideswiped a small vehicle in her blind spot. Its strident horn shook her back to reality. One of those Smart Cars? "Get a crash test, you dummy!" she yelled out the window.

As she passed OK Tire, then the defunct White Rose horticultural complex, she turned on the air conditioner. The van was warm, hot sun pouring like pernicious lava through the shaded windows. She felt sleep-deprived, though she knew that wasn't the case. Should she pull into the IDA parking lot and take a nap? Maybe Yoyo was right. Carlo the pharmacist gave free blood pressure tests. What was the matter with her? Surely she could hang on another twenty minutes. Maybe she'd had a stroke. What a ridiculous thought, but typical of a hypochondriac. She tried a facial test, smiling at both corners of her mouth.

Cruising through Garson, she found herself fixated on a large man in a motorized wheelchair navigating the sidewalks at a fast clip. Should she get her father one? When the concrete ran out, the man switched to the road, a Canadian flag waving from a six-foot fibreglass antenna. Then again, if her father putted out the side door when a resident deactivated the alarm, she didn't want to imagine the consequences. He might drive down the middle of the road looking for a barbershop on Yonge Street. Suddenly she was coming up fast at traffic waiting at a light. Belle jammed on the brakes, nearly plowing into the bumper of a truck. As her tires screeched, the driver gave her a scowl through the rear view mirror and an Italian salute out the window. How rude. Belle shook her head. Some of the signs seemed slightly blurry, as if she needed new glasses. Wouldn't that be a nice bite into her bank account?

As she left the final light, she rolled down the window to clear her head and speeded up, letting the wind rush through her hair. Who cared about the sixty kilometre per hour speed limit through the short, residential area? Police never patrolled it anyway. A strange euphoria was coming over her, though a sheen of sweat glazed her brow. Why had she been so worried about Mutt? He was off to Toronto, nearly fully recovered. Business was good, and Miriam would soon be back. She'd give Yoyo a bonus. How her eyes would shine at two thousand, no, three. Shoving in one of her homemade tapes, she started singing "Money, Money, Money" from *Cabaret*, banging her fists on the steering column in rhythm. A yellow helicopter buzzed overhead, heading for the Ministry pad to join the army of water bombers. Feeling grateful, she gave them all a welcoming wave. "Hello, boys...and girls. You stand on guard for me." In her exultation, the seatbelt seemed confining. Stupid invention. What had people done before it had been invented? She snapped it free and took a deep, liberating breath.

Then she was heading around a sharp curve, where someone had built a descanso in memory of a traffic victim. A pile of stones and plastic daffodils on the barren ground. The banking was wicked, and the cracked and leaning wooden guard posts looked like neglected teeth ready to snap at her. With the concentration of playing a video game, her tongue poking out the corner of her mouth, she tried to steer away from the yellow line as an approaching pick-up pulling a wider RV came whisper-close to her side mirror. Idiot. He should be jailed, pulling a big tin can like that at rush hour. A power surge came over her, and she felt like she could wrestle tigers. Her foot pushed to the floor, and her head rolled back. This baby could fly. Vans were no sissies.

How odd that she hadn't reached her road yet. Too much daydreaming. Snap out of it, girl. Grrrrl. That's what Yoyo would say. Yet nothing looked familiar any more, as if she were in a different country. She blinked and swallowed. Her throat was dry from that wretched coffee.

Ave atque vale. Edgewater Road on her left. The mailbox pavilion was gone, but that didn't fool her. Someone always slammed into it on black ice once a year. How would she get her mail now, though? The authorities would never spring for home delivery. And what was that sofa doing in the middle of the field? More dumping? She continued driving, pleased that the road was smoother than usual. Usually she navigated a Kosovo minefield. Had a regional truck arrived with a load of asphalt to patch the potholes? About time.

Where were the houses? And had she already passed the swamp and the new mine complex on the hill, towering head frames clad in Wedgwood blue and lit up at night like Coney Island? Despite her elation, a primitive urge deep inside sensed that something was wrong. Then the van began bucking and lurching like a rodeo horse. If only she could find her driveway, anyone's driveway.

Trees rushed by, closer and closer, their branches scraping her windshield. One axle ground on a rock. Then a miracle happened. Home at last, she spun the wheel and took a right turn into her yard, searching for her Horny and Corny sign.

The van soared over a hill, plunged down an embankment and stopped. As her head hit the padding, the front and side air bags deployed with a whomp.

Dazed and frightened, Belle began to moan. Fumbling with the ghostly air bags, she pushed against the door and fell out onto the ground, confused at the sand. Her parking lot had gravel. Was she on the beach? Had the retaining wall stopped the van? *On the Beach*. Deborah Kerr rolling with Burt Lancaster as waves rushed over their bodies. No, that was, that was...From Here to Maternity. If her body wasn't working, couldn't her mind take up the slack? If she had to crawl up to the deck, she would. Mother would know what was wrong, put her to bed, bring chicken soup and make her well. On her hands and knees she inched forward, reaching a patch of greenery under a copse of dwarfish birch and poplar. Her senses were at the same time sharpened and dulled, like a wide-awake drunk. Small rocks picked at her slacks, wearing holes in the knees, but she felt nothing. A good sign, or was it? The canopy of sibilant leaves whispered endearments, the waning sunlight blinking through like a thousand diamonds. From high above, three ragtag ravens chortled at her like a biker gang, while an effete chorus of King's College warblers spilled liquid tunes deep in the bush. She was surrounded by sound. It reminded her of the glory days of Dolby in the grand old theatres, but her ears were aching.

Farther and farther she crawled, swallowing acid at the back of her mouth. It was going to be a hot evening. The air conditioner in her bedroom would go on for the first time all year. Not all night, though. Too expensive. Before her, she saw blueberries nodding on their stalks. Weeks early. She extended her hand and plucked one. A singleton, but huge. Giving it a nibble, she spit it out, tasteless and foamy. Not a blueberry. A

Clintonia, blue-bead lily. Was it poisonous? Freya liked to munch them. She pressed her head against a soft clump of sphagnum moss dotted with the British-soldier cup lichens.

At last she was out of the blinding light, lying in a shady spot. She rubbed her eyes as she imagined the sounds of a brook. Babbling, like brooks always did. The water would be cool and tangy with the flavours of the woodland meeting the Cambrian Shield, a peat and granite martini. A real "dirty" martini, not with olive juice like Gary had suggested. She urged herself onto her elbows and crawled forward, blocked by a mossy log long fallen. With a painful groan, she dragged on. The lower grounds were wetter as she continued toward the creek by sound alone. Everything was as blurry as an Impressionist painting. She could almost taste the pure water trickling down her throat. That was all she needed. A drink. She had grown dehydrated. Everyone knew that could cause confusion. Her hands scrabbled along the forest floor like ragged claws. At the creek's edge, she met the cool, green overlapping mysteries of liverworts with their scaly lobes and umbrella-like stalked fruiting body. No fragrance when crushed, but what a texture. They were sending her messages, or was someone talking? Slowly she reached toward the rippling water with her cupped palm. It seemed to be bleeding.

"Stop!" Strong, tiny hands grabbed her shoulders. The goblins had found her.

NINETEEN

Yoyo knelt beside Belle and shook her vigorously. "Jesus. Here you are. What's the matter? Did you get dizzy again? I've been following you ever since you nearly cut that guy off on the Kingsway. Why did you keep driving? And this is a fine time to go on a hike in the bush."

Belle couldn't quite bring Yoyo's face into focus. It was distorting like a cartoon of a chipmunk wearing a Veronica Lake wig. Looking at only one eye was disorienting. She'd never realized how very blue Yoyo's were, like her favourite cobalt crayon.

"Can you hear me?" The woman's voice was rising in fear.

"I need...water. It's right here. Then sleep. I must be overtired."

"Don't drink that water. You don't know where it's been. I have some in the car."

Why was Yoyo being so mean? Pure spring water was the best kind. Rosaline had told her that. Yoyo returned with a bottle, opened it, and handed it to Belle, who swilled it. Mouthfuls dribbled down her chin onto her turtleneck. The fabric was scored by itchy leaf litter and twigs. Belle brushed at it half-heartedly. "That's good. Thanks. Now I have to take a nap. Just a short one." She pillowed her head in her hands and closed her sore eyes.

Yoyo pulled on her arms. "No way. I didn't follow you to hell and back to leave you for buzzard bait. Get up, and let's go to my car. Your van needs a tow."

"Please. I'll be fine in the morning. Where's my blanket?"

"It's thirty-two degrees, a heat wave. You don't need one. But I don't like the look of that sky."

Belle shielded her eyes and tried to look up. Dark clouds were gathering, and the wind was rising. A crash of thunder made her flinch, but she still couldn't muster the will to stand. Yoyo returned with another bottle, which she splashed on Belle's face.

"Stop that! You're drowning me." She shook her head like a wet dog and ran a hand through her hair. The ground was suddenly hard, and a dull pain was announcing itself in her hands, arms and down her legs.

Yoyo kept prodding Belle until she rose shakily, leaning on the younger woman. Slowly they made their way to the car as hailstones pelted the roof and bounced off the windshield. Some were as large as ping-pong balls. "What timing!" Yoyo yelled amid the deafening clamour. "If that isn't all my poor car needs."

Finally they reached the door. "Watch your head. You put this car on, instead of getting into it. I was a swinging babe, not a mother-to-be, when I bought it." She jack-knifed Belle into the passenger seat, belted her up with a grunt, went back around and started the vehicle. It squealed like a young girl. "Fan belt," Yoyo said. "She'll settle down." Then she thought for a minute. "We'll need your health card. Your wallet's in the van?"

Things were starting to make sense. And it didn't look good. "In the compartment next to the driver's seat."

The storm passed as quickly as it had arrived, leaving the atmosphere as sultry and oppressive as a night in a bayou. Yoyo rolled down her window as they drove off. "Air conditioner's shot."

Belle was drifting when they reached the main highway.

She could hear Yoyo talking into a cell phone. "It's a dirt road to the west about a mile past the airport. There's an old sofa twenty feet away in the bush. Follow the tire tracks in the sand for about ten minutes until you come to the van just over a rise on the right. Take it to Robinson Automotive." She rang off. "That's your mechanic, right?"

Belle heard only a few words. "They're repairing it in my yard? What service. How did you—"

"It's not in your yard." Yoyo spoke quietly and evenly, as if to a fretting child or a senile elder. "Somehow, drugs got into your system. From what I saw and heard at the clubs a few years ago, I suspect the date rape drug. I never can pronounce it."

"That's impossible. I haven't been on a date, and it's obvious I haven't been raped. I would know." Belle began to snore, and when she awoke, she was being placed on a gurney and wheeled into Emerg. Yoyo stayed by her side, giving particulars to the admitting nurse. Too tired to talk, Belle could only whimper when lights were shone into her eyes, answering questions with monotones. With her condition in question, she was fast-tracked through triage.

After an hour, as she lay in a curtained cubicle, Dr. Evelyn Easton, tall as an Amazon, with a long silvery blonde braid down her back, said to Yoyo, "From her symptoms, you were right about the Rohypnol, I suspect. The toxicity results take longer than the normal scans. Whatever's in her system, she's stable now and can go home. Her blood pressure's back to normal."

"How long before the drug wears off completely?"

"The effects start within half an hour, peak in two, and take six to eight to disappear. We found no alcohol in her blood, which is a good thing, because the interaction can be fatal."

"That stuff shouldn't be legal."

"It's not legal in Canada, but it's sold in Europe as a sedative.

The hypnotic effect is a bonus for abusers. At five bucks a pill, a cheap high. Tasteless, odourless and very soluble. Dizziness, confusion, visual disturbances, hallucinations. She's lucky you came along." She checked Belle's pulse again for good measure.

Belle felt better as she tried to focus on the doctor. Evelyn was a crack ER physician who'd attended both her father and Miriam. "I'm great, really. And I can go home?"

"Of course, but not alone."

Somehow Belle found herself unable to protest. Yoyo spoke in a whisper Belle strained to hear. "And the long-term effects?"

Evelyn packed up her pen and chart. "Memory impairment. Depends on the dose."

As she left, an officer poked his head into the cubicle and cleared his throat. A native man of about thirty, hair in a ponytail behind a square and honest face. Belle felt her eyes closing again. How humiliating to depend on others. But at least she was safe.

"Got a report of a Rohypnol poisoning from the admitting nurse. This the lady?" Officer Ray Redfern introduced himself to Yoyo.

"She's sleeping it off, so to speak. If she comes to, I can't guarantee anything will make sense." Yoyo explained the incident, from the office to the crash landing in the bush. "She was out all day on business, but she was fine just before five. The last thing she did before leaving was finish the dregs in our coffee pot. She got dizzy for a minute, but that passed. Honest, I'd never have let her leave if I'd suspected anything was wrong. Good thing I took off down the Kingsway to hit Costco before going home. Same way she was headed."

"She didn't stop anywhere else?"

"I was behind her all the way, except for when my car

stalled in a sand pit as she made the turn onto that bush road. Mom always said to carry a shovel."

"So someone spiked the coffee pot?"

"If they did, it was after I had my last cup around three." Yoyo perched her butt on the edge of the gurney. "I'd never have noticed. We had a mob scene for a couple of hours. People coming and going. I was a one-man band."

"Do you have the names in your records? Can you coordinate the times?"

She firmed up her lips. "I think so. Most of them. Maybe some people left and intended to return at a less crowded time."

"How about the pot? Any residue? I can send a unit out for prints."

Yoyo's shoulders sagged. "Cleaned and polished, along with Belle's cup. The one day I decide to play Martha."

The officer opened another page in his notebook. "We get several roofie calls a year, usually in a date-rape circumstance. This is very unusual and could be classed as assault with deadly intent. The victim was driving? She could have killed half a dozen people. Why would anyone do this to her? Does she have enemies? An estranged husband or boyfriend?"

A giggle came from Yoyo. "Whoa. Wait a minute. I can't..."

Belle had been listening to the conversation, fading in and out, too tired to join in until the word "enemies". Grunting, she forced herself to sit up and gather the ruins of the hospital gown around her. The paper slippers fell to the floor. "Joey Bartko. He's in custody, but check out his friends. Call Steve Davis."

"You know Detective Davis, do you? He's in Virginia at Quantico for a training project. Gone for another week."

"What about Bartko's mother?" Yoyo asked, her eyes widening.

She'd been in the office that day. Maybe he'd told her that it was a prank, like the old laxative ploys. What would a seventy-year-old woman know about the sedative-hypnotic Rohypnol? It might as well be Love Potion #9. Sitting up as she became more alert, Belle told the officer what had happened.

"We'll send someone out to talk to her," he said.

After the officer left, Yoyo said, "You're welcome to stay at my place tonight if you want, but what about Freya?"

Dangling her legs over the edge of the padded table, feeling for a footstool, Belle squeezed her eyes. "Poor girl. I remember leaving her outside. Where's your cell? And where are my clothes?"

Wheeled back downstairs and taken to the door, Belle checked in with Hélène as Yoyo took a hike to the far end of the jammed lot to get the car. She gave a taxi the finger as she wove her way through the traffic clogging the front portico and yelled, "Learn to read off a beer box? The signs say no parking and no *stopping*, buddy."

Resting on a bench, Belle smelled the tangy aroma of a pizza being ferried through the doors. If her appetite was coming back, she must be improving. She gave the particulars to Hélène. "I can't ask her to drive me all the way home, so maybe I'll take a taxi."

"A taxi? They charge forty dollars to come out here. That would give you a heart attack." Hélène's voice assumed a soothing tone used by seasoned mothers. "We're on our way. Give Dad an excuse to stop making love to the refrigerator. He's been eying the beef roll for a sandwich. And how about you? It's nearly nine, and I'll bet you haven't eaten."

Yoyo drove up and got out to open the door for her passenger. Belle felt all eyes on her, being waited on by a pregnant woman. She explained about the DesRosiers. Yoyo looked around as a queue of walking wounded wheeled their IVs along the sidewalk two hundred feet to the smoking hut for pariahs. "I don't like to leave you here—"

"It's a hospital," Belle said with a laugh.

"Okay. If you're sure about your friends. You know my number. But don't stay alone tonight. The doc said it wasn't safe." With a wave, she pulled out.

Belle weighed the possibilities of privacy vs. security. She'd be all right alone, or would she? Bits and pieces of the past few hours were beginning to pop up like annoying advertisements on a computer screen. Only now did she perceive her good fortune. With half an hour to go, she picked up an abandoned copy of the *Sudbury Star*. An emergency evacuation from the Kashechewan First Nations Reserve on James Bay had brought over two hundred residents to town. They'd stay until their water system got a temporary patch, if not a permanent fix. Officials were scrambling to arrange for hotels and motels. Water again. Could that trickle down a trail to the solution to Gary's death?

An hour later, ensconced in a fuzzy blanket on the couch, a tray with a bowl of homemade minestrone and a rye roll filled with spicy Italian beef in front of her, Belle thought about Yoyo as she munched. It was not an exaggeration to say that the woman had rescued her from great harm. She could have been crawling around the bush all night until she recovered her senses. She might have plunged down a ravine and drowned in one of the steep-sided kettle lakes that dotted the area. Wasn't there some idea about a bonus? Now it would look like she was paying Yoyo off for saving her life. And the van. Was it salvageable? Another rental charge.

Ed and Hélène were watching *One Hundred Objects Left Inside the Body After Operations*. Wincing at the sight of a fourteen-inch retractor, Belle excused herself. At least Hélène hadn't pummelled her after learning the basics, just fixed her with an eagle eye and left her beak closed. For the time being.

Despite the swaybacked bed and the birdcall clock in the

kitchen, she slept the sleep of the living dead in their spare room, Freya on the floor beside her. Several times she woke in the night and nearly panicked, had it not been for the familiar snuffling sound. Images of dark figures in the bush. Trolls under a bridge. Gary falling from a canoe, hitting his head. Then she saw his form underwater, his golden hair billowing like a medieval saint's halo, bubbles spilling from his mouth, his glazed eyes staring like maraschino cherries, weeds trailing his clothes like a winding sheet. Something was pulling at her. Hélène's nightie. Why did women wear these things? Every time she rolled over, it bound her like a mummy. Sitting up, her heart throbbing, she clapped a hand over her mouth to suppress a scream. *Get a grip. The nightmare is over.* Then she reached for the dog, felt her steady breathing. Unable to get back to sleep, she climbed out of bed, taking the comforter, and spooned next to Freya, one arm around the deep shepherd chest, their hearts beating as one.

Sun was streaming in the window when Belle awoke to a polite knock. "Brekkie. Hope you didn't check your appetite at the door." Hélène peeked in, an oversized mug of coffee in her hand. A wee frown crossed her pleasant face as she saw the empty bed. "What are you doing on the floor? That's our best mattress."

Belle yawned and stretched, burying her face in Freya's thick ruff. "Sometimes a friend is the best mattress."

She let the dog out into the yard with Rusty and went to the bathroom for a splash in the sink. The mirror reflected someone not too much the worse for wear, clean, her abrasions sprayed with some magic orange instant bandage. Her face bore a few scratches on the chin, and despite the quick shower last night, one cedar shred hid in her ear. The bug bites were bothering her, and the skin was swollen near her eye where several had feasted. Back in the bedroom, she changed to a borrowed sweatshirt and sweatpants from the DesRosiers' trip to Graceland.

Hélène sat her down at the kitchen table, putting a juice in her hand and refilling her mug. "No one likes to go straight from bed to a big meal, so wake up a bit. And tell me what's been going on."

From the clanks by the dock, Ed was outside fiddling with their party barge for a huge Canada Day bash. Belle gave a large sigh and gulped the juice, still dehydrated, and reached for the carton. The label promised that the product cleaned out arterial plaque. What was in it, drain cleaner? "First I reported some dumping near Skead. Then a high school boyfriend of mine..."

Hélène listened to Belle with a serious expression, leaving only to check on an egg-and-cheese casserole in the oven. Its savoury aroma filled the kitchen. "I've met Sophia Bartko at St. Bernardine's. That lady arranges the altar flowers. She'd never have anything to do with this. Sounds like teenagers. A person with access to that awful drug."

"I could have been killed and taken a few people with me." Belle nibbled on the toast. "Someone in the office that afternoon is responsible. The place was mobbed. Yoyo is checking her records."

"But how does all this fit in with your friend's drowning?"

"I'm not sure. The robbery followed, then Mutt's so-called accident. Dave disappearing. The missing notebooks. I was thinking about some kind of a cover-up." She wiped her mouth and shrugged. "But this attack on me. It could be connected with Joey and his friends. He admitted to cutting my brake lines."

"This is getting dangerous. Maybe you should...lie low? You could stay here."

Belle struggled to keep annoyance from her face. Hélène meant well, but hiding was no solution. "You're kind to offer, but I can't do that. I have a business to run." She rubbed at her bug bites, then stopped. "And I need to look around the area where Gary had his base camp."

"Where was that?"

"Burwash area." Belle struggled to recall her upcoming appointments. When could she get away?

Hélène ripped into a pound of turkey bacon and arranged it to sizzle in the pan while she popped more slices of brown bread into a supersized toaster. "That's strange. Did Dad tell you about his relative Mike? He accidentally shot himself while hunting there years ago."

"He did tell me. I forgot all about it." Belle nodded to herself, nosing the bacon smells with the boldness of a bear. Didn't someone else mention a disappearance or death in that area? Cyril, the wood man? Had the place been a Bermuda Triangle, or was she jumping to conclusions? People died in the bush all the time. But Gary made three, even over many years. She'd give the area a once-over, and for good measure, take some water samples from Bump Lake and other places on the connecting courses. But her canoe was too heavy on portages. It was one thing to slide it up and down from the lawn to the lake and another to hoist the big Grumman over her head for a couple of hundred yards tiptoeing through a boulder garden until she broke her leg. How could she...? Then outside she saw the inflatable double kayak that the DesRosiers had bought last summer for their teenaged grandchildren. It looked light and manageable.

"You're awfully quiet. That usually means you're thinking. And that means trouble." Hélène gestured with the spatula, then turned to knock on the window to call Ed in.

Belle sneaked a piece of bacon, chewing with approval. "May I borrow your kayak? Just for a day."

"No problem. But what do you..." She gave Belle a sideways glance of assessment. "You're not going to do anything—"

"I'm thinking of getting one for those water-access-only camps. Just a test drive." Then she rapped her temple and gave a bitter laugh. "I forgot about the van. When I get home, I should call—"

"Uh, about home. There is something we didn't tell you."

Belle stood at attention, one hand on her chest and her breakfast stuck in her throat. "My house? Is it..." With her luck, it had been vandalized or burned to the ground.

Hélène patted her arm, a reassuring smile wreathing her mouth. "No, it's fine. But your garden isn't. That damn storm rushed down the road like a tornado. Left piles of hail like snow. It stopped after your house, so we lucked out."

Belle blew out a long breath. She'd been dozing in their SUV all the way back. It was kinder of them to keep the news to themselves until she'd had a good sleep. After all, at this early stage, a garden was no more than a dab of sweat and a wish. "There's always next year."

TWENTY

The next day, Belle was hoeing under the ruins of her garden. Small piles of hail still dotted the ground with white. Only the sturdy rosemary had survived the assault. Rosemary for remembrance. But which memory of Gary did she prefer? The dream or the reality? What fool had said that ignorance was bliss? She plucked a thick leaf of the evergreen and crushed it to enjoy the lemony herbal flavour.

The portable phone in her sweatshirt pouch rang. It was Officer Redfern. "Thanks to the resident snitch, we ran a check on Joey's pals, Minor, Szabo and Flack. Traced Szabo's vehicle to the U.S. border yesterday down at Kingston, so they're out of the area. We'll keep tabs on them when they re-cross. They'll definitely be stopped for a search. They're not headed for Disney World, so we'll probably find something to send them to our free hotel for a few years. Lizards like that should learn to keep their heads low."

A muscle twitched in Belle's temple, and slang from cop movies popped into her mouth like a peppermint. "I still don't *like* them for drugging my coffee. My assistant would have noticed thugs like that. Did anyone talk to Mrs. Bartko?"

She heard a slow sigh. "Had a massive coronary last night. She's unable to be interviewed until her condition stabilizes. But we canvassed the area. Her neighbours say that the lady's a churchgoer, volunteers to take care of the elderly in Skead."

"That's what they said about Lizzie Borden."

"Sounds familiar. She a local?"

By Monday, life was back to normal. Robinson had opened his garage on Sunday to replace the struts on the van and polish out the scratches. Like Belle, it wasn't much the worse for wear. With her thousand dollar deductible to keep rates low, she swallowed the bitter pill like the dregs of the coffee. Making a claim with CAA might have elicited questions about why she was dune jumping in the bush.

As a singular bright economic spot, Rosaline Silliker had reconnected, and Belle had arranged to give her mother a tour of the Maki Cove model condo. She picked the old lady up at her home on Roxborough Drive. It was a lovely tan brick house with gingerbread trim, a whimsical fairy tale for stolid Sudbury. Plots of cheery multi-coloured zinnias were edged with white alyssum. Expensive baskets hung by the quaint rounded door and on wrought-iron stands on the manicured grass. Belle knew the perfect buyer, a lawyer. "What a wonderful home," she said, as she helped the woman into the van.

"I'll be sorry to see it go, but it's just my husband and I now. The children have been on their own for longer than I'd like to confess."

Eileen Gable, a well-preserved seventy-five, had once been taller than Belle was now, but time and osteoporosis had taken a toll. Her dowager hump reminded Belle of Terry Palmer and the reason for calcium-fortified orange juice. Eileen wore a tailored grey dress with a lace collar, low-heeled spectator pumps, and a broad straw sun hat. She set her purse on the floor.

Mrs. Gable was inclined to chat, nodding her powdered pink chickadee face, her crinkled eyes merry behind jewel-winged trifocals. As the family saga unfolded, Belle learned that the lady's father, Marshall Mincore, had prospected in the

Sudbury area, operating several small mines. "Of course that was before you were born, young lady. Twenties and Thirties. Filthy time with those roasting beds. Not like now. I was an only child, so my husband Robert carried on the business, and Gable Minerals was born. Long after the Old Batty by then, though."

Belle recalled overhearing Rosaline at the hospital. If Robert died, Eileen's plans might change. And what was the Old Batty? A nickname for her father?

Mrs. Gable tapped her bird-like chest. "Now Robert's not doing so well. Heart. Eighty years of bacon and eggs has its price. I prefer oatmeal. My Scottish grandmother lived to be ninety-five."

"Sorry to hear about your husband. And is Gable Minerals still in operation?" Belle asked. It didn't hurt to sound interested.

"Thriving, as a matter of fact. My son Barry is in charge. We have a mine in Manitouwadge. That's over by Marathon, past Wawa. Lovely little houses for the workers, a school and hospital." She began chuckling to herself. "Father had an old joke about going up by train and coming back by..."

Belle had heard that chestnut a thousand times, but she laughed as if it were fresh from *Saturday Night Live*. So that accounted for the family wealth. It sure didn't come from Rosaline's husband's job as a minister. He was no televangelist.

Mrs. Gable kept chatting as they drove, her hands fluttering in her lap like pale butterflies. "Barry's also running for MPP. Conservative, of course. That party's the best steward of our resources. With Rosaline working in the Ministry, our family does its part."

In love with the show model of the condo, Mrs. Gable gave Belle a cheque for thirty thousand dollars, ten per cent of the purchase price. She could move in by September. Easy as pie, Belle thought, driving back to the office with the paperwork to list the Roxborough home. A twofer, the realtor's dream.

Dancing an impromptu soft-shoe, she sang out, "Guess what? We're in the mon—" Then she did a double-take. Miriam was sitting in her chair, grinning."You look familiar. Do you come here often?" Belle asked, going over to give her a hug. Miriam had quite the tan, as if she and the recovering Jack had enjoyed themselves outdoors.

Miriam threw up her hands. "The darn poodle got me kicked out. A dog moved into the house next to the apartment, and she started shrieking whenever she saw it from the window."

The pitch of that mini-monster could shatter plate glass at a hundred paces. "So you're back for good?" Belle dared not ask the fatal question. She felt her blood pressure quiver.

"I'd better be, because I was a very *bad* girl up North. Nearly gave Jack a relapse." Chuckling, Miriam began to fumble under the desk. "Where is that foot roller? And why is my mug on your desk?"

As Belle passed over the mug, Yoyo came out of the back room, her small personals case under her arm and a woeful look on her face. "Guess that's it. Except for one thing." She pulled a book from her purse and handed it to Belle.

"Eats, Shoots, and Leaves?" Belle considered the panda on the cover and the offending comma. "Thanks. This looks hilarious."

"Figured you could use some laughs around here now that I'm gone." Yoyo tossed Miriam a moue and received a raised eyebrow.

Belle said, "You're entitled to some advance notice. How about...your salary to the end of the month? Come on Friday, and I'll have it." In the back of her mind, she remembered something about a bonus. Her memory still wasn't clear about that night.

Yoyo set down her case and parked her bum on the desk. "I hear they're hiring at Teletec at the City Centre. Night shift. It might tide me over until something more permanent turns up. I can't commit until after my girl arrives."

Miriam gestured to her belly. "So you got an ultrasound?"

"Naw. My mother does this thing with a string and a dime. Never fails. Has to be a pre-fifties coin, though."

Miriam polished the mug with a tissue, giving it some scrutiny. "Yoyo told me about the poisoning. I turn my back, and all hell breaks loose. Do you have any ideas?"

Yoyo handed Belle a list. "Here are the names of the people who came in. They all check out as legit except for one. Cassandra Lachance. The address on Second Avenue doesn't exist, and the phone number belongs to Sudbury Steam Cleaners."

"Good work." Belle flashed an okay sign. "What did she look like? Sounds like a lap dancer."

"It's really hard to put faces and names together. I called everyone, but I guess I didn't ask the women what they looked like. What an idiot." She crossed her eyes in a dimwit pose and screwed her finger into her temple.

"Take a guess. Think about clothes, too. You have a good...fashion sense. Do a little self-hypnosis."

Miriam and Belle watched as Yoyo placed her hands over her face. Silence filled the room like a wall of cotton batting: Then she slapped her palms on the desk. "There was one in her forties. Not very well-dressed."

"What do you mean? Sweat pants? Shorts?"

"I mean she looked like she came from the Sally Ann reject bin. A very shapeless dress in a pink flower print. Big floppy hat, more for gardening, covering up her face. Ugly shoes. Clunky. Not the type in the market for a house."

"That sounds stupid as a disguise, because it stands out."

Did Joey have a female friend they had overlooked? No one had mentioned a sister or an aunt. Clearly, Mrs. Bartko was not to blame here.

"Honestly, I never exchanged more than a few words with her. I was busy with a couple. She just left her name and number and mumbled about coming back later. Damn, if I hadn't cleaned that pot—"

"Chances are that whoever did it was careful enough not to leave prints." Belle looked over at the coffee station, now moved strategically behind Miriam's desk.

Miriam smiled, filling her mug and doctoring it. "By the way, what ever happened with that old...friend of yours? Was it an accident after all?"

Belle filled her in, noticing that Yoyo was reluctant to leave. She moved slowly around the office, straightening a file, closing a drawer. Belle hadn't really said goodbye yet or thanked her for her work. How did you thank someone who had saved your life?

Miriam's eyes narrowed, and her Roman nostrils flared. Question everything was her motto. "Two deaths and one disappearance in the same general area. That's a big red flag, even given the time span of over thirty years."

"And so many years between incidents? It sounds creepy. Like a curse." Yoyo made a woo-wooing sound.

"Two hunters and a zoologist. All strangers as far as I know," said Belle. "The only connection is the territory. So I need to check out the site where Gary was working, go a bit farther into the bush. I'm not sure what to look for, but water samples could be important."

Well-versed in the local geography, Miriam pointed at the regional map and frowned. "But how are you...I mean your canoe is too—"

242

"I've borrowed a kayak. It weighs less than thirty pounds."

Yoyo's eyes lit up. "Tom and I paddled kayaks in Algonquin Park on our honeymoon. It was so much fun. Can I go with you?"

Both women stared at her then at each other as Belle answered, "In your condition, I—"

Yoyo plumped out her bottom lip and gave Belle's arm a light punch. "Come on. Soon enough I'm going to be paddling in a diaper pail. Disposables are not allowed in my family. This could be my last chance for a long time to get outdoors. Besides, I know the area. Maybe I'd have some ideas. Pleeeeeeeeeeeease?"

Belle applauded the frugality and logistics of avoiding those plastic landfill polluters. Anyone who was prepared to handle baby hygiene the old fashioned way should be allowed one wish from the Eco-Genie. "The town has been razed," she said, shaking her head in stubborn resistance. "Demolished. There's nothing left."

Yoyo gave a sigh of nostalgia. "But the trees are still there. The big oak that was a billion years old. I had a swing, and my brother had a treehouse."

The trees did it. Belle rolled her eyes, and Miriam chuckled. "Just for a few hours, then. Sunday good for you?"

Yoyo clapped her hands. "Of course. As you say, I'm in no condition to camp out."

Belle eyed her stomach with wariness. They'd never be more than an hour from Route 69. She wondered if the Burwash area had cell coverage. "You're sure your doctor would approve of this?"

"Yes, I'm in great shape. Just had my check-up. He said to keep active. There's nothing to kayaking. The boat is so light. And hey, I'll bring lunch."

With that settled, Belle dialled Athena to ask for a set of

water-testing tubes. Her friend promised to drop them at the office on her way home later that afternoon.

*   *   *

On Sunday at six, just as the sun cracked its crimson-streaked egg into the sky, Belle chucked the bulky deflated kayak, its foot pump and two paddles into the rear of the van. More a child's toy, the boat was designed for small, calm lakes or slow rivers, since it had no keel or steering gear. Gusts of wind could send it sideways. There was no designated cargo space, as in a normal kayak, only a few zippered pockets. Fortunately for Yoyo, it had large, cushy seating areas.

Pacing around the yard, Freya eyed the procedure with some confusion. Usually she went along on Belle's trips. "There is a space for you, girl, but it's taken. When I get back, we'll try it out ourselves if you watch those clawbees."

At the old dog's hurt expression, Belle departed from custom. "Tell you what. You can stay out on the deck today. Special treat. Watch Nature Canada." Freya's doghouse was Belle's house, but the day was clear and the forecast warm and dry. It would take an earthquake to make the animal set one paw off the property. As a further bribe, she dug out a smoked bone intended as a present for Rusty's birthday and placed it between Freya's paws. The resigned animal gave it a token lick and turned her head away from her mistress.

In town, Yoyo was sitting on the steps of her apartment, rubbing sleep from her eyes, when Belle picked her up. At her side was a small daypack, which she hoisted. "Sunblock. Bug spray. Twenty per cent Deet. That's the max. I suppose there'll be hordes. When you live in town, you don't bother about them. But I remember Burwash." She rubbed her arms. "Makes me itchy just thinking about it." Belle looked at the woman's long-sleeved pink denim shirt and sensible cotton pants with a maternity panel. The neon-blue sky was dotted with high, harmless clouds. Still, a weather rock was more reliable than the local forecasts. Mix of sun and cloud was their default prediction. "Did you bring a jacket? You never know."

Yoyo waved a little nylon packet. "It has its own case. Neat." She tucked it into her pocket. "Mom made us cheese sandwiches. Apples, drinks. Sound good? I baked last night and brought a bag of Baron's bikkies for Freya."

"She loved the last ones."

Then Yoyo looked at the van. "But where's the kayak? Are we picking it up somewhere?"

"Blowing it up instead. It's inflatable. And you did tell Coco we'd be back by six, right?" She felt strangely protective, as if something precious was in her care. What if they had an auto accident and...

Yoyo's heart-shaped face nodded, totally devoid of makeup, healthy and glowing. The tooth whitener system had left her with a star-tingling gleam to the neat rows. "I can't wait to see the old place again. I was only a little kid when we left. Know what? I bet we'll find some raspberries."

"Maybe in a few weeks."

"Blueberries then. Around the rocky areas where it's hotter." Her deft tongue gave a sensual lick to her full lips.

On the road for a short time, they came to a halt behind traffic at Britt as an army of front-end loaders, backhoes and dump trucks rearranged masses of sparkling granite blasted from the Shield. Yoyo asked Belle to turn on the air conditioner. "Sorry, but it's kind of like hot flashes, you know," she said, fanning her flushed face and rolling up her sleeves. A wisp of a fruity deodorant tickled Belle's nose.

As she juiced the air conditioner, Belle reached around to put on a light jacket. She wore a T-shirt, convertible pants, and a brown suede cap from Meldrum Bay. "Hot flashes are lurking around the corner for me."

An hour later at the parking spot at the edge of the Burwash community, they began unloading the kayak. At the perimeters, meadows of hay and wildflowers had taken over, violet vetch, black-eyed Susans and hawkweed. The warm air was still with the aromas of fresh grass and the buzzing of bees on clover reconnaissance. Yoyo shielded her eyes to scan the remains of the town site, searching for landmarks. "Whooee. There's my big old oak. And a couple of boards still up from Nick's fort. Our house was a ways farther. Can't we—"

Belle locked the van with the remote and zipped her keys and wallet into her jacket pocket. "Plenty of time when we return. That roadwork at Britt delayed us half an hour. I want to get moving here. Let's carry the kayak as is, and we'll inflate it at the lake. I don't want to take off like a Zeppelin." Then her cell phone rang. "Damn. I'll check the voice mail later," she said. "If it's important, they'll leave a message."

The portage through the maple grove into Bump Lake was flat and easy. Belle hoisted the folds of kayak, and Yoyo the rest. The younger woman gave a bittersweet laugh as she puffed along. "Tom and I had our own baby kayaks. You could tuck one under your arm."

Finally they reached the shores of Bump Lake. Tied to an old dock, mere fragments of planks, was a small car-top boat with a 9.9 horsepower motor. They hadn't seen any sign of a vehicle. Either someone was nearby, or too trusting of other fellow men. Motors were portable and quite untraceable. Belle spent ten minutes operating the foot pump. Finally they positioned the kayak half into the water, paddles at the ready.

Belle checked the topo section she'd brought, cut down for convenience and laminated for waterproofing. Maps loved to fly out of boats, get soggy, or rip. "Portage to the next lake will be through those bulrushes on the far side. Only a hundred feet. First we'll take a sample here." She got out the package of test tubes, unstoppered one, and bent down to dip. Gary would have had a good laugh imagining her as Madame Curie.

Then they heard a roar as a man chugged up on a quad, a rifle strapped to the side and an expensive spotting scope hanging from his neck.

"I met this guy before," she told Yoyo. "Nearly blew my head off, but he's harmless. That's probably his boat."

"Hello there, back again?" he called, getting off the machine and punching the kill switch to return the scene to quiet. Again he wore full camouflage, but this time a light brown tree-bark pattern.

"No pup today?" Belle asked.

"Arthuritis got her down. Best to rest the girl. Vet said he had some meds that might help. Rima-something. Pricey, though." Walking over, he gazed at the test tubes with some curiosity. One bushy eyebrow rose, and the corner of his grizzled mouth flickered as he considered Yoyo. "Got your sister with you? You two don't look alike."

Belle laughed. "Two crazy but unrelated ladies. We're here to take water samples like Gary did. I had a hunch about something. Probably a wild goose chase." She made the introductions. "Yoyo used to live in Burwash. That's why she wanted to come."

Patch cocked his head at the nubile blonde in an appreciative evaluation. "All them years ago, little lady? Why, you don't look hardly old enough for that."

"My mother Coco was the cook." Yoyo's bright eyes wore a proud look.

Patch threw back his head and guffawed until his belly shook. He slapped a hand on his broad thigh. "Coco Caderette. God, could she whip up a Christmas turkey dinner to beat the band. Never saw the like before or since. Should have asked her to marry me after old Bruce took off." He gave a grunt of self-reproach. "Uh, no offence. Just that your momma deserved better."

Yoyo's dark, sharp eyebrows flickered, and she cleared her throat. "What did you say your name was?"

The water was murky at the trampled roil of the shore, but no help for that. Turning back to her work, Belle capped the filled tube, labelled it with a pencil, and tucked it into the carrying case. One down, three or four more to go. Then as she rose from her knees, her phone rang again. Would they never get this trip underway? And what was wrong with Yoyo? Her posture seemed defensive, and her wary expression was hard to decipher. Please no cramps, breaking of water, or whatever foretold birth. Belle was wondering about the wisdom of her decision to bring the woman. She glanced at the phone. Caller ID made her hesitate against ignoring it again.

"It's Rainbow Country," Cherie said after Belle hit the green button.

Belle's father had returned yesterday. Had the condition flared up again, or was he merely wondering if she'd be there Tuesday, Tuesday? Had he twisted the arm of a soft-hearted nurse to call her? "Tell him I'll be—"

"I'm sorry, Belle, but your father has developed pneumonia. Probably got it at the hospital, despite precautions. Seniors can be vulnerable."

"And he's going back to the same place? Tell me not." Her voice started to rise in panic. Pneumonia was one often fatal complication for the elderly.

"I'm afraid he had to. We're not equipped for anything that serious. We did our best until the paramedics arrived. Got him on oxygen right away."

"Where is he?"

"The geriatric wing at Memorial. Fifth floor."

In a mental limbo, Belle looked over at the pair. Patch seemed abnormally interested in what Yoyo was saying, but he kept glancing around at Belle. Yoyo scratched at her neck and grimaced. "Damn blackflies. I've got a little perfume for you. Eau d'Off." Snickering, she took off her daypack and rummaged around. Patch had been carrying the rifle on his back in a sling, but now he held it in front of him like a soldier guarding a prisoner. Belle didn't like the intimidating pose. He hadn't seemed like this last time, but Mutt had been present. The sooner they were gone, the better.

She looked out at the lake. Only one sample taken. Her father would want her to complete her mission, but if she didn't act fast, she might not see him again. Either that, or a grim bedside vigil might await. His heart was so strong that he would joust for days with death. Her mother had died in their home in Florida, refusing Belle's offer to fly down, probably to spare her daughter from seeing her in a wheelchair. Her father had done the caretaking as best he could. Now it was her turn. Couldn't the old man have another kick at the film can? He enjoyed his life, had made adjustments in good humour as his independence melted like Victoria Day flurries. Then she clamped her jaw in decision. Life had presented a defining moment. Even if the trip to the interior would delay her a mere hour or two, there was no real choice. "I'll get there as soon as I can, Cherie. Thanks for calling."

Then as she punched off and the merry jingle of Bell Mobility added a discordantly festive touch, a strong and hairy hand snaked over her phone and wrenched it from her. "I don't think you will." Patch tossed it far into Bump Lake, where it landed on a lily pad with a splash and sank into the benthos. Frogs set up a chorus of protest as he tickled the rifle barrel under her chin like a shy lover.

"Jesus, what are you doing?" Belle asked, her pupils larger than Kalamata olives.

An ugly leer came over his grizzled face, as instantly as John Barrymore had morphed without makeup from Dr. Jekyll to Mr. Hyde. He set the rifle butt on the ground. "One trip's not enough. Just hadda come back and spy on me. I'll take care of the both of you nosey little fuckers the same way I took care of the others."

Others? For a split second, Belle stood frozen, assessing the scene, tumblers in her brain falling into place like a lockset. Was the man crazy, protecting his territory, or even more sinister, both? What had he to gain or lose? Then she heard a hissing followed by a deep, low scream, as if from a wounded gorilla. Yoyo was deploying her superstrength dope canister into the old man's face. The pungent smell of citrus filled the air like a toxic bomb. He dropped his rifle, slumped over it, and began pawing at his eyes. The patch slipped off, revealing a stitched socket. "You bitch! When I get my hands around your—"

Taking the gun was impossible. At close quarters he had all the power, half-blind or not. In another minute he'd be capable of shooting, then running them down on the quad if they tried to backtrack over the portage to the van. "Into the kayak, Yoyo!" Belle yelled.

TWENTY-ONE

Awkwardly, she knelt to hold the boat while Yoyo tried to crawl into the tippy craft, her arms braced against the sides, one sneakered foot ankle-deep in the lake. At this critical point, Belle had landed in the water more than once. No rehearsals allowed now. Showtime. As the woman landed precisely into the hole with an "oomph," Belle added, "Pass me your backpack." Meagre as they were, here were their only supplies. Shaking with adrenaline, she tucked it in front of her, then handed Yoyo a paddle and grabbed the other one. As Yoyo fumbled to set her hands, the moment in slow motion, cursing and stamping came from the bank.

"Go!" Belle called, pressing fast-forward.

With an easy motion stressing balance over strength, keeping low as she'd been taught, she slipped in and pushed them away from shore as the craft scraped bottom on pebbles. One leak, and they wouldn't get fifty feet. Something white floated in their wake, but she dared not look back. As they powered ahead, she was amazed that Yoyo handled the paddle like a pro. No wasted movements. No miscalculated circles. Kayaks could be totally unforgiving. In half a minute, they were a hundred feet from shore, gasping for breath. Belle craned her neck to see Patch standing and shielding his good eye against the bright sun. His vision might be returning. Yoyo's action had bought them only precious minutes. Would it be enough to reach the protective reeds? She heard gunfire pops and saw bullets spit the water to the right. A .22, not a shotgun. A bonus for the vulnerable boat. They ducked and mistimed strokes. The kayak swerved like a drunk exiting a bar.

Belle did a compensatory motion to set them straight. "Paddle harder! We need to reach those rushes."

"I am!" Yoyo bent and continued to dig at the water with savage strength. Her sun hat lifted off her head as the breeze rippled the lake, but she brought the paddle shaft flat down on it and never missed a stroke. Smooth move, as a teenaged Belle used to say.

All was silence, except for their laboured breathing and the sleek cuts of their paddles, parting the water like chef's knives. Either they had drawn out of range, or Patch's vision was still impaired. Belle gave a momentary gulp of relief. Just as they neared the sanctuary of the rushes, they heard a few stuttered rips. It was the 9.9. The motor roared into action, and the small, flat-bottomed boat came streaking across the water, raising a pair of mergansers who flapped along then rose into the sky like British Harrier jets.

Belle's heart began to pound as she worked the paddle. One false stroke, and their chances at escape were over. She heard no more gunshots, but as she turned around at last, she saw Patch take his hand off the tiller and aim the gun. Twenty feet from the reeds. Was the proverbial fat lady tuning up? Would they soon be floating face down like Gary then find shallow graves where no man ever walked? Patch would know many secret places. Then, in a freakish break of luck, the unbraced motor hit an underwater spar, a deadhead, and pulled a ninety, sending the boat into wild, overlapping circles. Patch fell out of the rear and flailed around trying to avoid the propeller. But the lake was eutrophic, hardly more than a swamp. He found his feet and struggled to regain control of the craft. Then they glided into the heavy reeds and were swallowed up like Moses in the rushes. Whoever had chosen the colour army green for the boat got Belle's blessings.

Belle felt the boat slow as Yoyo stopped paddling. Aching muscles or not, this was no time to rest. She lowered her voice to a whisper to avoid telegraphing their destination. Perhaps he'd believe they were hiding. "Farther, keep going. We're not stopping until the portage."

Yoyo's breath came in short gasps as she resumed her stroke. "I know that bastard. Patch Wells was a sadistic prison guard. Mom told me all about him. He used to be a boogeyman to all the kids. Patch is gonna get you if you don't watch out. Old One-Eye."

The weeds parted between hummocks of grass, and sharp blades slashed their arms like whips. Belle aimed for the narrows at the confluence of two hills. Portages were located for good reasons. "I thought Burwash was a medium-security facility. No need for rough stuff. Why wasn't he fired?"

Suddenly the water became quite shallow, and the heat built up, sending sweat trickling down her back. She still wore her light jacket from the frigid van. Now she was glad of the protection. Belle felt the kayak ground as it scraped bottom. "We're not going anywhere," Yoyo said, her voice rising with frustration.

"Hold on." Belle muscled the paddle like a Cambridge punt pole, and they eased by as the disturbed muck bubbled and burped sulphuric swamp gas.

"Puke," Yoyo said, coughing. "One of the men he beat up nearly died. And he *was* fired. But they didn't have enough evidence to prosecute. Besides, the facility closed that year anyway."

Belle gave herself time to let this information sink in. So

he'd stayed in the bush in some shack all this time. Convenience? Habit? Surely after being fired, he wouldn't have had any pension other than the basic Old Age and the supplement for those with no other support. Was he a total mental case, or a gatekeeper protecting something?

Suddenly the weeds parted, and they saw the muddy shore. Scratches of aluminum and flecks of paint on half-buried rocks showed where boats had been dragged. "If I recall, this one's not long," Belle said as Yoyo rubbed her sore arms. "Cracker Lake's just beyond those trees."

Yoyo looked around with eyes wide as the lily pads at her side. From afar, the yellow bullheads had bright blooms, but nose-close, they festered with flies and stank like Shakespeare's flowers. "Shouldn't we get going?"

"We're safe for a minute. He can get here, but he has to be careful not to ground or choke the motor with weeds." She patted her coat pockets. "Now where was that map? I want to take off in the right direction once we're at Cracker."

Then in her mind's moted eye, she saw a white sheet floating in Bump Lake. *"Hostie."* She drew out the curse like an unanswered prayer.

"What's the matter? Where is it?" Yoyo asked in a hushed voice, poking around her own seat and finding nothing.

"The map fell out back where we put in. If he sees it and the notes and arrows I added, he'll know where we were going."

A tiny frown shadowed Yoyo's face. "We can't go back, can we?"

Patch would follow them as far as he could over short portages where he could haul that light boat. If he didn't find them, he would return and set up camp, knowing that they carried no provisions and lie in wait like a fat vulture. This was perilous country. Squeezing her eyes, Belle tried to recall the progression of lakes. Eventually the watercourses, including streams and rivers, led to the huge Penage Lake district and Killarney, the jewel in Ontario's crown of parks, then finally to populated Georgian Bay, but never directly. They might end up backtracking, mired in a swamp, losing precious energy fighting a log jam. A pregnant woman. Little food. No map. The last problem was the worst. It struck her like a pitiless arrow. Maps were light in a dark world.

"Owwww," said Yoyo and bent forward. Gritting her teeth, she took off her hat to fan herself. Sweat glued her blonde hair to her forehead and stained the light fabric of her shirt between the shoulder blades. Despite the heat, Belle felt a trickle of cold tighten her chest. Moderate exercise was one thing for a pregnant woman. Running for her life was another.

Yoyo bit her lip, then smiled and waved her hand. "Nothing. Gas. I had a big brekkie. Sausages even."

Belle blew out a relieved breath. "You had me going for a minute. Now let's follow the path to Cracker."

They climbed out, and Yoyo carried the paddles while Belle pulled the kayak. Dry grasses cushioned the dragging stern. If it got more than its share of scratches, she'd buy the DesRosiers a new one. If it deflated, she'd see her friends on the other side. Soon the glistening surface of Cracker appeared. Short and sweet, the way she liked portages.

At the bank in a clearing lay the remains of an old fire ring, nothing but ashes inside, no cans or bottles. People had been through here. But how often? Every ten years? And who? Gary, or just Patch Wells?

Cracker Lake, an oval with several twisted bays, was pristine and ringed with conifers. A beaver dam at one end kept the water high. She looked downlake to a misshapen lodgepole pine, one branch protruding like a fateful finger. Often the sign of a portage. "We're heading for that tree. Keep your eyes open for a gap," she told Yoyo. Here the crapshoot began, with odds slightly better than the lottery. If they wasted time, toured around without success, they risked meeting Patch. That first portage would be easy for a muscled man and a light boat, even at his age.

After ten minutes at top speed, they reached the end of the lake. Discounting the pine, Belle had noticed a piece of blue tape on a striped maple sapling, a good colour for the bush, neon and unnatural in all seasons. The kayak scraped on the bank, shifting their torsos forward, and like a pro, Yoyo hustled out and pulled up the boat. Quickly they marched down the peaty path, comfortable in their new roles. Belle listened for a sudden hiss that would whisper their epitaph.

The portage proceeded an easy fifty feet. Pot of jam for them, but also for Patch. Belle found herself in the odd position of wishing for a hell portage. Then they rounded a corner and fought through a stand of pesky, overhanging alders and beaked hazel. "Whoa!" Yoyo said, breaking the last branches. "Look at that mother."

Belle put the boat down and stared at the steep, rocky incline. Then she clapped Yoyo's shoulder. "He'll never get the boat past this. But first we have to move the kayak together. I can't drag it over these rocks. One leak, and it's all over for us."

Yoyo firmed her lips and flexed her tiny biceps. "No problem. I've been staying in shape with exercises."

Together they urged the kayak up the hill, treating it like a newborn. In some places they lifted it over their heads. Other times it rode at their sides. The paddles were tucked in the boat to free their hands and avoid a costly and dangerous second trip. For five minutes they laboured on. Then ten. Despite her conditioning, Belle's thighs were screaming with the efforts. Often she worked against herself, shifting the weight awkwardly to protect Yoyo. Sweat stung her eyes and fogged her glasses around the nose.

Yoyo had been humming a tuneless song, twitching her neck at the mosquitoes. Belle was approaching scream mode, heartened only by the fact that at the lake, they could take advantage of a breeze and dig the delta-winged deerflies out of their hair. Suddenly the kayak lurched.

"Stop! Have mercy! I need dope now, not later," Yoyo said between clenched teeth. The kayak wobbled precariously as she tried to support it with one hand while slapping her neck with the other.

"Easy," Belle said. "Don't drop it, or we'll..." She stopped short. Negative thoughts brought negative results, a self-fulfilling prophecy. Gently they set down the boat and sprayed liberally, coughing at the cloud. A sticky but necessary bargain. The effect would wear off within a few hours, especially with sweat.

"I forgot to compliment you. Nailing Patch with the can was brilliant. A truly Canadian touch," Belle said.

"Saw it on TV once." She giggled, a girl again. "Damn. The can's empty now." She flung it far into the bush, where it merged with the green leaves and couldn't be spotted.

Once at the top of the hill, in the distance behind, Belle heard the roar of that familiar motor coming across Cracker Lake. Then their path took a turn into the bush and plunged down. The last hundred feet were steep and perilous as they wound their way through a huge rockfall like giants' building blocks. She looked out over a long, narrow lake. Which one was this? Merit or Dooble? Didn't one have two portages, east and west? If so, which one should she take? The lady or the tiger? In her original plan, this had been as far as she'd intended to go. The last of three water samples. She remembered that

257

Patch had turned on them when he'd seen what she was doing. The blur of the mystery that shrouded this area was beginning to sharpen into focus.

Yoyo knelt to get into the boat. Belle put a hand on her arm. "We'd better drink while we can. He can't follow us over that, except on foot, and he's no slim jim. Maybe we'll catch a break, and he'll have a heart attack."

Popping open a couple of diet sodas, they quenched their thirst. "Keep the containers," Belle said. "You never know."

"Yeah, on that grilling show, the guy cooked a chicken over a beer can."

"If you're thinking of grouse, forget it." She held up her hands. "No matches."

"Should have brought Mom along. Smokers have good survival tools."

Then they resumed paddling and made the end of the lake in minutes, an Olympic team getting more proficient by the moment thanks to the best motivation, the desire to live. As the kayak reached shore and ground into the sand, suddenly Yoyo hunched over in pain. Her knuckles were white against the boat as she looked up with fear and frustration. "Bad timing. I think junior is knocking at the door. God, I wondered why my boobs were killing me."

Belle's mouth formed a silent scream. Bad timing? *Apocalypse Now.* She could feel Patch's bullet slamming into her back. Forward progress was impossible. They'd have to hunker down and hide somewhere. Then when the baby was born...born prematurely...she couldn't imagine a worse situation, except for being sick or injured. Pregnant women needed to be warm and safe. Why had she allowed Yoyo to come? She sat paralyzed by the scenarios, all bad. Her hands were shaking from the paddling, or something worse.

The silence was deafening as Belle's ears pounded with blood. Could this baby survive? Not without them, and their chances were dropping as fast as the American dollar. Yoyo's voice wavered. "It's my fault. I was close, but I thought—"

Belle lifted her head and locked eyes. "Close? Close to what? You mean—"

"Mmmmmmwuh. This is my last two weeks. I'm not supposed to get on planes or anything." She gave a weak laugh, then hugged her stomach. "As if."

"Last two weeks! When you hired on, you said that you were only...you told Miriam..."

Yoyo looked at the ground as if studying each stone for a geology midterm. Her chin wobbled, and she gave a pointed sniff, wiping her nose with a filthy hand. "I know. But I needed the job. And I worked hard, didn't I? You said so."

"But you didn't look that—"

"Neither did Mom. Guess I take after her. She was cooking lunch for two hundred the day she delivered my last brother."

Belle sighed. Suppose she had come alone and met Patch? This was the second time that Yoyo had saved her life. Now she was in far more danger, and so was the child, full-term or not.

"What's the plan, Belle?" She sounded like a little sister. Was she expecting miracles or just expecting? Yoyo's sang-froid was admirable, or maybe the pain was distracting her from their real dilemma. Perhaps she thought help lay around the corner, except that she'd lived in the area and knew its amoral soul.

Belle tried to calm her heart, will her blood pressure to stabilize. Now she was their only hope. "I'd say that depends on you. Are you sure about these pains? Remember last time."

"Not one hundred per cent. But I'm not nauseous." She sighed and straightened her back, stretching. "All gone now. Let's get over the next portage. Maybe we'll get lucky—"

Belle laughed in spite of herself, faced down the horror with irony. "Get lucky?"

"And meet someone. That's what I meant."

Talk about hope limping eternal. Still, it was an improvement over panic and tears. Relieved about the cramps for the moment, Belle heard a splash and a dripping of water. She turned suddenly toward the shallows, then spoke in a whisper and pointed. "Over there. It's Gary's elk."

A massive white bull plunged his muzzle into the lake and let water cascade from his fleshy lips. He grabbed a large mouthful of pickerelweed and turned to watch them as he munched, his eyes dark and deep. Magnificent beast. His antlers were as large as a moose's. Was this the dominant male in the neighbourhood, the father of the baby that had died? What Gary would have given to see this rare and noble sight. Then the stag threw back its head and bugled as if on cue. The eerie sound echoed over the still lake. It seemed to say "Go on. You are under my protection."

Miraculously, the final section of the portage was gently downhill and soft as a rubber running track. Belle took the kayak herself. But as they reached the next lake, now into unnamed territory, a blind country, Yoyo had fallen behind. Belle ran back and found the woman on her knees, crying softly. "It's for real. I've been counting. Only ten minutes between." She pounded the soft moss at her side. "Man, these pains are wicked."

Frantically, Belle looked around. It was early afternoon. Plenty of daylight. Giving birth in the dark would be a worst-case scenario. All she knew about labour was what she had seen on the silver screen. Prissy mewling in *Gone With the Wind*. Bette Davis taking a firm hand to whiny Mary Astor in *The Great Lie*. "You asked for a plan. We'll land the kayak somewhere unlikely, cover up the tracks, and head into the woods—"

Yoyo's voice trembled, and agony was etched on her cheery face. "Into the woods. But you said we were safe now after the last portage. That he couldn't..."

Belle gulped back a cry of pity as she looked at the woman's hand, the knuckles scraped and the jolly teddy-bear polish chipped and cracked. "Listen. Hunters and trappers sometimes cache canoes in the bush. I forgot about that possibility. We don't know where Patch is, except that he's God in this area. And anyway, you're not going anywhere until that baby is born. Let's move up the east side of the lake and scout the banks. It'll keep the sun longer."

They got back into the boat and slowly edged along the shore, in parts rocky but often opening to a sandy beach. "Sand we don't want," Belle said. "Might as well leave him a letter. I'm not saying Patch has the tracking abilities of a native, but he's lived in the bush and done plenty of hunting. And remember that spotting scope?"

They came to a jumble of slippery rocks half covered by steeplebush. A carpet of snaggy blueberry bushes traced over the ground, their green berries full of hard, round promise. "Not here. We don't want to crush the vegetation." She scanned down the shoreline, then fixed on a small point of grey granite entering the water on a gentle slope. "Over there. Good traction. No moss. No footprints. Nothing to be disturbed. But watch where you put your feet. A broken ankle is not on the agenda. Being in one piece is our only chip in this casino." She paused, and a ghost of a smile raised the corner of her sweaty mouth as she licked away the salt. "That, along with a double helping of feminine wiles."

In a dangerous slow-motion dance, Belle choreographed Yoyo's exit from the kayak, then her own, and finally lugged the boat up the rough bank, careful to avoid punctures or rips. Once off the shore, she reached for a large, twisted branch of dead red pine and placed it over their entrance. Plunging into the thick bush, predominantly white birches and poplar with an alder undergrowth, they stepped where their prints wouldn't show and finally found a narrow game trail leading past a grove of conifers. Belle swept a cedar bough behind them to disguise any tracks.

Yoyo sat down on a log and groaned. "I can't go much further, I mean farther, Belle."

Belle pointed to a giant balsam fir a foot wide at the trunk. "Home sweet whatever. Give me a minute before you come in." The dry branches at the bottom could easily be broken for access to the rude shelter. Underneath, the ground would be soft with a cushion of dried needles. Right now it didn't look like rain, but the thick overhang would afford some protection...if she could find sloughed-off birch sheets to use as impromptu shingles. She shook herself back to the present. This was hardly the time to contemplate constructing anything complex. Although they were in a small valley between ridges, Belle shoved the kayak underneath the tree to serve as partial wind protection. In the global warming that had unbalanced the climate in Northern Ontario, fierce gales and storms could spring up out of nowhere. Hail might be on the agenda twice in one summer.

Belle scavenged to find whatever would make Yoyo more comfortable. She settled on gathering brackens and ferns for a bed. Their smell reminded her of camping trips. Then she ripped up a large cushion of sphagnum moss, spongy and green.

Yoyo gave a long, low moan, a trickle of blood dripping down her chin from biting her lip. "Sorry. I know we have to be quiet. Jesus. What's the matter with me? Mom told me she never made a sound. Am I a wimp?"

A dead wimp, if a loud wimp. She watched Yoyo crawl forward as heavily as if she were hauling a bag of anvils. "How's your nest, little mother bird? Are you warm enough?" She knew the answer. It was nearly thirty degrees, their only good fortune.

"Real soft. Thanks." Then as a spasm hit, she clamped a hand over her mouth.

Belle had an idea and duck-walked out, then headed for the nearest yellow birch. Returning with a handful of thick twigs, she said, "Bite on this. It's like wintergreen."

Monitoring her breathing in measured huffs, Yoyo gave her an odd look and put it aside. "I'm no beaver. Maybe later."

Belle wiped her forehead with her sleeve. Mother Nature was writing the screenplay. They were mere attendants. And if the baby was born, and if it was healthy, and if it didn't make any noise...too many ifs.

A minute later Yoyo gave a relaxed sigh. "All over for now. Next round in a few minutes. Guess what? I'm starving."

"Coming right up." Lying beside her, Belle reached inside the kayak and pulled out the daypack. She retrieved a large green plastic bag from the LCBO and measured it with her eye. Bunting for the twenty-first century. Unwrapping the sandwiches, she handed one to Yoyo, who wolfed it down, licking the last crumbs from her fingers. Two cans of soda remained. Despite being made from white bread and processed slices, the cheese sandwich was so luscious that Belle forgot the painful brick in her empty stomach. They were burning calories like pine kindling. Two apples came with a plastic knife, so Belle cut them in quarters, nearly snapping the tiny weapon in her haste.

Suddenly they heard a crunch nearby. Belle put a hand on

Yoyo's shoulder, and the woman's anguished eyes went wide with terror. She bit down on the stick so hard that it broke, then spit out the residue as a brown rabbit hopped across the path twenty feet from them. "Isn't that cu—"

Without a sound, a red fox pounced and cracked the rabbit's neck with one efficient shake, hauling off its prey with a beady eye on the crouching women. A fast lesson in bush ethics.

"You'd better tell me what to expect before all hell breaks loose," Belle said. *I don't know nothin' 'bout birthin' babies!* "Better that you were a bear. Their cubs weigh only half a pound."

"I could handle that." Yoyo gave a light laugh, but then her eyes rolled back in torment.

As the afternoon wore into early evening, and the intervals between pains shrank, Belle unwrapped Yoyo's jacket and spread it over her. At least they had basic covering, but with the dope wearing off, the mosquitoes would regroup. No wonder moose ran berserk onto the highways to escape their tormentors. As she slapped at a sipper, she remembered the old trick of coating the skin with mud. Then Yoyo groaned. Prepared to help her, Belle shoved the pack into the recesses of the kayak, then had a second thought. Was it possible that something of value in the small boat had been overlooked? Crawling forward, she fumbled around in the zippered pockets. She didn't hold out hope for matches, but...then her fingers discovered a tiny Maglite, a toy in size but a serious one. It went on with a glow, and she grinned. At least they would have some company in the dark tonight. Until the batteries died.

"It's time, Belle," Yoyo said and squeezed her hand. "I think my water's breaking. Let me get my pants off. I don't want to lie in that."

TWENTY-TWO

Yoyo shuffled herself to the side as Belle counted to a hundred. Everyone had heard of the concept of the water breaking. To Belle it brought the image of floating away on a salty tidal wave. But the reality was smaller, a few cupfuls. Then Yoyo arranged herself in a sensible straddle that recalled the posture of a birthing chair. "Not long now. Hope I'm fast like Mom. Take a look and tell me how far I'm dilated. Say like a dime." At Belle's horrified face, she added, "Come on. When I was a little kid, I saw worse. Why one time—"

"Why do you think I never went to medical school?" Tentatively, Belle lifted the jacket aside, bent down and gulped. "Oh, my God."

Yoyo panted, counting to herself. "Well?"

"Uh." Belle tried to assess progress on the basis of snowfall. Hers was a generation caught between imperial and metric. "About...two centimetres. A quarter."

Almost an hour passed, and the yellow birch twigs Yoyo chomped flew by with no more than a hum and the occasional quiet growl. Belle gave Yoyo credit for her stoicism and for the primer in midwifery. Women had babies at home all the time, but they also died without medical help for breech births, haemorrhages, twisted cords. Why hadn't Mother let her watch Mimi delivering those kittens? Because that night after she went to bed, her father had taken a small bundle wrapped in a towel to the trash can? She'd seen him hunched furtively in the moonlight, opening and shutting the lid without a sound. How strange that Mimi had produced only one, but her parents told her it was common. After that first "right of all females" litter, the cat had been spayed.

Her father. Now he might be fighting his last battle, the old knight against the dark man with the scythe under his cloak. She preferred those images to the graphic reality. A tear seeped from the corner of her eye. She'd think about that tomorrow. Be here now. Make yourself useful, her mother always said. And the timing was good. The sun still glistened above the horizon in the cleft far down the valley. Night would be at least two hours away.

Belle looked at her watch, wondering how long this last act might continue. "Am I supposed to tell you to push or something?"

"Stop rushing me. What the hell do you think I've been doing?" Yoyo began puffing, the little engine that could. "Now. She's coming. They're coming. Holy shit, it feels like a basketball team."

On the fragrant green bed, Belle tried to position herself kneeling at the entrance to what Leonard Cohen called the delta, the alpha and the omega, to catch the slippery little fish on exit. The primal rhythms of the song soothed her, and she nodded in self-hypnosis. Her pupils pulsed with the dilation of the cervix, and she ground her teeth in empathy until they ached. Slowly the crown emerged, and she laughed. Hair as red as hers. So far, so good. Not feet first. She felt her adrenaline surge and hoped that Yoyo was getting a whacking dose of natural painkillers. No epidurals here.

Then a squirming parcel the size of a football with legs and arms lay in front of her, a cord dangling from the mother. Belle cleaned the mouth and nose with a paper serviette. It was breathing easily, nothing more than a confused look on its wizened face. Eyes as dark as plums. And it was a girl. Fancy that. Yoyo sat up with a grunt. "God. She's wonderful. Is everything there?"

Belle looked down. "All accessories accounted for. About this handy but now useless cord, though. The plastic knife is all we have."

"So go for it."

Belle bent to the gory task, then fashioned makeshift knots with loose threads ripped from the daypack zipper. What had Yoyo told her? Wasn't there something more?

Yoyo wiped the baby with a handful of soft fern, then pulled the tiny bundle to her with a dazzling and loopy grin. "Welcome to your first camp-out, darlin'."

Belle sat back for a moment, massaging her cramped thighs. Minutes later, the afterbirth arrived, and Belle tidied up, her sticky hands cleaned with a clutch of large striped maple leaves. A metallic smell of blood filled the air. Lest it fetch some beast, Belle collected the matter in a Ziploc, walked a hundred yards away and found a deep rock cleft with a foot of standing water. Letting out all the air in the bag, she managed to sink it under a sizable stone. She hadn't given a thought to their other predators, bears or wolves. On bush trips, tampons had to be burned in the fire or buried.

So far the baby hadn't made a sound other than a soft cooing when Yoyo "latched" it to her breast, another new term for Belle. "Hey, hey. Easy, little cub," mother said to daughter. She explained that the first few days of nursing brought out the colostrum, a weak and easily digested milk. Clearly she'd studied her books with diligence. Her lessons took their minds off the present.

"It'll get colder tonight." Belle picked up the LCBO bag and the last birch twig. "This is about the right size. Let's poke a few holes for ventilation and put her in here."

Then in the silence, punctuated only by sucking, the baby gave a small cry. "What's wrong?" Belle whispered, panic in her tones. "We can't have that. If Patch is around…"

Yoyo wrinkled her brow as she stroked the baby's back. "It could be gas. Come on, girl. Humpty dumpty." She gently moved the baby up and down. Finally, a small burp emerged. The girl opened her mouth to breathe, squeezed her eyes, then settled back in a nap, milk burbling at her rosebud lips. Apparently the baby would sleep much of the time and become more active once the true milk appeared.

"You passed the final with an A-plus," Belle whispered with a smile.

As the gold of the setting sun flared to burgundy and brought the slow darkness, they settled beside each other for warmth. Every inch of skin was covered against bugs, except for their faces and hands, oily with dope. The baby was wrapped under Yoyo's coat. Her button nose twitched, but she was well protected.

"God, I'm hungry," Yoyo said.

"But we finished the sandwiches. Maybe tomorrow I'll find some berries." And a campfire with boy scouts and a vat of stew and s'mores for dessert. Something lumpy was in her pocket as she shifted. Patch's whistle. No help there. The last thing they wanted to do was make noise.

A little cheer came across Yoyo's face, illuminated by the flashlight they allowed themselves from time to time. "Baron's Bites! The bikkies. I forgot about that."

Belle grabbed for the pack, her mouth watering in spite of herself. "But what's in—"

"All natural stuff. Whole wheat flour. Skim milk. Egg. Meat fat. Good for you."

"Speaking of meat, I could go for a hamburger." Belle tasted one, making it last nearly a minute. "Bland, but nutty. I like it. Nutritious, too." She counted the rest. Two dozen. A treasure chest.

Tired as they were, they talked to maintain a semblance of normalcy, to sustain their spirits. Plans for the next day went unmentioned. Too many unknowns. "So you write country songs? That's pretty cool," Yoyo said.

"It's not like I ever sold one." She recited the lyrics to "Come On Up To Mama's Table".

"I sent it to an address in *Writer's Digest,* but the whole thing was a scam."

"So you have just the one song? It's not like a passion or anything?"

"No, just a little moneymaker, or so I thought."

Then Yoyo gave a quiet laugh. "Of course, dear boss. But there are other easy ways to score a quick dollar."

Belle gave a scoffing gesture with her hand, barely able to see it in front of her face as the rising half-moon scudded behind a bank of silvery clouds. "Like what? Those TV come-ons? Work at home for a thousand a day? Or are you referring to gambling?"

To her credit, Yoyo ignored the bait. "You have an English degree, right? You've read tons of poetry. Why not try some limericks for *Playboy?* My brothers had a subscription. I read the articles...of course."

"Right, the limericks are in the joke section. But what money?"

"Hey, they pay a hundred dollars U.S. And how hard can it be?"

Belle pondered this. "The 'little old man from Nantucket' idea has been taken."

This got them both giggling. "Let's think of a place or a person first, then go from there. I used to write poems in high school. Perfect rhyming. I have a very good ear."

"I wrote poetry, too," said Belle. "Very gloomy stuff. 'Misery, companion mine.' What was I thinking? I wasn't unhappy."

"Listen," Yoyo said.

In the growing darkness, a song arose. A gasping buzz. Tuptup-sheeee. Belle pricked her ears. Not the Sam Peabody of the white-throated variety. "A sharp-tailed sparrow maybe. Must be a marsh nearby."

"Sparrow. Good name. There once was a woman named Sparrow." Yoyo clicked her teeth, shining in the ambient light. "That gives us narrow, arrow. Where can we go with that?"

Belle was enjoying the game. It was taking her mind off her aching shoulders. "Marrow, yarrow, barrow and harrow."

"What do those words mean?"

"I agree. Too obscure. But I like the sparrow. Maybe we should try Spanish. Many words end in 'o.' It's an American magazine, and L.A. is nearly half Hispanic."

"All I know is *salsa* and *buenos dias.*"

Belle paused to think while Yoyo gave her daughter another slurp. "How's this? 'A castanets player named Sparrow/ Invited a well-hung torero...'"

Yoyo gave a silent splutter, then tucked the girl back under the covers. "Well-hung. That's the idea. A guy thing. But invited him to what? A party? A dance?"

"You don't want to go with party. But dance lead to pants. Imagine the possibilities." She wiggled her eyebrows, though she knew Yoyo couldn't see them.

"A dance. What kind of music? Something sexy, I bet."

"Ravel. Everyone's fantasy." She snapped her fingers. "And played a two-minute bolero."

"Two minutes is more than a lotta guys can handle."

Finally, they slept, a bonded trio. Only once in the night did Belle twitch awake. An old nursery rhyme was stuck on her mental disc drive. "Bye, baby bunting. Patch has gone a-hunting."

As diffused light from the morning sun reached their shelter, Belle opened one eye, nearly swollen shut from bites. She was frantically thirsty, having rationed the last sodas. She watched Yoyo nestle with the baby under her chin. They had to move on. And the bugs would be fierce unless they caught a wind. She thought again of the early blueberries. A few would give them fresh heart, even if they were a bit sour.

Yoyo yawned and checked the baby, whose mouth opened. Before it could close, Yoyo had popped in a warm spigot. Way to go. No getting up in the wee hours warming bottles. Not to mention the cost of formula.

"I'm going to scout around for a minute, Yoyo. Open the last pop can. We'll get more water back at the river." Dehydration would punish them far faster than the perils of giardia.

"There's a stream where we came in."

"Larger sources are safer."

Belle rose stiffly and found the game trail. She squinted. It seemed a bit broader here than she would have expected. Was it more than an animal path? Then she saw the black scab of an old blaze on a white birch. Did it lead somewhere? She glanced back at mother and child, dozing again, then set off on a lope.

The path climbed a maple ridge, then down again, widening as it went. Checking her watch to monitor the time, she finally reached a clearing. Man had made his ugly mark here. It was an old mine site, now levelled and burned to nothing more than a few boards and bricks. Toxic pools seeped from the ground. A yellowish clay oozed at her feet, and she moved off. From the hardy poplars that had reasserted themselves in this hell, she judged that more than half a century had passed. In the trees at the edge, she saw the remains of a shack and went over, careful where she stepped.

Underneath the tin panels was a rusted metal sign with fractured letters. The Old...Batty. Where had she heard that? From Rosaline's mother. She had thought it referred to a person. Was this what Gary had found? Or discovered arsenic traces in nearby watercourses? Had its poisons killed the vulnerable baby elk? Then she froze. What if Yoyo wandered back to the river?

She began running, tripping over roots in the path. Finally she reached their tree and paused to catch her breath, bending over with her hands on her knees. Yoyo was still lying there, a contented odalisque. "The water...you didn't..."

"Huh? Did you bring some back? I'm parched."

Briefly Belle explained what she had seen. "We can't drink from anything around here. Once we get downstream a mile or so, we can risk it. I'm thinking that this is what Patch was hiding."

"But why? If it's that old, it had nothing to do with him."

They munched a few biscuits and shared the last can of pop. Then Belle scouted down to the river, happy to see nothing from her hiding place in a thicket. Patch wouldn't waste energy. He'd be waiting for them back at Bump Lake.

They set off in the kayak, the baby nestled between Yoyo's legs. From her bra and some moss, she'd fashioned a rustic diaper. Father of Industry, meet Mother of Invention.

A short portage took them over to a river, where they made faster time. They were travelling light, but quickly, the bonus of a kayak. At a few points, large dead trees had fallen into the river, blocking their path. "Lie down," Belle said, as she lifted the branches and they slipped beneath in a potentially fatal game of pick-up sticks.

At another junction, the logs were too large to move. Belle got out and stood on one, bending over to lift the boat and Yoyo over a few inches at a time. The effort was costing them. All of the biscuits were gone. Then the river disgorged on a larger body of water. Not Georgian Bay yet, but the Penage system. Farther to the west, the main lake was full of cottages, some of which she'd sold. Here, many inlets away, the shoreline was wild. At an island, they pulled in close and stopped to gather a few handfuls of blueberries, nature's debut ripening on a south bank with plenty of sun-collecting rocks. They drank thirstily from the big water and continued west, navigating by the sun behind them.

"Gotta be someone around," Yoyo said half an hour later, then wrinkled her nose. "But I have to change the diaper. Pull in somewhere."

With the lake came the growing chop of waves. They tacked and weaved in an effort to avoid swamping. They were navigating a knife edge and making little progress as the winds slewed the craft and their two compartments began filling with water.

Suddenly Belle glimpsed what looked like a small canoe disappearing around a point. They yelled, but the rising wind blew their words back. Then Belle pulled out Patch's whistle, and its shrill shriek shot across the water like an arrow. The canoe turned, and a person waved. So that they wouldn't be perceived as mere sightseers, Belle kept on whistling and flailing her arms until the canoe sat dead in the water. The paddler aimed something at them. Its large eye glistened in the sun.

TWENTY-THREE

Bonnie Fleischer was a wildlife photographer whose work had been featured on many nature calendars. She'd aimed her telephoto lens at them like a telescope. The float plane that had dropped her off was due back, and all of her gear was packed into the canoe. Her tanned and wiry body testified to a fitness far younger than her fifty-five years. A sensible brush cut of steel grey hair streamlined her intelligent face.

As they sat on the beach, Bonnie offered a litre of drinking water, beef jerky and two bananas. Belle wiped her mouth as she searched the sky and began calculating the weights. Bonnie's cumbersome Sportspal was built more for stability than lightness. "The boats can stay. We have to get this lady and her daughter back."

"I agree." Bonnie traced a finger over the baby's chin and smiled. "I can't imagine how you managed it."

The baby gave a lusty cry. "Let her exercise her lungs. She's been patient long enough," Yoyo said, waiting a minute before giving her the magic flute. Then she secured the baby in a soft bed of moss, and she and Belle went into the water to scrub off two days of dirt and sweat. They used nature's scouring pad, swamp horsetails growing at the water's edge, the original pop-it beads.

At three, when the pilot touched down and motored to the small bay where they waited, he got out onto the pontoon and tipped back his cap. "What is this, a party?"

Having been filled in, he asked the women their weights. One hundred and thirty for Belle, one hundred and twenty for Bonnie, and one hundred and ten for Yoyo plus about five for the wolf cub. "If you gals were a big man and we were taking the canoe, it'd be about the same. Hop in. I'll radio ahead."

Belle rode in the rear seats with Yoyo. The plane took off quickly, and within half an hour was cruising over Lake Ramsey. It landed at the Eagle Flight Centre's docks, where an ambulance was waiting. As Yoyo was being lifted onto a gurney, her daughter in her arms, she waved goodbye. "I thought of a perfect name. Cocobelle."

Belle groaned inwardly and blew a kiss. She made arrangements for the pilot to return for the boats, all expenses paid. Bonnie had been a lifesaver.

Then she took a quarter from her wallet and went to a pay phone. "Hélène?" she said as someone answered.

A shriek came from the receiver. "Where in God's name are you? Why didn't you call us? Freya was all night on the deck. We saw her in the evening, and she was still there next morning, but your van was gone. We left a note and took her—"

"Stop the presses. I have quite a story. But I have to see my father first. Then the police."

She took a cab to Memorial, well aware of the sweat reeking from her clothes when the driver rolled down the windows. She asked at reception for her father's room. He still had one, a good sign. On the way she passed a non-denominational chapel and slipped in to compose herself. She still recalled a few prayers from the wonderful Cranmer prayer book. But this time she addressed someone other than God. Her hands were shaking from running on a diet of adrenaline and dog biscuits. "If the old man can beat this, leave him with me. But if suffering will be his lot, come and get him now. Tonight. And I mean it, Mother."

As she entered 510 in the geriatric wing, she heard a familiar voice. It was hoarse but strong. "I saw every film ever made. Shake the hand that shook the hand of Gene Autry. Smiley Burnette, too. Didn't like Gene much. Too cold. But Smiley was a prince."

Her father was propped up in bed, his face pale but free of sweat and pain, his cornflower blues clear and sharp. He was talking to a young Filipina nurse who was taking his pulse and had probably never heard of the singing cowboy.

He looked up at Belle with a mild annoyance and shook one bony finger. "I thought you weren't coming. Where's my chicken? And double ice cream on the pie."

"Triple. Soon as you get...home. Your arteries have proved themselves."

He nodded toward some daisies in a vase by the next bed. "It's time to send Mary LaGrotta some flowers for her birthday."

Mary was the sweet Italian girlfriend he'd left behind in Florida. She'd made him laugh like a teenager. "December's a few months away, but a lady always appreciates a bouquet." She hugged him fast and long until he squeaked.

Next stop was the Sudbury Police Department. Belle gave her story to the detective on duty, and when he heard about the three other incidents in the area, he became very interested. "So I don't know if Patch Wells acted on his own or not. If he'd had his way, Yoyo, the baby and I would have been his fourth, fifth and sixth victims."

*   *   *

The next day, along with the OPP, who had jurisdiction

outside the city, Belle returned to Bump Lake. Her van was still there. Patch was gone, his cabin burned, and the authorities were making inquiries across the country. The Old Batty lurked deep in the bush, spewing its poisons. At last its secret was exposed.

The next day Belle contacted Larry Celeste, a professor of mining and geology at Nickel City College. He was kind enough to listen to her story and got back to her within twenty-four hours, inviting her to his crowded office.

"There are over ten thousand abandoned mines across Canada. Some of them are orphaned, the owner untraceable. Four thousand are contaminated. The total cost for clean-up could run over six billion dollars, at a conservative estimate. The boreal forest is especially vulnerable, fewer species, thin, acidic soils, slow recovery."

"I suppose they brought in the building material by barge. It was a hell of a mess, even after all these years."

"All stages from A to E, 'acquiring' to 'exit ticket', cause damage. Trenching, drilling, then when water comes into it, the real disaster. Acid mine drainage, metal leaching from uncovered tailings. Mines were nearly unregulated before the war. No rules, lost records," he said, leaning back in his swivel chair.

"And now?" She thought of the Nickel Rim South Development, high on its shiny hill.

"We made some progress in the Eighties and Nineties with MISA, the Municipal Industrial Strategy for Abatement. 'Exit ticket' means that the company has to put up a cash guarantee when the liability is transferred to the public."

"Sounds good."

He gave an ironic laugh and pointed to a map with hundreds of dots across Ontario. "Even that's losing its teeth lately. The Renabie Mine near Chapleau proposed a deposit of a hundred thousand dollars for clean-up. One single sinkhole that appeared later ate that amount."

They consulted a topo he pulled from a set of narrow drawers. "But there's no cross and pick to indicate the mine," she said. "That's what confused me."

"From the few records I've been able to access, the Old Batty operated from 1920-1939. That's a long time ago. Once the gold was gone, they dozed over the place and felled trees to block access. No roads. It's not prime fishing or hunting territory, so..." He spread his hands.

"I get it. They didn't expect anyone to come poking around in the area."

"The Burwash facility kept the place conveniently off limits for the next several decades. And all this time, elemental arsenic ions began to leak into the aquifer. Not for years, maybe, but once the drifts filled up with water. With no one around, who would ever know except the bottom feeders, daphnia and fish?"

Gary had mentioned daphnia. He had probably intended to test for accumulation of toxic elements in the famous benthos. She felt stupid for not pursuing it. "But again, why no cross and pick?"

Larry motioned to grease his palm. "Here's my suspicion. Gable Minerals was a small operation then. As it moved out of Sudbury and grew, it had enough money to pay someone to keep the site off the ordinance map in 1940. Then any revisions would have been moot."

She told him about Marshall Mincore and the politically ambitious Gable family with their gold mine and dream town for workers in Manitouwadge.

"Think what it would look like if news got out that their old site was polluting the edges of a reserve right in our backyard."

He pointed to a thick article from MiningWatch. "It's a

national crisis waiting to happen, and not just in remote areas like the Giant Mine in Yellowknife, where the cost of freezing the tailings may run higher than the value of the gold. Red Lake has a toxic plume underground waiting to envelop the city in another ten or twenty years. The Campbell Mine there closed in 1960, but it left a little time bomb."

"What is the North supposed to do, start growing more organic produce in the empty shafts?" Underground endive was already a hot commodity.

"'Right to mine' is the hot button. The prospect of putting jobs into the community, even for a short time, outweighs the long-term damage. Canada is the world's largest producer of gold and nickel."

*   *   *

Steve and Belle sat outside on the deck, enjoying a cold Northern Maple lager, their last. The landmark brewery downtown had failed to skirt bankruptcy and closed its massive doors.

"They found Patch? Where?" To express her delight, she whistled over the top of the bottle.

"Off his own turf, he didn't have the resources to hide. We picked him up on a bus to Prince George. I think he intended to disappear up into the remote lumber regions where no questions are asked. He's in remarkable shape for a man of seventy plus, and he's talking. Wants to make a deal that will give him the most comfort in his old age. You know what happens to guards who become prisoners." He sliced a finger across his throat.

Apparently Patch had discovered the Old Batty site on a hunting trip in the Sixties. Suspicious about the seepage, he had asked a few mining codgers at a local bar and drawn his own conclusions. Local history books from the Sudbury Public Library had mentioned the early gold efforts. With the help of an efficient librarian, it hadn't been hard to track Mincore Metals to Gable Minerals. With his father-in-law long gone, a nervous Fred Gable had started the payments to Patch the year the prison farm closed, and his son Barry had continued them. The modest sums, only five hundred dollars a month, were paid under the justification that Patch was prospecting for new mining claims.

"Prospecting for over thirty years in the same area? That's not going to wash. And Rosaline?"

"It's going to be Patch against the three of them. They're denying any knowledge of his crimes. The paper trail's cold. Cash every month by mail."

"What about the...cheap scotch? Did he explain that?"

"Seems he got Gary to have a quick belt with him just before he hit him with a rifle butt and set up the 'accident'."

She didn't want to imagine Gary fighting for his life in the water once the blow had disoriented him. Drowning was not as painless as freezing to death, but at least it was fast. "So Patch didn't stuff the furnace vent or doctor the coffee."

Steve chuckled and flicked a wasp away from his bottle. The little devils loved beer. "Rosaline *is* a zoologist. She'd have access to mouse nests, if anyone would. Plus she owns a white Buick. And she would have known how to cover up or misdirect Gary's research. But it could have been an accident. Remember that we also caught the kids that broke into the house. The fifteen-year-old leader told them that offices are a good place to hide money. That explains the riffling of the papers. And they had no vehicle to take away the heavy stuff like the generator or chain saw. "

Belle grimaced, her eyes narrowing. Down on the water, a family of mallards came by, eight babies scuffling to ride on the mother's dull and mottled back while the showy father in a black and white tuxedo bobbed his iridescent green head. She was still frosted about the poisoning. "Some things can't be proved, I guess. But what about my office? Maybe I should get a videocam."

"Silliker had nothing to do with the date-rape drug in your coffee. We picked up Joey's friends on a speeding charge on the 401 just east of Windsor. They had three kilos of coke in the car, along with a cocktail of designer drugs. One boy worked a plea deal by turning in an old girlfriend of Bartko's. Liz Ash. A real pistol. She was bragging about getting back at the 'ho' that gave her man so much trouble. She doctored your coffee and broke the sign as well." He shrugged. "Now she'll try to sell her information on Bartko. Women are fickle."

"The 'ho' begs to differ." Inside, she smiled. At last, some mystique.

"I know it offends your sense of justice, but Silliker, her brother and father probably won't see a day in court. They pretended to be horrified at what Patch had done. Maybe they were, for all we know." His chiselled lips curled at the edge as he hoisted his beer bottle. "And they're model citizens."

"The Old Batty is back in the news," said Belle. "A team of environmental assessors will be going over the property. A total reclamation is impossible, but the place will be made safer. Under the former rules, Gable Minerals won't have to pay a cent, but they'll be under much more scrutiny for their current operations."

"Your friend Gary played a part in this. That little pop can was a major factor. Where did he find it?"

"Not at the mine, I'd guess. He'd have reported the pollution. Patch probably left it at the site on one of his excursions, and one spring at high water, tangled in brush perhaps, it floated down the creek." Belle sighed, remembering how she'd said goodbye to Mutt. Another man sailing out of her life with the same ease.

Steve seemed to pick up on her sadness and changed the

topic. "So Yoyo's become a little mother now? A new career for you as a midwife?"

"Much too messy. Long hours, too. I owed her, though. And I gave her a couple of thousand dollars for her mother's eye treatments. We're hoping that the government will see reason and start funding that drug. Other provinces have."

"*Gave* her money?" Steve gave an exaggerated gasp and put a hand on his heart over the Sudbury Wolves logo on his jacket. "Going soft in your middle age?"

Locking eyes with him, Belle shook her head. "Yoyo insisted that it's only a loan. With her new job at RE/MAX, she's on her way to success at last. She'll pass the third qualifying exam with no sweat. How is your adoption working out? Any new developments?"

"Warm up your listings. We're going for a hat trick. Twin boys of four. Janet's never been happier, and Heather's over the moon."

Steve looked relaxed and confident. Her heart went out to him, and her fingers crossed in best wishes. His was a cherished friendship. And he hadn't said a thing about her reckless episode at Burwash. What did that mean?

With Steve gone, Belle went down to the garden with her latest purchases in a wheelbarrow. July 10th. Everything had been half-price and looked it. Scraggly and overgrown tomatoes, zucchini plants going brown at the edge, wilting lettuce. It was ridiculously late to try again, but she'd always had a garden, neglected or not. She knelt down and buried her hands in the warm earth like her forebears. Rutabagas had seen them through many bitter winters.

Humming softly, she tucked in her hopes. Then she realized what song haunted her thoughts. Lerner and Loewe were right. It *had been* almost like being in love.

BARON'S BITES

1 1/2 cups whole wheat flour
1 cup all-purpose flour
1 cup skim milk powder
1/3 cup melted meat fat (beef, lamb, or bacon)
1 egg, lightly beaten
1 cup cold water

Combine flour, milk powder and salt in bowl. Drizzle with melted fat. Add egg and water; mix well. Gather dough into a ball.

On floured surface, pat out dough. Roll to 1/2 inch thickness. Cut into desired shapes. Gather scraps of dough and repeat last two steps.

Bake on ungreased baking sheets in 350°F oven for 50 to 60 minutes or until crisp. Makes about thirty-six 2 1/2-inch biscuits.

(Recipe courtesy of Debbie Snow)

Photo by Jan Warren

LOU ALLIN was born in Toronto but raised in Ohio when her father followed the film business to Cleveland.

Armed with a Ph.D. in English Renaissance literature, Lou headed north, ending up at Cambrian College in Sudbury, Ontario, where she taught writing and public speaking for twenty-eight years before recently retiring.

Her first Belle Palmer mystery, *Northern Winters Are Murder,* was published in 2000, followed by *Blackflies are Murder, Bush Poodles Are Murder, Murder Eh?* and *Memories Are Murder. Blackflies Are Murder* was shortlisted for an Arthur Ellis Award in the category of Best Novel.

Lou has moved from the bush to the beach: the village of Sooke on Vancouver Island. She is beginning a new series featuring Holly Martin, a female RCMP corporal in charge of a small detachment in Fossil Bay, where the rain forest meets the sea.

Lou welcomes mail and can be reached at louallin@shaw.ca. Her website is www.louallin.com